SHADOWS

JONATHAN NASAW

A DUTTON BOOK

DUTTON
Published by the Penguin Group
Penguin Putnam Inc., 375 Hudson Street, New York, New York 10014, U.S.A.
Penguin Books Ltd, 27 Wrights Lane, London W8 5TZ, England
Penguin Books Australia Ltd, Ringwood, Victoria, Australia
Penguin Books Canada Ltd, 10 Alcorn Avenue, Toronto, Ontario, Canada M4V 3B2
Penguin Books (N.Z.) Ltd, 182–190 Wairau Road, Auckland 10, New Zealand

Penguin Books Ltd, Registered Offices:
Harmondsworth, Middlesex, England

First published by Dutton, an imprint of Dutton Signet, a
member of Penguin Putnam Inc.

First Printing, October, 1997
1 3 5 7 9 10 8 6 4 2

The epigraph on page 3 reprinted with the permission of Simon & Schuster from THE
COLLECTED WORKS OF W. B. YEATS, Volume 1: THE POEMS, Revised and
edited by Richard J. Finneran (New York: Macmillan, 1989).

 REGISTERED TRADEMARK—MARCA REGISTRADA

LIBRARY OF CONGRESS CATALOGING–IN–PUBLICATION DATA
Nasaw, Jonathan Lewis, 1947–
      Shadows / Jonathan Nasaw.
          p.   cm.
      ISBN 0-525-94065-0 (acid-free paper)
      I. Title.
      PS3564.A74S48   1997
      813'.54—dc21   97-8751
                                                                 CIP

Printed in the United States of America
Set in Bembo
Designed by Jesse Cohen

PUBLISHER'S NOTE
This is a work of fiction. Names, characters, places, and incidents either are the products
of the author's imagination or are used fictitiously, and any resemblance to actual persons,
living or dead, events, or locales is entirely coincidental.

"Are these the shadows of the things that Will be, or are they shadows of things that May be, only?"

Still the Ghost pointed downward to the grave by which it stood.

—Charles Dickens, *A Christmas Carol*

PROLOGUE

Santa Luz
U.S. Virgin Islands
October 29, 1993

The weed woman's grandson reported seeing the devil hiking down the trail from the Greathouse shortly before dawn. When she asked what he looked like, this devil, the boy replied that he was a white man, dressed in black, with eyes like dragon's blood.

He was not being fanciful here—dragon's blood is the island name for the *Cordyline terminalis*, a crimson-leaved plant used by the natives of Santa Luz to mark village boundaries. But inasmuch as the boy had spent the rest of the morning gathering a dizzying assortment of psychotropic substances for his grandmother's potions and amulets—psilocybin mushrooms, milktoads, devil's wort, that sort of thing—the weed woman was inclined to discount his story. After all, blood red eyes were not an uncommon sight along that particular rain forest track.

A few hours later, however, the old Rastaman who lived by the side of the trail in a hut built from a Volkswagen shipping crate came rattling down from the hills in his goat cart, shouting that the Greathouse was on fire. But the dundo track—the sunless rain forest road—was narrow and winding, and by the time the first fire truck arrived at the scene the entire compound had been engulfed in a firestorm so intense that the little yellow sugar birds were dropping from the trees within a radius of a quarter mile, unmarked but stone dead from lack of oxygen.

As for the inhabitants of the Greathouse itself, it did not appear that any living creature could have survived such an inferno. Upon this, everyone agreed—the local firefighters, the police, eventually the coroner from St. Thomas, the FBI arson investigators from Puerto Rico, and the Santa Luz stringer for the *Virgin Islands Sentinel*.

Everyone, that is, except for the weed woman, who was heard to remark to the Rastaman that she would believe Mr. Whistler was dead when she heard it from his own lips, and not before; and the Rastaman himself, who slept on the beach that night and returned to his hut the following morning to find evidence of an overnight visitor. A loaf of titi bread and a wax paper packet of homemade Jamaican-style jerky had disappeared, along with the stub end of a cigar-shaped spliff the Rastaman vaguely remembered having left in the conch shell ashtray.

Now it *could* have been the devil that had stopped by his hut, supped so meanly, and stolen a roach, the Rastaman reasoned—but if so, then the devil had fallen on hard times and was welcome to what he could carry.

As was James Whistler. But then, as far as the Rastaman was concerned there was very little difference between Whistler and the devil. Except of course that Whistler had more money.

PART 1

All the Wild Witches

All the wild witches, those most noble ladies,
For all their broom-sticks and their tears,
Their angry tears, are gone.

— W. B. YEATS

CHAPTER

1

For a woman about to take poison, Selene Weiss was magnificently calm. She fed the cat—which was only a cat—and took a cold shower out behind the A-frame, under the redwoods, hoping to get a jump on the fever that was reported to be one of the side effects of the Fair Lady, also known as belladonna, deadly night-shade, death's herb, devil's cherry, and witch's berry.

Or, as the Auld Buik, the *Herbalis Malificarum* put it, somewhat pessimistically, "Burning with fever, nane to relieve her." The other side effects weren't much more encouraging:

> Dry as a bone, mad as a hatter,
> Blind as a bat, crimson as madder.
> Burning with fever, nane to relieve her,
> The witch maun fly, ithers will die.

What it really comes down to is, am I a witch or am I an ither? Selene mused as she toweled off on the redwood deck. Of course there was no way of knowing for certain, short of the Fair Lady's test. But that was a gamble she was ready to take. Selene had been prac-ticing the Wiccan religion for thirty years—twenty-five as high priestess—but it was time to acknowledge to herself that for the past year or so she'd only been going through the motions. Or worse: during the previous Sabbat Selene had been unable to get through the backward Lord's Prayer without giggling. *Muck mudgnik eyth*—thy kingdom come—got to her first, though she'd said it a thousand times before. And when she tried to start again, she couldn't even get past *Nemma, livee morf.*

That was six weeks ago. Tonight's Sabbat was Hallowmas, when the veil between this world and the next was thinnest, and yet here was the high priestess of the coven no longer sure there even was a veil—or a next world, for that matter. The only thing she was sure about was that she couldn't lead a Sabbat in this condition— she loved those most noble ladies too much for that.

So what do you do when you can't go back, and you can't stand still? she asked herself as she stepped into her hiking boots. She already knew the answer: *Either you dance in place like a fool for the rest of your life, or you go on.*

Onward it was. And upward: naked down to her unlaced boots, Selene clomped up the path behind the A-frame that led to the herb garden on the southern slope of the hill. She unlatched the chicken wire gate in the pungent and forbidding rosemary hedge and stepped from dappled shade into the thin yellow light of the clearing. The sun felt voluptuously warm on her bare skin after the morning chill under the redwoods.

Four feet high by now, the bushy, hairy-stemmed nightshade had fruited only recently. The new berries were purple, almost black; Selene noticed that the deer that regularly jumped the hedge to browse the garden hadn't nibbled at them, famished though they must have been after the dry spring and parched summer.

Selene asked ritual permission of Hecate, under whose dominion the Fair Lady lay, before testing each berry by rolling it lightly between her fingertips. The first five that were firm and meaty to the touch, as the *Herbalis* suggested, with their skin unbroken, she plucked from their five-lobed calyx.

Cupping her harvest carefully in her hands, Selene hurried back down the hill, toed off her boots, backed through the kitchen door, set the berries down on the cutting board next to the stove, and turned on the burner under the small slab of Crisco she had pre-

viously melted and left to reharden in a Corning Ware saucepan—
the three-hundred-year-old *Herbalis* explicitly forbade metal pots. It
also called for rendered fat of virgin lamb rather than Crisco, but
even if she'd been willing to slaughter and render a lamb, Selene
couldn't see any way of assuring its chastity, short of raising it herself.

While waiting for the shortening to melt again to the point of
fragrance, Selene quartered the berries with a silver knife. After donning her consecrated black leather apron to protect her bare torso
from spatter burns, she dropped the pieces into the saucepan, stirring
gently clockwise with a wooden spoon until the melting Crisco was
briefly marbled with red streaks. Then, before the shortening could
liquefy completely she scooped as much of the streaky concentrate
as she could into a miniature apothecary jar, which she corked and
left to cool for an hour and twelve minutes—the twentieth part of
a day glass, as the *Herbalis* reckoned it. The remaining bits of berry
she mashed into the leftover Crisco, which had melted to a clear
liquid; when this had turned pink she poured three teaspoons into
a miniature pastry shell, then washed up scrupulously before climbing the ladder to the sleeping loft at the apex of the A-frame.

Selene had intended to spend the next hour meditating, but
instead, lying naked on her back on the waterbed, feet together,
right hand covering her privates, left hand over her heart, she found
herself thinking about a tidbit she'd come across in her research:
according to Plutarch, Marc Antony's army had been involved in
one of the few mass belladonna poisonings in recorded history. *He
that had eaten of the nightshade lost all memory and knowledge, and would
occupy himself in turning every stone as if it were an entirely engrossing
pursuit.*

But it was Plutarch's understated description of the aftermath
that sent shivers up Selene's spine: *The entire camp soon resembled an
overturned anthill of unhappy men, bending to the ground and digging up
stones as though their very lives depended upon the successful completion of
the task.*

If it came to that, Selene decided, she'd try to make her way
up to the rocky vegetable patch on the south slope—it could use a
good obsessive picking over.

⬳

After an hour, the ointment in the tiny apothecary jar had turned to pink cold cream. Seated cross-legged before her black damask-covered wicker altar, Selene uncorked the jar and dipped her pinky in, grimly applying a dab to the pentacle points of her body: wrists, ankles, the hollow of the throat.

But as always, the *Herbalis* required one final touch—*the witch's daub,* it was called—to the genital region. The more benign ointments could be applied to the clitoris or labia, sometimes with interesting effect, but the indications for the Fair Lady called only for *the weeist drap 'tween portals.*

'Tween portals—a portion of the anatomy the books never named. But Jamey Whistler had had a lover's name for it once, a quarter of a century ago; lying back, thinking of him as she leaned back to apply the witch's daub, Selene felt her grimness ebbing.

"It's known as the tizzent, m'dear," Whistler had explained patiently in the Oxford accent he'd been perfecting since his expulsion from that university. " 'Tisn't pussy, 'tisn't asshole." This had been 1967. Oh, but he'd been a striking man, his eyes wide-set and amused, the color of solder, and his upper lip long and sardonic, more sensual than severe.

He'd been employing the tizzent more or less as a chin rest at the time—Selene smiled, remembering, as she worked the cork back into the apothecary jar.

Another hour had passed. The middle-aged witch wandered out onto the deck naked and stoned, her miniature belladonna tart in hand. The trees had a bluish cast in the late morning air, and she could sense a connection, a pleasant fellow feeling with the Steller's jays swooping busily among the redwoods. That would be an effect of the scopolamine, she decided—scopolamine, sometimes used as a truth serum, was one of the active elements in belladonna. Another was atropine, and considerably less benign: the ancients had named it for Atropos, the Fate whose task it was to cut the thread of life after her sister Fates had spun it out.

But so far the high was strictly a sewing-circle buzz: apparently the ointment alone wasn't going to do the trick. Selene looked down at the custardy pink filling in the fluted pastry shell; she was about to try a nibble when the calm of the redwood grove was broken by a shrill scream and a percussive beating of angry wings: the jays down the hill had taken indignantly to the air to report an intruder. As Selene put down the tart and reached for one of the towels drying across the top rail of the deck, she heard a familiar voice from around the side of the house, scolding the jays right back.

"Oh, don't get your tailfeathers in an uproar." A slender girl of seventeen or so stuck her head around the corner. She wore a T-shirt and cutoffs; her hair was corkscrewed into dark honey blond honky dreads on top, and cut close around the sides and back. "Selene? You back here?"

"Martha, my dear! You have always—"

"Been your inspiration," said Martha Herrick pleasantly. "Yeah, I know." In her arms were three fat bundles wrapped in blue paper—Selene's laundry back from the cleaners. Martha balanced them with her chin as she climbed the last few redwood steps to the deck. "If I had a dime for every time Daddy Don quoted that, I'd be shopping at Nordy's instead of Penney's. And you know what he told me the other day? The Martha in the song was one of the Beatles' *dogs.* Where do you want these?"

"Over on the bench will be fine." Selene finished wrapping the towel around her. "How's Don doing?"

"Sleeping when I left." Sleep was as close to peace as Daddy Don ever got anymore—the tumor wrapping itself around the old biker's cervical spine like a boa constrictor around a tree made sure of that. "The pain was getting pretty bad, so the doctor let us double up on the morphine drip. It helped a lot, but god, he gets so dopey. Last night he thought I was my mother."

"*That's* a compliment." Moll Herrick had been a renowned beauty in her day—might still be, for all any of them knew.

"Do I look that much like her?" Martha, who'd been raised by Moll's sister, Connie, and her husband, Daddy Don, hadn't seen her mother since infancy.

"Oh, there's a resemblance, all right. Especially around the mouth." Selene reached out and brushed a coil of hair away from Martha's face. *Ah, but the eyes,* she thought affectionately. *It's your father looking out from those gray eyes.*

Martha glanced over at the tart resting on the railing. "I looked up belladonna in *Cunningham's Magical Herbs.* He says the shit'll kill you dead."

Selene dismissed the notion with a flap of her wrist. "Your godmother's a tough old witch, dearie. It'll take more than a little nightshade to finish me off."

"Fly or die. That's a bitch of a final exam, Selene."

"I know. I've about decided they ought to have one in every profession. You know, inject the doctors with a fatal disease. If they can diagnose and treat it in time, they pass."

"And lawyers who flunk the bar get life without parole," suggested Martha. "They have something like that for mountain guides. The last part of the test, you have to hang from your own belay."

"Well there you go."

Martha peered a little closer at her godmother. "Wait a minute—are you stoned, Selene? Did you already take it?"

Selene laughed gently. "Just the daubs. Why, is there a problem?"

"Sort of." Martha turned away shyly. "I was thinking about it all last night, and I'd kind of decided I wanted to take my initiation at the Sabbat tonight."

"But darling, that's *wonderful!*" Selene crossed the deck, holding her arms out to her goddaughter for an embrace while trying to keep the towel in place with her elbows. "Where's the problem?"

"What if you don't make it to the Sabbat?" Martha muttered into Selene's wild graying hair.

"My poor baby." Selene patted the girl's shoulder, then stepped back, tugging at her slipping towel, hiking it up under her armpits again and tightening the wrap. "You know I wouldn't miss your initiation for the world."

Martha brightened, made a feint toward Selene's towel. "Then what are you fussing with this stupid thing for? Like we're not all gonna be bare-ass at the Sabbat anyway.''

Selene clamped her elbows against her sides. "Watch it, petunia. You're not a witch yet.''

But Martha had thought of another problem. "I almost forgot —what about your Tale? Are you too stoned for that now?''

"Oh dear.'' The older woman leaned against the railing, feeling light-headed, light-bodied. As part of the Dianic tradition, the initiating witch was required to relate the story of her own introduction to Wicca to the acolyte. Selene had heard Moll Herrick's Tale, Moll had heard Bensozia's, and so on, back to the dawn of Wicca. And even if in this instance the telling might prove somewhat awkward—Selene's introduction to Wicca had featured Martha's birth mother in a story of seduction, attempted rape, and revenge —still the thread could not be broken. Not even after a healthy dollop of truth serum to the Teller's tizzent.

2

"In a way it's like a fairy tale, dearie, only bass-ackwards." Selene and Martha were lying side by side on padded redwood chaises, Selene in the shade with her watch and tart on the arm of her chaise, and Martha in the pale autumn sun. "Brave witch rescues maiden in distress from evil knight. The maiden in question— that's me. Helen Weiss. Fresh out of Ludman, Ohio, in my third week of classes at Barnard—oh my dear, I was a miserably unhappy child. . . ."

—

Unhappy was an understatement. Homesick for Ludman. Lonely—Helen Weiss's roommate hadn't spoken to her since Helen told her that if she played that Leslie Gore song one more time on her little pink record player, she would be strangled in her sleep. And as for the academic side of things, Helen was already desperately disillusioned. She wanted to be a poet, but Barnard wanted her to become a lady first—etiquette and tea pouring were still required courses for all incoming women in 1963. And it didn't take long for Helen to learn that the closest she was likely to get to a famous professor at Barnard was if one of the Columbia boys invited her to a lecture—they thought of it as a cheap date—and as for the nearest real poet, why, they were all living and working and reading in Greenwich Village anyway.

It took her a little while to work up her courage—finally one Saturday afternoon a few weeks into the term she copied three of her shorter poems onto one piece of paper, dressed in her notion of a Village outfit—black Danskins leotard under a ribbed black sweater, tight black capris, bare ankles, and Fred Braun sandals—stuffed everything she might conceivably need, *including* a toothbrush and a change of underwear, into an enormous purse, and took the subway down to the Village.

It was Helen's first time underground—the signs seemed so exotic—*el via del tren subterraneo es muy peligroso.* And as for the Village, it soon had her goggling like Dorothy opening the door onto Munchkinland. An outdoor art show was set up in Washington Square Park, spilling out onto the side streets—more paintings than she'd ever seen in one place, and more people than they had in the whole town of Ludman, filling the park, parading around the fountain, beatniks, bums, tourists, chess players, moms with strollers, little kids, high school students trying to look like they were in college, college students trying to look like they weren't. Music in every corner, folksingers, conga drummers, black jazz men in shades and porkpie hats.

Paris, she thought, gawking up at the Great Arch. *This must be what Paris is like.* She wandered the crooked streets for hours with her purse tucked under her arm and her mouth wide open, past bars, sidewalk cafés, tiny shops with handmade jewelry and second-hand clothing in the windows, spiry churches, private parks behind spiked wrought-iron gates, crooked old houses with high stoops, art galleries, little theaters.

And poetry everywhere, in the bookstores, the coffeehouses, the streets, the parks. One old man sat on a folding chair on the sidewalk outside Judson Church selling poems taped to the church fence. Ten cents apiece, three for a quarter. And there were fliers and handbills advertising readings posted from one end of the Village to the other. One spot, the Café LePetomane, looked especially promising, if only because the address on the flyer was Second Avenue and Ninth Street, and since she was standing on the corner of Third and Seventh reading the flier on a light pole, she decided she could find her way there without getting hopelessly lost.

The Pet was a dark joint with brick walls, tiny tables, and mismatched chairs. There were price tags on the chairs, which puzzled her at first—she later learned that if they pretended to sell the furniture they could get around needing a cabaret license. The place was about half full, but even though it was going on suppertime, the denizens were huddled over their coffee as if they'd all just awakened. She found an empty table in the back, under a bunch of charcoal portraits Scotch-taped to the wall, and sat down, hoping alternately that no one would notice her, and that someone would talk to her.

Someone did—a tall, handsome waitress in a scoop-neck burgundy leotard, black tights, and purple wool leg warmers (exactly the look Selene had been going for), who informed her that coffee cost fifteen cents and espresso a quarter. Helen ordered the espresso, paid with a dollar bill, dropped the change into her coin purse, and was about to drop that back into her shoulder bag when she was overtaken by the strangest sensation. It was like the roaring sound a seashell makes when you hold it to your ear, only it wasn't a sound—more like a feeling. But if it had been a sound, there would have been a voice behind it, a tiny voice like a Who from Whoville shouting over a hurricane. And at its wordless bidding Helen found herself removing a dime from her coin purse and placing it carefully on the table, next to her saucer. The waitress scooped it into her apron and moved on to the next table before Helen had quite grasped what had just happened. She started to call the waitress back, but just then a poet climbed up on the stage, which was only a wooden platform raised about a foot above the floor at the far end of the room, and began to read.

And he stunk. As did the second, third, and fourth poets, in the considered opinion of the Poet Laureate of Ludman High, class of '63, as well as that of the majority of the audience, which chattered noisily through the readings. But when a wild-haired man in his late twenties or early thirties, wearing a wrinkled white long-sleeved shirt with sweat stains under the arms and a pair of khaki pants held up by a fraying canvas belt, more or less wandered up on stage holding a fistful of lined loose-leaf paper, the room grew quiet. . . .

" 'Lincoln sat still as a stone,' was how his first poem began," Selene told Martha.

"I know that one," the girl interrupted. "We had to read it in sophomore English. 'Martin's Dream.' "

"By Stanley Kovic. Everyone knows it by now—it's in all the anthologies. But that night was the first public reading ever. . . ."

—

It was scarcely a month since the March on Washington—the now famous poem didn't even have a title yet. When Kovic was done, instead of applauding, the crowd at the Pet signaled for him to read it again by rattling their cups. After he finished the second time and left the stage to another cup-and-saucer ovation, Helen got up to visit the ladies' room, which was behind the stage. When she returned there was a fresh cup of espresso at her place, and the poet was sitting halfway between her table and the next one over. She started to get out her change purse but the waitress shook her head. "It's on Wordsworth, there." Indicating Kovic with a contemptuous toss of her head.

He turned to Helen. "Well, what did you think?"

And there she was, exactly where she'd once dreamed of being—in a coffeehouse in Greenwich Village, talking poetry with a real poet. Unfortunately she was so intimidated that she couldn't think of a single intelligent thing to say. She mumbled something; he turned away to talk to some people who'd come up to congratulate him. When he turned back, Helen had finally gotten some thoughts together.

"See, I'm a poet, too," she told him. He looked disgusted. Blushing, she stumbled on. "But something that's always bothered me—I've been trying to figure it out since I was a freshman in high school—is whether the emperor really has any clothes on."

He looked down his long curved nose at her. "Oh? And who's the emperor?"

"No, not like that. Not an individual poet. Just poetry in general. I mean, in school they give you this book that they say has 'Great Poems' in it, but I always wondered what would happen if there weren't any anthologies, or critics, or English teachers. Would there really be any such a thing as a 'Great Poem'? And now I know the answer."

He scraped his chair a little closer and leaned his elbow on her table. "Do tell."

"It's yes. There is such a thing as a Great Poem. I just heard one, and nobody had to tell me it was great, or what it meant, or who the poet was, or the scansion, or any academic booshwa like that."

He looked deeply into her eyes. "That was the most meaningful compliment anyone has ever paid me. Only around here, when we *mean* bullshit, we *say* bullshit." He stuck out his hand and introduced himself as Stan Kovic. Helen told him she was Helene Weiss—she'd decided Helene sounded more sophisticated. Never could have gotten away with it in Ludman—or perhaps even uptown—but this was the Village, and a girl could be anyone she wanted to be.

He asked her if she had any of her poems with her. "Yes," she replied—Helene replied. "But I couldn't, not now, not after your poem."

"Don't be such a child, you're among poets here."

So she brought the envelope out of her purse—he tucked it into his shirt pocket and said it was too noisy to concentrate, and why didn't they go upstairs so he could give her stuff the attention it deserved. . . .

—

Martha sat up and tied her T-shirt into a makeshift halter to get some autumn sun on her flat belly. "Don't tell me you didn't know what 'stuff' he was talking about," she said with a snort.

Selene shrugged; she was sweating more in the shade than Martha was in the sun. "Different times, dearie. I was practically a virgin—my high school boyfriend and I had done it exactly once, and got caught by my parents to boot, which was why I had to go to a women's college in the first place. I wasn't a complete ninny, mind you. I pretty much knew when one of the *boys* was coming on to me—their idea of seduction was telling you how beautiful you were over and over while they tried to get their hand under your bra—second base, they called it—"

"Still do," Martha informed her.

"—but grown men were still a mystery to me. . . . Now where were we again? It's getting harder to concentrate."

"You were going upstairs with him."

"Oh yes—upstairs." Selene closed her eyes, seeing it all again. . . .

Village walk-up. Bathtub in the kitchen doubles as a dining room table. Living room through a curtain to the left of the kitchen; a double bed took up most of the bedroom to the right of the kitchen. Tiny bathroom off the bedroom—when you sit on the toilet your chin is pretty much resting on the sink.

This last detail Helene discovered almost immediately, because the first thing she had to do was pee again—nerves and coffee. It was obvious from the clothes lying around the bedroom that a woman lived in the apartment as well—Helene was young and naive enough to find this reassuring.

Kovic was in the living room; he looked up from her sheet of poems. "*You* wrote these?"

She nodded dumbly and plopped into the other chair, steeling herself for scathing criticism, and was astounded when he dropped to his knees. "Then you're a real poet, and I salute you." He kissed her hand. "Not a great poet yet—I'm not saying that—but a real one." Turned her hand over and kissed her palm. "And in my humble et cetera, you've got a better chance of maybe someday writing something worthwhile than all those other clowns down there put together."

She had the steel of a poet, he went on to say, but it needed to be tempered by experience and adventure; she had to learn to say yes to life. And what could she say in return—that she wanted to say *no* to life? That she had to be back in the dorm by eleven? That she didn't really want to be a poet if it meant *doing* anything?

Then, once she had agreed in principle to saying yes to life, he reached under the armchair, pulled out a shoe box, twisted up the very first marijuana cigarette Helene had ever seen, stuffed a towel into the crack under the front door, and fired it up, as if *that* was what he was really talking about all along, *that* was the life she was to say yes to.

She did know what pot was, vaguely—she'd read the Beats—they were part of the reason she'd chosen Barnard, which was the sister school to Columbia, from which the best poets were always being expelled. So she tried to look casual—she'd smoked a few cigarettes in her time—took a big drag, coughed it out. He pretended not to notice, got up to put on a Miles Davis record. By the third or fourth toke she'd figured out how to take in small sips of smoke and mix them with air. Not bad. She closed her eyes, and after a few minutes was seeing the music dancing on the back of her eyelids—*Fantasia* had nothing on Selene, her first time on pot—and *feeling* it, too. Then she felt something else—his hands sliding under her sweater, his thumbs brushing her nipples through the leotard until they were hard as pebbles. He began tugging her capris down past her hips; soon his lips were kissing her sex through the wet nylon of the leotard. . . .

—

"Oh my." Selene interrupted herself—she'd forgotten to whom she was telling the Tale. "Pardon me, dearie. I must be higher than I thought."

"No, I love it, I want to hear all the good stuff."

"The good stuff? Unfortunately, dearie, that was about as good as it got. A few minutes later we're in the bedroom, he's lying on top of me. My leotard is dangling off one ankle; his pants are around his knees but his shirt is still buttoned—even the cuffs. I can feel his pelvis grinding against me—he's pushing, pushing—I close my eyes—I keep expecting his penis, but nothing happens.

"After a few minutes he climbs off me—I can't tell what he's doing—then he's sitting on me—he's sitting on my stomach and his hands are squeezing my breasts together so hard it hurts—I open my eyes and look down—he's trying to shove his penis in between them—I don't know what the hell is going on, what he was trying to do—"

"He was trying to—" began Martha.

"Yes, dearie," replied Selene tolerantly. "I'm well aware of what he was trying to do now. But it came as a complete surprise to me at the time." She glanced down at the towel covering her chest, and laughed. "I wasn't exactly endowed for it, either. So the next thing I know, he's scooting farther up, sitting on my chest, waving his dingus in my face—"

Martha started to interrupt; Selene stopped her with an upraised palm. "Yes, dearie, this time I knew what he wanted. But I'd never done it before, and wasn't all that eager to try it. I started crying, turning my head away, but I couldn't make him stop, couldn't get him off me. By now I was scared to death—he was swearing at me, calling me a witch—'It's your fault, you fucking witch. You and your fucking curse.'

"And when he hit me I didn't even know what had happened at first. I heard the slap, and my head jerked left to right before I felt the pain. So now he's sitting on my chest, I can't breathe, I think this is it, he's going to kill me now, he's going to smother me for sure. But when I open my mouth for a gulp of air he raises up on his knees to put his penis in. I accept it—at least his weight is off me—I can breathe through my nose.

"Then I hear—feel—that roaring noise again, the one that's not a noise, the one with the little voice I can't quite make out. I try to concentrate, but there's this *thing* in my mouth, distracting me. Finally I understand, though not quite in words—more like a sudden, almost irresistible urge to clamp my jaws together.

"*I could bite it off, couldn't I?* is what I'm thinking—I open my eyes—I'm looking up at the beautiful waitress from the Café

LePetomane. She's winking down at me. 'You surely could, honey,' she says—out loud this time. He jumps about a mile. 'Right in half. And it would serve him fucking right, too.' ''

Selene's voice trailed off; her eyes had closed. A minute went by, then another. Martha, who'd been basking both in the sun and in the warmth of her godmother's attention, began to grow alarmed. Finally she propped herself up on her elbow again. "You okay, Selene?"

The older woman shook her head sharply, trying to clear away the pinkish haze. "Fine, dearie. But it's getting awfully hard to concentrate—where was I?"

"The waitress. That was my mom, right?"

"It was indeed. Moll Herrick in all her glory." Selene blinked again. "Listen, dearie, I'm definitely starting to lose it here—I think the only way for me to get through this is to go to trance."

"Okay. What do you need me to do?"

"Just give me a few minutes to drop through, and then when I start talking again, don't interrupt me, no matter what. That's the most important thing. Some of the stuff I'm going to be telling you might be a little shocking even by modern standards, but it's absolutely critical that I not be interrupted. It's hard enough on the psyche to be jerked out of a trance—I don't know what the effects would be when you're on belladonna on top of all that."

"You can count on me," said Martha.

"I already do," replied Selene. "More than you'll ever know." She closed her eyes again, and began to slow her breathing.

3

As she dressed hurriedly in the living room, Helene could hear Kovic's voice from the bedroom:

"I knew this was your doing, you fucking witch!"

She was a little afraid for the waitress—he had looked so frightening when she scrambled off the bed and raced out of the room, his face gone gargoyle—all bumps and bulges—from anger. But he'd also looked slightly ridiculous, with his wild hair frizzed up around his head and his skinny legs sticking out from under the shirttails, and the waitress's voice didn't sound frightened in the least: "I told you what would happen if you ever cheated on me again. And to do it in *my* bed, you miserable limp-dick motherfucker!"

The man's voice: "Take the curse off, or I'll kill you right here and now."

And the woman's: "Stalemate. If you kill me before I remove the curse, you'll *never* have another hard-on. Now get the fuck out of my apartment."

"It's my apartment too."

"Not anymore it isn't."

Helene heard doors next: the bedroom door opening and closing, the front door slamming, then a refrigerator door. A moment later the waitress entered with an ice pack for Helene's cheek.

"Are you really a witch?"

A laugh; a picturesque toss of the long hair. "I suppose I'll do until the real thing comes along."

"And you put a curse on him?"

"Damn straight."

"It wasn't straight at all." Helene couldn't believe she said that. She felt her face growing hot, except for the cheek with the icebag.

A dismissive flap of the strong-wristed hand. "Kindergarten stuff. Suggestion. The easiest spell there is. You could learn it, you know. In fact, you'd make quite a witch yourself—you're already tele-pathic—that bit with the tip tonight? Most people don't pick up on what I'm putting out anywhere near as strongly as you did."

Helene gathered her sheet of poems off the floor and stuffed it back into the envelope. "I didn't exactly pick up on what Stan was putting out."

"College girl, eh?"

"Barnard."

"A chickie fresh from the Barnyard. Stanley, Stanley, Stanley." The waitress sighed—her chest heaved impressively under the le-otard. "Tell you what, chickie. How about I make us a cup of tea while you ice your eye there, and I'll hip you about all them big bad wolves out there drooling for such a tender young pullet."

"I'd rather hear about the witches."

"That too."

━

"The first thing you have to get out of your head is the idea of the wicked witch from fairy tales. That's just Christian propaganda —although the Crone *is* one of the aspects of the triple Goddess. Wicca is a religion—it's older than Christianity. Lots of tradition, lots of ritual, pantheistic, animistic, neopagan for the most part. But no dogma—faith is not required, and every coven gets to define itself. Nobody even agrees about where the word *Wicca* comes from. In Old English, *wit* is the root for wisdom, same as today, but in Indo-European *wic* had two meanings. As a noun it meant 'religion' or 'magic,' but as a verb it meant 'to bend or shape.' In my coven's tradition, Dianic—women only—we say a witch is a wise woman who uses magic to bend or shape reality.''

"What do you mean by magic?" Helene wanted to know. The two women were having their tea in the cozy little kitchen. A plywood board over the bathtub served as their table; the green Melmac cafeteria-style cups were from the Pet.

" 'The science and art of causing change to occur in conformity with will.' " Moll was quoting Crowley, though Helene didn't know that yet.

"But what sort of magic? Like spells and stuff?"

"Spells, prayers, potions—they all work together. Although as Bensozia always says, potions work without spells a lot better than spells work without potions."

Moll drained her teacup, then set it down decisively on the bathtub table. "But I really can't say any more about that." Then, casually, "Unless of course you decided to take initiation, join the coven."

"What's involved in that?" asked Helene, also casually. But she was being coy—somehow she already knew she was going to do it. For all the wrong reasons, no doubt: because she hated Barnard; because she already had a crush on Moll, though she'd never had any leanings of this sort before—or experience, except for one summer at sleep-away camp when she was twelve; because she was still in shock; because she was a silly goose of a girl, eighteen years old and green as grass; whatever the reason, it was as if past and future had switched places. Her past, Helen's past, was blurry and unreal, while the future seemed as sure as if it already happened.

And Moll must have known she had her hooked; still she played the line out with great care. "Not much. But it would have to be tomorrow—that's the Equinox Sabbat. If not, you'll have to wait until Samhain for the next Sabbat, and maybe there'll be another candidate by then." She stood up, towering over Helene. "But this is all going too fast for you—I'm sure you have to get back to your dorm."

Helene glanced at her watch, a Lady Bulova, a graduation present. "Uh-oh. Too late for that. I haven't even signed out, so I sure can't sign back in after curfew."

Off-handedly: "You can crash here if you'd like."

"Crash?" It was the first time Helene had heard the word used in that context.

"Sleep over. C'mon, help me change the sheets so they don't smell like Stan."

Not a word was mentioned about sex. While the two women stripped the soiled bedding, Moll explained to Helene a little about the initiation ceremony (by and large, it would be the same ceremony Martha would undertake this Halloween night thirty years later), about the Misikidak Helene would have to memorize. But the clincher as far as Wicca was concerned came in a remark Moll called through the bathroom door while Selene was brushing her teeth.

"If you were a witch, you know, you could never allow something like what Stan Kovic did to you to pass unrevenged. It would weaken your power. And all the other witches in the coven would be bound by oath to help you take that revenge—it would be their religious duty."

Although she had brought her toothbrush and a change of clothes, Helene had neglected to pack anything to sleep in, so Moll lent her one of her own denim shirts. In Ludman a denim shirt marked you as a farmer's kid, but Moll's denim was soft and smooth and as blue as her eyes. Helene changed into it while Moll was in the bathroom. She was already so excited about the prospect of joining a coven of witches that it hadn't occurred to her—not consciously, anyway—that that night might be something beyond a pajama party sleepover.

But when Moll emerged from the bathroom stark naked and climbed straight into bed Helene's whole body started trembling. Moll must have felt it—the bed was only a rickety double-wide cot on casters. She rolled onto her side, facing Helene. "I think we'd better have a little talk, woman to woman."

"Okikikay," was all that Helene could manage, and the way her teeth were chattering she barely got that out.

"Just nod—I'm afraid you're going to bite your tongue off—and you might need it."

The trembling worsened.

"Joke. That was a joke. You are scared, aren't you?"

A nod. "Ninininervous."

"Well I don't blame you. After all, you were nearly raped tonight. But this is different. I'm not gonna rape you, I'm not going to seduce you—shit, I can't believe I'm saying this—I'm not even going to touch you. Unless you want to. Now here's the deal. . . ."

It was not a very complicated deal. If Helene rolled onto her left side, facing the wall, they would sleep. If she rolled over onto her right side, facing Moll . . .

When Helene awoke the next morning, she was still lying on her right side. *I'll never sleep on my left side again,* she promised herself sleepily. Moll told Helene the Tale of her own initiation over breakfast (bagels, the first she had ever seen, much less tasted) and afterward brought her to the strange little bookshop called Covenstead and introduced her to Andred and Bensozia, the two old witches who owned the place, and served as joint high priestesses of the Village Coven.

She purchased the tools for her initiation—a dagger and cords and an incense holder and a silver cup—that morning. Andy and Benny, who reminded her strongly of the two sisters in *Arsenic and Old Lace,* agreed to let her pay them off on the installment plan, then showed her into the back room, which really *was* a covenstead, the place where a coven meets. It was bigger than the front of the shop, furnished in thrift-shop Victorian: thick Oriental rugs, soft chairs, flocked wallpaper, bric-a-brac by the carload. In one corner the walls were covered with silk hangings, like the Gypsy fortune-teller's tent at the county fair back home.

There was yet another room behind the covenstead where the

witches kept their herbs, potions, powders, and poisons, as well as a cabinet containing—oh good heavens—dildos. It took her a moment to even think of the word; Helene had never actually seen one until she found herself in the back room of the covenstead staring at a whole dick museum—a collection of wood, stone, rubber, wax, and primitive battery-powered plastic phalluses in every shape, size, and color imaginable.

She spent the rest of the morning and afternoon studying for her initiation. Andred—the rounder, softer of the pair of priestesses—helped her with her Misikidak, her witch's catechism, while Benny and Moll pored through the ancient tomes looking for just the right potion for her to use against Stan.

Around two o'clock the other witches began arriving; Andy and Benny locked the store at three, formed up the circle, and kicked off the Sabbat celebration in the back room with the initiation ceremony; by four-thirty Helene was Selene, thirteenth witch of the Village Coven, signed, sealed, and named for the Goddess of the Moon.

Afterward about half the coven stuck around to help their new sister plan her revenge (as well as the post-Sabbat orgy—women only—scheduled for midnight). They cast a few spells, of course, the way Selene had always imagined witches doing, but the most important element of her revenge proved to be much more down to earth. It was a potion, a powder made up of a whole cocktail of different herbs and substances, some of which, like brucinetta and cantharides, were deadly poisons in stronger doses; she ground them up herself in the back room using a medieval mortar and pestle, while Moll explained how the potion was to be administered.

"It won't be easy. You have to get him to drink a whole glass of wine with the powder in it without stopping, then get him naked while keeping as many of your own clothes on as possible—I suggest you make him think you're still scared of him from last night—and masturbate him as long as possible without letting him come."

I'm a long way from Ludman, thought Selene when the jerk-off lessons began, Moll demonstrating on a dildo from Andy and Benny's collection. Some of the other ladies had different suggestions. They passed the dildo around, and everybody showed her a favorite grasp or technique. Selene got the benefit of a hundred and fifty years of experience all at once. Poor Kovic didn't stand a chance.

The effects of the potion were supposed to be temporary. Not that Selene gave a damn. She was *digging* this. Born to be a witch. No fear, no second thoughts—zapped with adrenaline, a warrior on her way into battle.

Around six, Moll called Stanley—he'd taken a room at the Chelsea Hotel—and told him to come over and pick up his shit right away or she'd throw it out in the street. They yelled at each other over the phone for a while, then Moll cast the hook, telling Stan that if he apologized sincerely to both women while he was here, she'd take the impotence curse off him.

He swallowed it hook, line, and sinker, and was over in a flash, apologizing his ass off. When he'd finished grumbling, Moll mumbled some made-up Wiccan at him—she'd never actually bothered to curse him or dose him; suggestion alone had done the trick—and told him all was forgiven and the curse was lifted. She threw his stuff into boxes—books mostly, some clothes; Selene offered to help him carry it over to the Chelsea Hotel. Told him she'd always wanted to see it on account of Dylan Thomas had died there.

It was a long walk up to Twenty-third Street carrying those heavy boxes, but Stan insisted he couldn't afford a cab. Once Selene saw his room she believed him—if Dylan Thomas's room had been anything like Stan's, she could see why he drank himself to death. The color scheme was pea green and mustard yellow. Beat-up old bureau, narrow bed. Not even a chair. She set her box down on the floor and collapsed on the foot of the bed. She didn't have to do much acting to convince him she was exhausted.

He brought her a murky glass of water. She caught her breath, they talked about Dylan Thomas for a while, then poetry in general. He asked her if she wanted another stick of pot. She told him it made her dizzy, but if he had any wine . . . ? He did, of course: Moll had thrown a bottle of Mateus into one of the boxes, along with two wineglasses wrapped in an old *Village Voice*.

While Stan was in the bathroom rinsing out the glasses, Selene removed the paper bindle with the powder from her purse. "I'll pour," she told him when he returned. "I'm studying tea pouring at Barnard." Next came the sleight of hand: while he was trying to find some jazz on the clock-radio, she palmed the bindle and poured the powder into his glass. It dissolved immediately, and they toasted each other to the music of Coltrane.

Selene followed Moll's instructions to the letter: "Maintain eye contact during the toast. Drain your glass in one long swallow— breathe through your nose if you have to. If you don't stop drinking while you're holding eye contact, neither will he. Don't worry about getting a little drunk—it'll help with the next part. There'll be an aftertaste; when you're done, make a face if he does."

It all went off without a hitch. So did his clothes. By eight-thirty the innocent college freshwoman had the worldly-wise poet bare-ass on his back, penis in the air, while she gave him—it— every bit of that hundred and fifty years' experience. It wasn't too revolting, probably because she was a little drunk, and also because she kept reminding herself of something else Moll told her: "The sex isn't personal. Just the revenge."

Selene found herself performing the last tricky part of her mission as coolly as a veteran. She took his hand and placed it around his penis, began squeezing the hand rhythmically, and started it going up and down, up and down, until it was moving on its own. She delivered the line Moll had suggested: "You show me. Show me how to make it come." Then she pulled her hand away quickly and watched as he began spurting semen the color of blood.

Oh, it was glorious. Glorious. She couldn't tell whether he felt any actual pain; the way he started screaming when he saw himself coming in technicolor—crimson gobs at first, then red, fading to watery pink—it was hard to tell what he was feeling, other than sheer terror. She hurried out of the room; the sound of his howling followed her through the door and down the hall.

Of course it looked a lot worse than it was: the brucinetta and cantharides, along with the hard stroking and the prolonged erection and excitement, had caused just enough urethral bleeding to turn his seminal fluid the color of blood. It was sort of like dyeing his sperm. And unless he had sex too soon, which didn't seem likely, the effects of the potion would clear up within a few days. . . .

A few more minutes passed in a silence broken only by the burbling hot tub and the posturing jays. Eventually Selene opened her eyes. "I slept over at Moll's again that night," she continued. "The third week of classes started the next day, but I didn't. Instead I moved in with Moll. She got me a job waitressing at the Pet, and I spent all my spare time studying Wicca. Never wrote another word of poetry. My parents never forgave me. Just dropping out of school against their wishes would have been bad enough in those days, but when I told them that I also wouldn't be celebrating Christmas anymore because I was a Wiccan now . . . ? Oh my oh my oh my. Suffice to say I never even got around to telling them about me and Moll before receiving what we used to refer to back then as the *Never darken my towels again* speech."

Selene seemed to have come out of her trance, but Martha didn't want to take any chances. "Selene?" she whispered tentatively.

"Dearie?"

"Was it worth it?"

Selene tried to laugh, but her mouth was so dry it came out more like a caw. "If I knew that, little witch-to-be, I wouldn't be lying here with belladonna smeared all over my tizzent." She sat up slowly, tightening the towel around her torso. "Which reminds me—I've got one more appointment with the Fair Lady, and it won't do to keep her waiting."

"Aren't you going to help me with my Misikidak?"

"Sorry dearie. That you can do on your own. You've heard my Tale, now off you go."

"Wait. One more question. What happened to that guy Stan?"

"The word on the street was that he left for San Francisco the next morning. And all he'd say to anybody was that when he got there he was going to ship out with the merchant marine, because one continent wasn't enough ground to put between him and those witches. Now run along and study your Misikidak—I don't want you embarrassing me tonight."

"So you'll be there, right?"

"I'll do my best."

"Witch's Word?" Martha asked. The look she received from Selene in reply had so much love in it, mixed with so much sorrow, that it frightened her a little. "I said, Witch's Word?"

Selene took Martha's hand, brought it to her lips, kissed it gently, and sighed. "You win." She crossed both hands over her heart. "Witch's Word. If I'm alive, I'll be there. If I'm dead, I'll give it my very best shot."

～

The soft slap of Martha's sandals died away. Selene lay back, feeling the heaviness overtake her again. She wondered whether she'd done the right thing, encouraging Martha to join the coven though she herself was ambivalent to the point of apathy. Then she found herself remembering how it had felt to be a witch back then—not just the orgies and the fellowship, but the sense of purpose. She remembered how comforting it had been to feel oneself in the arms of the Goddess, to feel that every casting of the runes in the morning was a cosmic event, that every ritual was sacred, that every moment of every day was invested with magic and meaning according to some grander scheme of things.

"Ah well, onward and upward," she sighed, reaching for the belladonna tart and raising it to her lips. There was no invocation for the Test of the Fair Lady—if there were Powers and if They were with her, she'd know soon enough. And if she was really lucky, the auld buik had suggested, not only would she not die, but the Fair Lady might show her . . . well, something important, though it was rather vague as to what. Purposefully vague: *A task and a path by the Fair Lady's light,* the last couplet in the book promised. *The deeper the dark, the truer the sight.*

She took a bite. Bitter. Brack and bitter as the book had promised. A series of shudders wracked her as she forced herself to swallow. Realizing that she'd never be able to get the whole thing down a bite at a time, Selene carried it over to the railing so that if she puked it would be into the azaleas, then held her nose with one hand and crammed the rest of the pastry into her mouth with the other, working her jaws furiously, gulping the crumby clotted mess down as fast as she could swallow.

Within minutes her body was reeling from the insult. She sat down heavily on the wooden rim of the covered hot tub and dazedly began brushing the pastry crumbs from her chest. Soon she broke out into a fine sweat from the crown of her head to her bare toes; when she looked down she saw that the skin of her torso had taken on a red blotchy glow.

She started to mop herself off with the towel she'd donned for Martha, but quickly soaked it through; she draped it over the railing; it slipped off and fell into the bushes on the other side. Her mind seized on the need for a dry towel. She tottered into the house, sweat pouring down her face, dripping from nose, chin, and nipples, but by the time she reached the bathroom out behind the kitchen she had sweated out every drop of moisture her body could spare, and the heat from the fever had cooked it away.

Her face felt like parchment, and when she brought her hands up to her eyes, she saw through a quickly darkening rosy glow that the skin of her fingertips had begun to pucker.

Selene looked up and caught a glimpse of her face in the mirror: her long witchy gray-black hair had frizzed out wildly, and her face was indeed crimson as madder. Then she couldn't see anything: an angry red haze had washed across her vision.

—

Somehow Selene must have managed to stagger to the ladder —she had a vague memory of a black reeling time—and climb to her loft, because when she regained what passed for consciousness she found she was lying facedown on the waterbed, her nose buried in a soft canyon between two pillows.

She rolled onto her back, fighting against a sudden wave of dizziness that worsened as the waterbed rocked and rolled. When she opened her eyes she saw only the red haze at first, but gradually it parted to reveal the jagged crimson branches of the redwood trees outlined against a garish pink and violet sky.

She reached a hand up toward the domed skylight directly over the bed. To her mild surprise it slipped through as easily as if the Plexiglas were spun sugar; she felt her spirit drawing out after it with a rush, flowing freely through the illusory hole, wobbling and shifting shape like a great bubble of lucid oil rising up through water.

4

The view of San Francisco at night was breathtaking from Aldo Striescu's corner suite at the Fairmont. The neighborly hills, the cold starry towers, the great sweep of the bay spanned by bridges strung with scalloped strands of light, gave Aldo the same tender feeling in his chest as hearing the divine Callas singing "O mio babbino caro" from *Gianni Schicchi*. Soaring sweetness, a core of innocence and sorrow, but with an edge to it that never let you forget why La Divina had also been the preeminent Medea and Lady Macbeth of her day.

"Cruzime si inocenta." He said it in Romanian first, then repeated it in English—"Cruelty and innocence"—in order to practice his mush-mouthed California dialect. Sounded too sibilant to his trained ear. He repeated the troublesome word—"innocence, innocence, innocence"—until he felt ready for a field test, then picked up the phone and punched a button at random.

"Housekeeping, this is Rosa."

"Rosa!" As if he'd reached an old friend by mistake. "I'm trying to reach room service. . . . Sure, thanks."

"Room service, this is Hector."

"Hector! Do you serve crabs—and don't tell me you serve anybody!" For Aldo, the ability to pun was a measure of his mastery over the language.

An obsequious chuckle. "We do have a crab cocktail, sir."

"Fresh?"

"Previously frozen."

"As opposed to what? Still frozen?"

Silence.

"Just kidding, Hec." He ordered two, along with the Surf 'n' Turf combo, a bottle of Napa Chardonnay that Hector had seemed quite enthusiastic about, and a slice of the delightfully named Chocolate Decadence for dessert. "And coffee—make it a cappuccino. Forty-five minutes? Swell. Room nine twenny-two."

He hung up. He wasn't really hungry—but then, his room number wasn't 922, either.

"Chahklit decadince, chahklit decadince . . ." He practiced that one on the way to the bathroom, then tried out the whole order again in front of the ornate bathroom mirror, where the sight of his reflection reminded him of the boy by the side of the rain forest path who'd run away shouting about the devil Friday morning. The goatee Aldo had grown to match the photo on his American passport, along with his wide forehead, impishly arched eyebrows, and permanently bloodshot eyes, made the comparison all but inevitable.

Generally speaking, he wasn't pleased with the look. It robbed him of some of the easy—and incongruous, to those who knew him—Striescuan charm. But the passport had been too clean to pass up—and free. It occurred to Aldo that he should have chased the Luzan boy down, eyewitnesses being something of an impediment in his line of work, but he'd been on a tight schedule at the time —as it was, he barely made it back to his hotel room before sunrise. Ah well, perhaps someday he would return to Santa Luz and finish the job.

Not that his schedule was any more forgiving tonight. Aldo had *two* of Whistler's properties to torch before driving up to Lake Tahoe, and according to the maps splayed out on the marble-topped coffee table over by the window they were two counties apart, with the San Francisco Bay between them.

After showering and dressing—black slacks and a worn black pullover—Aldo removed his silver thermos from the refrigerator built into the wet bar in the living room and carried it over to the sofa by the picture window. He took his first swallow of the night while comparing the maps with the computer printout he'd brought with him from London, by way of Santa Luz, detailing James Whistler's worldwide real estate holdings.

Aldo traced tonight's route with his finger: across the famous Golden Gate Bridge and up Route 1 to the redwood A-frame near Bolinas, then clear across Marin County and over the Richmond–San Rafael bridge to El Sobrante, where Whistler owned a clapboard farmhouse. He might even have time to watch that one go up before leaving for Tahoe, where Whistler Manor was located. The manor itself he would save until the following night.

—

The roadbed of the Golden Gate Bridge was wet and shiny with fog; overhead the towers disappeared into the mist. Aldo slipped a disk of Callas singing "L'altra notte in fondo al mare" into the CD player of his rented Mercury Sable, then changed his mind, and the disk. *Norma* would be a much better accompaniment for what the guidebook promised would be a winding and spectacular drive up the coast—he would save *Mefistofele* for the flames.

Aldo grinned at the thought of the flames; his grin widened when he discovered that there was no bridge toll for northbound travelers. Growing up an orphan, Aldo had learned to appreciate these little bonuses in life. Despite years of living high off the Ceauşescu hog, he had never entirely overcome the poverty of his upbringing. Even now, on the brink of the biggest payoff of his life, he still begrudged every dollar he couldn't charge directly to his new employer's Platinum Card.

His new employer: something else to grin about. And to make a poor orphan boy shake his head in wonder over the vagaries of fate. Just a little over a month ago Aldo had still been living hand-to-mouth after nearly four years in England, doing shit work, mostly collection and protection, and the occasional torch job, for the Suterana, the Romanian criminal underground, which for the most part did shit work for the English criminal underground.

So things could have been worse. Aldo had a decent, sound-proofed apartment in Chelsea, and when funds did run low it was always possible for a man of his peculiar talents and abilities to obtain cash. But in his opinion he should never have been allowed to fall into even such modestly straitened circumstances in the first place. For without Aldo and his Third Branch colleagues in the Securitate guiding the so-called spontaneous December Revolution that followed the slaughter in Timisoara, the Communists would never have been able to rid themselves of the old peasant Ceauşescu, who'd become an embarrassment anyway, while still managing to coopt the National Salvation Front, thereby maintaining themselves in power without missing a meal.

So as far as Aldo was concerned, he should have been back in Bucharest helping to run the new government along with the rest of the conspirators who'd engineered the phony coup d'état. But more scapegoats were needed, and who better to sacrifice than the field operatives, men who knew too much anyway? The double-cross had turned into a triple-cross: Aldo had barely managed to escape to England with his life and his Callas collection, leaving his life savings behind. Hence the one-bedroom flat in Chelsea and the shit work for the Suterana.

And then one September night he'd popped into the Cock and Fender for a pint, was told by an old buddy from Bucharest of a mad old fellow with a fierce interest in certain Romanian folk legends, and suddenly everything changed. Now, a month later, here he was driving a fully loaded Sable with creamy leather seats and a sound system worthy of La Divina across the celebrated Golden Gate Bridge, getting paid more money than he'd ever dreamed of to do a job he'd have gladly done for free—or at least for expenses: burn a *striga*—a witch.

According to the maps the turn-off for Bolinas was just north of the town of Stinson Beach. Aldo was nearly to Olema before he realized he'd missed it. He turned around and soon found himself back in Stinson. Somehow he'd managed to miss his turn again heading south.

There was nothing for it but to ask directions. How bloody

unprofessional! He executed his second U-turn of the night, pulled up in front of a bar called the Sand Dollar, pressed the button to lower the passenger-side front window, and hailed a hippie-looking fellow in a tie-dyed shirt who was just reeling down the steps. Time to try out his California accent for real. "Hey dude, can you tell me how to get to Bolinas?"

"Sure can." But no directions were immediately forthcoming —the fellow just stood there, swaying and giggling.

"Oh, I get it," said Aldo. "Like, I said 'can you?' and you could. Right?"

"Riiight!"

"Very funny. How about *would* you tell me how to get to Bolinas?"

"Sure. Jus' drive straight through town"—the hippie waved vaguely to his right—"pas' the lagoon, pas' the Audubon Ranch, hang a lef' on the Bobo road."

"That's what I thought—but I didn't see any sign or anything."

"That's 'cause the Bobos take the signs down as fas' as Caltrans can put 'em up. Don't like tourists much in Bobo-land. Jus' look for a busted-off sign after the lagoon."

"Great. Thanks."

"No prob. Hey, how about you buy me a drink for my condition?"

"What condition is that?"

"Not drunk enough."

Aldo laughed and pulled away from the curb, tires squealing. When he passed the wide flat lagoon for the third time he slowed the Sable to a crawl. Eventually he made out the broken signpost across the highway; the road to Bolinas was right where the maps and the hippie had said it would be. *Batardes*. He flipped a finger, American style, to all the Bobos in Bobo-land: they had cost him precious time. Now he'd have to rush both this job and the one in El Sobrante if he hoped to make Tahoe before sunrise.

Ah well, perhaps there would still be time to have a little fun with the striga before he torched the building. Because in Aldo's experience the only thing that could equal the orgasm potential of watching an old wooden building going up in flames while listening to La Divina sing *Mefistofele*, was the release that could be achieved during even the most hurried of smotherings, if the victim put up a decent fight.

But it seemed Aldo was doomed to be disappointed once again. First he missed the driveway and drove halfway into town before executing yet another U-turn. Then when he finally located the A-frame at the top of the winding drive, he discovered that there was nowhere to hide the Sable while he went about his business. This one would have to be extra quick, to reduce the possibility of someone driving up and spotting the car. Aldo muttered a quick oath—oh, how he hated to torch and run.

And such favorable tinder, too: he'd never burned redwood before, but if it flared like other dry evergreens, the conflagration would be spectacular. Not that he would have time to watch it. He backed the Sable around in the driveway, so it was facing downhill, took a healthy swig from his thermos, and climbed out of the car with his leather kit bag in hand.

The front door was unlocked. It was Aldo's first piece of luck all night. Another followed immediately: he sensed the presence of the witch. A third: he climbed the ladder to the loft and saw that she was lying across her bed, on her back, sound asleep, and—a fourth spot of luck—completely naked. He wouldn't have taken the time to undress her otherwise. Skinny old thing, but perhaps what she lacked in meat she'd make up for in fight. Without a good struggle he had no chance at an orgasm.

But there Aldo's brief run of luck petered out. He snatched up a pillow which had fallen to the floor, placed it firmly over the striga's face, and tensed himself for a resistance that never came; there was no reaction whatsoever. A minute went by, then another, without so much as a gasp or wiggle. Puzzled, Aldo tried to remember whether she had been breathing when he first saw her. But she must have been; she was still warm.

Warm? She was hot, and the sheets were soaked with sweat. Maybe she'd been in a coma or something. Whatever her problem, smothering her proved a dreadful disappointment. She never even kicked at the end. They were all supposed to kick at the end—it was a reflex, for God's sake.

But the striga was definitely not breathing when he removed the pillow after a few minutes, and when he put his ear to her bare chest he couldn't hear a heartbeat. Just to be sure, he plucked out a pubic hair. She didn't flinch. Dead as dead could be, and he hadn't even managed an erection, much less an orgasm.

"Oh well," said Aldo aloud, climbing back down the ladder. *"Alt noapte, alt flacara, alt femeie."* Other nights, other fires, other women. "And they'll all be kicking like the famous Rockettes of Radio City Music Hall. For now, there is work to be done."

Indeed there was. He took a toothpaste tube filled with jellied gasoline from the kit bag and began squeezing it around the base of the ladder.

5

The photo album discovered among Aunt Connie's effects after the beloved biker mama and her likewise beloved '57 Harley Sportster missed a curve in the fog (the bend of Highway 1 where she suffered the ultimate Wipe Out, and where her ashes had later been scattered, was still known as Dead Woman's Curve) was a typical Aunt Connie production. The oldest pictures—mostly of Martha's maternal grandparents, a pleasant-looking, clueless old couple—were pasted in carefully enough, as were Martha's first baby pictures, but all the later prints had been stuffed back into the Photo-Mat envelopes they'd come in, and the envelopes jammed between the glossy pages of the album.

Not that Connie wasn't sentimental about her photos—she was sentimental about everything. Just not very organized. And out of the whole collection, there was only one of Moll Herrick, immensely pregnant, standing next to Connie. After coming home from Selene's that morning, Martha had dug it out from the album and slipped it into the edge of the white wicker frame around the mirror atop the white wicker dresser in her bedroom. From time to time during the day, Martha had looked up from her Misikidak to inspect the snapshot, trying to gauge whether Selene had told the truth about the mother-daughter resemblance. Hard to tell what Moll looked like from that one picture; her features had blurred into the bovine placidity common among expectant mothers.

But the two sisters in the photo shared the pouty look that film stars were now injecting collagen into their lips to obtain, and when Martha glanced from the picture to her mirrored image one last time on her way out that evening, she was absolutely convinced she could see the same sexy lift to her own upper lip. Eat your heart out, Drew Barrymore.

The A-frame that Martha and Daddy Don shared was constructed according to the same general plan as Selene's up the hill: one big room on the ground floor, separated into kitchen and living areas by pillars that supported the sleeping loft overhead. Daddy Don and his crew had added the deck and hot tub to the upper house when Whistler purchased it for a honeymoon cottage for himself and Selene; the same crew had later converted the sleeping porch behind the lower house into a nursery when Martha arrived, then popped the top of that a few feet when she outgrew the nursery. (And done a creditable job all around, considering that what they were a crew of was motorcycle mechanics, not carpenters.)

After Connie's fatal spill, Selene had moved into the upper A-frame to help Daddy Don raise the six-year-old Martha. Between Selene and her circle of witches up the hill, and Daddy Don and his extended family of bikers, Martha's two surrogate parents had managed to raise what passed for a normal teenager, at least in Bolinas. Martha smoked pot but avoided stronger drugs; was sexually active but not egregiously promiscuous according to the mores of Marin County teenagers, and always used protection; and although she was an indifferent student, her grades through her third year of high school would have been good enough to get her into any of a dozen campuses of the Cal State system, had she not dropped out in September, a few weeks into her senior year, to help care for Daddy Don—against both his and Selene's wishes.

Whether she would return to school to finish up her senior year was a subject Martha refused to discuss, or even consider, involving as it did speculation about Daddy Don's eventual demise: on this topic the seventeen-year-old had raised denial to an art form.

Just before eleven o'clock on Halloween night Martha crept quietly out of her room and closed the door behind her. The only light in the main room was the pallid silvery flicker of the TV. She tiptoed over to the hospital bed, which had been cranked to a sitting position although the occupant was asleep, found the remote clipped to the sheet, and clicked off the television.

The dying man opened his eyes. "Who's that? That you, Marty?" Daddy Don's bed had been moved down from the loft when he lost the use of his legs entirely back in August.

"I'm here, Daddy Don." She reached across to the bedside table and switched on the Harley lamp that Selene had given him as a gift for his sixtieth birthday. It had a miniature bronze '56 Hydra-Glide for a base. "But where's that miserable Dirtbag? He's supposed to be staying with you till I get back."

The bikers were taking care of their own; rather than send Baechler back to the VA hospital to die after he'd refused palliative radiation, they had been helping Martha care for him at home. Dirtbag had always been a reliable night nurse before—a crankhead, he was considered as unlikely to fall asleep on the job as he was to raid Daddy Don's morphine infuser.

"Sent him on a beer run. Twitchy motherfucker was getting on my last nerve."

"You hurting much, Daddy?"

"Naw, I'm P-far." Pain Free At Rest was the best the doctors at the VA had been able to promise him. At rest meant not moving a muscle. The bitch of the thing was, the way the tumor was progressing, in a few weeks he wouldn't be *able* to move a muscle. "Just roll me back down."

Martha lowered the bed and adjusted the pillow under his head while he held his breath against the pain. "Arms in or out?"

"Out."

"Whiskers?" She pulled up the covers and began to tuck him in.

"Out."

The girl lifted the old biker's footlong ZZ Top beard out from under the sheet; it fluttered down like a ragged-edged white battle pennant across the army blanket. "How long ago did Dirtbag take off?" she asked, kneeling to check the urine bag tied to the bottom rail of the bed. She didn't like leaving him entirely alone, even for a few minutes.

"Half hour?" A barely perceptible shrug of the wasted shoulders, then a wince. "Me and time ain't exactly been tight lately, Sugaree. But you go ahead, I'll be fine."

"Naah, I can wait." A lie—if she didn't make it to Mill Valley by the start of the ceremony, her initiation would have to be postponed until the Yule Sabbat. And after hearing Selene's Tale, she was more eager than ever to join the coven. Imagine, not just rituals and incantations and praying to the Goddess, but powders and potions and revenge. She could think of a few boys who could stand a little brucinetta in their Long Island Iced Tea.

Fortunately, Dirtbag showed up within minutes, carrying a six-pack of Green Death, a carton of Kools, and a bag of Slim Jims; when he entered the house Martha was forcibly reminded of how he had earned his name—she blew him a kiss, but gave him a wide berth on the way out.

Martha drove to Mill Valley with the top down on the white VW Cabriolet Selene had given her for her sixteenth birthday. Due to the lateness of the hour and the chill in the air, there were only a few trick-or-treaters left on the streets. It was too cold to have the top down, really, but the stars were so splendid overhead that she couldn't bear to shut them out, so instead Martha zipped up her thin nylon jacket and turned up the heater and the blower. She tried to turn up the CD player too, to make up for the added noise of the fan, but by the time she got the volume cranked high enough to hear, it was so distorted she had to eject Counting Crows and punch up Primus. A little distortion never hurt Primus.

The most noble ladies, in hooded forest green robes, had already taken up their forked brooms when Martha arrived at midnight, as Samhain Eve turned to Hallowmas. The brooms, known as besoms, were for sweeping, not flight, as the witches prepared the already immaculate white carpeted floor of Catherine Bailey's living room for the casting of their circle.

After determining that Selene was not among them, Martha changed into her robe in the hall, folded her clothes and placed them under her purse, grabbed a besom, and swept her way alongside Catherine. "Heard from Selene?" she whispered from under her hood.

Catherine shook her head.

"She promised she'd be here for my initiation. Maybe she forgot about spring ahead, fall back?" Daylight savings had ended at 2:00 A.M. the previous morning.

"Then she'd have been here an hour early," the plump older woman pointed out sensibly enough; she stopped sweeping and drew Martha over to the side of the room, beside the cantilevered floor-to-ceiling, wall-to-wall picture windows looking out over a heavily wooded hillside north of Mill Valley. There were no neighboring houses to mar the view—or the privacy. "I know how you feel, sweetheart. But if she doesn't show up, we can go on with your initiation without her. The coven is what matters; this is not a cult of personality."

"But what if something's wrong—you know she took the Fair Lady today? What if she needs us?"

Catherine threw back her hood and brushed several unruly strands of *I Love Lucy* orange curls away from her face. "Do you remember when Selene was so badly hurt, about six or seven years ago?"

"When that guy who thought he was a vampire tried to rip her throat out?"

A barely perceptible pause. "Ahhh . . . yes. Nick Santos. It happened at the Yule Sabbat up at Tahoe."

"At Mr. Whistler's. I remember. I was like ten."

"And a few weeks later, after we'd brought her home, Selene threw a pulmonary embolism—know what that is?"

"An embolism's like a blood clot. Daddy Don had one in his leg."

"And your godmother had one in her lung. Selene was alone up at the A-frame. When the embolism lodged she was paralyzed by the pain. Managed to take in a sip of air every now and then, but other than that she couldn't move a muscle. Which they said later probably saved her life, because if she'd jarred the embolism loose, its next stop would have been her heart, and that would have killed her."

"So what happened?" asked Martha warily, not sure where the lesson was going.

"Half the coven showed up at her house within the hour. I'll never forget; I was watching TV, suddenly there was a roaring sound in my head—not my ears, my head—accompanied by this overwhelming sense that something was wrong with Selene. I called her number—no answer. Sherman was off somewhere" (Catherine's husband was Sherman Bailey, the eminent Mill Valley psychologist) "so I jumped in the car and took off. MV to Bobo via the Panoramic. I was over the mountain in twenty minutes, at her house in thirty. I still don't know how I managed it. When I arrived, though, Carol was already there, and had called the paramedics. And while we were waiting for the ambulance, the two Barbaras showed up, and we compared notes: we'd all gotten the same weird feeling at more or less the same time."

Catherine pulled her hood back over her head, picked up her besom again, and began sweeping. "Point is, sweetheart," she said over her shoulder, "if Selene wants us, one way or another, she'll let us know."

—

Martha had to wait in the kitchen while the others cast the sacred circle. She was in a state somewhere between shock and despair. It had been Selene who'd taught her everything she knew about Wicca, Selene who'd introduced her to the coven, Selene who'd encouraged her to take her initiation. Martha knew what was coming from studying her Misikidak, and it was hard for her to imagine accepting the five-fold kiss, much less a forty-stroke scourging, from anyone other than her godmother. When the bell rang in the living room Martha marched down the carpeted hall as though she were being summoned to her execution instead of to her initiation into the mysteries of Wicca.

Although she'd grown up around clothing-optional beaches, hot springs, hot tubs, and topless biker mamas, and attended one or two lesser sky-clad Sabbats as a guest of the coven in the preceding year (always leaving before the orgy), it still gave Martha a jolt of adolescent discomfort when she turned the corner of the living room to see the eleven other women, ranging in age from their mid-twenties to their mid-sixties, standing naked in their circle.

She wondered, not for the first time, if she were going to turn out to be a lesbian—not because she found the bodies sexually arousing or anything, but because they always fascinated and disturbed her so. She had time for a quick peep around the circle: Catherine was an opulent, heavy-breasted, round-bellied ur-fertility goddess; next to her old Faye was a dowager-humped question-mark crone; Carol, twenty years after childbearing, scored with stretch lines, was a brown tiger with black stripes; Heloise was pink, with white scars and wrinkles; and so on, all the way around to the two Barbaras, who were holding hands, their backs to Martha as she entered the room. One Barbara was pear-shaped from behind, a lush, blush-colored overripe Bosc pear with legs; the other, standing with her feet pressed primly together, was long-necked, narrow-shouldered, straight-hipped, graceful, and white as a lily.

Too weird, too funny, too mysterious. Too much flesh and too much shadow. There was something awfully powerful about a woman's body, something that included sex, but went beyond it as well. Martha couldn't name it, but she couldn't deny it either. The girl suppressed a quick shudder: it was her turn to join them.

Catherine took a formal step backward. Outside the circle, which had closed behind her, she and Martha exchanged passwords—"Perfect love," "Perfect trust"—and a quick peck on the lips. Then Martha produced from the pocket of her robe five nylon cords of red, blue, violet, green, and brown. Catherine took them from her. "Take your robe off."

Martha grabbed the neck of her robe in either hand and pulled it off over her head; embarrassed again, she busied herself in folding her robe and placing it with the other discarded robes on the table in the adjoining dining room.

"Now I'm not going to blindfold you," Catherine explained. "But you have to keep your eyes shut until the Ring of Power is actually on your finger. It's part of the test—if you open your eyes even once before then, you'll have to wait until the next Sabbat to try again."

Catherine stepped behind Martha, and with her left arm around the girl's waist tugged her gently backward through a gap in the circle. The Barbaras parted for them, and closed behind them. Then the older woman knelt before the acolyte and tied one cord around Martha's left ankle and the other around her right knee. "Turn around, and put your hands behind your back."

Martha obeyed and Catherine bound her hands loosely with the three remaining cords while delivering the charge of the Goddess, the one that begins, "Oh listen to the words of the Great Mother . . ." and ends, "So mote it be."

Charge completed, Catherine took the girl by the waist again and led her twelve times around the circle. Several times during the course of the circumambulation, Martha came perilously close to opening her eyes; she came even closer when it was time to receive the five-fold kiss. Ever since she'd learned of it, she'd assumed it would be her godmother's dry soft lips brushing her ankles, knees, vagina, breasts, and lips, and somehow that would have been okay with her. With Selene doing it, it would have been more like being born than anything sexual.

But instead it was Catherine's lips, full and warm, that were kissing her, first the bound ankle, then the unbound, and in between kisses it was the red-headed witch reciting the formula: "Blessed thy feet that have brought thee . . ." Next her knees were kissed and blessed; then—*whoaashit*—those soft insistent lips were pressed firmly against the front of Martha's pussy, a quick little **O** of a kiss. "Blessed the womb, bearer of life . . ."

Catherine stood, then bent to kiss each of Martha's nipples. "Blessed thy breasts, Goddess-formed in beauty . . ." Finally a brief pressure of the soft lips to Martha's own—"Blessed these lips, that would speak sacred names"—and the first part of the ritual was over.

Now came the scourge. "Will you suffer to learn?" was Catherine's ritual question.

"I will."

"Then kneel before the altar."

Martha almost opened her eyes again to look around for the altar, but caught herself just in time. Catherine took her by the waist and led her over, helped her kneel, then whisked her three times across her bare buttocks with the leather scourge.

It didn't hurt—not physically, anyway, not much, which was just as well, as the first three blows were followed by a series of seven, nine, and finally twenty-one strokes. But there was something so emotionally powerful about being whipped publicly—not just whipped, but whipped naked, kneeling, and bound—that Martha couldn't help sobbing anyway, tentatively and without focus at first, until her mind, casting about for a suitable sorrow to weep over, settled briefly on Selene's absence; halfway through the last round of strokes, though, Martha decided she was crying for Connie and Moll as well—for all her missing mothers.

But by the time it was over and Catherine, cautioning her to continue to keep her eyes shut, had helped her to her feet and untied her bonds, Martha was feeling much lighter, as if something had been released from deep inside, and she was even ready to consider forgiving all three mothers for having so cruelly deserted her.

The ritual anointing, although it also involved her privates, was a piece of cake compared to the kiss and the scourging. Catherine daubed her above each breast, then over the vagina, first with oil, then with wine, then with spit, nine daubs in all, while leading her through the oath: "May my own powers against me move / Should I false to this oath prove. . . ."

Martha sensed the commotion, rather than heard it. A soft shifting of weight as the circle parted after the final daub, and then Catherine must have stepped back: the girl stood alone in the circle for the first time since crossing into it. But only for a moment—then she felt a stirring in the air as someone approached her across the intervening blackness.

Martha's slender body swayed against an unsubstantial wind as she fought the instinct to open her eyes. It was Selene coming toward her, and yet it was not Selene. Or it was Selene gone to hell and back, a hot dry Selene with a scorched and bitter scent, kneeling before her, slipping a heavy ring onto the third finger of her right hand, kissing the back of her hand with lips so hot they left a burning sensation.

"Have you chosen a name?" A dry, pained whisper—but Selene's voice nonetheless.

"Hecate."

"Then welcome, Hecate, to the Coven of Diana. I bestow upon thee the Ring of Power."

Martha was seized, embraced briefly; she smelled smoke, felt a feverish body pressed against her and a birdlike heartbeat against her own.

Selene managed one last dry whisper—"My power I will unto thee"—before collapsing into her goddaughter's arms. Catherine sprang forward, and the two of them helped lower the high priestess's body gently to the floor.

6

When Selene came to she found herself lying on the floor of Catherine Bailey's living room staring up at a pair of watery blue bloodshot eyes magnified by round-lensed spectacles. "Sherman."

"Selene." Catherine's husband, a tubby man with a walrus mustache and sparse ponytail, stared down at her with practiced concern. "Are you back with us?"

"So far as I know." No throat pain as long as she whispered.

"Thank God for that. I don't know why people expect a psychologist to be any use in emergencies." He helped her to a sitting position; she indicated she wanted to stand, and he gave her his arm. "If you'd been conscious I could have consoled your inner child—beyond that I'm out of my depth."

"We'll take care of her now," said Martha, hurrying to Selene's side and taking her other arm.

"Are you going to be okay?" Sherman asked. "Do you want me to drive you over to Marin General to get checked out? What'd you take, anyway? Smells like you did a Richard Pryor with it."

"Belladonna," she whispered. "But I'll be fine."

No response.

"Really, Sherman. You can go on back to whatever you were doing."

He still seemed reluctant to exit a room full of twelve naked women—and one naked girl; eventually Catherine walked him down the hall, explaining that the orgy hadn't been canceled, just postponed for an hour or so. "The troops are getting restless," he replied.

With her loosely curled fist she demonstrated what the troops could do with themselves, then kissed him and gave him a gentle shove. When she returned to the living room, Selene was lying with her head in Martha's lap on one of the sofas that had been shoved back against the wall opposite the picture windows. The two of them were still naked, but the other ladies were rerobing and re-forming their circle, seated this time, in front of the sofa. Upon seeing Catherine, Selene sat up and patted the cushion next to her. "Cathy, over here," she whispered hoarsely. "I have to ask you something before we go on."

Catherine detoured past the dining room, grabbed the last three robes from the table. They were identical except for size; she donned the 16, carried one 6 over to Martha, and helped Selene slip the other 6 over her head before joining her on the couch. "What did you want to ask?"

Selene reached out and adjusted Catherine's hood, pulling it back from her eyes, fixing her with a meaningful if somewhat bleary stare. "After supper tonight, did you sneak down to the laundry room and eat a napoleon?"

Catherine's mouth fell open. Before she could answer, Selene turned to Martha. "And you, my darling—Daddy Don was asleep —you went out to the shed and pinched a bud from the drying rack, smoked it in your little silver pipe, the one with the turquoise beads. Yes?"

Martha nodded, her gray eyes gone round and solemn, just as Catherine found her voice. "Sherman and I," she began haltingly. "We're trying to lose weight. But no one could have—"

Selene turned back to her with a trace of the old twinkle in her eye. "While you were down in the basement with Napoleon, Sherman was in his study with Sara Lee."

"Why that cheating son of a bitch!"

Selene stroked the smooth satin over Catherine's thigh with a warm gentle hand. "I'll tell you something else. In the bottom right-hand drawer of his desk, Sherman has a stack of dirty magazines. He took out a few to browse through while you were doing the dishes. They were *Plumpers and Big Women, Meaty Mamas,* and *Fat Femmes.* So if you're dieting for your hubby, dearie, you're wasting your time."

Selene turned to the others, sitting in a flattened oval at her feet. The brief flash of merriment had died away. "Obviously, I flew. At first it was like Gertrude Stein's description of Oakland, only more so. There was no there *anywhere.* I began to wonder whether I *had* died after all—I was nowhere, out of time, disembodied, frightened. I wanted to go back, I didn't want to have to leave my friends yet. I especially wasn't ready to leave Martha behind."

She looked down at the girl, who had joined the circle on the floor. "And as soon as I thought of you, my darling, I saw you from above. Not too far above—a few yards, perhaps, but it was hard to tell—I had no body, no eyes, so there was no frame, no perspective. Wherever I was looking from, though, and wherever you moved, I could see through to you. I would have been above the roof of your porch, yet I could see you. When you went out the back door, then I could see the roof behind you. When you entered the shed, the shed roof disappeared, but I saw the smoke from your pipe flattening against it."

Selene took Catherine's hand. "When I saw Martha, and was reminded of the Sabbat tonight, I thought of you, Cathy, and then I saw you. Seeing you, I thought of Sherman, and no sooner did I think of him then I saw him in his study."

She leaned forward, still holding Catherine's hand, as if she were afraid she might float off again, and began looking around the circle, meeting each of the women's eyes in turn. "I visited most of the rest of you, too. I suppose it would have been between six and ten, your time. Or perhaps I should say, *time* time—there was no time where I had been. Then I went farther. I thought of . . ."

She had started to say "Martha's mother" but thought better of it. She had indeed seen Moll Herrick, but in circumstances some-where beyond compromising: the bed upon which the now heavy-set fifty-two-year-old woman was disporting nude with several other hefty older women was surrounded by a video crew, lights, booms, cameras and all; out of curiosity Selene glanced around the room to determine just where on earth she was, and saw a *New York Post* folded on a chair; a clapboard being wielded by one of the crew read "A-Mature Productions/*Moll Montana Experience, Vol. III.*" But that would have been quite a load to dump on Martha.

". . . of a friend I hadn't seen in years, and no sooner had I thought of her, then I was there. Clearly distance didn't matter any more than time did. But just to be sure—no, just because I wanted to—no, because I couldn't help it . . . You all know me well enough to know what Jamey Whistler means to me. . . ."

Selene stopped, swallowed. Her throat was beginning to burn again. She asked for water, and waited for Martha to return from the kitchen with a bottle of Evian before going on. "He's been away for a year now—I suppose that's why I didn't think of him sooner—but at any rate, as soon as I did, I saw him. But it was far from what I would have expected. He was sitting in the hold of some sort of wooden ship, surrounded by what looked like burlap-wrapped hay bales. His head was between his knees and his shoulders were shaking, and it wasn't until he looked up that I realized he was crying. Crying!" *Can you imagine that?* her tone of voice implied. She took another sip of water.

"I wanted to get closer, to try to contact him, but before I could, something pulled me back and I found myself floating high above my bed, watching a man in black bending over my body, pressing a pillow against my face.

"I started to try to figure out where—and what—I'd been, and for how long, and what it all meant, but I had to force myself to stop—clearly there was no end to the muddle my mind could make of the infinite. Or vice versa. After a minute or two he removed the pillow and stooped to put his ear to my chest, then stood up and reached down toward my crotch. I thought for a moment he was going to molest me, but he only plucked out a pubic hair, and nodded like he was satisfied. That's when I first saw his face. He looked a little like the devil—not the God of the Underworld or anything—more like a ham actor made up to play the devil in *Damn Yankees*—a cheap road-show *Damn Yankees* at that.

"That's also when I understood that he had only been reassuring himself that I was dead, that he had been listening for a heartbeat and had found none. An intense fear washed over me—was it too late to go back? Would I be trapped in a corpse for all eternity? But then suddenly, with no sense of in-between, no rush through space or anything—just *poof!*—I was back in my body staring up at the skylight through my good old human eyes. Then came a thought: *Welcome back, Selene.* I barely had time to consider who or what was welcoming whom or what when I smelled the smoke. It didn't occur to me at first that this man I'd seen, this road-show devil, or whatever the hell he was—had set the fire. I wasn't even sure whether he was real or a hallucination. Then I heard the front door slam, and a car start up, and the smoke came billowing up over the edge of the loft, and I was coughing and choking, and the waterbed was rocking, and I couldn't think about anything but fighting for air. I rolled over the side of the bed and dropped down flat on the floor, started crawling towards the ladder. But the flames were already licking over the edge of the loft, so instead I crawled in the other direction, over to the bureau, reached an arm up, felt around for my sewing basket, grabbed the scissors out of it, crawled back to the bed, took a deep breath, climbed up onto it, and started stabbing like a maniac at the mattress, rocking on my knees to make the water come out faster, sawing away at the mattress until there was a beautiful silver waterfall spilling across the floor and over the edge of the loft. It sounded like the hissing of a thousand snakes down below; black smoke was billowing up so heavily I couldn't get any air, so I wrapped one of the wet bedsheets around me, felt under the bureau for my rubber thongs, and started down the ladder.

"Halfway down, the rungs started collapsing under my weight; I fell through them one after the other, *clacketa clacketa clacketa,* until *whomp!,* I hit the floor still wrapped in the sheet, teetering, trying not to fall on my face onto the floorboards, which are so hot they're starting to melt my rubber thongs." She turned to Catherine. "That's when I remembered the fire walkers."

Catherine nodded in recognition. Walking on coals had been quite the rage in Marin County back in the late eighties. Sherman had conducted a one-day self-realization seminar with a troupe from Rishikesh; for three hundred bucks a head you got a box lunch, a secret mantra, and the sense of accomplishment and self-worth at having overcome your fears and performed the seemingly impossible feat of walking barefoot over a twelve-foot-long carpet of coals. Seemingly: as the always skeptical Jamey Whistler had pointed out afterward, the principle was the same as basting a turkey: anybody can stick a hand into a 450 degree oven without getting burned— the trick is not to leave it in too long.

Selene continued. "By now the thongs were completely melted to the floor—I stepped out of them and started through the smoke—I couldn't remember the mantra the fire walk facilitator sold us, but it didn't matter—the next thing I knew I was standing on my front doorstep shivering and coughing.

"All at once I remembered the Test of the Fair Lady, and won- dered how much of this had been part of it? Had I conjured up this man? This devil? Then I remembered Whistler in the hold of the ship. . . ."

A pause followed. All this, from rejoining her body to standing on her doorstep, Selene recalled clearly enough, but after that the memories came in chunks, like icebergs floating across a black dream sea. Afraid for Jamey. Afraid for herself. Cold and wet. The white sheet puddled around her feet. The dark steps leading around the side of the house and up to the deck. Stumbling over a paper- wrapped parcel—the laundry—she'd never gotten around to taking it in that afternoon. Dressing in the dark. The A-frame groaning and creaking alarmingly, sounding almost human in its pain. Her hiking boots by the back door. Feeling around for the car keys hanging from a nail just inside the door.

No memory of descending the path to the one-car garage built into the side of the hill, or of opening the overhead door, but a clear image of the long silver snout of Whistler's '58 Jaguar saloon gleaming in the darkness of the garage. A fervent prayer that the temperamental beast would start. . . .

The drive itself was a total blank. Had she been fleeing blindly? Honoring her witch's word to Martha? Impossible to say. The next thing she remembered clearly was standing in the doorway of Catherine's living room, looking at the circle of the coven from the outside, and understanding with an overwhelming sense of sadness that although the Test of the Fair Lady had indeed addressed the question that had been foremost in her mind—*witch or ither?*—the answer itself was virtually meaningless.

Witches fly, ithers die. She had flown because she was a witch; she was a witch because she had flown. No larger question had been answered directly, but even her brief tour of *there*-lessness had convinced her that whatever being a witch meant, beyond not dying from belladonna, it had fuck-all to do with a bunch of women standing naked in a circle in Mill Valley reciting the Lord's Prayer backward.

So, in the face of two revelations, one a tautology and the other unutterable, she had stripped off her clothes, entered the circle through the portal of the Barbaras, taken a ring from the right index finger of Ariadne, the most recently initiated witch, approached Martha standing blind, naked, and vulnerable in the center of the circle, shoulders squared, breasts thrust bravely forward, and then, just before everything went black, she had bestowed the Ring of Power upon Moll and Jamey's daughter. . . .

━

Selene looked down at the seated witches. How long the pause had lasted she could not have said. "Where was I?"

"You remembered Whistler in the hold of the ship," somebody said.

"Oh yes." Selene was parched again. As she took a last slug of Evian and looked down at the upturned ring of faces she realized that while she still had no idea what her path was to be, the task the Fair Lady had set for her was pretty obvious: Jamey Whistler was in trouble—he needed her.

She rose too abruptly and found herself swaying dizzily, colored stars exploding across her field of vision. Catherine's strong arms steadied her as her knees began to buckle; Catherine and Martha eased her gently down to the couch.

"Where do you think you're going?" asked Catherine.

Where indeed? thought Selene. Then it came to her: "The island of Santa Luz," she replied. "U.S. Virgins. Anybody know how the hell I get there?"

7

Seven hours later Selene found herself staring at a wild-haired witch in the dim mirror of an airplane bathroom, wondering just what in the name of the Great Horned God she thought she was doing. Was this only some sort of delayed midlife crisis after all? It wouldn't be uncommon; even if she weren't officially premenopausal (which she was, according to her nurse-practitioner: her mood swings were stronger and her periods weaker; she'd missed one entirely two months ago, and *not* because she was pregnant), clerics of all description were inclined toward midlife crises—the Catholic Church had spawned a whole cottage industry of retreats for vocationally troubled priests.

Wicca, though—a witch with doubts was on her own. Though she *had* flown; Catherine and Martha had confirmed that. And if she had flown, then Whistler was indeed in trouble. And that road-show devil: he'd been real enough. Apparitions didn't start fires. Although—

But there were only two coach bathrooms on the nearly full connecting flight to Denver; this was neither the place nor the time. She splashed some water on her face, retwisted her braid and pinned it up again, then returned to her seat in time for breakfast. Her first solid food in twenty-four hours, not counting the belladonna tart. No sleep, either. After canceling the post-Sabbat orgy—a first, as far as Selene could remember—the coven had departed in convoy for Selene's house, where the witches set to work cleaning up the ground floor with all the energy they'd been saving for the orgy, while Selene took a cold shower to cool herself down, shampooing repeatedly to get the smell of smoke out of her hair.

They had to bring a ladder up from Martha's A-frame to get to the loft. There was some question about the supporting pillars, which were badly scorched. In the end they decided that it would be safe for Selene to climb up there alone, but only for as long as it took her to pack. When she reached the top of the ladder she saw that while the fire damage was minimal, the smoke had rendered her best clothes unwearable. Fortunately, the gems of her T-shirt collection had been out on the deck in the bundles of clean laundry, along with her favorite shorts, jeans, panties, and socks, so she had no trouble finding enough casual clothes to fill the suitcase. But she'd definitely have to do some serious shopping in Miami. Or better still on St. Thomas, where she'd have to change planes again—Charlotte Amalie was a duty-free port, according to Catherine's year-old Caribbean guidebook.

Choosing which of her tools to take along proved more difficult. Alone in the loft, she knelt in front of her altar, threw back the black damask cover, and opened the wicker doors. One at a time, with a reverence that came of long habit, but that she no longer particularly felt, she removed her white-hilted, steel-bladed athame, her stag's-horn chalice, her shallow enameled thurible, her red silk cingulum and red velvet garter, and her loose-leaf Book of Shadows, placing them carefully atop the altar. None of them had been damaged, except by smoke, but all of them seemed somehow tainted, diminished by her recent loss of faith.

But it was not the loss of faith that kept her from taking them along; rather it was the dust mote of faith that remained to her. She was no longer sure that all the rituals of Wicca were worth more than the empty promises of her childhood Christianity—but she wasn't sure they weren't, either, or she wouldn't have been leaving for the Caribbean. All she knew was that using the tools and performing the rites out of superstition or habit would be a form of sacrilege, if indeed there was such a thing as sacrilege. And if not, then why lug them around?

In the end, she took only her goat-bladder sack of runestones, and that more for comfort than guidance. Selene had carved the tiles herself, so long ago that ivory had still been legally obtainable; her own fingers had worn them smooth. As to whether she would cast them tomorrow morning, as she had every morning of her life for over a quarter of a century, or cast them into the Caribbean instead, she didn't have the slightest idea. But they were as familiar to her as her own toes, and they didn't take up much room in her suitcase, so what the hell.

Saying good-bye to Martha was difficult too—and Martha hadn't made it any easier. A brisk handshake, eyes averted, had been the girl's farewell of choice as Selene tossed her suitcase into the trunk of the Jaguar. Then, pointedly: "I'll say good-bye to Daddy Don for you. *Please* take care of yourself, Selene."

Selene sensed that Martha's capacity for denial was stretched to the breaking point. This was as close as the girl could come to reminding Selene that she and Daddy Don were the closest thing to parents she had, and that she understood that she might be in the process of losing both of them.

"I will, dearie," Selene had replied gently.

"You shouldn't be driving, you know. Or flying, not until your temperature comes down."

"I know."

"Do you have your passport?"

"Don't need it for Santa Luz—it's a U.S. territory. But yes, I packed it anyway, just in case."

"Okay. See y'around." Martha had turned her back and started walking away.

"Hey you!" Selene grabbed her from behind by her sausage-length blond dreadlocks.

"Hey! Ow! What?" Martha turned to face Selene; the tears in her lovely gray eyes were not from the pain of having her hair gently tugged. They embraced. Selene took Martha's head between her hands and kissed her tears, then her forehead. "Bless you, baby. I'll call you—Witch's Word."

"I'll keep an eye on your place—Witch's Word."

"And the cat! I almost forgot Dunstan."

"And the cat."

Selene had opened the door of the Jag, then turned back one last time. "If I'd had a daughter of my own, I'd have wanted her to turn out just like you."

But Martha had the last word: "And if I'd had a mother . . ." she began, and they had both laughed tearfully.

—

It was as good a parting as any they could have engineered, given the circumstances, thought Selene as the stewardess set her breakfast down. It proved to be a Mexican omelette, with which Selene set some sort of speed record: ten minutes from tray to barf bag. It would have been five, but for the sake of her fellow passengers she managed to delay the inevitable until she reached the fortuitously unoccupied john.

One of the stewardesses was in the galley when Selene emerged from the bathroom for the second time. Selene asked her for some crackers and a glass of water; this second breakfast stayed down. They were an hour into the flight when Selene managed to doze off. Her dreams took her back to Whistler. This time she was with him in the hold of the boat, but he could not see her; when she tapped him on the shoulder her fingers went right through him, as if *he* were the disembodied soul.

Then she was awake again. The businessman by the window had leaned across the empty middle seat and was tugging firmly at the sleeve of her old black cardigan, staring at her in some alarm.

"I'm sorry. Was I babbling?"

"The babbling wasn't so bad, but the way you were flailing your arms I was afraid I'd get my nose broken." He was a jowly, lawyerly-looking man in his mid-fifties, with a laptop computer propped up on the seat tray in front of him. "Can I offer you a Valium?"

"Oh dear. No thank you." Selene apologized again. "I'm afraid I'm the seatmate from hell this morning."

He shrugged a polite disclaimer and turned back to his laptop. Selene reclined her seatback, folded her hands across her lap—under the seat belt, for the sake of her neighbor—and tried to go back to her dream. She wanted to see if she could pick up any clues as to Whistler's whereabouts. She wasn't expecting much—Selene had never been particularly strong on dream magic, having found the subconscious to be a powerful but largely unreliable ally. She succeeded in dozing off briefly, though, and when she did she dreamed up a powerfully evocative image.

Unfortunately, it was of eating a grilled cheese sandwich at the Ludman Diner. *American* cheese. Quarter inch of orange goo, tiny beads of buttery moisture sweating up from the toast. Vivid enough—she could hear the scritch-scratchy sound of the toast when she bit into the sandwich—but fuck-all to do with Whistler, she realized as she awoke.

Fuck all. Second time she'd used that expression since midnight. It had been one of Jamey's; he'd used it the very first time he'd spoken to her. The inaptness of her grilled cheese dream made her smile: somehow her subconscious had managed to select one of the few images floating around her universe that did *not* remind her of Jamey Whistler.

Selene closed her eyes again, and let her thoughts wander back to that first meeting. 1967. The Summer of Love. No, not the Summer of Love—they'd met at the Sabbat of the autumnal equinox. The Fall of Love, rather.

—

Yes, the Fall of Love. That would do nicely for a description of the whole Haight-Ashbury scene by September of '67. Selene's own situation was illustrative: She and two other witches, one of whom was dating an abusive speed freak, and the other who *was* an abusive speed freak, were sharing a basement apartment at the corner of Page and Central, but their landlady, anticipating that the recent appreciation of Haight property values would continue indefinitely (innocents and predators were still being drawn to the deteriorating scene like flies to a corpse) had announced her intention to raise the rent on the two-room flat.

Of the three roomies, only Selene had regular employment, and her job—cocktail waitress at the Hipper Than Thou in North Beach—was in considerable jeopardy. She got it through Moll's sister Connie, with whom she'd stayed when she first arrived in San Francisco. Connie would have had to give up the job soon anyway, because she and her new husband, Don, were about to move to Bolinas, so she was happy to recommend her sister's friend to the boss, a fabled North Beach character.

Unfortunately, he was also a fabled North Beach asshole. Selene had been working for him nearly two years by the fall of '67, but when she asked him if she could have Friday night off he had removed his cigar from his fat red lips just long enough to inform her that better-looking chicks than her were kneeling in line to suck his dick for her job.

On the other hand, it hadn't been a definite no, and given the choice between telling Morgana, the high priestess, that she would be unable to attend the Lesser Sabbat, or losing her job and possibly her apartment and starving to death on the street, she would take the latter every time. Less trouble.

And if she did return to work Saturday night to find her job had gone to a hippie chick with knee pads, then both her replacement and the fabled North Beach character were going to have a nice crimson surprise in store for them at the climax of one of their next backroom blow jobs.

Sometimes being a witch was inconvenient, but it was never without its compensations.

8

"Bad news and good news." On the evening of the autumnal equinox of 1967, High Priestess Morgana greeted Selene at the door of the Broadway House, a handsome old prequake black-trimmed gray Victorian on San Francisco's outer Broadway. It had been converted to a bordello in the twenties, and the floor plan had proved convenient for a covenstead. "Mr. Flood has sent his regrets—he will be unable to attend either the sperming or the Sabbat orgy this evening."

"Is that the good news or the bad news?" Selene was not particularly fond of Mr. Flood. Knowing this, Morgana had selected him as Selene's orgy partner for the last two Sabbats in a row.

"Depends upon how you feel about his replacement, I suppose. English fellow, comes with quite a recommendation from High Priestess Aphrodite in London. Here, take a peek."

Morgana, a robust-looking woman in her mid-fifties with upswept hair dyed midnight black, pulled Selene into the coat closet in the hall, where a one-way mirror looked onto the parlor. Lots of peepholes and one-way mirrors in the Broadway house. The property had cost the priestess a fortune. Providentially, she had two: Morgana had been widowed twice, each time by wealthy older men who had died of natural causes. ("All-natural causes," she used

to joke in the privacy of the coven. "No artificial coloring or pre-
servatives.") "Well, what do you think?"

Selene, who couldn't take her eyes off the young man in the
parlor, feigned indifference. "As the high priestess wills."

Morgana chuckled. "Don't bullshit an old bullshitter, sweetie.
You've been dreamy-eyed since you caught sight of him."

Selene didn't bother to deny it—she'd all but fogged up her
side of the mirror—but she did blush prettily when Morgana told
her it would be her job to brief the handsome young man in the
parlor (he seemed to be young, though his boyishly cut hair was a
becoming shade of gray) on what would be expected of him this
evening. Freshman orientation always embarrassed the hell out of
Selene, who still found it easier to have sex than to talk about it.

Robed and hooded, Selene waited for the grandfather clock in
the parlor to finish striking nine before entering.

He stood up—he was a lean six-footer; she was a lean five-
footer—and held out his hand, his wrist cocked at a donnish angle,
as if he were wearing an academic's gown instead of a soft-collared
periwinkle polo shirt and tailored wheat jeans. "Jamey Whistler."

"Hi. I'm Selene." Her hand slipped easily into his.

"The Goddess of the Moon?"

"Just a namesake." Her hand still in his.

He smiled down at her. "Not as far as I'm concerned."

She looked up, met his wide-set gray eyes, and felt a flutter
from her heart to her womb that was not lust, but included it. It
was like a foreknowing; she ducked her head, hiding her blush
under her hood. "Let's get down to business, shall we? How much
do you know about Wicca?"

"Fuck-all," he replied pleasantly. "And despite having attended
several orgies at your sister house in London, I have steadfastly re-
sisted all attempts to improve my knowledge."

Selene sat down on the loveseat and smoothed the lap of her
robe. "At least you're honest."

"At least?" Unbidden, he sat beside her on the yellow silk, his
knee only millimeters from hers. "Honesty is one of my chiefest

virtues. Born of not giving a shit, of course, but it's still a beautiful thing, if truth is beauty, and beauty truth."

"Actually, it's the other way around." She couldn't help it—there was something challenging in his manner. Even if she did have a crush on him the size of the moon. " 'Beauty is truth, truth beauty.' Keats. 'Ode on a Grecian Urn.' "

"I see. And how much *is* owed on a Grecian urn?"

Selene laughed in spite of herself—apparently freshman English jokes were the same on either side of the pond. "About three, four drachma."

"Sounds right." Then he did something quite unexpected—he reached out a long-fingered hand and gently pushed her hood back. "If beauty is truth, you must be the most honest woman in San Francisco," he said, with his gray eyes locked to hers. Not a color she'd seen before—metallic gray, but soft metal: solder, not steel.

"Don't bullshit a bullshitter," she retorted confidently, though she'd heard the phrase for the first time only a few minutes before. She liked the way it sounded coming out of her mouth.

But he hadn't bought it. "Firstly, *you're* no bullshitter. Though if you'd like to become one, I'm reasonably sure I can help you." He replaced her hood, as gently as if he were bonneting a baby. "Secondly, we've already established that I'm an honest man." His fingers brushed her dark, unruly hair tenderly. "And the truth, lovely witch, is that you possess the sort of delicate beauty best described as pre-Raphaelite. It may be uncommon in these rough parts, but a hundred years ago your lovers would have been queuing up to have miniaturists carve your likeness in cameo, for lockets to be worn close to their hearts."

If it is *bullshit,* thought Selene, *don't ever let it stop.* And then stopped it dead in its tracks, with another Morgana-ism she'd once overheard the high priestess use upon an importunate sperm donor. "That hand that's touching me without my permission—did that used to be yours?"

"Sorry." And suddenly the hand was gone, back at his side with inhuman speed, too fast even for a blur.

Somewhat rattled now, Selene struggled for control—if not of him, at least of herself. "Thank you for the flattery—"

"Compliments."

"All right, compliments. Now can we get down to business?"

"At your service."

"Okay. First: the sperming. I'll get you a robe, and show you up to your room. You're to put it on, nothing underneath, and wait there until someone comes for you. You'll be led to a room, and be allowed to provide sperm for the Sabbat. You're not to peek, nor to touch anyone, nor to address anyone. Afterwards, you'll be led back to your room, and when it's time for the orgy, you'll be summoned."

He hadn't said a word, nor could she read his expression. She went on: "Have you ever been to an autumnal Sabbat?" He shook his head. "No? Well you'll be representing the God of the Corn returning from the Underworld to claim his bride, and—"

He interrupted her. "May I claim you?"

If he *was* jiving, he was a master: the simple question had pierced her to the heart. *You must,* she thought, but said nothing. She didn't think her voice could handle the nuances.

—

Selene hurried through the rest of the instructions, then led Jamey up the back stairs to the attic. "It's the smallest room in the house," she explained in a whisper, opening the door, "but it's worth it for the view—whoops, watch your head."

Low slanted ceiling; a dormer window faced the west. Far out over the unseen ocean, the stars were struggling bravely; later that night there would be a moon for sex magick.

And a bed for it: king-size, with a stout brass head rail. Goose-down comforters, satin sheets, and all sorts of pillows, soft, hard, round, angled, cut-out. He tossed his overnight bag on the bed; she handed him the hooded crimson robe she'd selected from the linen closet on the second floor. "Here, put this on—hood up, arms in, penis out. I'll be back for you in about twenty minutes. Any questions?"

"Just one." He inspected the robe (wide sleeves, placketed crotch, executioner-style hood, but no eyeslits), shrugged, and started to pull his polo shirt over his head. "Do you want me hard or soft when you arrive?"

Selene, blushing under her own hood, fought back a grin. "Whichever you feel is to your best advantage." It was not a question that had ever come up before.

—

The customary practice was to dispatch a single witch to accompany each sperm donor from his room to the Circle Room, but when Selene told them about Whistler's question and her ad-libbed response, they immediately began laying bets—hard or soft, big or small, various parlays—and it was an entire delegation of green-robed witches that arrived at Whistler's door: Morgana, who'd wagered a full-body massage on hard against Selene's soft; Vivienne, an angular-featured blonde from Marseilles, who'd bet Sidonia, a former Las Vegas call girl, that any man who'd even dare pose such a question had to be hung like a baguette; Sidonia herself, who had no personal knowledge of Whistler, but had done enough gambling in her time, and seen enough penises, to know where the odds lay; and of course Selene, who had only bet on soft as a knee-jerk response to Whistler's arrogance, and was beginning to think she'd backed the wrong horse even before they'd knocked thrice and opened the door.

When the hooded, crimson-robed figure turned blindly to meet them, Selene, the youngest and least experienced of the four witches, had to stifle a gasp. Sidonia, whose bet with Vivienne involved the loser Easy-Offing the winner's oven, spread her hands wide, shrugged, and made a you-never-know face, while Morgana and Vivienne applauded each other—and Whistler—in mime.

Selene didn't care about losing her bet. What really galled her was the feeling, as she stepped forward to seize him by his protruding member and lead him down to the circle room, that under that crimson hood he was almost certainly grinning that infuriating, cocksure grin of his.

⬥

A ripple ran around the circle of witches when Selene led Whistler into the room. He was the third sperm donor of the evening; she positioned him in front of the cast-iron kettle, and expertly began masturbating him. She tried to keep her breathing steady and her mind on witchly matters—this was part of the Sabbat, and not part of the orgy—but was not entirely successful. It wasn't the act that had her nonplussed—in four years as a witch, she'd milked dozens of men—or the size of his penis, but rather it was the way this most detached of sexual connections was starting to feel intensely personal. She struggled to remain dispassionate, but through her hand, and the receptive powers of her psyche, powers she had barely learned to understand, much less control, she found her knees going weak and her sex going wet and soft, and her breasts going tender, as if they were making love face-to-face, staring into each other's eyes.

And when he finally came, when his penis swelled another improbable few centimeters in diameter, the veins distended like blue worms and the skin shiny and white and hard as ivory, when he moaned deep in his throat and began spurting gobs of thick white ejaculate so forcefully that she barely had time to adjust the angle of the shaft so that the arc of precious fluids splashed against the far side of the kettle instead of shooting over it, she found herself sinking to her knees in a near faint. For at that moment, impossible as it may have been, considering his penis was still throbbing in her hand, she could have sworn she felt him inside her, filling her.

It was a phenomenon she had read of—spirit filling spirit, was how the Book of Sex Magick phrased it—but Selene had never experienced it herself, nor met a witch who claimed to. She moaned involuntarily as the ghost of an orgasm, sort of like pins and needles as opposed to full sensation, seized her. Even kneeling, she could scarcely keep her balance; she found herself clutching his still erect penis as tightly as if it were a spar she'd grasped to save herself from drowning.

That must have been painful for him, Selene realized, but he hadn't uttered a sound. She loosed her hold and his penis sprang free, giving no sign of softening despite the orgasm. Selene climbed unsteadily to her feet; as she led him back through the circle of witches she realized she wasn't the only one who'd been affected —she could all but smell the pheromones bubbling out from under the green robes.

—

Morgana, never a speed demon, went through the ritual even more deliberately than usual that night. The opening form, which involved each of the witches kissing the high priestess's robed behind, then receiving upon their pentacle points daubs of Sabbath Oil (wolfbane, cinquefoil, mandrake, moonwort, poppy, saffron, and tobacco, ground into powder and mixed with the sperm of thirteen men), seemed to take forever. And then after the invocation Morgana insisted on narrating the long version of the story of the return of the Corn God, now Lord of the Underworld—as if they didn't all know it by heart.

But finally it ended, and the witches were dispatched to summon their Gods for the evening. This time Selene went alone. When she opened the door, Whistler was standing at the window, still in his robe, but with the hood thrown back and his gray hair catching the moonlight.

"Nice effect," said Selene.

"Beg pardon?" He turned around—no protrusions, no protuberances at the front of the robe.

"The moonlight. On the hair."

"I wasn't posing." Not quite pouting, but clearly his feelings were hurt. It made him look a lot younger. She began to suspect that he was nearer her age—twenty-two—than not. It also made him a lot more likable.

"Of course you weren't. Ready for the orgy?"

"I need to freshen up. Is there a bathroom nearby?"

"Right down the hall."

He took his overnight bag with him; his manner, languid when he left, was entirely assured again when he returned, his step more certain, and his color higher. After living for two years with Moll in the Village, and then another two in the heart of the Haight, Selene understood full well that he'd taken some drug or other in the bathroom, but which drug she couldn't imagine. If it were pot, she'd have smelled it; coke or smack or speed she'd have picked up on readily enough from his vibe alone. She was also a little puzzled that he hadn't offered her any of whatever it was. Perhaps customs were different in England; she decided to give him the benefit of the doubt.

The Circle Room was ready for the orgy, the gently curved, double-wide armless leather chaise set up in the center, and cushions and pillows strewn around the circumference of the high-ceilinged round chamber. Morgana clapped her hands sharply three times when Selene and Whistler appeared in the doorway. "Lords of the Underworld, that side of the room; Goddesses, this side."

Selene gathered with the other green robes. Her roommate Brisen, the one who was dating the abusive speed freak, seized her hand excitedly. "Oh my god, Sel—he's good-looking, too! You have all the luck," said Brisen, as Morgana returned from the red team's huddle on the other side of the room. She had assigned the men numbers from one to thirteen; now she gave the women numbers corresponding to the partners she'd selected for them. "Selene, you're one. Brisen, two; Sidonia, three . . ."

When she was done the women formed a circle around Selene, undressed her, and fastened the stiff, gold-embroidered white Goddess mask over the upper half of her face. Across the room, the men disrobed Whistler and helped him don his half mask—it was leather, with stumpy horns and oval brass grommets around the eyeholes. Then, as the women pushed Selene toward the center of the room, the men did the same for Whistler; the naked couple approached each other slowly, one measured step at a time.

The walk always made Selene self-conscious about her body—boyish forms had been no more treasured where she grew up than were pre-Raphaelite faces. She wondered if the gorgeous man approaching her, his remarkable erection bobbing at each step, was disappointed. But he gave no sign of being dissatisfied. Certainly his penis seemed enthusiastic enough, and he was concentrating fiercely on her body, his wide gray eyes round with desire under the mask, the pupils glittering blackly, filled with wondering lust. His body was lean and rangy, with long smooth swimmer's muscles, his pallor striking—not papery white like an old man but polished like ivory, chest hairless as a statue's.

They came to a halt in the center of the room, next to the couch, standing as close to each other as his erection would permit; she welcomed him back from the Underworld rather more loudly than she'd intended.

"I've returned for you," he replied, as he had been instructed, although with more emphasis on the "you" than was customary. He put his long arms around her and pulled her close against him. She could feel the shaft of his erection throbbing against her heart chakra; she turned her head so her ear was pressed to his heart. It was pounding like hers.

He bent down; she started to tilt her head up for a kiss, but that wasn't what he wanted. Instead he pressed his masked forehead to hers; his eyes sought hers through their masks. "There's only us," he whispered—not a trace of an English accent. "Only us, only you and me. Yes?"

Yes! Again she couldn't trust her voice, but knew he heard her anyway. They kissed, tilting their heads to avoid clashing masks; she let him lower her gently down to the armless chaise. To her left were the green-robed witches, to her right the red-robed men; but when she spread her legs and raised her knees it was for him alone.

CHAPTER

9

When the last couple, Morgana and a Mexican polo player, had finished Selene rushed across the room and grabbed Whistler's hand. It had been torture, being separated from him by the length of the room, watching the other couples make love. Laughing, she tugged him through the arched doorway; they raced up three flights of stairs to the attic without letting go of each other's hands, rushed through the door and froze in awe: the full moon was dead center in the western sky, the entire room aglow with moonlight.

"Have you ever seen anything like it?" Selene whispered, turning her face up to his for their first unmasked kiss.

But the buss was perfunctory on his part. "Have to go freshen up," he said, brushing her lips with his while reaching for his overnight bag. The English accent was back.

"Wait." She put her hand over his on the leather handle. "Whatever's in there, whatever it is you need from there, don't you know you don't have to hide it from me?"

He sat down on the foot of the bed; the room was so small that his knees were practically touching the windowsill. "I'm afraid it's not that simple."

She sat down next to him; she could feel the warmth of his long-boned thigh against hers. The moon, never so large, never so round, filled the dormer window.

"It's not that I don't trust you with my life," he continued, as she wriggled closer; he slipped an arm around her. "What complicates matters is that I'll be asking you to trust me with your life."

"But you know the answer!"

"Yes, but *you* don't know the question. Please, Selene, let me do this my way."

She looked up at him, and zipped her lips with a pursed thumb and forefinger. It was a gesture she hadn't made since she was a little girl in a pinafore. Her eyes were solemn but sparkling.

"Very well, then. Here's what we'll do. I'm going to tell you a little what–if story. No obligation whatsoever to believe in it on your part. And if you decide it's only a fairy tale, or a lunatic's raving, why then, I was only what-iffing, only joking. No harm done—I'm off to the loo and back in a mo."

"And when I believe you?" Her voice sounded strange in her ears.

"You're a stubborn one, aren't you?"

"Mister, you don't know the half of it."

"All right." He reached down and felt around in his overnight bag. She caught a glimpse of a thermos, but what he removed instead was a folding knife of some sort with a long mother-of-pearl handle. When he opened the blade, she saw that it was an antique scalpel. He presented it to her; she turned it in her hands. When the blade caught the moonlight, she saw from the glint that it had been sharpened to a razor's edge. "*If* you believe me (you see, m'dear, I'm quite as stubborn as you) then when I'm done all you have to do is hand this back to me—handle first, if you please—and I'll know what to do from there. Now, are you ready?"

She nodded.

He seemed nervous, younger again. "Right-o. Off we go. I told you earlier that I didn't know fuck-all about witches. What I do know about is vampires." Selene forced her body to be still. "Not just cinema vampires, or vampire novels, but the myths and legends behind them. Every culture has vampire folklore, you know—the *langsuyar* of Malaysia, the *lamiai* of Greece, the *strigoi* of the Romanians (they're almost always partnered up with witches, by the way), the *dhampir* of the Gypsies, the Drinkers of the Caribbean— different names, different manifestations, but what they all have in common is that they drink blood.

"Now, let's play our what-if game? What if there really were some factual basis for all these legends from all the civilizations of the world? What if there were some people upon whom, for whatever reason—some genetic factor, say—blood acts as a drug? Not *just* a drug, but a drug so powerful that all other drug highs are merely pleasant by comparison? Beyond that, what if when these people drank blood they not only got high—and extremely, extremely, extremely randy—but also gained certain physical powers —strength, speed, vastly improved sensory perception, and immunity to disease?"

He took her hand, the one without the scalpel; she held her breath. "And what if these people didn't need to kill anyone for their blood, what if they only needed a sip here, and a sip there— less than you'd give to the Red Cross."

Selene noticed that he had dropped the interrogatory rise at the end of that last what-if. She waited to see if there were going to be any more of them; when there weren't, she handed him the scalpel. She did not turn her throat up for him, but she would have had she been so instructed. It didn't have much to do with belief, either: this was for love, this was for trusting the Goddess. This was for the moon.

He took her hand as if he were going to kiss it. She started to turn it palm up for him, thinking he wanted her wrist; the ease with which he kept her from turning it gave her a hint of his true strength. He gathered a fold of skin from the back of her hand, pinched it hard so that all she felt was the pinch. She looked out at the moon as he made a drawing motion with the scalpel; when next she looked down he was sucking greedily at the back of her hand.

He drank from her for three or four minutes; she could see a dark red blush creeping up from under the neck of his robe; his face flushed. When he'd finished, he kept his face averted, closing the scalpel with one hand, stanching the wound, which proved to be a hair's-breadth slit about an eighth of an inch long, with a firm pressure of his thumb. Not a drop had he wasted. He closed the scalpel and dropped it into his bag, pulled out a tin of decorator Band-Aids, selected a little round one—blue with yellow stars—and pressed it into place with his thumb.

Only then did he raise his eyes to her. She gasped—the whites were red as blood. "Just a side effect," he assured her. "I can use Visine if you'd like." But his voice was thick with lust, and his erection was nosing its way out through the placket in his robe.

"Never mind," she said, reaching for it wonderingly. He tugged at the hem of her robe; she rose up so that he could lift it over her head. Again, the sight of her nakedness seemed to arouse him beyond mortal lust; for the second time that night—the second time in her life—she made telepathic contact with a penis.

He seemed to understand what had happened. "I believe an introduction is in order," he announced, raising himself up high enough to tug his own robe off. His penis was briefly out of sight; when it appeared again, it was pointing toward the moon. "Selene, I'd like you to meet the Creature." He circled its base with thumb and forefinger—they barely reached around—and made the Creature nod hello. "Creature, Selene."

Selene, laughing through the lump in her throat, nodded back. She climbed onto his lap, facing him, so that the Creature was trapped between them, its circumsized head velvety soft, firm and spongy, throbbing against the hollow of her sternum. "How do you do, Creature?" she said, adopting a clipped British accent of her own, as if she were a heroine in an Austen novel. "I think you and I shall prove to be the greatest of friends."

It was Whistler's turn to laugh. He lifted Selene up into the air as if she were light as a doll; she reached down to adjust the angle of the Creature. "Don't let me go," she whispered as he began to lower her—meaning, don't impale me all at once.

"I won't," he said. "I won't ever let you go."

"Oooweee," she replied, trying not to let the implications—among other things—overwhelm her. "You do talk pretty." But

she checked to be sure she could still reach the floor with her feet
—just in case.

—

"Good afternoon, ladies and gentlemen. This is Captain Thaw
again. We'll be landing in Denver in just a few more minutes. . . ."

The pilot's announcement called Selene back from her reverie;
her heart was pounding fiercely. Funny how the thought of
Jamey—and the Creature—still had this effect on her, even after all
these years.

So what had happened between "I'll never let you go" and
now? Wicca had happened. He hadn't let her go, after all; she had
let him go. Beltane; May of 1968—it gave her a jolt to realize that
it had been a quarter century since High Priestess Morgana had
passed through the veil. One unseen weakness in that robust body
—a tiny vein deep in her crafty brain had burst while she and a few
members of the inner circle were practicing an obscure and dangerous form of black magic divination known as orgomancy.

And Selene and Whistler's plans for the future had died with
her. He had proposed to her on Candlemas, back in February;
they'd had a hippie wedding planned for Midsummer's Night in
one of the great meadows of Golden Gate Park. (Midsummer was
an auspicious date on the Wiccan calendar. As for having the ceremony and reception at night, that was for Whistler, whose eyes,
like those of all long-term blood drinkers, could no longer tolerate
daylight.) And soon after she'd introduced him to Connie and Don,
who were having trouble meeting the payments on the property in
Bolinas, Whistler had arranged to buy the upper house and lot for
a honeymoon cottage—tea for two and me for you and all that.

But Morgana's death in May, and her last will and testament,
naming Selene as high priestess, had put an end to the wedding
plans. The high priestess could not, by coven rule, be a wedded
woman. Selene had chosen Wicca (and the Broadway house, as well
as a goodly chunk of Morgana's two fortunes) over marriage.

Now, twenty years down the road, Selene understood full well that if the same decision came up again, she might choose differently. But the point was moot: Jamey Whistler was already a married man. Married and uxorious—*and* a father. Lourdes Perez, a beautiful young vampiress from the Philippines by way of Modesto, had borne Jamey a daughter within months of their wedding. In fact, just a few weeks before Halloween Selene had sent little Corazon Perez Whistler a darling pink party dress for her first birthday. Lourdes had called Selene from Santa Luz to thank her. Afterward Whistler had come on the line, and he and Selene had chatted briefly. It was their last conversation.

Suddenly, the image of Whistler in the hold of the wooden ship popped into her head, as vivid as if she were still hovering over him. It occurred to her that he had been alone. Whistler, alone. Weeping. Grieving? For a moment, just for a moment, her heart leapt as she understood that something might have happened to Lourdes—something terrible. Possibly even something fatal.

It's an ill wind . . . were the words that came to mind. Confused, ashamed, she strangled the thought aborning; then, conscience-stricken, Selene forced herself to pray to the Goddess, in whom she no longer believed, for the protection of Lourdes and Cora as well as Whistler. But she felt like a fraud on several different levels, and was glad for the interruption when Captain Thaw came over the horn again to request that the passengers prepare for descent.

I'll try, thought the high priestess of Marin County, returning her tray and seatback to their original upright positions. *But I don't know how much lower I can get.*

10

Aldo Striescu had picked up his arsonist's skills (among others) while in the employ of the Romanian Securitate, which had plucked him from the Orfelinat Gheorghiu-Dej, the state orphanage, at the age of fourteen when his remarkable facility with languages had come to light. It was Securitate's Third Branch (counterespionage, which for the most part meant spying on any Romanian who had contact with foreigners) that had conscripted him. Could have been worse: back then most orphans were drafted into the Fifth Branch, which served as Ceauşescu's praetorian guard.

The Securitate, however, could not be blamed for either his pyromania or asphyxomania: by the time they got hold of him, Aldo's psychosexual twig was already bent. Flames had been giving him erections since the age of nine; the delights of smothering his partners he'd discovered somewhat later, as a bully of twelve or thirteen trying to keep the younger boys from crying out during the after-hour rapes. By the time he left the orphanage it had become an all but necessary adjunct to Striescuan orgasm.

But skilled as he was in arson, and much as he enjoyed it, not even Aldo was eager to attempt three major torch jobs two hundred miles apart in the span of a single night, so after burning Whistler's El Sobrante farmhouse (a glorious—and fulfilling—clapboard blaze) he slipped a bootleg of La Divina at Covent Garden into the tape deck of the Sable and drove up to Lake Tahoe with the cruise control set at a leisurely sixty miles per hour. He arrived well before daylight, checked into Caesar's, shot craps for a few hours, lost a few hundred dollars of his employer's money, then slept through the day and torched Whistler Manor shortly after sunset on Monday evening.

Unfortunately, he had no time to stick around and watch the mock-Tudor mansion go up—his schedule (as well as professional prudence) mandated that he leave for San Francisco shortly after setting the fire. Then, what with having to stop to pick up a hitch-hiker a few miles east of Placerville (Aldo's thermos had been nearly empty), then detouring off the highway a few miles later in order to drop off the body, he almost missed his flight out of SFO. As it was, he had to drop off the Sable at the curb, and boarded the red-eye to New York a good deal redder-eyed than any of the other passengers.

But rather than dose his bloodshot eyes with drops, Aldo donned his state-of-the-art wraparound black shades (as he did whenever his schedule required daylight air travel—his eyes hadn't been able to tolerate daylight for twenty years) and explained to the flight attendant that he'd recently had his corneas planed, and had to avoid bright lights in general, and ultraviolet rays in particular. Together they plotted out the point in the flight when the plane on its eastward journey would meet the westering sun. They were over Pennsylvania when the steward alerted him, and helped him secure his black sleep shades under his black-lensed glasses.

A representative of the airline met him at Kennedy and escorted him, thus blindfolded, to the Olympic Airways terminal. He probably could have made it on his own, so acute were his other senses on blood, but his collapsible white cane was packed in his trunk.

Aldo connected with his flight to Athens with an hour to spare, and although it was full dark by the time they arrived at Ellinikon airport, he kept up the charade of blindness, which had never failed to slide him through Customs with only the most cursory of examinations.

But the blind American who checked into the King George in Athens disappeared there. Instead it was a foppish upperclass Englishman who caught the last ferry to Lamiathos the following evening, just after sunset. (The blind American wasn't the only disappearance that evening: a few days later the body of a young prostitute was found floating in Piraeus Harbor, a ligature embedded so deeply into the puffy flesh of her throat that the medical examiner had to clip it free with wire cutters. The left carotid had been partially severed, but in the opinion of the ME, that had been incidental—the girl had died of suffocation first. Only lost a couple liters of blood—about a thermosful.)

Aldo stepped off the ferry, made a few inquiries, and checked in to a tourist resort with separate bungalows just outside of town at off-season rates. After freshening up with a splash of blood from his thermos, Aldo replaced the thermos in the small refrigerator and walked into town. His nose directed him toward the harbor, where he soon located a taverna that was both congenial and picturesque. He had a nasty microwaved gyro for dinner, but the ouzo was authentic, and after buying a few rounds for the house he used a lightly English-accented Greek to acquire some information about Whistler's villa that might prove interesting to his employer. He also acquired an equally congenial if less picturesque middle-aged whore willing to let him bring her back to his bungalow and asphyxiate her to the point of unconsciousness for an extra two thousand drachmas. About the price of a previously frozen crab cocktail at the Fairmont.

She was no beauty, but then, with the customary pillow over her face she didn't need to be. Aldo's resulting orgasm was greatly enhanced by La Divina's *Carmen*. (A concert tape—Callas, self-conscious about her fat ankles, never essayed the role in costume.) And although for Aldo release was ordinarily a product of grim effort, his climax, when it arrived during the soaring "Habañera," was all but merry.

The dazed whore regained consciousness a few minutes later, and to Aldo's delight she recognized the glorious voice coming from the tape deck. "Our Maria," she said hoarsely, rubbing her throat. She went on to explain that in the old days, before the skinny American bewitched him, Ari and Maria often visited Lamiathos, and that once ("I was only small child," the whore hastened to assure him), Maria Callas had sung for the village from the prow of Aristotle Onassis's great yacht *The Christina*.

Charmed, Aldo tipped her an additional grand (in drachmas, of course) before booting her out, and was still feeling relatively bubbly when he had the hotel operator place a call to his employer in London.

"Yes?"

Aldo recognized the voice. "Operator? I'll take it from here." Then, after he'd heard the click of the operator dropping off the line: "How are you doing tonight, Jo? I hope it's not too late to call?"

"Spare me the Transylvanian charm. It's never too late to call me—I haven't slept a bloody wink in months. Where are you?"

"Lamiathos."

"Is there a problem?"

"Minor. I learned in the taverna tonight that our mutual friend—our *late* mutual friend, I should say—never actually *owned* the villa here. He only leased it on a year-to-year basis, at a greatly inflated rate, according to my new chums. I wanted to know if that makes any difference as regards my business on the island?"

"Do you recall my instructions?" There was a quality of command to the voice, mad as it was, that reminded Aldo of Major Strada of the Securitate.

"How could I not?"

"Were they clear?"

"As glass."

"Then carry them out. This is not a bloody real estate transaction, man. Carry them out!"

It will be my pleasure, Aldo started to say, but the line had already gone dead. Aldo hung up the phone, then quickly lifted the receiver to his ear. Satisfied that the operator hadn't been listening in, he replaced the receiver again.

"My pleasure indeed," he muttered out loud. Of course Aldo recalled his employer's instructions—he'd all but put them in the man's mouth himself. *Exterminate the monster. Burn its nests.* Music to his ears. Music to rival La Divina.

PART 2

⮜

Echoes in the Forest

And the thicket closed behind her,
And the forest echo'd 'fool'.
—ALFRED, LORD TENNYSON

CHAPTER

1

Less than an hour after taking off from the dock at St. Thomas, the Blue Goose, a twelve-seater seaplane, banked gently to the left and Selene caught her first glimpse of Santa Luz, alone in a round azure sea, its wild tangle of rain forest rising from the tawny beaches and canebrake to crown the long central hump of the island.

There were three other passengers on the seaplane. One of them, a Luzan cleric with small round gold-rimmed eyeglasses and a high oval forehead that reminded Selene of an Easter egg—the shade of black you get when the egg sits in the purple dye way too long—had been on the flight from Miami with her this morning. As they skimmed low along the coast, Selene mentioned how alarmed she'd been by their landing at the St. Thomas airport.

"Do you know what de St. Thomas man say about dot airport?" he asked. "Say, 'Why did God put de mountain at de end of de runway?' "

Selene looked around the seaplane, which seemed to be made entirely of overstressed fiberglass. "At least if you survive the crash there, you won't drown."

The man smiled, and patted the threadbare seat arm like a trusty horse. "Safe as church."

Oh swell, thought Selene. "May I ask you a question, Reverend?"

"Ask away."

"Do you ever have . . . doubts?"

"Doubts?"

"About God. Your profession. Your belief."

"Oh dot. Sometimes. Of course."

"What do you do?"

"Pray to Jesus for more faith," he replied, as the pontoons hit the water with a thump and a groan, and the little seaplane bounced like a skipping stone through the breakwater into the harbor of the Old Town.

The larger schooners and sloops were anchored just inside the mouth of the harbor. It occurred to Selene as she peered through the clouded Plexiglas that perhaps Whistler was actually in one of them. What had she been planning to do, she wondered—hire a dinghy and row from one to the other? *Pardon me, mind if I check out your hold, Cap'n?*

The Goose puttered purposefully through the labyrinth of rickety wooden docks, past the sailboats with their bare masts sticking up like a forest of phone poles—almost all of them seemed to be under repair to some degree or another—while Selene tried to deal with her sinking heart. It wasn't that she'd thought it would be easy—just that up until this point every step had suggested itself. Of course, they'd been awfully simple steps.

Maybe that's the answer, she told herself. *Simple steps.*

⸺

The Kings Frederick and Christian Arms, the hotel the Reverend Edger recommended, was a charming, thick-walled, three-story castelled structure built on the foundation of the old fort constructed by the Spanish to guard the harbor from the English, rebuilt by the English to guard the harbor from the Dutch, then rebuilt again by the Dutch to guard against the Danes, and so on. (Apparently, Selene mused, it was not such a great location for a fortress.)

Selene's room had French doors that opened out onto a balcony overlooking the rustic harbor. Out beyond the breakwater the sea was bright blue, with turquoise streaks over the reefs and shallows; the sun was lemon yellow, low in a powder blue sky. As she opened the doors and stepped out onto the balcony Selene heard men's voices—deep, musical, unintelligible—punctuated by bursts of laughter and the slapping of wood on wood. Chickens were scratching in the dusty street below; across the street was a bar that was little more than a sidewalk shack with a few tables under a sagging wooden portico; at one of the tables four Luzan men in bright polyester shirts were playing a furious game of dominoes.

The late afternoon shadows were long and blue, and the air smelled like a flower shop. Selene took a deep sniff and had to grab onto the wrought-iron railing for support as shapes began to swim before her eyes. *Simple steps,* she reminded herself. *Unpack, shower, eat. I can handle that.*

But she couldn't. Suddenly it all seemed to catch up to her at once: hauling her suitcase around the Denver airport, a crowded flight to Miami, a febrile, all but sleepless night in a cheap motel room near the airport. Her belladonna fever had broken around dawn, by which time the couple next door who'd been bed-surfing all night had finally gone to sleep, but by then toilets had begun flushing all around her, and showers running and pipes groaning and elephants waltzing in the room overhead.

She'd made it back to Miami International in plenty of time to board the connecting flight to St. Thomas, which then sat on the tarmac for an hour, causing her to miss the first Blue Goose of the day on the other end, which gave her just enough of a layover in St. Thomas to wear the raised numbers off her American Express card at the duty-free shops. Normally a wary shopper and casual dresser, she found herself temporarily manic from exhaustion, and ended up having to buy another suitcase just to haul her stylish new wardrobe down to the Goose.

Okay, forty winks, then shower, then eat—I can unpack after dinner. Selene closed the dark green wooden doors and shutters, but left the jalousies open just a slit, and threw herself down on the bed. She awoke disoriented an hour or so later and saw to her horror that her nude body was streaked with vivid red horizontal stripes.

She would have shrieked, but her throat was still too sore from the smoke she'd inhaled—which was lucky in a way, because when she sat up she saw that it was not just her body, but the entire room that was striped with glowing red bands.

Feeling a little foolish, she climbed off the bed and opened the French doors upon a short-lived Caribbean sunset. Short but glorious—a Turner sunset would have looked like a Hogarth etching in comparison. Across the street the domino game was still going on in the failing pink light.

Selene dined alone that first night under a fragrant yellow trumpet flower tree in the sparsely occupied courtyard of the hotel dining room. Moist, white-fleshed snapper in a golden pecan croustade—real snapper, not the ling cod they called snapper in California; the side dish was a round scoop of some glutinous yellow stuff identified as fungi on the menu. A creamy mound of shivering flan drizzled with amber caramel finished off the meal.

Back in her room the maid had turned down the bed and lowered the mosquito net around it. Selene opened the French doors and stepped out onto the balcony. The chickens in the street below had been replaced by a pack of stiff-legged, feral-looking dogs; across the street three domino games were in full noisy swing under yellow bug lights, the players casting jerky shadows across the stucco wall of the bar.

She closed the doors behind her, undressed inside the mosquito net, changed into a ridiculously sexy nightgown she'd purchased in a fit of jet-lagged optimism on St. Thomas, climbed under the covers, and fell asleep listening to the men across the street swearing and laughing and slapping dominoes.

Selene awoke late the following morning feeling considerably refreshed. As for her next simple step, that problem seemed to have resolved itself overnight as well. There was really only one move that made sense, she realized as she climbed out of bed and headed for the shower. But underlying her new certainty and her sense of physical well-being was a different sensation: a feeling of unease that she couldn't quite place, but couldn't quite shake either.

It wasn't until she was going through her bureau picking out her clothes for the morning that she saw the goat-bladder bag in the back of the top drawer and identified the source of her unease. *The runes. Of course, the runes.* Her morning ritual. She'd thrown the bones every morning for over half her life. Selene started to close the drawer, then changed her mind. She was still feeling somewhat ambivalent about Wiccan ritual, but the runes were like old friends. *Don't want to throw out the baby with the bathwater,* she told herself as she pulled the bag out of the drawer, along with a sleeveless white cotton blouse and a pair of knee-length khaki safari shorts. *Or the baby's bath toys.*

She put the clothes on the bed, unwound the towel from around her wet hair, and sat down cross-legged and mother-naked on the floor. Without looking she selected three smooth tiles from the bag, laid them facedown on the beige carpet, shuffled them around like a three-card-monte dealer, then turned over the rune that had ended up on the left.

She wasn't expecting much—this was the quick-and-dirty method of casting—but the old bones surprised her once again. This first tile was supposed to represent her current situation: she found herself staring down at Raidho reversed. Raidho, the wagon. Travel. Journey of the body, journey of the soul. Obvious enough, if right side up. But Raidho reversed—that symbolized a journey that must be taken, no matter how inconvenient the time or perilous the way. Visit to a sick friend—that was a common interpretation.

So far, so good. The center rune would suggest a course of action. Selene turned it gingerly and saw her crooked old friend Nied—patience. Reversed, the skewed *X* would have meant think twice, turn back. But this morning it was straight up. Straight up meant straight on. Patience in the face of obstacles. Patience in the face of delay and despair. Patience while crossing the abyss.

The third tile was the outcome tile: what was supposed to happen if you applied the advice of the second tile to the situation in the first. She had a pretty good idea what it was before she turned it; after twenty-five years a witch knows her runes like a cardsharp knows a marked deck. The faintest mottle in the center of the tile

told her to get ready for Eihwaz, the symbol for Yggdrasil, the Great
Yew of the world. But which way would it be facing? Right side
up, Eihwaz promised protection no matter how fierce the storms.
All mysteries would be revealed—even delays would further. But
reversed? No shelter from *that* shit storm.

So what would be waiting for her up in the rain forest this
morning? Protection or betrayal? Triumph or tragedy? The lady or
the—

Oh, the hell with it. Selene closed her fist around the tile and
dropped it back into the bag, grabbed her hairbrush, gave her mane
a few whacks, then twisted it into a thick gray-black braid, donned
her spiffy new white blouse and khaki shorts, and went downstairs
for a cup of coffee. She asked the waiter where she might find a
taxi.

"No need, ma'am. Just step outside, and de taxi find you."

At first Selene thought she'd misunderstood, for when she
stepped out onto the raised wooden sidewalk there were no cars of
any description to disturb the chickens that were scratching at the
ocher dust in the road. But across the street at the bar three Luzan
men were playing—what else?—dominoes in the shade of the portico. When Selene appeared, one of them, a seedy-looking fellow
in a ratty aquamarine Miami Dolphins cap, poured himself a shot
of rum, downed it at a gulp, pushed his chair back, and disappeared
into the shack.

A few moments later an ancient yellow Checker cab came chuff-
ing and clattering down the left side of the street, sending the chickens scattering. "Taxi, ma'am?" asked the man in the Dolphins cap.

"Yes, please." The doors were so high that Selene hardly had
to stoop to climb in; the backseat of the cab was roomy enough for
a modest orgy, with a cracked leather seat facing two fold-down
jumpseats.

"Tour of de island dis fine mornin'?" the driver asked hopefully.

"Not this morning. Do you know how to find a place they call
the Greathouse?"

"Greathouse? How me ain' know dot?" he said scornfully.

Selene heard it as one word—*howmeeyainodot?*—and took it for an affirmative, but when he made no effort to start the car, she wondered if she'd misunderstood. "Well that's where I need to go."

"Nobody ain' *need* a go deh, ma'am." He turned around to face her again, the smell of Luzan rum sweet on his breath. "Ain' no stone left standing, deh."

Selene thought about *ordering* him to drive her, then recalled something Whistler had told her once, about the reason Santa Luz had never seized its share of the tourist trade that supported the other U.S. Virgins. "The entire population of the island is passive-aggressive," he'd explained. "It's like a G-rated horror movie, unless of course one is a Drinker. Then they'll hop to smart enough."

But Selene was not a Drinker, the Caribbean term for a vampire of Whistler's persuasion, nor could she pretend to be one, given that she had emerged from the hotel into the bright sunlight. "So I understand," she said to the driver. "But I'm with the insurance company, and you know how they are—don't trust anybody—dot the *i*'s and cross the *t*'s."

The driver narrowed his eyes. "Dey pay expenses?"

"Naturally."

His face brightened. "Fine and dandy. Me ga take you up de dundo track for double de fare, an' *twice* double de receipt, what you tink?"

"Fine," agreed Selene.

"*And* dandy!" declared the driver, throwing the old heap into gear; they lurched off down the empty street, sending the chickens scattering again.

—

By the time the Checker turned off Mainline Road, the island's major artery, Selene was ready to start praying to the Goddess again. It wasn't just that the Luzans drove on the left side of the road, but that they did it in left-drive American cars. A few miles out of the Old Town, Selene's driver—Rutherford Macintosh, according to the license clipped to the sunvisor—found himself behind a wide-bodied panel truck. There was no way he could have checked for oncoming traffic, short of sliding over into the passenger's seat, but that didn't stop him. He pulled out blindly to the right, into the path of an oncoming Volkswagen. Selene screamed and closed her eyes.

When she opened them again the Checker was roaring down the right (wrong) side of the road, and the Beetle had pulled off onto the dusty verge. Its driver shook his fist at them, and Rutherford laughed as he pulled back into the left lane. "Ain' no bitty bug ga tangle wit me tank," he said, patting the dash proudly.

So Selene was glad enough when they turned off the two-lane blacktop onto a dusty lane that cut through a flat cane field toward the dark forested mountain ridge on the horizon. The lane was bordered by palm trees and telephone wires, the wires draped at intervals with dry clumps of old man's beard, a rootless air plant. After a mile or so they passed about a dozen wooden shacks with tin roofs raised on poles. The boundaries of the little village were marked with red-leaved plants; bedraggled chickens and scrofulous dogs shared the road, yielding it disdainfully at the last moment as Rutherford steered straight for them, honking maniacally.

Both the road and the temperature began to rise after they'd passed through the village; by the time they reached the edge of the forest Selene's sleeveless blouse was soaked through, her khaki shorts had ridden up, and the backs of her thighs were stuck to the leather seat. They passed one last dwelling, a log cabin in a small clearing, window boxes bright with flowers, before the trees closed around them and the forest canopy blocked the sky overhead. The air was wet and heavy in Selene's lungs as the Checker made its way up the steep narrow track of dundo road, and the light grew so dim she could no longer read the name on Rutherford's license. Then suddenly the air turned luminous, blindingly bright; a great column of sunlight streamed through a wide round hole in the forest canopy, dust motes dancing in the dazzling white shaft of light.

"Eames Greathouse," announced the driver as the Checker rolled to a stop. "Previously." He jerked the hand brake, which made a ratcheting sound that was echoed in the depths of the forest by a cruelly deceived parrot. "See? Nothing. Let's go."

"I just need to look around for a minute," said Selene, climbing out of the driver's side door. "Wait here for me."

"Like fuck," muttered Rutherford.

Lack fuck, was how Selene heard it. "I beg your pardon?" She turned back and saw him releasing the hand brake.

An abrupt change of tone. "M'say, bad luck. Bad luck to wait here, ma'am."

"Please. Just give me ten minutes—I'll give you an extra ten dollars."

He appeared to be mulling it over. Finally he agreed, but insisted on being paid in advance. She gave him a twenty; he tucked it into the pocket of his short-sleeved white shirt and drove off. Stunned, Selene listened as the sound of the Checker's engine receded; she heard the gears grind around the bend, then the sound of the engine grew louder again. *Thank Goddess,* she thought. *He was only turning around.*

Yes and no—as the Checker rolled slowly by, headed downhill, Rutherford stuck his head out the window. "You ain' no *in*-surance lady," he yelled to her on his way past.

"What—why do you say that?" called Selene, trotting after the retreating taxi, inhaling exhaust fumes to go along with her incipient heatstroke.

Rutherford sped ahead to put some distance between them, then leaned out the window again and called back to her. "You know who lived here. You ain' a Drinker yourself, but you know. 'Cause if you ain' know, you ain' say 'M'give you ten dollars to wait.' You ga say, 'Why you ain' want to wait here, Mistah Driver? What you scairt of, jumbies?' "

She had nearly reached his bumper; he increased the distance again. "Me whole life, me ain' had no dealings wit Drinkers—now ain' de time to start."

Selene watched the Checker until it disappeared around the bend of the narrow trail. She sat down dazedly on a wide mossy stump with delicate ferns growing from the center. Her scalp was tingling; dark shapes swam across her vision. She put her head between her knees, breathing deeply and slowly until the light-headedness passed.

2

The abundant ivies and climbing vines that had once obscured the high stone wall surrounding the Greathouse compound were shriveled into crispy black ropes, but the forest was already at work reclaiming its own: green shoots crept across the path that circled the old plantation grounds, and a few had even begun climbing the scorched wall. Selene followed the path halfway around the compound until she found the entrance, a high, wide archway cut half into, and half under, the wall.

The walkway dipping under the arch was paved with moss-covered bricks so slippery she had to put out her arms like a tightrope walker to keep her balance. Her eyes scarcely had time to adjust to the dank darkness before she was in the light again, staring openmouthed at a Hiroshima-like landscape, a garden of gray ash and broken walls, freestanding chimneys scorched and blackened.

Here and there the ash assumed fantastic shapes, like a surreal topiary; Selene poked at one of these with a charred stick until the overlay of soot crumbled away to reveal a refrigerator. She tugged at the handle; the door yielded grudgingly, to reveal three shelves of Clamato jars, most of which had shattered in the heat of the fire. The sticky crimson residue spattered all over the inside of the

refrigerator bore little resemblance to Clamato juice: she had stumbled upon Jamey's private stash.

Quickly she shut the door again. She'd guarded Whistler's secret
for so many years that it had become a reflex. After looking around
for something to wipe her hands on, Selene settled for clapping
them together, producing a sudden cloud of gray dust; as she did
so she caught a flicker of movement out of the corner of her eye
and wheeled around. Nothing there. She tried to tell herself it was
only a puff of smoke, cinders stirring in the breeze, but the pounding of her heart suggested otherwise.

Her knees grew weak again, and her head began to swim, but
here in the garden of ashes there was no place to sit. At the other
end of the compound a giant gray wedding cake arose from a wide
flat ashen plain. Selene scuffed her way across the courtyard, kicking up puffs of smoke. *There go my new Mephistos,* she thought. A
hundred-and-forty-dollar pair of sandals. Not even broken in yet.
Then a self-conscious laugh, and another prayer: *Let that be the worst
of my problems.*

As she neared the wedding cake, she saw that under the shroud
of ash was a two-tiered stone well covered with a conical roof. From
the roof a bucket was suspended from a pulley rig; the bottom tier
of the well was a circular bench. With her stick she beat and scraped
away a clear patch, then sat down with her back to the well. Her
mouth was dry. It occurred to her that all she'd had to eat or drink
that morning was a single cup of coffee. No wonder she was feeling
faint.

Selene climbed up onto the bench; kneeling with her back to
the courtyard, she looked down into the well. Couldn't see to the
bottom, but she could smell the water. The bucket was suspended
from a chain, and the chain tied off around a rusty spur of metal
on the inside of the well. She unhooked it and lowered the bucket
down until she heard a splash, then began hauling up. The bucket
was heavy now; she leaned away, putting her back into it.

"Need some help wit dot, lady?" said a voice behind her.

With a cry Selene let go of the chain; it whipped through her hands and the bucket hit the water again with a hollow splash. She turned to see a Luzan boy standing at her elbow. "Oh my," she gasped, clapping a hand to her chest. "Where did you come from? You scared the p— the life out of me."

"Come from? Me bahn heah, lady," the boy said indignantly, his fists resting on his narrow hips like the old TV Superman. "Where *you* come from?"

He was a skinny, shirtless black kid in a pair of baggy red shorts and a faded red baseball cap jammed over jug handle ears. He looked a little like Stan Laurel, if Laurel had been a ten-year-old Luzan.

"California." She stuck out her hand. "My name is Selene."

"Joe-Pie." He took her hand by the fingertips and shook it vigorously.

"Pleased to meet you, Joe-Pie," she said, smiling inwardly. According to the lore, a few leaves of joe-pye Weed—*Eupatorium*—carried in the mouth would inspire love; carried in the pocket, they were said to guarantee respect for the bearer. "I'm afraid my taxi driver drove off and left me."

"You ain' so afraid as he," said the boy. "Dot mon haul ass so fast his shadow ain' cotch him yet." He hopped up onto the bench and began hauling on the chain; together they drew the brimming bucket from the well. Selene took a careful sip from the rim, half expecting a mouthful of ashes, but the water was sweet, with only a trace of ferrous aftertaste. She tilted the bucket to her lips and drank greedily, spilling half the contents down the front of her blouse, which was now a see-through (she was ever so glad she'd worn her new lacy brassiere), and soaking her shorts and her poor sandals in the process.

"Better so?" asked Joe-Pie.

"Much better," she replied, handing him the bucket.

He poured a narrow trickle of water directly into his mouth without spilling a drop, then lowered the pail, regarding her solemnly over the rim. "You still look green as goatweed," he decided. "You best come home wit me. Me Granny, she's de oldest weed woman on de island—she ga fix you right up." He put the bucket down, hopped off the bench, and held his hand out for Selene.

Stuck in midquest, fresh out of ideas, simple or otherwise, Selene hardly had to think it over. The mythical aspects of her plight were all but unavoidable. *Here I am, lost in the forest. A little boy appears out of nowhere to guide me. Ecce puer. Like I have a fucking choice, right?*

"Best offer I've had all day, Joe-Pie," she said, taking the small hand in her own.

—

A few hundred yards from the Greathouse Joe-Pie ducked off the dundo track, and Selene followed him down a verdant footpath that narrowed to a tunnel through a world gone altogether green, every shade imaginable, emerald, kelly, lime, moss, avocado, olive, jade, leek. Even the air was green, a pale hue like the inside of a cucumber.

It was all terribly disconcerting. Selene felt a little like Alice chasing the White Rabbit as she ducked under overhanging branches and dodged dangling vines, trying to avoid the roots and rocks underfoot without losing sight of Joe-Pie's bobbing red cap as he darted ahead of her down the warrenlike trail. She kept calling to him to take it easy, but asking a boy that age to walk is like asking a hummingbird to fly slowly. Hover or zip, that's the extent of their capabilities. By the time they'd reached the bottom of the trail Selene was bathed in sweat again, but no cooler for it; the extreme humidity of the rain forest prohibited evaporation. The tunnel gave out onto the road directly across from the small clearing with the log cabin that Selene had noticed on her way up into the forest. Joe-Pie was waiting for her.

"Is this your house?" she asked him, bending forward with her hands on her knees, trying to catch her breath.

"Me and Granny." He pointed to a column of smoke that seemed to be coming from behind the cabin. "See?" He tugged at her wrist and she followed him around the side of the cabin. When she turned the corner Selene saw the source of the smoke. Across a small dirt yard, an enormous iron cauldron was suspended by chains from a tree limb over a smoldering fire of lignum vitae wood;

behind it, through the blue haze, she could just make out a silhouetted figure in a wide bonnet and a long black aproned dress stirring
the cauldron with a wooden spoon the size of a canoe paddle.

"Granny," called Joe-Pie excitedly. "Look what I—"

"Cheese and bread, boy!" The woman bustling around from
behind the cauldron, wiping her hands on her apron, adjusting her
stiff black-ribboned straw bonnet, was a brown-black crone, tough
and rubbery and wrinkled as a dried currant. "M'send you out for
ladyroot and you come back wit de whole lady. Good ting me ain'
send you to fetch goatweed or elephant-leg."

"Dis is Selene, Granny. Taxi man left her up by Greathouse."

Granny stopped in her tracks. "Greathouse, you say?"

The boy explained about hiding in the bushes when he heard
the sound of a car engine climbing the dundo track toward the
Greathouse; about seeing two people drive up the hill, but only one
drive down; about following Selene into the compound, and spying
on her long enough to see that she needed help. "Don't fret none,
Granny," he concluded. "It's all bald daylight up deh now—she
ain' be Drinker."

"Boy, you ain' know *what* she be, or ain' be." She peered across
the yard at Selene. "What were you doing up by Greathouse, you?"

Quickly, Selene considered her response. She didn't want to lie
to the crone—things were getting too freaking mythical for that—
but she didn't want to appear cowed, either. She opted for a bold
joke: "I dunno, picking goatweed?"

It must have struck the right chord—the weed woman came
closer. "Oh? And what you do wit goatweed after you pick it?"
she asked slyly.

Mythicaler and mythicaler, thought Selene. She had presented herself as a woman of knowledge, and been challenged accordingly by
the crone. Fortunately goatweed, the smallest member of the Saint-
John's-wort family, known as sinjinweed to the English, corrupted
to injun wort in the States, was a staple of the Wiccan pharmaco-
poeia. "If I were feeling sad, I could make an amulet of the flowers
to wear around my neck. If I needed protection, I'd dry a branch
and hang it over my window to keep evil spirits at bay. Or maybe

I'd give a few leaves to a maiden to put under her pillow so that she could see her future husband in her dreams."

The old woman had listened politely, fiddling absently with her bonnet, removing one of the pins that secured the dangling black ribbon; when Selene had finished, she turned to her grandson. "Leave us now, Joe-Pie."

"But Granny—"

"Don't *but* your Granny. You want to listen to woman's talk, Granny ga make a woman out of you wit me razor. Go fetch me de ladyroot me ask you to fetch previous. And dis time don't come back without, else Granny can't make Berta Robinson no love-powders, and she ain' ga pay Granny no money, and you ain' ga have no new Beebops on Christmas Day."

"Reeboks, Granny, Reeboks," the boy called cheerfully over his shoulder as he left the yard. "De kind you pump."

The old woman smiled fondly as the boy rounded the corner. "Friendly boy," she said, but the instant they were alone she seized Selene's wrist tightly in one hand and jabbed the pin she'd removed from her hat ribbon into the back of Selene's hand. Selene sprang back, but it was too late—her arm was numb to the elbow.

Out of the frying pan . . . she thought, confused but surprisingly peaceful as the yard began to spin around her. She never did manage to finish the thought.

CHAPTER

3

Technically, the villa on Lamiathos appeared to be a difficult job, even for as skilled and passionate a firebug as Aldo, as he'd discovered when he went out to reconnoiter late Tuesday night. Unlike the redwood Marin A-frame, the clapboard El Sobrante farmhouse, or the wood-beamed Tahoe Manor, the stone walls and terra-cotta tiles of the villa would make poor tinder. (The Greathouse had been another matter: constructed in the Danish fashion, the walls were two-foot-thick stucco, but a stucco with a molasses base. Thrifty bastards, those Danish sugar planters. So once the propane, gasoline, and oil tanks had been blown, the rest of the place had burned spectacularly. Or so Aldo had read in the *Virgin Islands Sentinel*: he'd used time-delayed fuses in order to catch the vampires asleep during the daytime without getting caught by daylight himself, and was back in his bedroom at the Kings Frederick and Christian Arms with the curtains drawn long before the Greathouse had gone up.)

But the villa on Lamiathos was wired for electricity, so there weren't all those lovely tanks to blow. And since he'd been seen making inquiries about the place, he couldn't use any sort of explosive or accelerant—better if it appeared to be an accident. But it was difficult to effect an accidental-looking fire in an empty dwelling, unless the wiring was either very old or very new. Fortunately the villa was occupied by the lessor's son, who lived there when Whistler was not in residence—nine or ten months a year. Even better, Aldo had observed for himself, the young man was a smoker. As so often happened, it would prove to be a fatal habit.

Late Wednesday night Aldo returned to the villa on foot. A two-mile hike, but as he'd polished off the contents of his vacuum bottle before leaving his room, it proved to be an enjoyable and soul-stirring walk indeed, even on such a starless night. The inky sea stretched to the black horizon; wind-whipped waves broke against the foot of the cliffs that dropped sharply from the edge of a goat path hugging the rocky shore of the island.

The path ended abruptly at the border of Whistler's, or rather, George Demetrios's, property, where a barbed-wire fence had been erected across the ancient right-of-way. Aldo dropped his kit bag over the top strand of wire and vaulted the four-foot fence easily. His original thought was to jimmy the sliding glass door that led directly from the patio to the master bedroom, but when he saw a light on in the living room he changed his mind and rang the front doorbell instead, using his elbow so as not to leave a fingerprint.

"Hey English, you loose?" Georgie Demetrios, the ne'er-do-well son of the wealthiest property owner on Lamiathos, came to the door in pajamas patterned like mattress ticking. He and Aldo had met briefly at the taverna the night before when Aldo had purchased his round for the house.

"Loose as a goose," replied Aldo promptly, surprised at the greeting.

"I mean loose—you loose your way?"

"Lost," Aldo corrected him. "You mean lost."

"Yes, lost. You lost?" Bleary-eyed, his glossy black hair night-tossed, Georgie was still not a bad-looking fellow, Aldo thought, though starting to run to alcoholic bloat.

"No, not actually." Aldo smiled disarmingly, dropped his kit bag, raised two fingers into a peace sign, then jabbed them violently into Georgie's eyes with savage speed and pinpoint accuracy. The Greek shrieked, grabbed his eyes, dropped to his knees. In an instant

Aldo was on him from behind, reaching around his rib cage with both arms and squeezing the air from his lungs with a whoosh, taking great care not to break any ribs. This way, when they found what was left of the body, there would be no obvious marks on it —not even the eyes, which would have melted as the heat from the fire neared the hundred degrees Celsius mark.

Aldo kept squeezing until the young man was unconscious, then eased off. He knew better than to strangle his victim this time, forensic pathology having reached the point where a cause of death could be determined for even the most pathetically charred of corpses. Georgie would have to die by either smoke or fire. Aldo couldn't even risk smothering him with a pillow. A damn shame. Aldo preferred women victims, but there was an added bonus to asphyxiating men: the male victim's involuntary erection and seminal emission at the moment of death could be quite a treat if you timed it right.

But he could still make use of the body—would have to, now that his thermos was empty. He grabbed his kit bag off the doorstep, locked the front door behind him, knelt at the side of the fallen man, and removed from the kit bag a pair of surgical gloves and an enormous veterinary syringe used for drawing fluid from horses' knees. The glass barrel would hold a half liter of blood, but he didn't want to be greedy. A pint—not quite a full syringe—would be enough to get him back home to England.

Back home to England. Never dreamed as a child in the Bucharest orphanage that he'd be saying that someday, Aldo thought as he donned his gloves and unbuttoned Georgie's pajama top. He drew his pint through an axillary vein, so that the armpit hair would hide the puncture mark. It was almost certainly an unnecessary precaution, as the body was to be torched—but then, as he'd been taught by Major Strada, no precaution was ever unnecessary. (Advice the major should have heeded himself. Had he done so, he might have survived the fall of Ceaușescu as successfully as most of the other Securitate functionaries of his rank.)

After filling his syringe and allowing himself a quick squirt as an aperitif, Aldo replaced the syringe in the bag, rebuttoned Georgie's pajama top, carried the still unconscious body into the bedroom, and laid it on the bed. There was already a pack of cigarettes, a lighter, a half full bottle of ouzo, and an empty tumbler on the bedside table. This was going to be almost too easy, he thought, pouring out a glassful of Georgie's favorite beverage, then using his own Zippo to fire up one of Georgie's nasty unfiltered Greek coffin nails.

His next move was to pour most of the contents of the glass carefully along the front of the pajamas, from throat to crotch, then splash the last of it into Georgie's face. At that, the man started coming round. The eyelids fluttered, opened, as Aldo tossed the empty glass onto the bed while puffing furiously on the cigarette without inhaling—he'd given up smoking a few months before, except for the occasional cigar.

The two-finger fork didn't seem to have done any permanent damage to Georgie's sight: the puzzled brown eyes widened as comprehension began to dawn, at which point Aldo dropped the cigarette on the front of the pajamas, just below the throat. *Whomp*— a beautiful blue sheet of flame played all across the man's chest. Then, as the pajamas caught, the flames turned from blue to a smoke-smudged black and yellow, and the body jackknifed into a sitting position.

Aldo hopped back from the bed and stood with his back to the curtained sliding glass door that led to the patio, adjusting the crotch of his trousers—his erection had begun to swell. "Over here," he called, waving both arms over his head.

The body, by now fully engulfed, was in the process of flapping its arms and beating its hands against its breast, trying to smother the flames. It lurched off the bed, in the direction of Aldo's voice. Behind it, the bed was aflame. Aldo freed his engorged penis from his trousers, pulled off his left glove, and began masturbating earnestly with his bare hand as the burning man-shape lurched around the bedroom.

"No, this way," Aldo shouted over the Greek's high-pitched

whistling shriek; again and again he called, until finally the flaming body began staggering in his direction, arms reaching blindly like Frankenstein's monster.

"You're getting warmer," joked Aldo, tucking the glove into his pocket. Just before Georgie reached him, Aldo let go of his penis and stepped aside, nimble as a matador. The burning man crashed into the sturdy glass door and bounced off it, but not before setting the curtains on fire, which was what Aldo had in mind in the first place.

"Hoop-la. Colder now." Aldo backed out of the bedroom. "Over here, this way." The blazing thing seemed to hear him, even spun in his direction before toppling over onto the bed again.

"Oh, bad luck," said Aldo philosophically. He'd been hoping the human torch would do him the favor of setting the living room afire as well, but obviously it was not to be. Then, encouragingly, "Good show, though!"

For it looked as if the bedroom curtains were by no means fire retardant. They had gone up in a white blaze. Aldo backed across the living room in a hunched stoop, masturbating furiously again, picked up his kit bag from the floor, one-handed, and without taking his eyes off the flames that were now licking their way through the bedroom door, made his way backward to the front door. When he reached it, rather than let go of himself, he transferred the heavy kit bag to his mouth, biting down hard on the leather handle while he used his gloved hand to unbolt the door.

Once outside, he hurried back around the side of the house, gripping himself tightly. By the time he reached the patio the glass door had already exploded, and the flames in the bedroom were dancing madly. Aldo dropped his kit bag, peeled off his right glove, and soldiered on two-handed, squinting from the effort until the fire was only a warm red blur in his vision.

Then all movement stilled for a moment. His face raised to the warmth of the fire, the smell of the smoke sharp in his nostrils, Aldo squeezed himself tightly with one hand, using a peristaltic milking action, and grunted as he spurted into his other hand. When he was done, Aldo licked his hand clean, picked up his kit bag, and loped off into the night.

4

It was late afternoon when Selene opened her eyes and found herself staring up at the rust-flecked underside of a corrugated tin roof raised on corner poles for ventilation. Narrow-meshed plastic screening filled the gap between the top of the wall and the roof.

"Where—" She started to ask where she was, then, at the sight of the weed woman bending over her, remembered, and changed her question. "Why?" She lifted her hand weakly to check out the bluish discoloration surrounding the pinprick.

"Why you tink?" Granny asked, amused, as she helped Selene sit up. "You show up—poof!—where de Drinkers burn. Bewitch Joe-Pie—dot boy know better den bring a stranger to me house. Den you know all tree use of goatweed. How m'know you ain' obeah, you ain' sent by de mon burn Greathouse down?"

Even in her dazed condition it struck her. "You mean you know who burned the Greathouse?"

"Same mon burn your house."

"How do you know about my house?"

"Same way m'know you ain' obeah. Cha-cha bark."

Selene thought about it. *Some kind of truth serum? Cha-cha? But of course!* Her mind went back twenty-five years. An outing with Morgana in Golden Gate Park. "Behold the *Distachya*," Morgana had declaimed, pointing out a stand of small fernlike trees with velvety dark green leaves. "Also known as the plume albizia. *Albizia distachya* in the Latin. Cha-cha in the Caribbean. Native to Australia. One of Mother Nature's gifts to witches. The seeds make a nearly undetectable poison; the victim drowns in his own fluids, but on the cellular level. The bark, however, makes a handy truth serum. The aborigines call it the Talking Tree."

"How much did I tell you?" Selene asked the old woman, swinging her legs down from the old army surplus cot.

"Everyting." Granny had a hand at the small of her back, steadying her. "Fire and Fair Lady, Mr. Whistler, devilish mon—oh, every damn ting."

"And you think it was the same man who burned the Greathouse? Somebody saw him down here?"

"Joe-Pie!" the weed woman called, by way of reply.

The boy skidded through the back door of the cabin. "Miss Selene! Oh good, you're up. Granny said you was tired, was all dot was wrong wit you. Did you have a good sleep?"

"Apparently," replied Selene. She didn't remember a thing— but as she was beginning to appreciate, any sleep you woke up from was a good one.

"Joe-Pie, tell Miss Selene about de mon you saw coming down de dundo track last week."

"Ain' no mon," the boy asserted to his grandmother, then turned to Selene and repeated it. "Ain' no *mon*, Miss Selene. He de devil for damn sure."

"A white man? Slightly built? Light hair, goatee"—she stroked her chin by way of illustration—"pointy eyebrows?"

The boy nodded, eyes wide. Granny gave him a pat on the head. "Tank you, m'son. Now go back out in de yard and mind kettle." When he was gone, she turned back to Selene. "Child ain' need to know what we know—he still of an age where he troubled by dreams."

"You mean you grow out of it?" joked Selene. The room had stopped spinning, but she was still woozy. "What was on that pin you stuck me with first, anyway?"

"Dis 'n dot," was the self-satisfied reply.

Selene recognized the smug tone: she'd been guilty of employing it herself from time to time. "Please. If you know what I'm doing down here, then you know I need your help."

A chuckle, and a pat on the knee. "True as cha-cha." Then the smile faded; the crone leaned forward and peered into Selene's eyes. "If you want help from Granny, you must ask for it."

Again, Selene drew on her only point of reference—the crones in the myths weren't exactly warm and fuzzy nurturers either. "Will you help me, Granny?"

A shrug. "Might be. Might be too, you can teach me how you fly?"

"The Fair Lady? I'd have to send for some. But sure, why not?" Selene found herself searching the bright black eyes that were searching hers. It occurred to her that as long as she found herself in such a *mythic* damn situation, she might as well see if she could pick up any pointers as to the direction her path might be leading, as well as get some help with her task. "Can I ask you something, Granny? What you do, what you practice, how you use the herbs? Does it have anything to do with . . . you know, *religion?*"

The old woman thought about it for a moment. "One time Reverend Edger come to Granny for bed trouble. Give him caperberry. Missus Edger bear him a fine son nine months later."

—

Shortly before midnight a three-wheeled cart drawn by two goats clip-clopped straight down the middle of Three Kings Street, the Old Town's main drag, scattering yelping dogs in its path. The dogs that did not scatter quickly enough felt the bite of the Rastaman's whip; the alpha male of the pack held his ground, yellow teeth bared, and got himself butted halfway down the block for his pains, to the great amusement of the loafers outside the saloon.

The cart pulled to the curb at the entrance to the Kings Frederick and Christian Arms and Selene hopped down from the buckboard. "Thank you for the ride, Mr. Munger. And for everything else."

"De pleasure's ahl mine, Miss Weiss." The Rastaman tipped his battered white yachting cap, and his dreadlocks spilled out around his face like a lion's mane. His eyes were red as a vampire's, but then so were Selene's: they'd shared a spliff the size of a cigar on the ride down from the rain forest.

Selene, who rarely smoked, was good and blitzed, in a contented sort of way. After she and Granny had concluded their business, they had dined on fresh island lobster snared by Joe-Pie that afternoon and boiled alive in the great cauldron. Then Granny had sent Joe-Pie to fetch the Rastaman, who at Granny's urging told Selene all about his unseen visitor the previous Friday night. It was nice to have a little evidence—or in this case absence of evidence: the missing titi bread, etc.—to shore up her conviction that Jamey Whistler had survived the fire.

And the ride home had been memorable: the hypnotic clip-clopping of the goats' hooves, the flat round stars above, the cane-brake stretching to either side, the graceful roadside palms silhouetted against a soft gray-black horizon. She could have done without the odor, though; either the Rastaman had begun to smell like his goats after all these years, or else his goats had begun to smell like him.

But never mind—the man's heart was sweet as the perfumes of Araby, and his weed beyond reproach. She leaned over and gave him a quick peck on the cheek, then mounted the wooden sidewalk and waved good-bye as the Rastaman lifted the reins and clucked his tongue; the goats executed a smart U-turn and parked themselves in front of the bar across the street, where the usual domino games were in full noisy swing.

Selene was just about to step into the shower a few minutes later when the phone rang. "Taxi driver here to see you, Miz Weiss," the desk clerk informed her. "He say urgent business."

"Tell him I'll be down in a few minutes," she replied, smiling inwardly.

A muffled whisper; then: "He say he ga wait."

I bet he will, thought Selene, on her way into the shower. She made it a long one—it was badly needed—then donned a clean "Free Tibet" T-shirt and jeans and took the stairs down to the lobby, where Rutherford Macintosh was waiting for her with his Dolphins cap in one hand and her twenty-dollar bill in the other.

"Me ain' know you be friends wit Granny Weed," he said hurriedly, thrusting the bill in her direction.

"I'm sure you didn't. But that doesn't justify stranding me in the middle of the rain forest."

"Sometime a mon just act from fear."

Selene's first instinct was to go easy on the fellow—the same sort of counterinstinct that had kept her from praying to the Goddess lately, or turning over Eihwaz that morning. Then she remembered how it had felt running after the taxi, sucking exhaust, the sense of powerlessness, hopelessness. She looked down at the proffered bill disdainfully. "I don't think I'll take the money back, Mr. Rutherford. Or is it Mr. Macintosh?"

"Rutterford is me Christian name, ma'am, but everyone call me Tosh."

"Tosh, then. I'm afraid just giving back the money isn't going to cut it, Tosh. But I do believe in second chances, so I am going to give you an opportunity to redeem yourself. You see, I'm going to be on the island for another few days, and I can certainly use a driver, but I have no use for the sort of driver who steals off and leaves me in the middle of the forest, forcing me to hike all the way down to my old friend Granny Weed's house to tell her my troubles again. Because according to what Granny tells me, that's the sort of driver whose balls are apt to swell up to the size of coconuts in the middle of the night, for no reason any doctor will ever be able to figure out. Or cure. Granny also tells me they call such a condition *bamacoo*, and they call the man who has it a *windward gobi*. Windward Gobi—do I have that right?"

Rutherford opened his mouth, but the rest of the speaking apparatus was not under his control. He settled for nodding, his jaw dropped foolishly. Gobi was the Luzan name for the calabash.

"And if that happened, such a driver would be of even less use to me," continued Selene. "As I understand it, with his balls blown up like that a man can't sit. And if he can't sit, he can't drive, don't you agree?"

Another nod. One of his drinking buddies had come down with bamacoo once. A St. Vincent man who'd never done any harm to the weed woman personally, but whose wife had stiffed her for the price of an herbal menstrual tonic. Poor bastard required two chairs at the saloon for the next few weeks, one for himself and one for his testicles. Eventually the wife, at great trouble and expense, had been permitted to settle up with the weed woman. Not long after that the husband recovered, but the haunted look never quite left the fellow's eyes. Reluctantly Tosh stuffed the wrinkled Jackson back into his pocket and raised his eyes to meet Selene's. "At your service, ma'am."

"Good. Be here early tomorrow morning—I'll need a ride back to Granny's. Oh, and one more thing, Tosh. Granny tells me you taxi drivers know more about what's going on around here than the police. I want you to ask around for me, see if anyone has any information about Mr. Whistler. Did he have any unusual visitors in the last few months? I'm particularly interested in a white man with pointy eyebrows and a pointy goatee, but anything else you can find out, anything out of the ordinary . . ."

Tosh flashed her a wry look as he settled his cap on his head. "Anyting *not* out of de ordinary up deh be out of de ordinary, ma'am."

As soon as she got back to her room, Selene placed a call to California. Martha answered on the third ring. "Selene, are you okay? We were so worried when you didn't call last night."

"I was going to, honey, but I pretty much collapsed from exhaustion."

"I'm not surprised. Hey, good news: Carson went up with me this afternoon to check out your house—he says structurally the place looks pretty good. You might need some new beams to shore up the loft, but the roof's fine."

"Be sure to thank him for me. How's Daddy Don doing?"

"He misses you. We both do. How's the search for Mr. Whistler going?"

"I've made some progress, but I need you to do something for me. First thing tomorrow morning I want you to go up into the

herb garden and pick five ripe cherries from the nightshade bush."
She described the technique for determining if a cherry was ripe.
"Be very careful not to crush them, or get any juice on you. If you
do, wash it off right away. Wrap them in something sturdy—maybe
hide them in a videocassette box—and overnight them to me."

"You're not going to take belladonna again, are you? It practically killed you last time!"

"It's not for me, it's for the weed woman."

"What's that?"

"Like a witch, but without the Wicca. She's forgotten more
about herbal lore than I'll ever know, but she was fascinated by the
idea of flying. We're swapping a few recipes, is all."

"Okay, but be careful, Selene. That guy hasn't shown up around
here again. Maybe he's back down there."

"You be careful, too: I'm pretty sure this thing isn't over yet."

"Yeah, but Selene—*what* thing?"

A sigh. "I wish to hell I knew, dearie. I wish to hell I knew."

5

The next morning Selene awoke just before dawn, donned safari shorts and a lightweight, long-sleeved khaki blouse over her bathing suit, crept down the stairs, and tiptoed past the sleeping night clerk and out the front door. The yellow Checker was parked at the curb, the cabbie asleep behind the wheel.

Selene opened the back door and slid in; Rutherford Macintosh awoke with a start. "Mornin', ma'am."

"Good morning, Tosh. Have you been out here all night?"

"You say you ga leave early, ma'am, but y'ain' say *how* early. M'tink, better ready den gobi." He made a cupping gesture in the vicinity of his crotch.

The sun was just coming up over the mountain when the Checker turned off the highway; the dew on the canebrake was sparkling like refined sugar. Joe-Pie sat waiting for her on the front steps of the cabin. He sprang to his feet waving a machete half as long as he was. "Mornin', Miss Selene!"

The boy opened Selene's door for her, leaned in to tell Tosh that Granny said he wouldn't be needed again until midafternoon.

Tosh touched his cap brim with two fingers, and the Checker roared off; the morning dew damped its standard cloud of dust as Tosh executed a five-point turn and raced back down the track.

"Dot mon *still* scairt," grinned Joe-Pie, waggling his eyebrows comically under his worn red Hess Oil cap; an oversized "Santa Luz: The Last Unspoiled Virgin" T-shirt, yesterday's baggy red shorts, and last year's shredded Nikes completed his ensemble. "Ready?" Without waiting for an answer, he slung the machete over his shoulder, darted across the road, ducked through the feathery divi-divi trees that camouflaged the entrance to his footpath, ducked back to beckon Selene, then disappeared again up the green tunnel.

Selene caught up to the boy a few hundred yards up the trail. He had a finger to his lips. She held her breath and peeked through the wall of brush to see three tiny rain forest deer drinking at a shallow pool that was no more than a wide spot in a sluggish stream. She smiled and touched her hand to her heart.

When the deer had drunk their fill they bounded off across the stream; a clatter of pebbles, a flicker of white tail, and they had disappeared into the bush. Joe-Pie ducked under a low-hanging branch, lifted it for Selene, then led her down to the edge of the little pond. He knelt and whisked his hand around in the green scum that covered the surface; beneath it the water, only a foot or so deep, was so clear that she could see the delicate stems of a watercresslike plant undulating in the gentle current.

The boy plucked a few of these, slipped them into a Baggie, slipped that back into his pocket, and stood up. "Dot's just for go-wit," he explained.

"What's gowit?"

He rolled his eyes. "Go *wit*—a ting what go *along* wit a ting."

"Oh."

The next stop was a stand of gray-green bushes growing by the bank of the creek. Joe-Pie plucked a few leaves, stuffed them into a separate Baggie, then led Selene farther up the stream, where he shinnied up a tall tree with a slender trunk that bowed and swayed under his weight, and returned with a handful of brilliant purple flowers. "More go-wit."

They rejoined the trail back by the shallow pond. The invisible sun was over the forest now; the tunnel had taken on a paler green glow, almost chartreuse, and dark sweat stains had begun to blossom under the armpits of Selene's blouse by the time they reached their destination. This was a dense patch of jungle by the side of the trail, which to Selene was indistinguishable from the rest of the forest except for a greater profusion of overhanging liana vines.

"Cure-root," said the boy, pointing to a brown vine as thick as Selene's ankle dangling through the bottom-most layer of the forest canopy, twining around the base of an elephant-leg tree inches from the forest floor, then climbing the trunk back up into the canopy. "Know why dey call it so?" He unslung his machete and hacked once at the woody vine where it joined the trunk of the tree, then once again a few feet higher; he pried the severed section of vine away from the tree, and handed it to Selene. " 'Cause a little of dis ga cure you of livin'."

She took it, examined one of the cleanly cut ends, from which a candy-cane pink sap was beginning to ooze. *Cure-root,* she thought. *A liana vine. Instant paralysis.* As she put two and two together the root began to tremble in her hands. It occurred to her that she was even luckier to be alive than she'd first suspected. She wondered if anybody else had ever been dosed with belladonna, distachya, and curare in the space of three days and lived to tell about it.

Oh my poor, poor liver! she thought shakily, handing the vine back to Joe-Pie.

━

The process of preparing the curare took about two hours. Granny worked under the shade tree in her backyard. First she shaved the bark off the cure-root and put it aside, then shaved the rest of the root into a small iron kettle. That she hooked onto a small chain hanging from a pulley over the great cauldron, and had Selene lower it partway down into the boiling water. Then at intervals she sprinkled into the bobbing kettle first the crushed leaves from the water plant, then the gray-green leaves from the bush, then the bark shavings, and lastly the purple flowers.

It was Joe-Pie's job to keep the fire up. Selene was given charge of the chain, maintaining a constant temperature in the kettle by lowering or raising it at Granny's instructions, while the weed woman danced with surprising spryness around the cauldron as the blue smoke shifted, tossing in leaves or stirring the kettle with one hand, holding the skirt of her black dress out of the fire with the other.

At the very end of the process, Granny had Selene lower the kettle into the cauldron all the way to the lip while Joe-Pie worked a hand bellows to raise the temperature of the fire. Selene secured the last loop of the chain to the nail at the base of the tree, then approached the cauldron. Granny warned her to hold her breath, then let her peek in. A violet-white paste in the bottom of the kettle was being condensed at a rapid boil. Granny sent Selene back to the chain, and at the precise moment that the last of the moisture had cooked away, signaled Selene to raise the kettle as high as it would go.

Granny backed away a step. Using her long wooden paddle as leverage, she overturned the heavy cauldron, sending the boiling water pouring down on the fire. A dreadful hissing and billowing ensued. Selene gasped—it looked as if Joe-Pie had been steamed alive, but gradually he reappeared, grin first, through the blue-white smoke. "Dot's de best part," he assured her.

———

When Tosh arrived to drive Selene and Joe-Pie to the beach, he was bursting with news. According to Francis Sylvester, a cab-driver who had served the Drinkers at the Greathouse both as a Drink (sort of a feudal blood donor) and a chauffeur, there hadn't been any unusual visitors at the Greathouse—or at least not any who had taken cabs. But something out of the ordinary had taken place in the past few months: around the end of August Mr. Whistler himself had flown to England to visit his father.

Just how out of the ordinary that was, though, was something perhaps only Selene could truly have appreciated. Jamey and his father hadn't seen each other in thirty years. He never talked much about his old man either. It occurred to her as Tosh dropped them off at a small lagoon protected by a grove of poisonous manchineel trees just south of the Old Town that she didn't even know his first name; he'd always been referred to facetiously as Whistler's Father. Oddly enough, she did remember his address, though—No. 11 was how Jamey always referred to the home of his youth. No. 11 Cranwick Square. She reviewed what little else she knew about Whistler's Father while floating on her back in the blood-warm Caribbean while Joe-Pie snorkeled for lobsters.

Like the son, the father had been born wealthy. The bulk of the Whistler legacy came from the building of the trans-Russian railway, a fortune that was enhanced over a hundred years later with the discovery of a trunkful of genuine James Abbott McNeill Whistler drawings in a Baltimore attic.

What else did she know? Jamey was born in Baltimore, she remembered; the family vacationed on Santa Luz, where Jamey was cared for by a Luzan nanny. But when Jamey was around twelve the old man, who fancied himself a painter, had moved the family to London to carry on the Whistler tradition. Went ten years without selling so much as a cartoon. How had Jamey put it? "Failure is always a tragedy. Even a rich man's failure is a tragedy. Unless he hangs on to all his money. Then it's a comedy—he gets to keep everything but his self-respect."

Jamey's mother died when he was nineteen, whereupon his father had suffered some sort of nervous breakdown; according to Jamey the old man had been on antipsychotic medications ever since. As far as she knew, he had never remarried. When Jamey turned twenty-one, Nanny Eames invited him back to Santa Luz for a visit and initiated him as a Drinker. Within a year of his return to London he was expelled from the country for the crime of curing his father's housekeeper of migraine through the use of an old English folk remedy: bleeding. It was quite an amusing story, the way Jamey told it. "So what if I drank the stuff?" he had protested to Selene years later. "The bloody megrims went away, didn't they?"

But the old man had gone ballistic when Jamey was arrested. "Monster was the kindest thing he called me. Oh man, his meds weren't working that day. That's when I got *my* never-darken-my-towels-again speech. Haven't seen or spoken to him since."

Jamey had always left Selene with the impression that he had been permanently eighty-sixed from the UK, as well as his father's presence. But if that were true then Whistler and his father must have reconciled, or Jamey wouldn't have risked reentering the country in order to see him.

Just then Joe-Pie interrupted Selene's train of thought with a shout of "Lobster!" She swam over to him; he pointed down to the ocean bed. Her mask and snorkel were hanging around her neck. She spat into the mask and swished the spit around to keep it from fogging, the way Joe-Pie had taught her, slipped it over her head, took the snorkel between her teeth, and blew it clear. When she rolled over and peered under the water she could make out on the bottom a tailless, bluish-white carapaced critter hunkered next to a pile of rocks or coral that resembled ossified human brains.

"Watch me," said Joe-Pie. He swam a dozen yards parallel to the shore, in the direction that the lobster was facing, taking a loop on a pole from behind his back, then diving straight for the bottom. He approached the lobster from the front, and when he'd gotten close enough, extended the pole so that the loop was immediately behind the crustacean. Then he propelled himself forward, and the lobster scuttled backward into the loop. The boy pulled the pole up sharply, tightening the wire; the lobster, claws scrabbling frantically, was lifted from the ocean floor.

Joe-Pie swam to the surface, waving the lobster at the end of the pole in Selene's face; she yelped and splashed away from it. "It may not be much of a nose," she informed him, swimming farther out to sea, "but it's the only one I've got."

"You got two ears," Joe-Pie pointed out gleefully. She ignored him, and he left her alone to reboard her train of thought. Now where was she? Oh yes—was there any chance it was Whistler's father who was behind whatever had happened to Jamey? Had the old fellow gone round the bend again? Or perhaps something had happened during Jamey's visit. Another quarrel over blood? Couldn't have been over money—both Whistlers had more money than God. And from what Jamey had told her about his grandfather's will, one of those WASP-y generation-skipping trusts, Jamey would get the rest of the money when the old man died, but it wouldn't work the other way around: when Jamey died, the Whistler Legacy would go to his children, not his father.

Suddenly it dawned on Selene that circumstances had changed considerably in the past week. If Lourdes and little Cora had indeed perished in the fire, then Jamey's only living heir was Martha Herrick. But there were only two people on earth who knew that Jamey was Martha's father: the long-lost Moll Herrick, and Selene herself. And the only proof of Martha's paternity was a letter from Moll to Selene, a letter that was sewn safely into the lining of Selene's Book of Shadows.

Which was where it would remain for the time being, Selene decided, rolling over onto her stomach and striking out for shore. Martha Herrick might be a wealthy woman someday soon, but until Selene knew just who was trying to kill Jamey, and why, she would keep that knowledge to herself.

As for her next step, once again she'd found a simple one. And fortunately, she *had* brought along her passport.

━

Tosh insisted on driving Selene down to the seaplane dock on Saturday morning, though it was only a few blocks from the hotel to the harbor. She tried to pay him for his services, and had just about talked him into taking at least his gas money when they heard the clip-clop of goat hooves on cobblestones. Tosh caught sight of Granny in her black dress and bonnet. Hurriedly he thrust the money at Selene, ducked back into his cab, and steered one-handed away from the seaplane shack as the goat cart approached—Selene had the distinct impression that the other hand was cupping his balls.

Joe-Pie couldn't wait for the goat cart to reach the dock. He jumped off the little backward-facing rear seat and raced across the cobbled square toward Selene as if he were going to jump into her arms. As always, however, he stopped short and thrust out his hand; she shook it solemnly.

"Thank you for coming to see me off, Joe-Pie." His eyes darted down to the shopping bag at her feet. She reached down and handed him his parting gift as the Rastaman and Granny climbed out of the cart; he had the paper off and the box open before their feet hit the ground. Reeboks, of course.

"Wit pump," he breathed reverently. "Cool."

For the Rastaman, Selene had purchased a new yachting cap with an anchor patch at the front, navy blue to replace the white one gone yellow from age and smoke, and for the weed woman, she had a bag of devil's cherries. In return, Granny handed her a paper of pins. Selene opened her bag, found the little "For Our Guests" sewing packet from her hotel room, opened the cellophane package of needles, and slipped Granny's present inside.

"Be careful now," Granny warned her.

"You be careful with those," Selene replied.

Another round of formal handshakes, Luzan style, then a round of hugs, California style, before Selene boarded the gently rocking seaplane. She looked back once as the plane taxied toward the mouth of the harbor—the three of them were climbing back onto the goat cart—then hurriedly fastened her seat belt as the Goose gained speed, pontoons thumping against the waves, each bounce a little higher than the one before, until at last they were airborne.

The plane banked in a circle and flew back over the island; Selene pressed her nose against the Plexiglas for a last glimpse of the cozy little harbor. She could make out the goat cart crossing the square far below, the Rastaman in his blue cap, and Granny in her black bonnet facing forward—a blue dot and a black dot. Joe-Pie was a red dot perched on the backboard, his new shoes bright white dots on his feet.

Selene waved through the salt-rimed window. He couldn't have seen her, but perhaps something got through, because as the Blue Goose flew over the island the boy took off his cap and waved it over his head in a wide circle. Then he leaned back, stuck his feet straight up in the air, and waved his new Reeboks too.

6

"Mr. Yardley? If you'd come with me, sir?"

If Aldo had been higher when the Customs official at Heathrow took his elbow he might have taken his chances and made a break for it, but as he hadn't had a drink since just before boarding the plane in Athens, he meekly let the man lead him to a holding room that was bare save for a wooden bench and a wall-length mirror—one-way, no doubt.

Aldo's first thought was that his passport had soured for some reason. He should have had more than a few weeks with it. Yardley, a gay American from San Francisco, had been traveling alone, was estranged from his family, had lost most of his friends to AIDS, and was not expected home until spring. In fact, the way Aldo saw it, he'd been doing the fellow a favor. Instead of a prolonged and agonizing death (Yardley had scrupulously warned Aldo of his HIV-positive status—not that Aldo cared, blood drinkers being as immune to AIDS as they were to other diseases), the man had died suddenly, the last words he heard were tendernesses whispered into his ear as Aldo tightened the garrote, and he died with an erection that would have been the envy of any *living* man. And if his final emission had been involuntary—well, in the larger sense, what orgasm wasn't?

There were, however, other reasons for Aldo to have been detained, he recognized, shifting uncomfortably on the hard bench. He hadn't been holding any explosives or incendiaries, having used up the last of his Plastique Jesus statue, dental-floss det cord, and toothpaste napalm in Tahoe, but it was always possible the customs-house dogs had sniffed some residue. He refused to panic, though: for Aldo, fear was an intolerable sensation, fear was the orphan he'd left behind him when the Securitate had plucked him from under the grim roof of the Orfelinat Gheorghiu-Dej. Besides, whatever it was they were detaining him for, it *couldn't* be anything as serious as murder or arson, otherwise they'd have cuffed him already—and they'd certainly never have left him alone like this.

Then he caught sight of himself in the mirror across the room and realized that of course they *hadn't* left him alone. Aldo immediately rearranged his features to communicate anxiety to the unseen observers on the other side of the one-way glass; he had been on that other side often enough with the Third Branch, where the rule of thumb held that the more innocent a suspect was, the guiltier he or she would act, and vice versa.

Just then one more possibility occurred to Aldo. The only person on earth who knew that Aldo was traveling as John Yardley was Aldo's employer. Could the old man have turned him in for some reason? But why? Surely not to avoid paying Aldo—with the old man as wealthy as he was, and in this thing as deep as he was, it would be crazy for him to take a chance like that. Then Aldo remembered, with a sinking heart, that he'd known that his employer was *nebun*—crazy as a shithouse rat—from the very first. He found his thoughts drifting back to their first meeting, six weeks ago. . . .

—

It had been an unseasonably cold September night, and Aldo had popped into the Cock and Fender as much for the fire as for the pint or the companionship. As he walked into the pub, Danny Dimitriu, a sneak thief and pickpocket who resembled Peter Lorre on a starvation diet, and was even lower on the *Suterana* totem pole than Aldo (his only talent was with dead bodies: Danny was a wizard at making a *cadavru* disappear), had hailed him from a corner booth. "Striescu! Over here!"

He hurried over and clapped Danny smartly on the back of the head.

"Hey, what was that for?" whined Danny in Romanian.

"For calling my name aloud, you idiot," replied Aldo, also in his native tongue. *Idiot*—the word was the same as in English.

"Sorry. Buy me a beer and I'll tell you something to your advantage."

And over a pint of Guinness—Romanian beer was one thing no Romanian every waxed homesick over—Danny told him about the *nebun*—the nutcase—who'd been in earlier that evening, expressing an interest in Romanian folktales. "I gave him the usual story about the *nosferatu*, but he's done his homework. He wants to know about the real thing. I thought of you right off."

"Sounds interesting," Aldo said, while trying not to *look* interested. Though neither man had mentioned it, both knew that the haggling—the Romanian national pastime—had already begun. "Maybe I'll give him a call. I don't suppose you happen to know the number?"

"Oh, but *do* suppose, my old friend," Danny had replied. "Suppose away!"

It only took another pint—and a menacing look—to obtain the number. The *nebun* was there within twenty minutes of Aldo's call. It wasn't hard to spot him—the old man was six and a half feet tall, wearing a topcoat over what appeared to be pajamas; his ankles were bare, and on his feet were soft tan sheepskin bedroom slippers. A pair of cheap plastic sunglasses, the kind you grab off a drugstore rack, obscured his eyes.

Aldo raised a forefinger discreetly; the man picked up the gesture from all the way across the bar, through the smoke and the dim light and the black lenses of the sunglasses, and made a beeline for him, moving with a graceful ease that would have been remarkable for a man half his apparent age.

"Are you Aldo?"

"If you're Jonas."

"Call me Jo. I understand you're an expert on v—"

Aldo cut him off. "Perhaps you should order a drink and we can continue our discussion at a more private location—say that last booth in the corner." He was employing what would have been his own natural Romanian accent, had he not been cured of it in the Institut Limba Strain, the foreign language school run by the Third Branch.

"But it's occupied."

"They'll be leaving soon."

"When?"

"When they understand I want the booth."

Aldo signaled for another drink for himself; Jo asked for a single-malt Scotch, the oldest they had. "I haven't had a Scotch under twenty years old since the war," he explained to Aldo as they approached the booth, which magically emptied itself at that moment. "Second World, that is." He took a tentative sip as they sat down across from each other at a dark booth. "How do people drink this stuff? Ah well, I suppose I'll just have to rough it. Let's get right to business, shall we?"

"Which business would that be?"

"What we discussed over the phone. I'm interested in learning something about . . . I believe you call them the *nosferatu* in your country?"

"Nosferatu? Paah!" Aldo blew an imaginary bubble into the air. "Nosferatu is bullshit. Nosferatu is Dracula, and Dracula is a creation of an Evreu Englese, an English Jew by the name of Abraham Stoker."

"Are you telling me there are no such things as vampires?"

"I'm telling you there is not such a thing as nosferatu. What we do have in my *former* country are legends of creatures known as the *strigoi*. Strigoi are said to be mortal creatures who drink blood to attain supernormal powers. They are not immortal, neither do they sleep in coffins or fear garlic or crosses."

The old man took another sip of Scotch. "*Not* immortal, you say?"

"Not according to the legends."

"So if a strigoi, for instance, were diagnosed with some incurable disease, he would be as likely to die as anyone else?"

"I did not say that, my friend. So long as a strigoi has human blood to drink, he is said to be immune to any form of disease."

"But if someone, say, wanted a strigoi dead, there *are* ways to kill them?"

Aldo tossed off his Stoli at a gulp, then leaned across the table. Sounded like a job might be in the offing, but he needed to be sure. "Before I answer that, *Jo*, I would have to know in what spirit you are asking the question."

The old man finished his drink as well, then signaled the bartender for another round. "Let me answer that with a question in return." He leaned forward as well, until their foreheads were nearly touching over the scarred wooden table. "Do you believe in vampires—strigoi, nosferatu, whatever you want to call them. Do you *believe* in them?"

"*Believe* in them?" Aldo said triumphantly, placing both hands flat on the table, and half rising until he was leaning over the old man. "*Believe* in them? My dear Jo, I've been hunting strigoi for over twenty years, both in the service of my former government, and more recently in the private sector. You might as well ask an exterminator whether he believes in cockroaches."

"I'll take that for a yes," replied the old man, drawing back. Then, nervously, as he started to slide out of the booth: "Thank you so much for your time."

Aldo stopped him, reaching across the table and placing a hand on his arm. His improvisation appeared to have backfired. "Please. I seem to have frightened you. Perhaps you misunderstood. I have nothing against strigoi personally. If a man wants to drink blood, as far as I'm concerned, that's his own business. Please, have a seat— see, here comes our next round of drinks."

The old man sat back down, but Aldo had the feeling he was regarding him warily from behind the black lenses of the sunglasses. "I thought you said you hunt them down like cockr—"

Aldo raised a hand again to cut him off as the barmaid arrived with their drinks. "Thank you, my dear." Then, when the girl was again out of earshot: "I said I *believe* in them the way an exterminator *believes* in cockroaches. But it is true, I hunt them for the same reason: because it is my business."

"I see," said the old man doubtfully, knocking back his second Scotch of the evening while Aldo sipped at his third Stoli. Neither man was showing much effect from the liquor. "Just out of curiosity, how much do you charge?"

"For believing in them? Nothing. For exterminating them . . . ?" With only the briefest hesitation, Aldo picked the first figure that came to mind: "One hundred thousand pounds." The figure had, of course, been an opening gambit. When old Jo evinced no shock at the grandiose sum Aldo had quickly added, "And expenses."

"Of course."

It wasn't much fun, dickering with this wealthy *nebun*—like playing table tennis with an armless man. But haggling was part of the Romanian's nature. Aldo decided to take things a step further, to chance mixing pleasure with business. "And you know, of course," he went on smoothly, "that the only way to be sure a strigoi is truly dead is to burn him alive."

The old man in the pajamas swallowed that too without choking, so Aldo hurriedly ad-libbed: "And all his dwellings as well." Ambitious—but ah, to be out torching again! And at that point he hadn't even known about Selene. Didn't find out about her until later that evening. They'd both had a few more drinks, and Aldo was riffing on Romanian folklore when he happened to mention that the word *strigoi* was derived from *striga*, the Romanian word for witch, because so many strigoi were thought to have witches for companions.

The old man almost choked on his Scotch. "This is astounding!"
"Oh?"

"The very strigoi I want you to take care of told me he'd once been engaged to marry a witch. I believe they're still close—in fact, if I remember correctly, she lives in one of his houses."

"Then we'll have to burn her as well," replied Aldo without missing a beat. He'd given the old man a break, though: he'd thrown in the striga for half price. Practically lagniappe. . . .

━

And now, six weeks later he'd fulfilled his part of the bargain to the letter—the strigoi and all his dwellings were burnt to ashes. The striga as well—it wasn't Aldo's fault she was dead when he got there. Besides, nobody could say he hadn't burned her. So the question remained: was the old man *nebun* enough to turn Aldo in to the authorities just to avoid paying the piper his hundred and fifty thousand pounds? Aldo was still trying to decide when the door to the holding room opened.

"Mr. Yardley? Can you explain what you were doing with *this* in your luggage, sir?"

When Aldo turned and saw that the Customs official was holding—of all things—his oversized veterinary syringe, it was all that he could do to keep from breaking into a grin. "Of course," he said in American. "It's for my old football knee." He bent over and rolled up his left pant leg to the knee, revealing a ragged scar from a childhood soccer injury. "Here, let me show you." Aldo took the syringe from the astonished official, jabbed the needle into his knee (which hadn't given him any trouble in thirty years), worked it around, and managed to withdraw a few cc's of cloudy fluid. The customs man almost tossed his scones, the bloody fool, and then, quick as you please, it was, "Welcome back to the UK, Mr. Yardley, and have a lovely stay."

"Oh, that I will," replied Aldo, thinking of the hundred and fifty thousand pounds that would be transferred into his bank account on Monday morning.

CHAPTER

7

The daylong drizzle had let up a bit by Sunday evening, but the streets of London still gleamed darkly and a fine pearly mist hung in the air around No. 11 Cranwick Square. Selene paused at the bottom of the steps leading up to the modest-looking row house. The cream-colored facade of No. 11 was as genteelly grimy as the rest of the row, but unlike most of the other town houses, which had been chopped into flats decades ago, No. 11 was intact. Between two Tuscan columns, four shallow tiled steps led up to a stucco entrance portico; there was one ornate brass letter slot to the left of the door, one doorbell to the right, attached to a white-washed, metal-grilled speaker. Selene paused under the dripping portico with her finger on the buzzer; she could feel her heart pounding as she jabbed at the button.

"You're early," squawked the intercom. "Entrez-vous."

"Mr. Whistler?"

"I *said* entrez-vous. That means let yourself in, you ignorant trollop," was the tinny reply. "I'm upstairs."

Selene pushed open the heavy door. "Hello?"

No answer—only the stouthearted ticking of the grandfather clock in the dark entrance hall. She closed the door behind her and stepped back into the nineteenth century. Parquet floor strewn with densely patterned Oriental rugs. Dusty oak baseboards. Dado panels overlayed with leathery anaglypta. Between the dado rail and the elaborate plasterwork of the cornice, the walls and friezes were covered with green and gold flocked Morris paper; a converted Beethoven gasolier hung from a gilded ceiling rose.

Selene hung her damp trenchcoat, a Lady Burberry she'd purchased at Heathrow, on a towering mahogany coat rack, and made her way down the narrow hall and up the staircase, taking note of the curious state of neglect into which the old house had fallen. A layer of dust had settled over the woodwork and furniture, from the Prussian clock to the walnut hall table with flanking side chairs, from the coat rack to the smooth banister and spindled balusters of the staircase. But when her fingers brushed the staircase railing, Selene saw that beneath the dust the wood retained a dark polished luster, and overhead the cobwebs clinging to the corniced ceiling were intact and confined to the corners. Up until a few months ago, she decided, there must have been servants, else the state of disrepair of the venerable furnishings would have been a good deal more advanced.

The staircase turned, and turned again. The second story was dark, the open drawing room deserted. The stairway narrowed as she continued climbing; she began to hear a faint, rhythmic squeaking from overhead. When she reached the third floor she saw yellow light spilling from an open door across the green and cream hallway rug. It was from this room that the squeaking emerged. Bedsprings, judging by the high-pitched, breathy squeals that accompanied them in perfect time. Selene waited in the hall for a few minutes, but the squeaking and squealing neither slowed nor accelerated. Finally she peeked in.

The bedroom was decorated in higgledy-piggledy High Victorian. A massive, elaborately carved, double-fronted, ebony-inlaid wardrobe took up most of one wall, its leaded central mirror reflecting the matching ebony bedstead across the room. As she peered around the corner of the doorjamb, Selene saw the source of the noise revealed in the mirror: a nude Asian girl squatting on the bed, bouncing up and down, squealing at the bottom of every bounce.

She couldn't see the girl's face, only her determined, wide-waisted torso rising and falling, and her long black hair bouncing. How long could she keep it up? Selene wondered admiringly. Must have been hell on the thigh muscles.

But she had leaned too far into the doorway. "Come on in," said a querulous old voice. "If you're waiting for *me* to finish, you'll be standing out there all night."

Selene approached the bed as the old man shoved the Chinese woman off him. She had a brief glimpse of the ancient but still impressive penis, heavy and substantial enough to have filled the woman, but not hard enough to stand on its own, as it plopped out of her like an elongated, partially filled water balloon, falling across the old man's thigh with a fat slapping sound.

In its youth the thing must have been truly imposing, Selene reckoned, before turning her attention to the Chinese woman, who had fallen back against the high footboard. She saw before the woman turned her back and climbed wearily off the bed that the slim girlish figure in the mirror had been an illusion—the face was lined, the slack belly and small breasts sagged softly.

"Where do you think you're going?" snapped the old man.

"To 'ave a pee, guv," was the response as the Chinese woman trudged off—Cockney, not pidgin, to Selene's mild surprise.

The old man stuck his tongue out at her retreating back, then turned his attention to Selene. The only light in the room came from a small lamp on the bedside table. His face was in shadow, his fine hair tufted up into a white corona around his head. "Damn, you're an old one, aren't you? How long have you been in the business?"

Selene, though she'd been attending orgies of one sort or another for over thirty years now, found herself blushing and stammering. "I'm afraid there's been some mistake. I'm not"—she nodded in the direction the Chinese woman had gone—"one of those."

"You mean Chinese? That's rather obvious."

"I mean a prostitute," said Selene.

"Neither was she." As he lay back against a mound of pillows Selene saw his eyes for the first time. They were gray, like Jamey's,

but so bloodshot and debauched they looked like pearl onions floating in tomato sauce. "She was my housekeeper before all this happened. Best I ever had. Never occurred to me to lay a finger on
her. Now instead of a crackerjack charwoman, I've got an indifferent whore, and my house is falling down around my ears. As for
you, if you're not a whore, who the bloody hell are you and what
are you doing in my bedroom?"

At the sight of those eyes Selene understood instantly that everything had changed. "My name is Sarah Stone. I'm in your bedroom because you insisted I come into your bedroom. Believe me,
I would have been just as happy to meet with you down in the
parlor."

"On what business?" replied the old man, leisurely tugging his
nightshirt down over his lap.

"I'm trying to locate your son, James. He owes me a rather
large sum of money."

"If you took all the information I have as to my son's whereabouts and stuffed it up a flea's arse, Miss Stone, you'd still have
room up there for how much I care. I have neither seen nor spoken
to Jamey in thirty years. And if you think you're going to get a
brass farthing out of me, you're sadly mistaken." But as he spoke,
his glance was slithering down her body—her outfit, a sheer white
silk blouse over an ankle-length beige skirt, was a souvenir of her
second tour of the duty-free shops of Charlotte Amalie, this time
stoned on the Rastaman's righteous weed. There seemed to be little
doubt that although Selene was nearing fifty, and Whistler's father
would never see eighty again, the old boy was definitely checking
her out. And apparently liked what he saw, for he quickly added:
"But I'm being rude. Obviously you've come a long way. Have
you had supper yet?"

Selene smiled flirtatiously. "Why no. No, I haven't."

"Excellent. Then perhaps you'll do me the honor of dining with
me." Without waiting for an answer, the old man called in the
direction of the bathroom: "Mrs. Wah. I'll be having a guest for
dinner this evening."

"Wot?" came the reply. "Oi let you stick 'at fing in me all afternoon, now you fink Oi'm cookin' bleedin' supper for you and your 'ore? Bloody 'ell Oi am!"

"Servants," said the old man, shrugging apologetically. "Perhaps you'd be more comfortable waiting down in the drawing room."

—

The drawing room was in no better condition than the rest of the house. Selene looked around for a dust cloth; finding none, she used a tissue from her purse to dust off a yellow wing chair as best she could. She perched gingerly on the edge of the chair, mindful of her light-colored skirt, and began trying to evaluate this new piece of information: judging by both his eyes and his behavior, Whistler's father was almost certainly a full-blown, degenerate, balls-to-the-wall blood drinker. And if she had to make a guess, he was definitely off his antipsychotic medications.

Whether this meant he was more or less likely to have been involved in the attempts on her and Jamey's lives, however, was not at all clear. On the one hand, there didn't seem to be much chance he was still pissed off at Jamey for having drunk blood thirty years ago, if he was now drinking himself; on the other hand, if he was as far gone as he appeared to be, there was no point looking for rational explanations for his actions. It occurred to her that perhaps her best move would be to get the hell out of Dodge. But then what? Call Scotland Yard? Fly back home and wait around for the road-show devil to return? Or perhaps he knew that Jamey had survived, and was out looking for him. She decided instead to stick around, act flattered at the old man's attentions, even flirt with him a little, and find out what he knew about Jamey—if indeed he knew anything. She also decided to keep the news that Jamey was still alive to herself for at least a while longer.

Fifteen minutes later, Mrs. Wah, clad now in a circumspect housedress, but reeking of gin and sex, appeared at the door of the parlor to inform her that dinner would be served downstairs in twenty minutes or so, and that if she wanted to wash up, there was a bathroom at the end of the hall. The woman then waited in the doorway for her, and as Selene brushed by her the housekeeper hissed into her ear, "Keep yer 'ands orf, 'e's mine."

Selene spent a few minutes in the bathroom trying to repair the damage the rain had done to her mane; when she emerged she found the old man waiting for her by the landing, dressed in a dark suit cut from an expensive-looking black wool fabric with a subdued gray pinstripe. The coat bagged on him, as if he'd recently lost weight; his white shirt was loose as a horse collar around his neck and his striped tie was wrinkled just below the knot, as if he had slipped it over his head already tied. But his shave was impeccable, his thin white hair combed back with care, and there was no sign of the stiffness of age in his movements as he stooped to give her his arm.

Thus cleaned up, he was a much taller Jamey—or Jamey in thirty years, at any rate. Same long jaw, same long, sardonic upper lip. His eyes were gray like Jamey's, but unamused and of a steelier metal; the worst of the red-eye had been washed out by Visine, or whatever they used in this country.

They descended the staircase together, turned left at the bottom, and he led her into an overdecorated, high-ceilinged formal dining room. Two places were laid at one end of a heavy-legged mahogany table; the place settings were Wedgwood and Sterling, but the serving dishes were white cardboard cartons with red pagodas printed on the sides.

He shrugged another apology. "Cook's night off. Hope you like Chinese. Never recognize any of the damn dishes, myself."

Selene had already determined to select food out of cartons from which her host had already eaten—this occasioned a brief Alphonse and Gaston *after you; no, after you* duel that Selene won with the *age before beauty* ploy, an unanswerable card when played by a woman. She watched his hands as he served himself. His long fingers were so like Jamey's. She thought of something: "Do you still paint, Jo?" By now they were on a first-name basis.

He paused with a silver serving spoon in midair. "How did you know I used to paint?"

"Jamey told me."

"In the course of your . . . *business* relationship? Odd that he'd mention that."

"To tell you the truth, Jo, our relationship was both business *and* personal."

"Then I was right? You are a . . . working gal?"

"Was. Gave it up when my looks started to go."

"Nonsense!" declared the old man.

"You're too gallant," protested Selene. "I thank you anyway. Actually, I've been in management for a number of years. I own an establishment in San Francisco."

"And you let Jamey run a tab?"

"Alas."

"More's the pity. But you do understand it's not my problem?"

"I do, Jo. I do." They'd begun eating now—with cutlery, not chopsticks. "But we were talking about painting."

"Ah yes, painting. Odd that you should ask. I'd given it up entirely—hadn't lifted a brush since my wife died back in sixty-four. But a few months ago, as I was recovering from a rather serious illness"—he raised his hand, palm out, against her protestation of concern—"quite well now, thank you. But it was the most peculiar thing: within moments of coming out of what the doctor had assured everyone would be a final, fatal coma, I called for paper and pencil and began drawing. Quite astonished Mrs. Wah, it did. Perhaps you'd like to come up to the atelier with me after dinner to inspect the results?"

Was he flirting? Selene wasn't sure. She tried a joke—"Come up to your room and see your etchings, eh?"—and punched it up with a leer and a waggle of bushy eyebrows that had never known tweezers.

Old Whistler had turned his attention to peeling the sticky paper from the bottom of a pork bun. "Not etchings; sketches." He corrected her in a slightly annoyed tone, then looked up and caught sight of her eyebrows. "Are you all right, Sarah?"

"Fine, fine." She found herself blushing. "Just kidding around."

"Ah, humor," he said, as if it were a quaint American custom.

It took her a moment to realize that he too had been joking—at least this last time. Sly old fellow.

Just then Mrs. Wah entered with a pot of green tea. They would be drinking from a common container, so Selene didn't have to worry about the tea being doctored; all she had to do was wait for Jonas to drink first. But there was another way to doctor a drink, as Stan Kovic had learned to his great discomfort so many years before. And yet a third method: put the poison in the pot, some sort of antidoting or neutralizing agent in your own cup, and give the clean cup to your victim.

But upon inspection, both cups were dry and empty. "I'll be Mother," said Jo. Fortunately Selene had learned the phrase from Jamey; it meant he'd pour. Selene sniffed the delicately scented steam, keeping her eye on the old man. He sipped, swallowed; she followed suit. Then, with the taste of the bitter tea still in her mouth, she had a dreadful thought. What if the housekeeper had meant to poison both of them? What good would all her precautions be against that?

She caught herself. It was a fine line between caution and paranoia. But once you start poisoning people, as Andred and Bensozia had warned Selene so many years before, you will never enjoy a meal to quite the same degree again.

After dinner the old man showed Selene up to the second-floor parlor, then excused himself for a few minutes—to take his medicine, he explained. She had a pretty good idea just which medicine he had in mind, and wondered whether she oughtn't simply take her leave before it took full effect. But she hadn't learned anything about Jamey yet. Jonas continued to insist he hadn't seen his son in thirty years. Selene decided to string him along a little further. Perhaps the blood would loosen his tongue as it made him hornier.

"Feeling better, Jo?" she asked him when he returned, though it was obvious that he did.

"Yes, much, thank you Sarah." He pulled a second wing chair closer to hers and sat down with their knees touching. "I was thinking, while I was upstairs, that perhaps it isn't entirely fair to let you take this entire loss. If I may ask, how much did Jamey owe you?"

Selene didn't know much about prostitution, much less what would be a reasonable tab for a madam to have allowed Jamey to run up. It would have to be enough to make a trip to England worthwhile. "Ten thousand dollars," she replied after a moment's hesitation.

"Tell you what I'll do," said Jonas, patting her on the knee with those long-fingered hands that reminded her so of Jamey's. "I'll give you half."

"That's very generous of you, Jo." She put her hand over his. "I accept."

"He *is* my son, after all." Somehow the old man smiled without changing expression, placed his free hand over hers, and pressed it warmly. "And if I may say so, for all his faults, Jamey always did have excellent taste when it came to women."

So he *was* flirting. "Why thank you, Jonas."

"Which brings me to my next question . . ." His bottom hand slid a little higher up her thigh, and he leaned forward to stare into her eyes. His own eyes were a washed-out shade of pink. "Would you like to stay the night?"

Well, perhaps *flirting* wasn't exactly the word. Time to start stalling. Selene squeezed the hand squeezing her thigh, before lifting it away. "Weren't you expecting someone?"

He was puzzled for a moment. "Oh! You mean the hook—the woman I mistook you for. I called to cancel that visit before we sat down to supper."

Selene stalled some more. "I'm afraid I'm well past the age where I can still pack all my overnight things in my purse."

"Not a problem. We can send for your things."

"I . . . I don't . . ." She screwed her features into a thinking-it-over face for a few seconds, then clucked her tongue against the roof of her mouth. "I don't think so." In as reluctant a tone as she could manage without leaving him an opening.

He saw one anyway. "Just for a few hours, then. I'll make it worth your while."

Selene was almost offended; then she remembered she was supposed to be a madam—and a former hooker as well. "I'm sorry, Jo. I'm afraid I'm quite retired from that end of the business."

"Not even for the other five grand?"

"It's tempting." Another thinking-it-over face. "Tell you what *I'll* do. Let me go back to my hotel tonight—I *am* quite exhausted—and then tomorrow night, if your offer still holds, perhaps I'll take you up on it—be able to give you your money's worth by then."

He gave her thigh another squeeze; his hand reached most of the way around it. "I'll have Mrs. Wah call a taxi for you, then." He inclined his head a few degrees—a delicate, understated nod that brought Jamey sharply to mind. But she felt a sudden chill come over her when he added that perhaps while they were waiting for the cab would be a good time to show her his recent sketches.

Impossible to refuse, though. She followed him up another two flights of stairs, the last quite narrow, with a ceiling so low he had to hunch his shoulders. The atelier proved to be a thoroughly charming, if dusty, room with dormer windows cut into either side of a high peaked ceiling. To the south she could make out the Chelsea embankment and the wide black ribbon of the Thames; to the north the sky glowed mistily above what might have been Victoria Station. He indicated a sketch pad that was propped up closed on a dusty drafting table. She picked it up, blew away the dust, and began flipping through the sheets.

The drawing on the first few was shaky; she could well believe they'd been done by a man coming out of a coma. But after a few pages the hand grew firmer, the line more fluid, the figure on the page more fully realized, until by the fifth or sixth page the slim reclining nude had taken on a life of her own, her arm raised languidly, her fingers curled in an invitation that would have been unmistakably sexual even had the figure been fully clad. All in all it was an astonishingly skillful effect to have achieved with a quick pencil sketch; Selene found it hard to believe it had been executed by the failed—and talentless—artist Jamey had always made his father out to be.

Moreover, this madman with whom Selene had made no discernible telepathic connection whatsoever, had spoken to her clearly through his art. "This was your wife," she said, without a hint of a question in her voice.

"It was," he said simply.

"She was very beautiful."

"She was." He had turned his head away as if he was unable to bear the likeness.

"You must miss her very much."

His head jerked up, and he stared at her intently for a moment, as if she'd said something astonishing; then he shook his head as if to clear it. "How odd," he murmured. "That's exactly what Jamey said when *he* saw it."

"I thought you said you hadn't seen him for thirty years," said Selene, much too sharply. Her words hung in the air, obtrusive as a cartoon balloon. Their eyes met. It was one of those she-knew-that-he-knew-that-she-knew moments, and what they both knew was that they had each come within a whisker of having successfully duped the other, and had both failed.

She allowed herself one shot at denial. "I must have misunderstood. My cab's probably here by now, don't you think?"

He shook his head. "I'm sorry," he said. "That was clumsy of me." He took the sketch pad from her hand, and closed it carefully. "It's the damn blood—clouds my judgment." Then he reached for her purse. "If I might just have a look in there, Sarah? Just to be sure you are whom you claim to be?"

"Why Jo, what—"

He cut her off, snatched the purse out of her hand with a speed that belied his age, then with his back blocking the door he removed her wallet and flipped it open to her California driver's license. "Selene Weiss," he murmured, as much to himself as to her. "The *striga*. I'll have to give my employee Aldo a call. He'll be quite surprised to learn you're here. In fact, he'll be quite surprised to learn you're anywhere. He informed me just the other evening that he'd smothered you in your bed and burned your house around you. Good thing I haven't paid him off yet."

CHAPTER

8

"I'll have you know that up until quite recently, I'd lived a largely exemplary life," remarked the old man, glancing around the atelier for a length of twine or cord with which to bind Selene's wrists. Finding none, he nodded toward the daybed. "Sit down."

She stood there for a moment, arms folded across her chest, too angry to think clearly. She realized she was glaring at him, dropped her eyes, and turned toward the daybed. He reached for the stool by the drafting table and started to slide it across the room, obviously intending to position himself in front of the door. Seeing that he was off balance, she tried to dart around him; he snaked out his other arm and grabbed her by the sleeve of her blouse. As she tried to pull away she felt the shoulder seam beginning to tear, and the first glimmer of a plan began to form in her mind. She threw herself back violently; the sleeve tore away and her momentum sent her flying across the room.

Selene fetched up sprawled against the daybed, breathing hard. "Damn you to hell," she muttered, sitting up. "That was a two-hundred-dollar blouse."

In an instant he was standing over her. "Don't try that again," he said sharply. "Next time it'll be your arm." He tossed the sleeve into her lap. "And as for damning me to hell," he continued in a more reasonable tone, turning his back on her and rolling the stool

toward the door again, "even if it weren't a ludicrous notion, coming from a witch, your old friend Jamey has already seen to that."

"What do you mean?" asked Selene.

"I mean that last year I was diagnosed with an incurable form
of leukemia." Jonas Whistler settled onto the stool, his back planted
firmly against the door. "And if it hadn't been for my son's med-
dling, my body would be lying beside Alice by now, and my soul
would be with my Maker. Instead I've become a monster like him.
If I had any character, any character at all, I'd have done away with
myself months ago. I still intend to—but not until I've sent Jamey
to hell first."

⟶

Jonas had wished to die at home, he told Selene, and was more
than wealthy enough to see his wishes carried through. But soon
after he'd slipped into what the doctors presumed would be his final
coma, one of his nurses had taken it upon herself to notify his next
of kin. Jamey, of course. A week later he was at his father's side, a
little of the Whistler fortune having greased the wheels of British
immigration, or perhaps purged a few incriminating records. The
next night the old man woke up calling for his sketch pad, feeling
better than he had in years. The doctors proclaimed a miracle—
they wanted to write him up for the medical journals—but Jamey,
whose presence Jonas seemed to have taken for granted, would have
none of it. He threw them out, gave Mrs. Wah the night off, and
father and son spent the evening catching each other up on their
lives, making up for lost time.

The reconciliation was going well—better than Jamey had dared
to hope for—at least until he told his father the truth about the
miraculous recovery: that shortly after arriving, Jamey had stolen a
blood sample off a nurse's tray and drank it down. This was the
only reliable method by which one Drinker could recognize another: a vampire couldn't get high drinking another vampire's
blood. And when his father's blood failed to give Jamey so much
as a buzz, it confirmed something he'd suspected ever since the old
man had overreacted so dramatically to Jamey's arrest for stealing

blood from one of the servants so many years ago: that the father, like the son, was a natural born blood drinker.

"Had you known before?" Selene asked, casually beginning to unbutton her blouse. "About yourself?"

"Yes, I— What are you doing?"

"I'm going to baste my sleeve back on, if you have no objections," she replied. "Toss me my purse there, will you?"

The purse had fallen by the door. Jonas picked it up and started to hand it to her, but when she reached for it he pulled it back— "Tch-tch-tch, not so fast"—dumped the contents on the floor, and began searching through them.

Selene shrugged as if it were no big deal. "All I want's that little sewing packet there. The one that says 'For Our Guests.' " She nodded toward it, with her fingers poised on the third button of the blouse—this one would show, if not cleavage, at least the lacy top of her bra, and considering what she knew about blood drinkers' sex drive, she wasn't just flattering herself by imagining that the prospect might sway him.

And it did—he scooted his stool a little closer and handed her the packet. She dropped it into her lap, and continued with her unbuttoning. "You were saying?"

"Where was I?" He brought his eyes back to her face, but they kept returning to her torso as she began taking her blouse off.

"About to tell me whether you'd known about your . . . tendency before Jamey."

"I did. It's a story I've never told anyone."

"I'd like to hear it," she said, sticking out her chest as far as she could without being obvious about it; a girl had to do the best she could with what she had. But it was enough, apparently; his attention seemed sufficiently diverted for her to risk picking up the sewing packet.

"Not a chance."

Selene's heart was beating so hard that she could hardly hear him over the pounding in her ears as she felt around in the packet for the weed woman's paper of pins. Five of them, each smaller than the next, and of a lower potency. The largest for the largest man, the smallest for the smallest woman—but even that one would kill a child, Granny had warned her. "Beg pardon?"

"I said, not a chance. I'd have to be a good deal higher than I am at the moment to blab *that* story."

Selene shrugged, and his eyes dropped to her chest again. "That can be arranged," she said, turning her wrist up and showing him the tiny scars from years of serving as Whistler's donor.

He narrowed his eyes. "Why are you suddenly so cooperative?"

"I figure as long as you're talking—or drinking . . ." She hesitated, not wanting to go too far—then went there anyway. ". . . or getting what your son used to call the world's best blow job, then you're not killing me, which is what I presume you have in mind eventually."

She bent forward, subtly pressing her elbows against her sides, thereby manufacturing enough cleavage to distract his eyes again as she selected the two largest pins from the paper—however much weight he might have lost recently, he was still an awfully tall man. She would try the second-largest first, she decided, but promised herself that if the first dose didn't drop him like a stone she wouldn't hesitate to use the second. The combination of the two would kill him for sure—hell, it would probably kill a horse—but if the alternative was being murdered herself, well . . .

And as she slipped the pin between the ring and middle fingers of her left hand, the point peeking out just below the first knuckle, Selene's mind dredged up a stray line of Browning: "Life's business being just the terrible choice."

She glanced up to see if any of her propositions had caught his interest. If he wanted blood or sex he'd have to come within reach of her pin—but to her surprise, he seemed to want to talk. "World's best, eh? Well, you know what the Bible says: 'All our righteousnesses are as filthy rags.' "

Selene didn't recognize it. "Old Testament?"

A nod. "Isaiah, sixty-four six. 'But we are all as an unclean thing, and all our righteousnesses are as filthy rags; and we all do fade as a leaf; and our iniquities, like the wind, have taken us away.' I committed it to memory on the day Alice passed.

"Not for her," he added hastily. "For myself. I was as responsible for her death as if I'd put a bullet in her head."

Selene was mystified. Jamey had never hinted that his mother's death had been anything but a heart attack. "I'm so sorry," she said, placing the larger pin in her mouth, fitting the sleeve against the torn shoulder of the blouse.

He didn't seem to notice that she hadn't started sewing yet. His gaze had turned inward, backward in time. "We met in Manhattan. I was just back from the Eritrean campaign—and looking rather dashing in my lieutenant's uniform, Alice later confided."

"I'm sure you were," said Selene.

"I was supposed to be joining some friends for drinks at the Hotel Pennsylvania. In nineteen forty-four it was one of *the* places to meet in New York. When I arrived to meet my friends I saw, hiding behind an enormous rubber tree plant, a little bitty slip of a brunette in a shiny green dress. I could tell she was hiding because she kept circling the plant to keep it between her and someone else. Of course I sidled over to her to see if I could be of some assistance, and learned that she'd arrived somewhat early for a dinner engagement and spied her lover, an officer, but obviously no gentleman, having a drink and a bit of a cuddle with a WAC with whom he was obviously on intimate terms. She asked me to give her my arm and walk her back through the lobby; she marched past the bastard with her chin up, making damn sure he saw her, but not giving him so much as the benefit of a glance.

"Is it any wonder I fell in love with her that night? And she with me, before she even knew about my wealth. I was in uniform, remember—well tailored, to be sure, but otherwise just another shavetail lieutenant. We had supper at the Morocco that evening, made love that night, and were married within a month. Our son, James, was born the following year, and if there was ever a more blessed union in the world than ours, I've never heard of it."

"How long did you have together?" asked Selene; she had let her sewing fall to her lap as if mesmerized by the tale.

"Her heart started to give out when she was only forty-nine. After we'd been through all the specialists in London, I took her to the best doctors on the Continent, and then back to the States, but it was the same everywhere—there was nothing any of them could do. It was still the Dark Ages as far as her medical options were concerned. No open-heart surgery, no transplants. We came back to London, I surrounded her with the best nurses, round the clock, and tried to keep her quiet and comfortable—any sort of exertion taxed her terribly.

"And as for making love, it was out of the question. She wanted to, for my sake, but it was too much for her. For me, it was another test of character—all I had to do was remain celibate for another year or so. And of course I failed. I couldn't even wait until she died—I had to go off with a woman who picked me up in a bar. A rather expensive bar, but a bar nonetheless.

"Her name was Theresa. Countess Theresa di Voltera. She was from an old Tuscan family—maintained pieds-à-terre in Paris and London, as well as the old homestead in Tuscany. Listened sympathetically while I rattled on about my beloved invalid wife—as if she gave a good goddamn—then dragged me up to her flat, overpowered me as easily as if I'd been a child, and withdrew a pint of blood from my vein while I watched as if in a dream.

"Theresa was delighted to discover I was a vampire as well. She fed us both from one of her earlier conquests, and we began a torrid affair that went on every night for weeks, always with her supplying the blood. And every morning I'd go home to Alice, sometimes napping on the daybed in her bedroom, the picture of the devoted husband.

"Then one evening I let myself into Theresa's flat with my key and found a note on the dining room table—she'd gone off to South America with a donor. Help myself to the blood in the fridge, she informed me, and she'd give me a ring when she was back in town."

"Were you terribly hurt?" cooed Selene.

"It wasn't as if she'd led me down the primrose path," replied Jonas. "She'd never made any bones about how she lived her life. But I was a bit angry—I thought I deserved at least a good-bye. Still, it was rather a nice gesture, her leaving me a milk bottle full of blood. I brought it back home in a paper sack, took a shot glass up to my room, and proceeded to drink myself into a wretched, and quite unexpectedly randy, state. You see, for those first few weeks I'd associated the unbelievable state of lust I was in with the Countess Theresa as much as with blood.

"But that first night I soon learned differently. I wasn't sure what to do—I didn't know any prostitutes myself. Not that finding one would have been a problem—there were a dozen friends I could have called for a reference. It was the embarrassment of making the call that held me up. By the time I decided I had to do something about my state, it was getting on to dawn. My eyes were already exquisitely sensitive to light—I could still get about on a cloudy day, but full sunlight was too painful, so I decided to hold on until the following evening.

"And hold on I did—with both hands, if you get my drift. And when my own fantasies no longer satisfied me, I went digging up in the attic for some pornographic magazines I'd confiscated from Jamey years before. I had them spread out across the bedcovers, and was sitting naked among them with a jar of face cream I'd stolen from Alice's dresser, when suddenly Alice appeared in the door between our adjoining bedrooms: she had come to say good night, because I had quite forgotten to say good night to her. I'd never forgotten before, not even the past few weeks when I was creeping out to see Theresa every night."

By now Selene's interest was quite genuine. "What happened?"

"She burst into tears and sank to the floor. I pulled up my pajamas and carried her in my arms to the bed. I started to call for her nurse, but Alice stopped me. She wasn't horrified or disgusted or any of the reactions one would have expected. Instead she blamed herself. She knew what sex meant to me, she said—she should have seen to me somehow, or freed me to find someone. She said that would have been all right—said she knew how much I loved her. Said she'd rather die than see me reduced to . . . well, she didn't have the words for what she'd seen."

Not much expression, either on his face or in his voice. "I didn't tell her about Theresa or the blood, of course. Just let her blame

herself, and weep, and I held her, and comforted her, and before
long—remember I had already drunk more blood that evening than
Theresa had ever allowed me at a sitting—before long the comfort
turned to caressing, and the caressing to . . ."

Finally words had failed the old man.

"Is that when she died?" There was no hidden motive behind
the question; Selene simply had to know.

He shrugged. "I don't know precisely when. We made love for
hours, and the next morning I found her cold in bed beside me."

"May I say something," Selene asked rhetorically, after a deathly
long silence. "If it was me? If I was dying slowly, like her? I would
pray for somebody to fuck me to death too."

His face was in his hands; he looked up as if he'd forgotten she
was in the room. "World's best blow job, you said?"

"So I've heard."

"A drink first."

"Absolutely. Do you have a knife?" asked Selene out of the
corner of her mouth—the other corner held the largest pin.

There was an intercom by the door; he pressed the button and
spoke into it. "Mrs. Wah?" he called. "Would you bring me my
pocketknife from my bedside table."

"Get it yerself," was the answering squawk.

"Never mind," said Selene. She'd forgotten about the housekeeper momentarily. With her free hand she dumped the contents
of the sewing packet into her lap—there was a tiny plastic scissors,
far too dull for comfort. But this was no time to be squeamish.
"Never mind," she told Jonas, again out of the side of her mouth.
"This'll do." Pressing her lips even more firmly together against the
pain, she forced herself to snip a little bite out of the tender skin
just below the heel of her hand.

Jonas, turning back from the intercom, saw the blood welling
and crossed the room in two strides. He dropped to a knee and
took her arm, brought it to his mouth, began sucking from the
wound at the inside of her wrist. Selene curled her fist, tightened
and loosened it a few times as if she were pumping blood to the
wound for him. What she was actually doing was bracing the back

of the pin more securely against her palm. When it was firmly in place she suddenly rotated her wrist a hundred and eighty degrees: the pin scratched a shallow furrow down the length of his cheek.

The effect was immediate and profound: he toppled over onto his side without so much as a sigh. She dropped the pin, knelt, felt for a pulse. Shallow, as was the respiration, but at least she hadn't killed him.

Thank you, Granny, thought Selene as she applied pressure against her own wound with her other hand. The bleeding had just stopped when the door burst open.

"You bloody bitch," screamed Mrs. Wah, fumbling to open the blade on the pocketknife she'd brought up for her employer. "If you've 'armed 'im—"

But she never finished the sentence. With one motion Selene had grabbed the larger pin out of her mouth and lunged across the room. Her momentum jammed the pin through the other woman's apron and blouse with such force that it lodged in the soft tissue of her breast. Selene drew her hand back in horror: for an instant that seemed more like a frozen slice of eternity, Mrs. Wah remained standing, her dead brown eyes staring into Selene's own. Then the body crumpled to the floor, the knife still clutched in its hand.

Think. Don't panic, think. Selene remembered stepping over Mrs. Wah's corpse—there was no other way out of the atelier—then fleeing down the carpeted hallway. But of racing down three flights of stairs and grabbing her trench coat off the coat rack she had no memory whatsoever. And yet here she was standing shirtless and breathless in the entrance hall of No. 11 Cranwick Square with her Lady Burberry in one hand and her purse in the other.

She forced herself to take a deep breath. First thing to do was figure out how much time she had before the old man came to. She tried to remember how long she'd been out at Granny Weed's. Two, three hours? Minimum. Which meant she had a little time. But for what?

To clean up after yourself.

The answer chilled her. *Oh no. No way I'm going back up there.* But she had already turned and started up the stairs; she slipped the trench coat on as she climbed, and by the time she reached the door of the atelier she had the inner lining zipped and the outer buttons buttoned. Not much use: the chill was coming from the inside.

The hardest part was stepping over that body again. Once in the room she gritted her teeth and did what she had to do. *Just function, dearie,* she told herself as she knelt beside old Jonas. He was still breathing so slowly and shallowly it was all but undetectable, and his jaw had dropped at what appeared to be an odd angle until she realized it was only his lower plate protruding crookedly—must have jarred loose when he fell.

It took her a few minutes to find the needle. As she searched the carpet she kept glancing at those stupid false teeth jutting out of his mouth. It was like having a picture hanging crooked on a wall: she just had to straighten it. She couldn't bring herself to stick her bare hand into his mouth, so she used his pocket handkerchief. It was after she had finished adjusting the teeth and was replacing the handkerchief that she finally spotted the needle, which had somehow slipped under the fold of his lapel. *Good deed rewarded—for once!*

She knew where the second needle was—embedded in Mrs. Wah. Holding the first one carefully between thumb and forefinger, point out, she knee-walked over to the corpse. Selene tried not to look, but her eyes were drawn irresistibly to the dead woman's face. The sight was shocking enough—the Oriental features were still contorted with rage—but even worse was the creepy sensation that came over her as she grasped the blunt end of the pin protruding from the black bodice and began working it free. It was as if her own breast had gone acutely, morbidly sensitive; Selene could feel the needle sliding out, millimeter by millimeter. She had never experienced telepathy with a corpse before. Not a pleasant form of extrasensory perception; she found herself praying unashamedly to powers in whom she no longer believed for the strength to keep her dinner down while she completed the awful task.

—

The rest didn't take long. Obviously the first thing to do was to get rid of the needles before she pricked herself accidentally. Had to step over Mrs. Wah again—second time was easier. She found a water closet at the end of the hall and flushed them down; on her return to the atelier she stepped over Mrs. Wah without a moment's hesitation. Jonas still hadn't budged. Selene took off her trench coat long enough to put on her blouse; the torn sleeve she stuffed into her purse. Then, after one last look around, as coolly as if she were

checking out of a hotel, she made one final traverse of the dead
housekeeper, and a few moments later Selene was striding purposefully through the dark streets of London with her coat collar turned
up against an implacable November drizzle.

Selene headed toward a faint glow in the sky, and found a cab
on the Belgrave Road. And if the *veddy British* night clerk at her
Park Lane hotel was surprised to find a guest desirous of having her
luggage brought down from her room shortly before midnight, he
gave no indication beyond an infinitesimal lift of one eyebrow.

The bellman, however, was West Indian, and curious as hell.
She told him her daughter had been in an accident back in the
States, then repeated the fib to the doorman who hailed her taxi,
and to the Pakistani who drove her to the airport, and to the first
uniformed airline employee she saw behind a lighted counter at
Heathrow. There were no seats available on the first flight out the
next morning, destination JFK, but the ticket agent, who had a
daughter of her own about the same age as the distraught woman's
in front of her (for in the telling and retelling of the tale, Selene's
phantom daughter had taken on an identity—guess whose?),
promptly bumped Selene to the top of the standby list.

Which should have justified injecting a dash of verisimilitude
into her scenario. All the same Selene felt uncomfortable, as if by
casting Martha as her unfortunate, if imaginary, daughter she'd
somehow put her in harm's way. Oh well, one more thing to obsess
over during the long wait; obviously sitting on a bench in Heathrow
for six or seven hours expecting a tap on the shoulder at any moment from either the police or Jonas Whistler or Aldo, her road-
show devil, wasn't stressful enough.

The cost of her ticket to the States, on top of all her other air
travel, and her shopping binges, meant that for the first time in years
she'd have to draw upon her principal in order to pay her American
Express bill next month, but she figured it would be worth it just
to be out of England.

Tired as she was, she found it impossible to sleep. It wasn't just
the horror she'd been through, or the fear, but rather a sense of
being somehow outside her life. It was as if the life she had come

to take for granted was still going on back in Bolinas, as if some other Selene was waking up in her A-frame, throwing the runes, gardening, planning the next Sabbat.

She reviewed what she knew for certain. One, it was definitely Whistler's Father who had sent Aldo after both her and Jamey. Two, Jonas and Aldo might or might not know that Jamey was still alive, but they certainly knew she was—and where she lived.

So wherever she went next, it couldn't be home—not right away. Whatever reason Whistler's Father had for wanting her dead before, he had double or triple the motive now. But within a few hours she'd be landing at JFK. *Can't go home, can't go back, don't know a soul in New York after all these years.* Then it occurred to her that that wasn't precisely true. She did know someone—or at least someone who'd been in New York exactly one week earlier—on Halloween.

⏤

Once through Customs—she had only her new trench coat to declare—Selene stopped at the first wall of public phones she saw and dialed 411, then slid a few quarters through the slot and punched in the number the information operator had given her.

"A-Mature Productions."

"I'm trying to reach Moll Montana."

"Who's calling, please?"

"Just tell her Selene."

"Oh, hi! Sorry dear, din' recognize your voice. Loved your spread last month. I'll tell her you're on the line."

"Wait—" But a digitized rendition of *Eine Kleine Nacht Muzak* was deedling in Selene's ear.

A few seconds later Moll was on the line. "Is this my plump 'n' pretty centerfold?" The purr was perhaps a pitch or two lower, but there was no mistaking the lioness.

"Neither plump, pretty, nor a centerfold, I'm afraid."

"*That* Selene! Oh my dear Goddess, *that* Selene! It's so wonderful to hear your voice." Then, alarmed: "Martha? Is Martha all right?"

"Martha's fine. She's not mixed up in this—yet."

"Mixed up in what?"

"Long story. I'd rather tell you in person."

—

The address Moll gave Selene over the phone proved to be a three-story brick-faced building in an ill-defined neighborhood that was not quite SoHo, Greenwich Village, or Tribeca. Selene tipped the driver and carried her suitcases up the steps and through the glass entrance door, feeling desperately grungy, wishing she'd been able to catch a quick shower—and about ten hours' sleep.

It was impossible to tell from the lobby whether the building had originally been a warehouse, a lodging house, or a private dwelling. Behind the low, peach-colored reception desk, a matronly Hispanic woman was engaged in conversation with a blue-shirted security guard, also Hispanic. When they were done she turned to Selene. "Can I help you?"

"I'm Selene."

Chuckling, the receptionist—Mrs. Torres, according to the nameplate on the desk—said something in Spanish to the security guard; then, in what for New York was an unwonted show of good manners, she translated her comment for Selene. "I tole him abou my mistake over the phone—how I thaw you were the other Selene." She chuckled as she punched a button on her console. "Funny thin is, your voices soun alike. Hi, Ms. Montana. Selene is here. . . . No, your frien Selene. . . . Okay."

Mrs. Torres smiled up at Selene and, turning to her right, indicated a modern-looking, open-treaded, spiral staircase. "She says go on up."

Selene climbed the stairs warily, hauling her suitcases in both hands, with her purse slung over her shoulder. Moll was waiting for her at the first landing, looking considerably more soignée in her long-waisted, cream-colored linen pantsuit than she had looked on Halloween, stark naked on her hands and knees. If Selene hadn't overflown her old friend a week before, she might have been more shocked at Moll's weight gain. But then it occurred to her that Moll was probably just as stunned to see her. It had been nearly eighteen years: they had each aged an entire generation.

After a hesitation that would have been imperceptible to anyone but the two principals, Selene dropped her bags, stepped forward into Moll's open arms, and they embraced. Solid woman, Moll: hugging her was like hugging a rolled-up mattress drenched in Chanel. Eventually Moll released her; Selene stepped back; they regarded each other at arm's length.

"How I missed you!" Moll announced dramatically, tears swimming in her blue eyes; her hair was a costly dark blond. She stepped backward through a pale orange door with MOLL MONTANA, EDITOR AND PUBLISHER on the brass name plate, ushering Selene into a large office decorated in shades of beige and avocado, with a palette-shaped, glass-topped desk so large it had to have been built inside the room; the desktop was buried under stacks of magazines, manuscripts, contact sheets, proofs, and glossies.

"Now what . . . ? Why . . . ? Oh, who cares! I'm just so glad to see you." Moll's voice was shaking with emotion as she led Selene over to a couch the size of a kneeling water buffalo.

"Who is this other Selene everybody keeps confusing me with?" Selene asked as the sofa enveloped her.

Moll laughed, and fanned out the pile of magazines on her desk; when she found the one she was looking for, she brought it over to the couch. Selene glanced down at the cover—*Fat Femmes*, though not the issue Sherman had been reading. A morbidly obese brunette wearing a pitifully inadequate black lace bra and barely visible black panties that were rendered quite superfluous for purposes of modesty by great dimpled rolls of suet, grinned up at her over the legend: "Selene: 401 Pounds o' Fun."

"I guess that answers my next question," remarked Selene.

"Which was?"

"What exactly you edited and published. By the way, is Selene her real name?"

Moll grinned ruefully, shook her head no. "What can I tell you? It's always been one of my favorite names." She took the magazine back, held it up by the spine, and with a practiced flip of the wrist let the centerfold flop free. The other Selene again, minus bra and panties.

"Oh *my!*"

"She's the dearest woman," said Moll, redoubling the centerfold and closing the magazine in one motion. "Pulls in a nice living with her videos. But if she ever decides she wants to lose weight, she's out of business."

"How many years could she make a living at this anyway?"

By way of reply, Moll went back to her desk and selected a handful of other magazines, brought them back, and spread them out across the Danish steel and glass coffee table. Selene read the covers aloud— *"Foxy Forties? Fabulous Fifties?"*—and opened a few at random. Women—fat, thin, busty, flat, naked, costumed by Frederick's of Hollywood or Victoria's Secret or J. C. Penney or Whips 'N Leather. Some were conventionally attractive, some plain, others downright homely, but each and every one of them was within ten years of Selene's own age—either way.

Selene laughed weakly. "You mean it's not too late for me to be a porn star?"

Moll put her hands in front of her face, thumb tips touching to form the rectangle of an imaginary viewfinder, and did a rough impression of a Hollywood producer. "Take a Lady Remington to those pubes, sweetheart, and I'll make you a star."

Selene joggled the magazines into a neat stack, and handed them back to Moll. "I don't even like to shave my legs."

"In that case . . ." Moll started back to her desk.

"Wait." A raised hand. "I'm absolutely convinced you have a magazine over there that features hairy middle-aged women—I honestly don't feel the need to see it."

Moll shrugged. "Up to you. But you ought to try posing sometime—it can be a kick. Stills, anyway: video's grueling work."

"Really? It appeared to me as if you were enjoying the hell out of it on Halloween, on that round bed with those three other women."

Moll blanched under her salon tan, and sat down heavily; she laughed shakily as the leather sofa made an ungracious farting sound.

"I do try to keep my hand in—so to speak. But the video won't be out until March. How did you . . . ?" Then she brightened. "You flew! Of course—you flew!" She leaned away from Selene and looked her over again. "No offense, honey, but you *look* like you *crawled* here from 'Frisco. You did remember to take an airplane?"

"Yes, but from London. By way of Santa Luz." As briefly as she could, she recapped her adventures since Halloween night. When she'd finished, Moll patted her on the knee, picked up the phone from the coffee table, and speed-dialed a two-digit number with the knuckle of her thumb so as not to chip one of her wicked-looking inch-long mauve fingernails.

"Hello, darling!" Shouting exuberantly into the receiver. "Guess who showed up on my doorstep? No, Selene—Selene Weiss. . . . Yes, she did. . . . Hold on."

"When did you take the Fair Lady, hon?" Moll asked Selene; she repeated the answer into the phone, then squinted nearsightedly at Selene. "She *appears* to have survived. . . . But she's gotten herself. into a hellacious situation. Can I bring her over? . . . That'll be great—she looks like she could use a few hours' sleep anyway."

—

The rather plain young woman who showed Selene up to the third floor was costumed in a white blouse and a short plaid parochial school pinafore, with her hair done up in schoolgirl pigtails. "I had a shoot this morning," she explained, when she noticed Selene looking over her outfit. "Three hours—I went through two of those big swirly round lollipops." She stuck her tongue out for Selene's inspection—it was still cherry red. "And I fucking *hate* lollipops."

Selene shrugged. "I guess it's a living, huh?"

"Actually, I'm a secretary over in ad sales. But Ms. Montana encourages us to moonlight. I used to be a fluffer, but I was getting carpal tunnel."

"What's a fluffer?"

The girl looked as surprised as if Selene had asked her what a secretary was. "For videos," she explained. "In between scenes, sometimes the men need somebody to keep their interest up, if you know what I mean." She mimed a jerk-off motion, and winced. "Like I said, carpal tunnel. Here we are."

She pushed open the door and saw the room she'd flown over on Halloween—looked like a cheap motel room with an enormous glass shower stall in the corner, a round bed, and enough track lighting on the ceiling to cook eggs on the shag carpet. Selene looked around dubiously.

"Don't worry," the retired fluffer assured her. "They change the sheets after every shoot."

⸺

Once she got over the feeling of being watched, Selene had to admit that the shower was sublime—plenty hot and plenty of it, water pressure like a fire hose, adjustable hand-held massager. The bed was quite comfortable too, though the mirror on the ceiling was a bit discomfiting. She awoke sometime later to the sound of Moll opening one of her suitcases.

"I let you sleep an extra hour, so we have to hustle the buns. Let's see what you've got to wear that's clean." Moll started going through Selene's new clothes, laying out a pair of cashmere-and-wool-blend tan slacks, a russet silk blouse, and a cashmere cardigan, beige with rust-colored buttons. "These'll do. I called a cab for us —meet me downstairs in fifteen minutes."

Same old Moll. "Sure you don't want to pick out my under-wear, too?" muttered Selene.

She waited until the door had closed behind Moll before slipping out from under the covers. She wasn't sure why—partly modesty, but with a component of embarrassment, an unwillingness to bare her middle-aged body before a lover who had known it in its youth. But after donning the wispy, silky, apricot-colored bra and matching panties, she couldn't help checking herself out in the full-length mirror against the wall opposite the bed. Funny how just knowing that magazines like those she had seen in Moll's office existed gave her a whole new perspective on her body. She tried out one of the poses she remembered, cocking her hip to the side, resting her hand on it, arching her back. Not bad. Not bad at all.

The slim woman in the mirror smiled back knowingly. Foxy forties, indeed—no wonder Jonas Whistler had . . .

At the thought of the old man, the smile faded.

CHAPTER

10

"Pleuraaaay mes yeux. . . ." Late Sunday night the aria from *Le Cid* issued from Bose speakers the size of doghouses installed in every room of Aldo Striescu's soundproofed flat a few blocks off the King's Road, Chelsea.

Aldo himself was installed in his clawfoot tub listening to his new Callas CD (Hamburg '62) while sipping Stoli out of the bottle in his left hand and O-positive out of the bag in his right. What a glorious weekend it had been. After maxing out the daily cash limit on his employer's credit card Saturday night (how Aldo was going to miss that thing), and visiting the little shop on Neal Street near Covent Garden that specialized in hard-to-find (read: bootleg) opera tapes, CDs, and even vinyl, he had popped into the Cock and Fender and bought a round for the house, then doubled back to visit his connection at the Royal Free Hospital on Gray's Inn Road, then back to the C and F—all of this by cab, crisscrossing London without regard to route or fare, and even tipping the drivers a generous (for him) five percent. Not that the bastards ever thanked him.

He could have picked up any number of hookers of either sex, had he been so inclined, but as always, after an extended spree of arson and asphyxiation, Aldo's sex drive was all but nil. Instead he returned home alone after the pub closed, and popped a tape of *Red River* into the VCR. Aldo was a fervent John Wayne fan—had been ever since the Duke had rescued him from the Orfelinat. (Indirectly, of course: three or four times a year the orphans had gathered in the gymnasium to watch old movies projected onto a bedsheet screen. These were almost always pirated prints of American movies, with inexpensive and inaccurate Romanian subtitles. It was after one of these, *Stagecoach,* that Aldo was overheard by the *matrona* amusing his buddies with a letter-perfect imitation, in English, of the Duke. The *matrona* quickly informed the *sef,* the principal, of their little prodigy. The sef of course immediately informed the Securitate, and it was good-bye Orfelinat, and hello Institut Limba Strain.)

When *Red River* ended, shortly before dawn, Aldo swallowed a handful of sleeping pills and slept soundly straight through that rainy Sunday afternoon, awakening shortly before sunset well rested but famished. As soon as it was dark enough to leave the apartment, Aldo had maxed out the cash limit on the credit card again and treated himself to a steak dinner at the Chelsea Chop House around the corner from his flat before dropping by the Cock and Fender to attend the regular Sunday night poker game in the back room. Normally a cautious—and successful—poker player, he found that the prospect of being rich had thrown his game off: he was tapped out by midnight; Danny Dimitriu had to lend him cab fare home.

No problem, he told himself, kicking back in the tub: in a few more hours, when the banks opened, he'd be a wealthy man. He closed his eyes and let Maria's glorious voice wash over him like a mother's lullabye—and of course the phone began to ring. *Never fails,* he thought. He let his machine answer it, but a few minutes later it rang again, and again a few minutes after that, and eventually curiosity got the better of him. He climbed out of the tub, wrapped a towel around himself, and padded into the bedroom. Before he could reach the answering machine the phone rang again.

The conversation was curt at first. "Yes?"

"It's Jo."

"Do you know what time it is?"

"Yes I do. Do you know your ass from a hole in the ground?"

"I take it that's a rhetorical question?"

"The striga was here."

"What? But that's impossible," replied Aldo, though the sinking feeling in the pit of his stomach told him it was very possible indeed.

"Try telling that to my housekeeper; she's lying on the floor of the atelier, stone dead."

Aldo shut his eyes like a man with a sudden migraine. He didn't like failure. Failure led to fear, and fear was the orphan, etc., etc. "Where's the striga now?"

"How the bloody hell should I know? All *I* know is that a woman you'd assured me was dead showed up at my front door pretending to be someone else, scratched me with a pin—some sort of nerve poison—instant paralysis, followed by unconsciousness— 'straordinary sensation—and I came to twenty minutes ago to find my housekeeper dead on the floor beside me."

"Twenty minutes ago, you say?"

"That's when I came around."

"Just how much of a lead does she have then?"

"Hard to say. We finished dinner around eight or so, Mrs. Wah and I went upstairs. . . ." The voice trailed off.

"Jo?" Aldo prompted him.

"I'm thinking, I'm thinking." A hint of a quaver in the old voice—whether from anger or sorrow, Aldo couldn't say. "I'd estimate she attacked me somewhere around nine o'clock. I don't know how long after that she got to Mrs. Wah. Not long, I should think, otherwise she'd have already left the room."

"Is the body cold? Stiff?"

"I don't know. D'you want me to go up and feel her?" No mistaking the barely contained fury.

You can screw her for all I care, thought Aldo. "Never mind. Just wait there, I'll be right— Hang on, what's the address?" He had just realized he had no idea where the old man lived—up to now they'd transacted all their business at the Cock (though with Jo fully dressed for their subsequent meetings).

"Eleven Cranwick Place."

"Wait there, I'll be right over."

—

The front door opened before Aldo had a chance to ring the buzzer; Jonas was in his face before the door had closed behind him. "If you think I'm going to transfer that money for you now, you bloody fool, then you've got—*arp!*"

For Aldo had reached up, grabbed the club tie, and tightened it until the old man barked like a seal. "I don't like to be sworn at," he informed the rapidly bluing Jonas. "Whatever's gone wrong, we'll handle it. These strigas can be tricky—I warned you about that."

Jonas staggered backward, grabbed the heavy mahogany coat rack to steady himself. "How dare you put your hands on me!" he managed, in a choked voice. His face was still dark, except for a livid scratch the length of his cheek.

Aldo looked up at him steadily. "Just how long have you been drinking blood, anyway?"

The old man swayed, and the coat rack with him. His mouth opened and closed, but no sound came out.

"Not long, eh? And this 'housekeeper' of yours, this Mrs. . . ." He prompted with a beckoning gesture.

"Wah. Mrs. Wah," whispered Jonas, in shock.

"She was probably your only source, am I correct?" He waited for a nod. "I thought so. Now listen to me. You've got yourself three serious problems: a body in your atelier that will begin to stink soon, a craving for blood that will have you climbing the walls even sooner, and a woman who already knows enough to send you to prison for the rest of your natural life."

Aldo caught his breath—his *s*'s had grown quite sibilant. "Is that enough reason to be civil with me?" He waited for another nod. "Good. Because if you want my help, you're going to have to mind your manners, and you're going to have to level with me. I want to know everything there is to know about you and your son—the truth, the whole truth, and nothing but. I'll sort out what's important. Last but not least, you're going to have to pay me what I ask without complaining. I'll need some help cleaning this mess up, and it won't come cheap. Now, have I made myself clear?" Another nod. "Good. Where's your phone?"

By the time Danny Dimitriu arrived, Aldo had calmed Jonas considerably with a sip or two from the flask he'd brought with him. He listened to the old man's life story in the bedroom while overhead Danny performed the preliminary work involved in his only magic trick—making dead bodies disappear—and whether it was the new blood that rendered the old man so talkative, or the near-death experience, Aldo soon found himself wishing he hadn't been quite so insistent on the *whole* truth. He interrupted Jonas in the middle of a diatribe against the philistine art establishment in London in the late fifties. "Just skip to the blood, Jo. I'd like to get home before daybreak."

As for the next part of the story—married man isn't getting any at home, picks up a woman in a bar, finds out she's strigoi, finds out he's strigoi, comes home and screws his sick old lady to death: *Ho-hum and lah-de-dah,* thought Aldo. *Welcome to the world on blood.*

Aldo interrupted Jonas once more to help Danny carry his rubber-lined sack out the back door and around to the Freddie Forth's Fresh Fish van that Danny used for his work. Nobody ever noticed the smell of a body in a fish truck. When he returned Jonas had poured out two glasses of elderly single malt. Aldo settled himself back down on the tufted horsehide cushion of the balloon-back side chair and took a respectful sip while the old man went on with his story. He had to admit that compared to this stuff, the best Scotch at the Cock and Fender was swill indeed.

"Our son, Jamey, was in his first year at Oxford when his mother died. I don't know how he took her death—I'd gone into such a deep state of depression and guilt that I was sent to a 'rest home' in Sussex, for my own protection. The psychiatrists, of course, were of no help whatsoever. All I could tell them was that I was responsible for her death—true enough—but of course I couldn't tell them about the blood drinking, so their reassurances —that my feelings of guilt were only natural—never touched the root of the problem.

"Unbeknownst to the doctors, however, the drugs they gave

me did help ease the blood withdrawal, and along with my Bible saw me through the sheer shock of the entire experience of the previous month, which you have to remember included both my own fall from grace *and* Alice's death—nor could I have told you at the time where the one began and the other left off.

"In the end, though, it was an altogether different sort of medicine that carried me through. It was either my second or third week in hospital; I was drifting off to sleep in the arms of Sister Seconal when there came to me what I can only describe as a vision, a bright blur of light that in outline was both feminine and angelic— not like any illustration I've ever seen. But I saw her; she was as real to me as you are, and I saw her with these same eyes.

"She spoke not a word, but when she left (I can't say how she left, whether she disappeared, or turned back somersaults through the wall—I never saw her—I was weeping into my hands at the time) it was as clear to me what I had to do to atone with God as if she'd given me written instructions. And the penalty for failing to atone was clear to me as well. She hadn't told me about hell, nor described it, nor shown me a vision, but I knew it was waiting for me, and that it was hell.

"As for how to stay out of it, there was nothing very complicated. I was to read my Bible, and disdain the pleasures of the flesh. No more blood, no more sex. I didn't even think about disobeying. I couldn't begin to, because as soon as I did the spiritual agony would come lapping at my feet, and if I didn't abandon the thought—even thoughts that included sex in the confines of an honorable remarriage—the agony would threaten to wash over me entirely.

"Within six months I was out of the hospital and back to work. My life was free of joy as well as despair—the only way I could get through it was to stay numb. Every morning, although I knew I was far from mad, I faithfully swallowed whatever combination of mind-numbing, soul-destroying antidepressants and antipsychotics and mood elevators and tranquilizers the quacks and pharmaceutical companies were pushing that year, then showered and shaved and showed up at the office. I guided the affairs of the Whistler trust so efficiently that it has more than doubled during my stewardship—to Jamey's eventual benefit more than mine.

"As for Jamey, I saw him during term holidays, and we would dine once or twice a month. We weren't particularly intimate, for father and son, but then we never had been, so it came as a complete surprise to me a year or so later when he was arrested for having duped my Bahamian housekeeper into giving him her blood under the guise of treating her for migraine headaches. He freely admitted to having drunk it.

"My solicitors were able to have the complaint withdrawn, on the grounds that Jamey leave the UK. Those terms he agreed to readily enough, but *my* terms—that he abstain from drinking blood—he rejected with an oath. I asked him to leave; he stole my watch on his way out.

"I didn't see him again until last summer. I was in a coma—dying, according to all the quacks. Jamey fed me blood without my consent, just to see if it would do me any good—naturally I'd never told him about my experience with blood. And naturally I recovered. At first he said nothing about still being a drinker—or what he'd done to me. We spent a lovely night talking. He told me all about his life—that's how I knew about the striga—and his new wife and child. The last thing he told me, shortly before dawn, was that he was still a blood drinker, had never stopped being one, and that I was now a drinker again as well. When I'd recovered from the shock I sent him away again with my curses.

"And I remembered my angel. I tried not to drink again, and failed, largely due to Mrs. Wah's intervention. She brought me her own blood disguised in tomato juice, and after I'd drunk it she climbed into bed with me, and to my shame I was too weak to resist. Every morning for the first month after Jamey revived me I would vow not to drink that night. Surely, I would think, God would not hold this involuntary addiction against me. But every night, just as the need came over me, Mrs. Wah would be there with her blood pulsing in her veins, and I'd be helpless as a drunk in a vat. It was not until I was quite addicted both to her blood and the sex that she told me that her murdered husband had been a blood drinker too. I suppose my addiction must have seemed like some sort of godsend to her, if you'll forgive me the expression.

"In any event, after a month or so there was no point kidding myself any longer—I had voided my contract with my angel. If I'd had the courage I'd have ended my life then, but I swore that before I died I'd see *him* dead, the man who'd already interrupted my death, denied me peace in life, and damned me to eternal hell in the process—my son. I began making inquiries—didn't have any notion as to how one goes about having a vampire killed. Couldn't be easy, I knew that from my own example. It was Mrs. Wah who suggested I begin my inquiries among the Romanians."

This was all somewhat baffling to Aldo—that anyone would rue being a blood drinker. But he didn't give it much energy; he was quite used to learning that other people didn't share his own enthusiasms. After all, even nondrinkers rarely appreciated a good blaze, not to mention a satisfactory garroting. He listened with greater attention when Jonas described his encounter with Selene, concluding with his discovery of Mrs. Wah's body.

"Did Mrs. Wah have any family left?" was Aldo's first question. "Close friends? Anyone who might send the police nosing around?"

"A sister in Brighton, I believe, but they weren't particularly close. No friends to my knowledge—the poor dear had quite dedicated herself to my service."

"We've got some time then. Do you have any samples of her handwriting?"

"I'll look around her room."

"Do that before I leave. I'll have a friend of mine run up some docs in her handwriting—letter of resignation dated a few days ago, having-a-wonderful-time cards we can have posted from ever more northerly locales. Now, as to your next most immediate problem. Do you have any blood stored away? Or anyone else you can procure from?"

The old man shook his head. "No. I'm afraid I hadn't thought that far."

"I'll make a call for you then. Young woman I've used myself. I'll have her ring you up tomorrow evening. Pay her what she asks for the blood, and if the two of you hit it off, she'll be more than willing to take on some of Mrs. Wah's other, er, *duties* as well—for a price, of course."

"Of course," replied Jonas. "And as for yourself?"

"Why, I'll be going striga hunting."

Jonas smiled coldly. "Bring me back her broomstick."

—

Aldo spent what remained of the night arranging for his new passport. Mr. Yardley had attracted too much attention already, and if his comings and goings grew too frequent or too closely spaced, he might draw more. Besides, Aldo was still shaken from his recent brush with Customs, brief though it had been.

No, this time he wanted a virgin—a well-aged, well-stamped passport, but one that had never actually been used. That meant a trip all the way across town to Islington, where Manny the Mocker, once the finest forger in all of Romania, now lived in suburban exile behind the walls of a modest cottage intended to deflect the notice of the Inland Revenue. It occurred to Aldo in the cab, however, that he was still looking a little too much like Mr. Yardley. On the other hand he didn't want to look too much like himself either, so he had the cabbie stop off at an all-night chemists on Guilford Street, where he used his credit card (which, it occurred to him gleefully, it looked as if he'd be keeping now) to purchase shaving supplies and barber's scissors along with a bottle of walnut brown hair dye and a coordinated tube of mustache dye.

Aldo trimmed his hair and eyebrows in the back of the cab. By the time he got to Manny's there was scarcely time to shave off his goatee, apply the dyes to hair, eyebrows, and mustache, and have the forger snap his photo, much less wait around for the passport. They made arrangements to have it messengered over, along with the forged documents in Mrs. Wah's handwriting, as soon as Manny had finished.

Aldo made it home with only a few minutes to spare before sunrise. After admiring his new look in the bathroom mirror—striking, if not downright handsome—he washed down a handful of sleeping pills with a shot of Stoli, and as he dozed off to sleep fantasizing about Selene struggling beneath him with a pillow pressed tightly against her face, a precious, sleepy, half-smile lifted the newly walnut brown mustache and a drugged snore set it fluttering.

11

The windows of the shop on the side street in Greenwich Village were whited out behind rusty grilles secured by a permanent-looking padlock, but Selene could still make out the outline of the old gold-leaf lettering. COVENSTEAD BOOKSHOP. CURIOS AND PARAPHERNALIA. Her lips formed the words as Moll fit a key into a warped, peeling door; a little drift of paint chips had settled like black snowflakes under the lip of the doorsill.

The storefront was dark, the light fixtures stripped from the ceiling, paler patches on the wooden floor and walls where the counter and shelves had rested. Where once a beaded curtain had clacked gently, a hulking metal fire door with a breaker bar now blocked the entrance to the back rooms. Moll had a key for this as well; for all its bulk the heavy door swung open easily, and Selene followed Moll through, returning to the first covenstead she had ever known.

The inner room was only a little less dark than the storefront. On a nightstand beside a four-poster bed in the corner of the room where the Gypsy fortune-teller's tent had once stood, a small pink-shaded lamp spilled a pool of warm rose light across the faded Persian carpet, silhouetting a nightgowned form sitting up behind gauzy age-yellowed bed curtains.

A clawed hand drew back the curtains a crack; crooked fingers beckoned stiffly. "Come closer," demanded a querulous old voice. Selene stepped into the light. "It certainly *looks* like you," allowed the voice grudgingly.

"Hello, Benny."

But there was still no welcome in the quavering reply. "Never mind my name. Say your own, first."

"Selene."

"And before Selene?"

"Helen."

"No!"

"Helene, then." Mystified, Selene corrected herself. "But only for a day."

"That's better. Can you kiss me?"

"Of course."

"Do so."

Selene parted the curtains a little farther. It was indeed old Bensozia, her white nightgown and her wispy white hair as yellowed as the bed curtains. She was propped up against a small mountain of pillows and bolsters, under a patchwork quilt she and Andred had sewn together during the Depression. Selene bent to press her lips against the powdery old cheek.

"No, on the mouth."

Selene brushed the cracked dry lips with her own; impatiently, the other woman grabbed Selene's face in both hands, her grip surprisingly strong though her fingers were crabbed like twigs, pulled her closer, and kissed her hard upon the lips. Selene inhaled a scent of old face powder and Johnson's baby shampoo as she returned the kiss, closing her eyes and parting her lips slightly, softening them against the crone's insistent pressure.

Finally Benny let her go. "Selene Weiss," she said softly. "Blessed be."

"What was that all about?"

"I had to be sure it was you."

"As opposed to?"

"Any number of things. A shade, a wraith, a daimon, a fetch."

"You can tell from a kiss?"

"Ghosts cannot kiss; wraiths will not."

"Even succubi?"

"Not on the mouth," Benny replied. "But they can lick the black off licorice." With what sounded suspiciously like a cackle, the old woman reached for an unlabeled medicine bottle of antique brown glass on one of the spindle-legged nightstands. Her stiff fingers pried at the cork futilely. Moll stepped forward and took it from her, poured a scant finger of slimy dark green liquid into a gold-rimmed shotglass.

"Tom Tyffin's Tonic," Benny explained, draining the glass and falling back against the pillows again, the color beginning to rise slightly in her ancient cheeks. "For my arthritis." She smacked her green-flecked lips.

Selene nodded. " 'Rosemary, Rue, and Life Everlasting / Mashed and pulped, and ta'en after fasting . . .' " She quoted from the formula in the *Herbalis*.

Benny nodded approvingly. "That's the exoteric recipe. But I'm glad to see you kept up with your studies."

"I had some very inspiring teachers," smiled Selene, as Moll walked around the bed, drawing back the heavy curtains. Then she thought of something, and the smile faded. "I'm so sorry about Andred."

Tears filled the dim old eyes. "I'm very angry with her." On the other side of the bed Moll had taken up a hairbrush from the opposite nightstand and begun working on Benny's sparse, flyaway white hair. "She passed over a year ago, and I still haven't heard a word from her." The old woman turned quaveringly on Moll. "Stop *fussing*, won't you?"

"Sorry." Meekly, Moll put down the brush.

"You're always *fussing*." Benny took a few deep breaths; her bony chest rose and fell under the yellowed bodice of the old-fashioned nightgown. "Here, you two." She gestured toward the medicine bottle with a clawed hand. "Pour yourselves a finger of friend Tom there—you both look as if you could use a belt. I assure you it tastes every bit as nasty as it looks."

Selene went first. "Nasty is not the word," she croaked when she had regained feeling in her tongue. She handed the bottle to Moll, who had removed her wrinkled linen jacket and climbed onto the bed. Moll held her nose and took a slug from the mouth of the antique bottle. By the time Selene had removed her own jacket and climbed up onto the bed beside Benny she was feeling mellow and buttery, yet strangely energized. It occurred to her that friend Tom was packing quite a wallop for rosemary, rue, and life-everlasting. "Okay, what else is in that stuff, anyhow?"

Moll answered as soon as she'd finished gagging. "The esoteric recipe includes paregoric and a syrup of coca leaf extract."

Selene smacked her lips tentatively. "Oh yes." Definite licorice aftertaste. "Oh my, yes."

Benny had fallen back against her mountain of pillows and bolsters. She took the bottle back, took another healthy draft, then clapped her hands softly three times. With each clap she seemed to regain a little more vigor, and drop a few more years. "Ladies, a trine."

Selene and Moll arranged themselves cross-legged at Benny's feet so that the three witches formed an isosceles triangle. Benny closed her eyes again and reached out her hands. "Where gather three, there Goddess be," the eldest witch intoned solemnly. Then she opened her eyes and grabbed Selene's thigh just above the knee, gave it a hard squeeze. "So good to see you, dearie."

Dearie, thought Selene dreamily. *So that's where Moll and I got that from.* Then something occurred to her: "Is this all that's left of the coven? What happened to everybody?"

Benny sighed. "Don't get me started."

"It's the goddamn New Age," Moll explained. "Everybody wants to worship the Goddess and cast spells, but nobody wants to memorize the ninety-nine names, or actually milk the toad. 'And why should I hand-write my own Book of Shadows when I can buy one in Waldenbooks?' she added in a mocking falsetto. " 'What? Orgies? I could catch AIDS.' And now there's always another coven around the corner where the Goddess is soft and fuzzy and, and *nurturing*, and they meet once a week for a healing circle and make it home in time to watch the eleven o'clock—"

Benny squeezed Moll's more substantial thigh with her other hand. "Patience, dearie. It's only a cycle." She turned to Selene. "Now, tell me what brings you to visit an old woman in her solitude?"

Selene started to recount her shrinking faith, her inability to believe in the existence of the Goddess, her search for meaning, for her path. . . .

"Whoa there, Nellie." Benny touched Selene's lips lightly with a forefinger as dry and crooked as a twig. "A path is a journey—you set out on yours thirty years ago, long before you plucked your first devil's cherry. As for the Goddess, I wouldn't worry about Her—She's certainly not going to worry about you." The old woman cackled, reached out a crooked hand, and tousled Selene's hair—which was far from in need of tousling. Then, abruptly: "What sort of danger are you in?"

Selene thought about it. "Mortal."

"Is there another witch involved?"

"Not so far as I know."

"And how much time do we have?"

"There *is* a little hurry-up involved. My old friend Jame—"

"Hush—I don't want to be muddled with details. Have you heard of the practice of orgomancy?"

Selene could feel the color draining from her face. "Heard of it? I was there when Morgana died."

But to Selene's surprise, Benny only laughed. "Is it true the undertaker couldn't get the smile off her face with a trowel?"

Selene forced back a smile. "Benny, I won't let you take that chance."

Another cackle. "First of all, dearie, I've been practicing orgomancy for over twenty years—if I'd an aneurism it would have burst before now. Secondly, once you've asked a crone for help—"

Selene interrupted. "I never called you a crone."

A third cackle. "Don't look so alarmed, dearie. A crone is not a bad thing to be; you'll find out soon enough. Now where was I? Oh yes—once you've asked a crone for aid, the manner of the help is not a matter of your choosing. You must accept what's offered.

And thirdly, if the Fates have decreed that it's my time, I can't think of a better way to go."

"But—"

"But me no buts, Goody Weiss." Bensozia started to pour herself another shot of tonic, but only a drop of sludge oozed into the shot glass. "Here, make yourself useful," she said, handing the bottle to Selene. "There's a jug in the icebox in the back room. Fill 'er up with ethyl, as we old dykes used to say."

Selene could hear Benny and Moll conversing in low tones as she made her way to the back room. How strange it seemed after all those years, and yet how familiar. The glass-fronted pharmacist's hutch still stood against the opposite wall, but its shelves and drawers and pigeonholes were mostly empty now. From an old round-shouldered Amana refrigerator standing in the corner that the dildo cabinet had once graced, Selene removed a gallon-sized plastic milk carton full of tonic. With some difficulty, she managed to decant about a cup of the stringy sludge into the narrow-mouthed medicine bottle, occasionally clearing clots the color of oobleck from the neck of the bottle with the tip of her little finger. When she had finished her pinky was stained a deep unhealthy shade of chartreuse that looked fearfully permanent.

When she returned, Benny was lying naked in the center of the bed, her feet together and her arms at her sides. As sometimes happens with slim older women, the process of aging had turned some sort of corner: on her back, Benny looked almost girlish in the dim light, her breasts and belly flattened by gravity and her pubic hair sparse and pale.

Not so Moll, who was undressing at the foot of the bed; when she reached behind her to unsnap her industrial-strength brassiere her breasts rolled free like melons, coming to rest against a triple-spare-tired swell of belly. A woman of substance; Selene couldn't help thinking about what it would be like to nuzzle up to all that flesh, to bury one's face in that smothery softness.

But this was not a Sabbat orgy, and it was not Moll's body that required attention. Selene handed Benny the refilled medicine bottle and undressed quickly; she and Moll joined Benny on the bed, kneeling on either side of her, and after another round of Tom Tyffin, the two middle-aged witches exchanged a kiss over the body of the last high priestess of the Village Coven, then stretched out beside her and went to work.

Selene wasn't sure how to proceed at first. Morgana had always used nine witches to achieve the altered state that prolonged orgasm could invoke in the adept. She would lie on her silken pallet in the middle of the Circle Room floor with a witch at each hand, foot, and breast, one leaning upside down over her face, one at the crotch, and one free to roam, and every so often they'd rotate, as in volleyball.

But now it was only herself and Moll. Their eyes met. *Mirror me,* said the once-familiar voice-that-was-not-a-voice inside Selene's head, and with lips, tongues, and fingers the two women began pleasuring Benny's body, starting at the ears, meeting briefly at the mouth, smiling at each other across the papery-soft folds of the ancient neck, kissing the trembling clawed hands, working their way down the torso to the toes, then all the way back up to the ears. When the old woman began to moan rhythmically Moll buried her face between Benny's thighs while Selene positioned her ear near Benny's mouth.

The crone's orgasms began building not long after that—the abdominal muscles tightened under the slack belly skin, the thighs began to tremble, the toes curled; even the clawed old hands had unclenched, and were opening and closing as rhythmically and peacefully as undersea flowers in a tide pool. Eventually the soft explosions of breath in Selene's ear turned to utterance, mere vocables at first, musical but meaningless, but as the orgasms rolled on and the slender body began to buck, the syllables turned to iambic glossolalia, the rhythm of her speech conforming to the rolling two-beat rhythm of her orgasm, of her heart—da-*dum,* da-*dum,* da-*dum,* da-*dum,* but in no known tongue. Selene leaned even closer, felt the warm breath against her ear as the gibberish resolved itself into words—Se-*lene,* the *God*-dess *of* the *Moon*—and the words into verse.

Selene had always suspected Morgana of faking this part; how could it be that each of her foretellings just happened to come out in the same meter, iambic, and of the same length, quatrain: the classic witch's quartet described in Enfernelli's Bible as the hallmark of true orgomancy? But Morgana's orgasm had always seemed real enough.

So did Benny's. And sure enough, her prophecy ran four lines, then stopped abruptly—her teeth snapped shut—Selene barely escaped with her ear intact. She turned her head to see the crone's mouth pulled back in rictus, her back arched painfully, shoulders, head, and heels pressing hard against the bed, pelvis rising in spasm toward the ceiling. Alarmed, Selene grabbed Moll by the hair. Moll's eyes were open, but rolled back, only the whites visible; her tongue continued to thrust rhythmically, involuntarily as Selene tugged her head away from between Benny's thighs.

Gradually the old witch's spasms subsided; Benny lay on her back, breathing hard, her hands contracting into arthritic claws again. One hand seemed to be beckoning, and she seemed to be trying to speak. Selene leaned closer again. "Tom?" said a weakened, barely recognizable voice.

"No, it's Selene."

"She *knows* who *you* are," said Moll from the foot of the bed, climbing dazedly to her hands and knees. "What she wants is her goddamned tonic." She swayed there for a moment, jiggling like a seismic event. "And when you're done, dearie, I could use a shot myself—my heart's still somewhere down around my womb."

A few minutes later Benny was back in her nightgown and Moll in her slip; Selene had put her russet blouse on and buttoned a few buttons at random. The way her hands were shaking, that was all she could manage.

"Well, how'd I do?" Benny asked Selene.

"Don't you remember?"

"Never do."

"You about scared me to death, for starters."

"But the oracle? In four?"

"Witch's Quartet. Letter perfect. Right out of Enfernelli."

Benny turned to Moll. "I guess the old gal's still got it, eh, dearie?" Then, to Selene: "Let's hear it."

She closed her eyes to recite: "Selene the Goddess of the Moon / With two men more must lie / The first of these she must betray / The second man must die."

When she opened her eyes again the other two women were looking at her strangely. "You just made that up, right, Benny? Tell me you made that up."

"I don't know anything more about what it means than you do," replied Benny, reaching her hand up to Selene's face, stroking her cheek gently. "But if I were you, dearie, I'd be awfully careful who I slept with."

PART 3

Your Book
of Shadows

*Even as a novice witch, you will recognize the importance of shield-
ing your Book of Shadows from prying eyes. As for letting it fall
into the hands of a foe, you would do better to go directly to the
devil and save yourself the intervening strife.*

—E. BEATRICE ENFERNELLI

CHAPTER

1

Manny the Mocker had done his usual bang-up job: on Tuesday, November 9th, Mr. Leonard Patch of Croyden, complete with passport, driver's license, and credit cards, slipped out of the UK and into the U.S. as a tourist without attracting more than cursory attention from officialdom, then flew straight on to San Francisco without seeing daylight, thanks to the long night and the westward flight. As the plane passed over the great Midwest he popped a CD of La Divina singing "Dov' è l'indiana bruna?" into his Discman, chuckling delightedly at his own pun.

A car had been reserved for Mr. Patch at the Enterprise counter at SFO—only a Corolla, but with quite a good sound system, as he had requested. Aldo reached Corte Madera shortly before dawn on Wednesday, and checked into the Travelodge by the side of the highway. His room was plain but quite comfortable; nevertheless he slept fitfully, awoke disoriented, snatched off his state-of-the-art sleeping mask (with thin rubber baffles to shut out even the thinnest sliver of peripheral light) and discovered, to his immediate discomfort, that the Travelodge drapes did not block out the daylight entirely. Quickly he grabbed his watch off the night table and ducked under the covers to check the time—it was only three in the afternoon.

Aldo's sheets were soaked with sweat. The nightmare that had awakened him, a recurring dream of the Orfelinat, had been un-usually vivid. He was around ten years old, he had done something bad again, and the *matrona*, who hadn't been able to make him cry since he was five, had tied him to his bed and gone off to fetch the sef. Fortunately, he'd awakened before they got back.

Two hours to kill before sunset. Aldo made good use of the time listening to the radio talk shows, noting local usage and ref-erences, mimicking the various local accents and dialects, and left Corte Madera for Bolinas shortly after six, stopping only once to refill his thermos—another hitchhiker—this one he picked up by the side of Highway 1 and discarded over a cliff.

Aldo spotted the broken signpost that marked the road to Bo-linas on the first pass this trip, and when he reached the drive that led up to the A-frame he didn't make the mistake of turning onto it again. Instead he drove on another few hundred yards and pulled off by the side of the road under a stand of eucalyptus, stowed his thermos in his kit bag, then set out on foot for Selene's A-frame, climbing the hill at a bias, using his night vision and other blood-honed senses to find his way through the dark woods. He circled around in order to approach the house from above, and was just about to leave the cover of the trees when he first heard the noise from below—girlish laughter, the hum of a motor, and a roiling, burbling sound that took him a moment to identify, until he re-membered the hot tub on the deck.

Grinning, Aldo picked his way through the woods, paralleling the path, and stopped behind the last redwood tree before the clearing.

"So how long before Selene comes back?" asked a girl's voice —she sounded as if she was wearing teeth braces.

"Who knows?" replied another girl. "Last time I heard from my dear godmother she was on some godforsaken island in the Caribbean, looking for her old boyfriend."

"Lucky witch," said a third voice.

Aldo doubled back up the hill a few yards and found a tree that would provide him with both cover and a view of the deck; as he climbed it the girls chattered on, and he was able to match a name to the goddaughter's voice: she was Martha. A few minutes later he was perched high in a fork of a redwood tree, looking down on the softly lit hot tub. It was a situation that would have been a bonanza for most perverts, but coming as it did during the low point of Aldo's cycle, he wasn't noticeably aroused.

But he did record every detail of the scene as grist for his fantasy mill: the steam hovering above the black water, the young girls sleek and shiny like some new breed of pale aquatic mammal, their nipples pink and plump on their glistening breasts. California girls. How did that song go? Wish they all could be?

Aldo watched, as still as the great trunk he clung to, until he had matched the name and voice with a face and body—Martha was the slender, boyish, dreadlocked blonde in the middle. When the girls began climbing out of the tub Aldo shinnied around to the far side of the tree and descended to the lowest branch, waited until the girls had begun giggling loudly at something, then dropped the last six feet, landing lightly on his feet. He waited behind the tree listening to his little birds chirping merrily while they dressed. When the sound of their footsteps had retreated around the front of the house he hurried after them and tailed them from a distance.

Not the toughest shadowing he'd ever done. The three girls yakked their way down the winding dirt driveway until they reached the A-frame down the hill, where the other girls piled into a Volvo station wagon and drove off, while Martha went inside. Aldo grinned when he realized he'd tailed the girl back to her own house, and although he'd been trying to think in English—or rather, Californian—the phrase that popped into his mind sounded so much better in pure Romanian that he couldn't resist saying it aloud. *"Drac noroc,"* he whispered. The luck of the devil.

—

Twenty minutes later the grin had faded, and there was no more talk of devil's luck. Aldo stood at the kitchen counter of Selene's house up the hill, his finger still frozen on the play button of Selene's ancient telephone answering machine. There had been several messages, most of them casual—"Where are you, just called to chat, gimme a call when you get back." But the last message had been far from casual:

"Selene, are you there? It's Jamey. If you're there, pick up. I haven't much time. It's Tuesday, the . . . what, the second? I'll try to call again."

A better than amateur, but to Aldo's trained ear somewhat grating Oxbridge accent. *Tuesday the second?* he thought, reaching shakily for the thermos in his kit bag. Tuesday the goddamn-it-to-hell second was four days *after* he'd burned the Greathouse.

As always, Aldo forced himself to banish his fear, send it right back to the orphanage where it belonged. *So he's alive? So what? No change in plans—find the striga—the rest will fall into place.* He fitted a collar onto his flashlight to keep the beam narrow, and began searching, starting with the base of the ladder where he'd squeezed out the jellied gasoline. The char marks were deep scored and well defined—whatever had gone wrong, it wasn't the fault of Dow Chemical.

The bottom five ladder rungs had all collapsed. Aldo studied the stub edges under the beam and saw they had broken off downward and inward, noticed the pale splintered wood beneath the layer of char. Somehow she had extinguished the flames before climbing down. But how? Then he remembered the way the bed had rocked beneath her limp form as he pressed the pillow to her face, and shook his head, disgusted at his own carelessness.

Ignoring the painter's ladder leaning beside the burnt one, Aldo grabbed the charred edge of the platform with both hands and chinned himself up easily. Unlike the ground floor, the loft hadn't been cleaned up after the fire—sure enough, he saw that the plastic mattress of the waterbed had been dragged off the frame. He crawled over to it with his flashlight. The thick plastic was slimy with mildew, and he could see the puncture holes, the long rips; the scissors she must have used still lay beside the bed.

Clever old thing—had she been in a trance, or only lying doggo? Playing possum, they said here. No matter—he wouldn't underestimate her a second time, not with Whistler on the loose too. For a start, he determined to go over the A-frame with a fine-tooth comb. *Informatiune este putere,* as they used to say in the Third Branch. Information is power.

But it wasn't until much later, after he'd gone through the house once top to bottom, glancing at books, patting through clothes, checking into drawers and cabinets and finding little of value to him, then systematically backtracked, bottom to top, going over every item he'd gone over the first time, but on this second pass giving it the full Third Branch treatment, looking *under* the drawers, tapping the doors and walls and cabinets for hollow hidey-holes and false bottoms, slitting the seams and linings of clothes, and carefully opening and shaking out every one of her books, that he discovered the letter hidden under the snakeskin inner lining of the silk-covered loose-leaf notebook in the damask-draped wicker altar not far from the bed where he'd begun his search hours before.

This must be my lucky day, thought Aldo as he read through the letter, which was handwritten in faded lilac ink, and began to appreciate just how much information he had attained. And how much power as well. Then he glanced at his watch and saw that it was nearly 3:00 A.M. But it was the date and not the time that caught his attention. November 11th. Armistice Day. Better known as Piss-Pants Day in the Orfelinat.

Aldo winced at the memory. In the sixties, as part of the drive toward "National Communism" as opposed to the preceding, but now entirely discredited "Proletarian Internationalism," only Romanian history was allowed to be taught in the schools—or at least in the orphanage schools. And only positive aspects of Romanian history at that, which drastically limited the curriculum.

So every Armistice Day the orphans were forced to sit in the auditorium and listen to hour upon hour of boring speeches celebrating the heroic defenders of Moldavia, without whom the war would surely have been lost, etc., etc., during which time the children were not permitted to go to the toilet. Hence, Piss-Pants Day.

After all, it's not as if the fucking day doesn't owe me, thought Aldo, folding the letter carefully, and slipping it back under the inner cover of the loose-leaf. Then he slid the book into his kit bag, blew a kiss to the heavens, and climbed back down the ladder as far as the rungs would allow before leaping lightly to the charred floor.

And his heart was as light as his leap, for he could see it all clearly now. The letter would fetch him the girl, the girl would fetch him the striga, and the striga would fetch him the strigoi.

"Drac noroc," whispered Aldo again, delightedly.

CHAPTER

2

"Oh my stars and garters, that feels good," moaned Selene.

Wednesday evening. She and Moll were on either end of the white sectional sofa in the living room of Moll's apartment on the Upper East Side, watching the sun set over New Jersey through a picture window the size of a multiplex movie screen. Selene's bare feet were in Moll's lap; Moll was massaging them with the balls of her thumbs only, so as not to bring her wicked mauve nails into play.

The next time Selene spoke both the park below and the sky above were dark, while the rest of the city was lit up like—well, like the New York skyline. "You know I'm going to have to leave soon," she said softly.

"Why?"

"You know why: because I have to find Jamey before they do. I'm worried about Martha, too."

Moll slid over to the middle of the couch and slipped her arm around Selene. "Martha's not involved in this. You said it yourself, nobody besides the two of us even knows Jamey's her father. Besides, you've been calling her twice a day. You're the one who might be walking right into a trap."

"So what do I do? Disappear? Just walk out of everybody's life the way you did?" It was the first time since they'd reconnected that Selene had brought up the topic that had never really been out of her mind.

Moll pulled her arm away. "I had reasons."

"So you wrote me—a month after disappearing without a word to anyone. From Winnemucca, as I recall."

"Yes, from Winnemucca. And if I'd taken Martha with me, she'd have grown up in a whorehouse." Then, when Selene said nothing, "Didn't know that, did you?"

"I suspected. I didn't judge you, though."

"You didn't have to. I judged myself plenty. I sure judged myself unfit to raise a child."

"So you let us raise her for you. Fine. But let me ask you this: just exactly who was it who forced you into that life in the first place? It couldn't have been money; all you'd have had to do was let Jamey know he was Martha's father. The child support alone would have . . ."

"It was the Test."

". . . been enough— What?"

"The Test. The Test of the Fair Lady."

"I think I'll stop talking now," said Selene.

"You always were a smart one," Moll replied.

It was quiet inside the apartment for a few minutes; through the thick glass of the picture window New York sparkled like a diorama in a World's Fair—a vast silent clockwork city. "At thirty-six I'd about reached the point you did at fifty," Moll said eventually.

"Forty-eight."

"Sorry, forty-eight. First the coven started falling apart, then I lost every cent I had when the club went belly-up. I came out to the Coast, you took me in—"

"You'd have done the same for me—hell, you *did* do the same for me, back in sixty-three."

"Whatever. But in a way that made it harder. I'd attend the Sabbats, and it was all I could do to keep from laughing—or crying. Meaningless ritual—dumb show—I'd be lying there at an orgy, bodies all around me, dead from the neck down, with that stupid Patti Page song running through my head—"

" 'How Much Is That Doggy in the Window?' "

"No. The one about is that all there is?"

"That was Peggy Lee."

"Well excuse me. You're forty-eight and it's Peggy Lee. Now if you'll let me finish . . ."

Selene ran a finger across her lips. "Zzzzip."

"Thank you. Anyway, I'm thinking *Is this all there is?* and the answer's coming back *At best*, but what's left if I give up Wicca? My waitressing job at the Trident? So I do the same dumb thing women have been doing since the dawn of time when they're feeling lost and empty—I get myself knocked up. Won't feel empty any more. I thought I was being so clever. I waited until you were out of town and seduced Jamey—oh, I was shameless—cut my finger carving my runes—*Silly me, look what I've done.* And of course it didn't work—I hated being pregnant. You and the ladies fluttering around me—oh, let me feel it kicking, oh the miracle of life—and it's like, *What miracle?* A cockroach can reproduce. A dog does it six at a time."

"But you never let on, we never had the slightest idea—"

"It wasn't as if any of you really wanted to hear it, you know. I cried through half the pregnancy and everybody said it was only hormones. I don't know, maybe it was. And I figured it would all change once the baby was born, that I'd look down into that little face and feel that serenity and that sense of meaning and accomplishment I always associated with new moms. . . . Hell, I was going to be the fucking *Madonna*—the real one, not the singer.

"Only of course it didn't happen like that. Fourteen hours of agony, then I'm holding this little wizened, bloody, hairy, crusty thing and everybody's going ooh and ah, and I'm thinking *It might as well be a monkey. We might as well be monkeys.*

"So I'm living at the Broadway house on your charity, I can't even waitress anymore, I haven't had a full night's sleep in a month, and I'm praying to the Goddess, whom I no longer believe in, for something, anything to take away this dead feeling and on top of everything else Martha gets the colic and I'm up pacing the floor with her for the third night in a row and she's screaming her lungs out and there comes a point where I'm holding her over my head and I swear to you I was *this* close to smothering her with a pillow.

"Instead I call Connie. She hops on the Sportster; in an hour she's sitting on the edge of my bed rocking Martha in her arms and looking down at her with so much love and longing—you remember she and Don couldn't have any kids, and with his prison record nobody was going to let them adopt—and I feel like a color-blind woman watching a sunset.

"Next morning Don brings the pickup and me and Martha move into the shed behind the 'frame. Time passes—soon Martha's spending most of her time in the house and Connie on her worst day is doing a better job of nurturing than I am on my best, and within a couple of weeks Nanny the goat has taken over my only remaining function. It was sort of a defining moment in my career as a mother: replaced by a goat.

"But when I try to tell Connie what's going on, what I hear is still, 'Hormones and postpartum depression and what you really need is just a little time to yourself and why don't we take Martha off with us on the spring run to Mendocino?' and in the back of my mind all I'm thinking about is that belladonna bush you planted up the hill behind Jamey's A-frame, and it wasn't so much a matter of caring whether I would fly as it was not caring if I died.

"They left on Saturday morning. When I went up to the herb garden the black cherries were shriveled up like raisins. I didn't know whether this would make them more or less potent. I followed the directions in the *Herbalis*, but instead of a tart shell, I used the base of an ice cream cone."

Selene's professional interest was piqued. "Cake or sugar?"

"Cake. Sugar soaks through and leaks. Didn't help, though; to this day the thought of that godawful glop still gives me the shudders. I ate my cone at sunset, in the woods behind Don and Connie's—a decision so flawed it is now enthroned in the Bad Idea Hall of Fame. An hour later I was lurching around the gazebo buck naked with the staggers and jags. That's when I separated. I remember floating through the gazebo dome and looking back down at my body lying where it had fallen, scratched and scraped from wandering through the woods. Then that terrifying sense of flying through nothingness—what did you call it? Oakland?—and the fear came down on me like a two-ton fly swatter.

"I was sure I was going to die, and all I could think about— not in words, mind you, but on a deeper level, I'd say middle to lower chakras, only I didn't have a body—all I had *time* to think about, was that I'd never fuck again."

Selene started to snicker, tried to turn it into a cough. Moll wasn't fooled; she nudged Selene lightly in the ribs. "I know, I know: it's the spiritual equivalent of walking out of the ladies' room trailing toilet paper from your panty hose. And it was even odder, because like I told you before, I'd been feeling dead to sex for a good year before I even got pregnant."

"So? What happened next?"

"So? I flew. But I didn't see the people I cared about, the way you did, Selene. I didn't even see any people I knew, or very many places I recognized. Bedrooms, mostly, and hotel rooms and motel rooms, and in every room there were strangers . . . I don't want to say fucking, or making love, or having sex, because that doesn't begin to describe what was going on, what I was seeing.

"At first, I have to admit, once I had decided that I wasn't dead, but flying, just the way all the ancient witchlore had described it, there was more than a little element of pure voyeurism to it. I started off by playing around: I'd think about a mommy/daddy type couple, look down, and there they'd be in the missionary position, pajamas and all. I'd think about men together, and *whoosh*—off I'd go to the Castro, looking down through the roof of a bathhouse. Or I'd think about a threesome, say, or an S and M orgy in a private club, or a twenty-dollar hooker giving a guy a backseat blow job. *Whoosh, whoosh, whoosh.*

"Then, as I gained confidence, I got a little more imaginative. I'd think about transvestites, and *whoosh*, I'd be looking down on a drag queen stripping at the foot of a bed. Bestiality—*whoosh*. Kids, virgins, wedding nights—*whoosh, whoosh, whoosh!*

"Then, after I'd gone through every variety of sex I could think of, I really went baroque, seeking out variations on variations. Old folks in threesomes. Pubescent boys—a dormitory circle-jerk. Women with women, but this time diesel dykes having rough sex, then a couple of preteen girls practicing kissing, getting hot, pretending one of them is a boy. Transsexuals—man-to-woman with man, man-to-woman with woman, woman-to— Anyway, you get the idea. But the most peculiar part—"

"Oh *please* don't get any more peculiar," whispered Selene. "I'm about peculiared out."

"Ironic, then—that's a better word. What I mean is, it wasn't until after I'd thoroughly exhausted my entire life experience *and* my imagination, and was just sort of floating around, looking down when the spirit moved me, that I finally saw what I think the Fair Lady wanted me to see all along.

"It started off, I was looking down on a woman gliding along a linoleum corridor in an electric wheelchair, steering one-handed with a joystick. I couldn't tell her age because of the way all the muscles of her face were working continually, like pudding coming to a boil—my best guess'd be late twenties. My other best guess is some severe form of cerebral palsy. It's late at night. Some kind of hospital or long-term care facility. At the end of the corridor she pushes a door open with one foot and rolls inside; I float over the top. Inside, in the dark, a man in a bed says something—I can't make it out—his voice is slow, slurred, distorted, kind of like a forty-five rpm record played at thirty-three and a third.

"She says something back—she's not any easier to understand than he is."

Selene shifted uncomfortably on the couch. "I think I see where this is going," she whispered, feeling a little like Scrooge pleading with the Spirit of Christmas Yet to Come. "And I really don't think I want to go there with you."

Moll clenched her fists as tightly as she could without impaling her palms. "If I could only make you *see*," she whispered passionately. "Please, Selene, let me try. I promise you, it wasn't grotesque at all—a little funny maybe, but what sex isn't?"

Selene put a finger to her own lips. "Not talking, me."

"She rolled her chair up to the side of his bed. With his hand controls he lowered the bed to wheelchair height, and she transferred over. They did the oddest thing before kissing—put their hands up in front of their faces as they brought their heads together. Like bumpers, I figured out, watching them lock lips and chow down: at any moment, the head of either one might jerk forward uncontrollably. If they hadn't worked out this thing with their hands they'd have continually been butting each other.

"They kissed long and slow and pretty sweet, considering all the spittle flying around. It took them forever to undress; having only two good working hands between the two of them—her left, his right—they had to work together to get her bathrobe off and her nightgown over her head. She was glowing with perspiration by the time they finished. And he got his nightshirt stuck over his head with his good arm trapped in it, and she tugged it the rest of the way off with her hand and her teeth. But they weren't impatient about it—they'd done it before—they showed each other a thousand little kindnesses. It was sweet, and moving, and if I'd had a body it might even have made me hot. She had cute little dangly breasts that brushed his chest when she leaned against him to help him out of his shirt, and he had a respectable hard-on.

"But oh, what they had to go through to actually get him inside her. She had to help prop him up and keep him from slipping over sideways; he had to help her get her leg over him so she was sitting on his lap; she had to close her fist over his dick so as not to bend it in half until they got it properly situated and aligned.

"As for the actual fucking, that's what I mean by funny. See, she couldn't exactly raise and lower herself, and he sure couldn't pump her, but between the two of them, their tics and jerks, all the spazz moves we used to make fun of when we were kids"— Moll mimed the old joke of the spastic boy rewarding himself with an ice cream cone to the forehead—"they had more moves than a sack of Mexican jumping beans."

"I get the idea," said Selene.

"Hush. I'm about done. When they came, I left, and the next

thing I knew I was hovering over a body lying on the hard floor of the gazebo. As soon as I recognized it for mine, I was back in it—and oh was it sore.

"But by then I'd seen what the Fair Lady wanted me to see, and I knew what my task was going to be. Find out about sex magick. Whatever it was that was the difference between being dead like I'd been for a year, and being alive the way those two poor lucky souls were, it had something to do with sex. Of course, I had no idea what that *meant*, choosing sex magick for my life's work— or having it chosen for me. About all I had figured out was that it was like gravity—the only way you even know it exists is by the effect it has on passing bodies.

"Not that I was phrasing it—or anything—all that elegantly back then. In fact, there was very little difference between the frame of mind I was in and a flat-out psychotic breakdown. Those first weeks when everybody was looking for me, I was hanging out in bars in San Francisco—straight bars, lesbian bars, even gay bars— and taking on all comers. It was a steep slide to a deep bottom— two or three years spiraling down, two or three years in the Underworld like Persephone, two or three years climbing back to the light. Talk about a long strange trip—doesn't get much stranger than that road from the Tenderloin to Winnemucca to Vegas to that fancy office of mine. I keep telling myself that someday I'm going to write a book about it. I will, too, after a few gentlemen of respect whose names end in vowels have passed through the veil." Moll bent the tip of her nose sideways with her forefinger, the traditional sign for wise guys.

Selene had to interrupt again. "And in all that time—I'm sorry for sounding like a Jewish mother—but in all those years it never occurred to you to get in touch with the people who loved you? Never mind me, never mind your sister—what about Martha?"

"I thought about her. Of course I thought about her. That's why I sent you that letter, so that I knew she'd be taken care of no matter what happened. But as for getting in touch, it didn't occur to me those first few years that there was a soul on earth who

wanted or needed me. I was way past low self-esteem by then: I
had no esteem whatsoever, and very little self."

"When did you find out about Connie?"

"A year or so after she died. I was running a legit house in Nye
County, and one of the fringe bikers—remember Hank the
Crank?—just happened to show up. I comped him to keep his
mouth shut, and sent Don a letter. Told him if Martha needed me,
I'd come back. I also told him you knew who Martha's father was,
if money was needed. I didn't want him to know what I was doing,
so I used a P.O. box in Vegas as a return address. He never
answered."

"You don't know, then?"

"Know what?"

"Don's dying, Moll. The doctors give him another couple of
months at best."

"Oh shit."

"My sentiments exactly. But there's something else we have to
consider here. I don't know how the actuaries work out the tables
for people being stalked by murderous arsonists, but when you factor in the belladonna, curare, and distachya, I imagine it's somewhere in the don't-buy-green-bananas category."

"All the more reason for you to disappear."

"But either way it works out exactly the same for Martha—
she's fast running out of surrogate parents. And she's seventeen years
old and not a virgin and if I had to predict how she'd react to
hearing your life story, my guess would be a range somewhere between *yuck* and *cool*, which is how all teenagers feel about their
parents anyway."

"So you think she'd want to hear from me?"

"I don't know. She might tell you to fuck off. But I've read a
lot on the subject, and one of the few things all the so-called experts
agree on is that there's not a kid in the world who was
abandoned—sorry, dearie, but that's the word, Fair Lady or no Fair
Lady—who doesn't on some level think it's their own fault. So
whether she wants to hear from you or not, I'm pretty sure she

needs to hear from you. You owe her that much, Moll. And if anything happens to me, I want you to promise me you'll get in touch with her—no, that you'll go to her. You owe *me* that much, for taking care of her all these years."

"You're going back then." It was hardly a question.

"Of course."

"Want company?"

Selene shook her head. "I just want to know you'll be there for Martha."

"I'll be there. Witch's Word. When did you want to leave?"

"Soon as possible. Which reminds me, I was going to ask you, have you got a good travel agent? I'm thinking about heading home by way of Santa Luz."

"How come?"

"I want to pick up a few items from Granny Weed *before* I run into Aldo or Jonas again."

Moll seemed to be resigning herself to Selene's leaving. "Good idea," she said brightly. "I can have my secretary make the arrangements for you in the morning. But there's something you can do for me in the meantime."

"And what might that be?" asked Selene.

Moll, grinning: "Rub my back the way you used to."

"You got it. Lie down and roll over."

"I love it when you talk dirty," joked Moll. "Let me draw the shades first. Half the apartments in New York have telescopes and the rest have binoculars."

"What do *you* care?" retorted Selene. Then, hastily: "I'm sorry. I didn't mean that to sound—"

"No offense taken." Moll reached for the Lucite rod to close the blinds. "And Goddess knows I don't mind a little exhibitionism—exhibitionism been bery bery good to me. But I don't like to encourage Peeping Toms. It's not only immoral, in my case it's theft of services. If somebody wants to get their jollies seeing me naked, they have to pay A-Mature Productions fifty-nine ninety-five for the privilege."

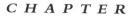
The lights were on in the A-frame when Martha returned home from her not-a-date with just-a-friend-who-happened-to-be-a-boy Friday night. When she saw the strange Toyota in the driveway her breath caught in her throat—*Daddy Don!* She tried to calm her fears. It couldn't be a doctor's car, she told herself, because all the doctors drove Beemers or Benzes or at least four-wheel drives. But neither would any self-respecting biker have been caught dead in a beigey-tan Corolla.

So she was pleasantly surprised when she opened the front door to see Daddy Don propped into a sitting position, conversing wooz-ily with a man she'd never seen before. Neatly spruced brown hair and mustache, black pullover, black slacks, ankle-high black boots. His head was a little too large for his body, but otherwise he was okay looking. "Martha!" he cried unexpectedly, jumping to his feet as she entered the room. "Thank God."

She couldn't think of a reply. He crossed the room with an athletic stride, took her hand almost before she could extend it, and shook it warmly. She threw Daddy Don a questioning glance over the stranger's shoulder; Baechler gave her a loopy morphine smile. "Honey, this is . . . this is . . ."

"Len. Len Patch." He let go of her hand, peered earnestly into her eyes. "Did you have any trouble tonight? Anyone approach you, anyone seem to be following you?"

"Not that I noticed." She hurried across the room to Daddy Don. "What's this all about, Daddy? Is something wrong?" His pupils were absolutely pinned. "Wait a minute, where's Dirtbag?"

The old biker struggled for focus. "Something . . . something happened?" He looked past her to Patch for confirmation.

"Everything's fine," said the stranger soothingly. "And I'm here to see that everything stays that way." He waited while Martha fussed over Daddy Don for a moment, fluffing his pillows and tidying the covers. When she straightened up, the man caught her eye. "Is there somewhere we can talk?" he whispered.

She cast her eyes up to the underside of the loft, then pointed to the ladder. "Go ahead," she whispered back. "I'll be up in a minute."

He darted over to pick up a leather bag—like a doctor's, but bigger—on the floor next to the bed, then started up the ladder, climbing as nimbly as a monkey with his one free hand. When he was out of sight, she bent over the bed. "Daddy, what's going on?"

But it was no use—Daddy Don had lost touch again. It had been happening a lot lately. "What?"

She sighed, stroked his stubbled cheek lightly. "Never mind, Daddy. You comfortable? Need anything?"

Another stoned smile; the eyes lost focus. Martha lowered the bed back to a gentle lean, tucked the pillows tighter around him, and clicked both side rails into place. She could hear the breath rattling in his chest as she started up the ladder. She climbed slowly, stalling. She missed Daddy Don so bad—somehow it seemed almost like she'd have missed him less if he were already dead.

The man was looking out the back window. She crossed the loft, trying to tread lightly on the wooden platform—she knew from experience how loud footsteps in the loft sounded down in the living room—and had just grasped the beaded pull chain hanging from the overhead bulb when he wheeled around. "No, leave it off."

She froze. "What's going on?"

"Your life may be in danger." He took a step toward her; the light leaking up from below made it look as if he were shining a flashlight under his chin. A surefire effect when telling ghost stories, but not terribly reassuring under the circumstances.

"Is somebody out there?" Martha took a step back, dropping the chain.

"Don't know. But let's not silhouette ourselves, shall we?"

The pull chain tapped the bulb, swung back gently toward her. Martha fought a rising panic. "Who are you? What are you doing here? And what happened to Dirtbag?"

She took another step back as he started toward her again. "I've already told you my name. What I'm doing here is trying to keep you alive. And if by Dirtbag you are referring to the pungent gentleman in the motorcycle jacket who was passed out in a chair when I arrived, I took him by the seat of the pants and the scruff of the neck and tossed him out the front door."

"Are you a cop or something?"

A modest chuckle. "Hardly."

"Who's after me? The man who tried to kill Selene?"

The man's eyebrows shot up. "Precisely."

"Did she send you?"

He shook his head.

"Who then?"

He smiled—an unfortunate effect given the eerie underlighting. "Your father."

Martha's eyes darted downward involuntarily, as if she were looking through the floorboards at Daddy Don.

"Not *him*," said the stranger, following her glance. "I'm talking about your real father." Then he clucked his tongue and slapped his forehead with the flat of his palm. "Oh! But of course. How stupid of me. You don't know who your real father is, do you?"

Numbly, she shook her head as he crossed the loft toward her, opening his kit bag as he approached. With his face only inches from hers he stopped and peered into her eyes; she could not tear her gaze away. "Would you like to know?" he whispered. His breath was sweet and coppery, a little rank, but oddly comforting, almost familiar, as he reached into the kit bag and pulled out a loose-leaf notebook with a black silk cover. "Recognize this?"

"Selene's Book of Shadows." Her voice wasn't working, but her lips had moved to form the words.

"There's a letter hidden under the inner lining. Why don't you take it down to your room—you'll probably want to read it in privacy," suggested Len Patch thoughtfully.

———

Martha sat cross-legged on her bed with the thick loose-leaf closed in her lap. Through the closed door she could hear Len conversing softly with Daddy Don. It occurred to her that although the book was as familiar to her as a childhood friend, she had never actually looked into it. She passed her palm thoughtfully across the silky black cover as a toddler memory surfaced. . . .

Lying on her stomach playing with her plastic Little Pony doll on the floor of Selene's big house in San Francisco. Selene sitting on the rug nearby, gluing a new cover onto her book. Something iridescent, magical to a three-year-old, with a hint of rainbow like Little Pony's mane and tail.

Martha slipped off the hand-sewn black silk dust jacket. Sure enough, there was the old rattlesnake-skin cover Selene had glued on so painstakingly years before. It was dull and cracked with age now, and starting to peel back from the original canvas-covered cardboard binding. She could just see the corner of the one-page letter Len had told her about, peeking out from under the snakeskin; with trembling fingers she pulled it out.

The cream-colored paper was soft as tissue, white and threadbare where it had been folded. Carefully she carried the letter over to her white wicker desk, carefully spread it open across the glass top. The lavender ink had faded to a nearly illegible gray; she switched on her tensor lamp and twisted the flexible gooseneck until the light was blazing directly down onto the letter.

April 5, 1976

Darling Selene,
    Know I love you. Know I appreciate everything you've done for me. I've either lost my mind or found my path. Please believe

me when I tell you I have my reasons. Perhaps someday I'll be able to tell you.

My original plan, insofar as I had one, was to drop clean out of sight—less painful for all concerned. I did call Connie a few minutes ago. It was as awful as I thought it would be, but this much we agreed on: she and Don will raise Martha as if she were their own child. I know this will work out for the best. You know how hungry they've been for one. They'll give her everything I couldn't—wouldn't. And as her godmother, I know you'll always be there for her too.

As you know, I've never told anyone who the father is. It seemed irrelevant. Wasn't his fault anyway—I told him I was on the pill. And now Connie's told me she and Don don't want to know and don't want Martha to know either. I agreed—I had another reason for keeping his identity to myself anyway. Martha's father was the lover—more than that, the one true eternal love— of my dearest friend in the world, the woman I've always thought of as my one true eternal love, and even though all I wanted was his sperm, and those lovely WASP genes, I couldn't take the chance that you'd think I was trying to steal him from you. How could I, Selene, when I know that Jamey Whistler is yours, marriage or no marriage, for richer or poorer, for better or worse, until death do you part. If then.

So why am I telling you now? Because I keep getting these scary thoughts about all the bad things that could happen down the line, some tragedy involving Connie and Don, or Martha comes down with some hereditary disease, or any one of a billion possibilities where somebody might need to know the identity of Martha's father. And if something happened to me before that (not very far-fetched), the secret would go to the grave with me.

But enough of borrowing trouble—sufficient unto the day and all that . . . So for what it's worth, to whom it may concern, etc., etc.: James Whistler is Martha Herrick's birth father.

Please keep this letter somewhere safe, and please keep our secret unless something dire happens. Tell the most noble ladies I love them all to the extent I am capable of loving. Tell them to pray for me. You pray for me too.

> *Your other eternal lover,*
> *Moll*

The look on Martha's face when she emerged from the back room was everything Aldo could have hoped for. She marched straight to Daddy Don's bedside. The old biker was asleep, breathing so shallowly that she had to stare at his beard intently to see any movement whatsoever. She touched him lightly on the cheek.

"Daddy Don?"

He opened his eyes. " 'S happenin', Sugaree?" Stoned.

"Is Whistler my father?"

"Beats the shit out of me. Ask your Aunt Connie." And he nodded off again.

Her back was to Aldo, but he saw her fingers clench as if they wanted to grab the old man and shake him awake—which was not part of Aldo's plan. He stepped forward and whispered into her ear, "You read the letter. Do you have any doubt?"

"Not really." She squared her shoulders and turned. Their faces were only inches apart.

Good-looking kid, thought Aldo. Then he remembered her in the hot tub, and smiled inwardly as he stepped back. *Little birds—give them room and they'll come to you.*

And sure enough: "Thanks for letting me know the truth," she said. She led him away from the bed, into the kitchen area on the other side of the pillars. "You said Whistler sent you to protect me. Then he must know now."

"Now, yes." Aldo had his story prepared; he hoped it was seamless. If not, he was ready to do some quick stitching. "I don't know if you know, but he's been in hiding since this all started. When he learned Selene was looking for him, he contacted her. That's when she told him about you, asked him to look after you. When he asked her for proof, she told him about the letter in the book in the trunk. He sent me to check it out, and in any event to take whatever steps were necessary to see that you were protected."

"But I spoke to Selene last night—she didn't say anything about any of this."

"Whoever is behind all this has cast his nets widely. Perhaps she was afraid the line wasn't secure. Was there anything at all unusual about the call? What did she tell you?"

"Just that everything was okay, that she'd be back in a couple days."

It was all Aldo could do to keep his inward grin from spreading outward.

"But now that you mention it," Martha continued, "she did keep asking me if I was okay, if any strangers had been around. I thought she was talking about the guy who set the fires."

"There you have it," said Aldo. "She was probably trying to find out whether I'd shown up yet, without tipping anybody off that I was coming." He could see in her eyes that she'd bought it, that she was leaning his way: time to pull out the props and drop her into his lap. "But now here I am. And if I fall down on this job, if I let anything happen to Whistler's daughter, he'll have me skinned for seat covers." He'd almost said *have my guts for garters,* but seat covers was better—more Californian.

Whistler's daughter. Martha liked the sound of that. "So what do we do first?"

"Obviously, the first thing to do is get while the getting's good." A phrase he'd heard on the radio this afternoon, in reference to American troops in Mogadishu.

"But I can't leave Daddy Don," she whispered, peering around a pillar to be sure he was still asleep.

"As long as you're here, he's in danger too."

"I guess I could call Carson—that's his partner. He could be over in like five minutes."

"Make the call and then we're out of here. We'll make a big show of leaving by the front door, so if there's anyone staking the place out, we'll draw them away with us before he gets here. Daddy

Don will be okay for five minutes, and this way we won't be putting your friend Carson into jeopardy as well."

"But then they'll be following *us*."

They. Us. Aldo couldn't have been more pleased. "And we'll lose them, too," he assured her. "The shadow hasn't been born yet that Len Patch can't shake."

CHAPTER

4

After her initial comment about the gentlemen of respect whose names ended in vowels, Moll had made no further reference to the subject, other than to assure Selene that with Gianni—again the sign of the bent nose—living in the penthouse, hers was far and away the most secure apartment building in New York.

So when Moll offered to have a car take them to Kennedy— Moll was just going along for the ride—Selene assumed she was talking about a cab or a car service, and was totally unprepared for the streeeetch limo waiting for them at the curb on Friday morning. She was about to ask Moll how much this was going to cost, but stopped when Moll greeted the driver familiarly as he came around to open the door for them.

"Hey Joey, how's it going this morning?"

"Any morning's good when I get to drive you, Miss Montana. You know I'm a fan."

"Well bless your heart. And be sure to thank Gianni for me."

"Aah, you know it makes him happy when he can do something for you."

"Well thank him anyway." She slid in after Selene.

"I have to ask," said Selene as the limo pulled out into traffic. "Who on earth is Gianni?"

Moll replied in the voice-that-was-not—*Il capo di capo di tutti capi*—then asked the driver to roll up the partition. "Got to get in a little girl talk, Joey."

"No problem, Miss M."

"You've gotten so good at telepathy," said Selene when the glass was up. "It's coming through so clearly now. And in Italian, yet. After all these years of work, it's still hit or miss with me."

"It'll come," replied Moll.

"When?"

"With menopause."

"I didn't know that."

"Sure. There's a lot of other good stuff that comes with it. Orgomancy, for instance. Can't even start *learning* that until after the change. Remember the part in Enfernelli where she talks about not being afraid of the crone?"

Selene nodded.

"Well she ain't talking about some other crone over in the next county, Selene—she's talking about the crone you're gonna turn into some day. Listen up, dearie—the crone is the toughest aspect of the Goddess to love. She ain't young and gorgeous like Persephone, she ain't regal like Maeve. But her magic is the most powerful magic of all, and it doesn't have diddly to do with good or evil or belief or unbelief. 'Mother of Darkness, Mother of Night, witchcraft neither black nor white.'

"Selene, my love, if you want to, you can abandon everything you've been working toward for the past thirty years because the Goddess didn't pop up in front of you wearing a fucking sandwich board every time you prayed, and you can find something else to do with the rest of your life. Needlepoint. Marriage. Volunteer work with the Cancer Society. Or you can travel; they have lots of tours designed for women of a certain age. I understand the Pyramids are a popular destination.

"Because you see, dearie, the alternative to becoming a crone isn't staying young and beautiful. No matter what you decide to do you're going to turn into an old lady if you live. You might as well tap into some magic, get some power to go along with those gray hairs."

"Thanks for the pep talk, Moll," replied Selene. "I'll keep it in mind. But at the moment I've got a problem that won't wait for menopause. *Now* is when I need some real magic."

Moll thought it over. "Remember that first night, when you asked me to define magic?" she said after a moment.

"Of course," replied Selene. "You quoted Crowley: 'The science and art of causing change to occur in conformity with will.' Why?"

"Frankly, dearie, if your will was any stronger, you'd own the fucking franchise."

—

Compared to her last flight to the Caribbean, the nonstop from JFK to St. Thomas was a piece of cake. It even arrived on time, enabling her to catch the last Blue Goose of the day to Santa Luz without doing too much damage to her American Express card in the shops of Charlotte Amalie.

The Goose skipped into the harbor shortly before sunset; the clerk at the Kings Frederick and Christian Arms greeted her warmly and assigned her her old room. There had, of course, been no way for Selene to call Granny Weed in advance. Her plan was to whistle up Tosh on Saturday morning and get a ride up to the rain forest, so the last thing she expected to hear when she went out onto the balcony to catch the last few minutes of the short but breathtaking tropical sunset was the clip-clop of goat hooves.

But when she leaned over the railing and peered to the left, here came the Rastaman's cart rolling down the middle of King Street, scattering chickens and dogs. She waved; he tipped his blue yachting cap. "Good evenin', Miss Weiss."

"And a lovely evening it is, Mr. Munger." Didn't take long to fall into the courtly rhythms of island speech.

"Granny Weed say, if you ain' dine yet dis evenin', would you do her de honor?"

It was one of those heart-stopping moments that even longtime witches honor by humming the *Twilight Zone* theme in their heads: da *da* da dum, da *da* da dum. "How did she know I was here?"

An eloquent shrug from the buckboard. "Sometin' about flyin' while sleepin'. Me ain' know more, me ain' *want* to know more."

Selene changed into her safari shirt and khaki slacks and hurried downstairs; after another delightful ride beneath a sky of tropical splendor, they arrived at the dark wooden cabin by the side of the dundo track. Joe-Pie and Granny were out back; when she stepped out from behind the fire and into the flickering light of the kerosene torches planted around the little yard, the weed woman's complexion was a dusky reddish-brown.

"Been flying, Granny?" asked Selene, opening her arms for a hug, then stepping back in mock alarm as the crone approached her. "Not going to stick me with any pins this time, are you?"

"Ain' wearin' me bonnet dis evenin'." The two women hugged while Joe-Pie, who had been using the bellows on the coals beneath the cauldron, ran into the cabin barefoot and emerged wearing his Reeboks.

"How's that pump working?" asked Selene as he skidded up to her, stopping just short of hugging distance and shaking hands formally.

"Real good."

"Too good," said his grandmother. "Last week he pump it up so hard his toes turn blue."

"And how are you doing?" asked Selene. "You must have taken the Test pretty recently, if you saw me on my way here. It knocked the shit out of me for two days."

"Because you ain' know shit about how to prepare it, and you take too much," replied the old woman scornfully, then called to the Rastaman. "Feed y'self, mon. Blue runner in de kettle." She turned back to Selene. "M'take just a little, fly just a little, not far —round de forest while Joe-Pie and Mr. Munger watch over me body. Saw where de most hidden tings be—dumbcane and nettle, hidey-toad to make balm for swell-toe—all sorts of tings. Last ting m'saw was you, steppin' off de Goose. Wake up, ask Mr. Munger a fetch you, ain' dot so, mon?"

The Rastaman had grabbed a machete leaning against the trunk of the shade tree from which the cauldron was suspended. "Dot's true." He speared a tiny blue fish, slipped it off the machete with thumb and forefinger, then held it up in the air, making it wriggle as if it were still alive, laughing uproariously at his own joke. Next he popped the whole fish into his mouth like a canapé, bit off the head and spat it out into the darkness of the bushes beyond the lighted clearing, then worked his jaws furiously, separating flesh from bone with delicate motions of his teeth and tongue, and spitting the bones out, rat-a-tat-tat, in the general direction of the head.

"I don't think I can do that," said Selene dubiously, when Joe-Pie offered her one of the little fish on the end of his own machete.

"Sorry, Miss Selene. Dey all got bones—we ain' cotch no jellyfish today." He and the Rastaman both laughed at that; then the boy sat down on the back steps with the cutting board in his lap; he beheaded, butterflied, and deboned the tiny fish with the tip of his machete—an astounding feat to watch, like seeing somebody fillet a sardine with a saber—and offered it to Selene wrapped in a slice of Wonder bread.

It was delicious.

After treating himself to a few more fish (by this time some creature, either a large rodent or a small dog, had stationed itself in the bushes and was catching the fish heads before they hit the ground, then snarfing them down noisily), Mr. Munger left for his cabin, promising to return in a few hours to take Selene back to her hotel.

The mosquitoes had begun to swarm in clouds. Granny, Selene, and Joe-Pie retreated inside and lit dark green mosquito coils; apparently the fierce Luzan breed were either beneath or beyond the power of Granny's weed magic. After Granny sent Joe-Pie off to his cot behind the green army blanket that screened his bed from the rest of the cabin, she boiled water on her old cast-iron woodstove, and she and Selene sat at the kitchen table (a board that folded flat against the wall of the cabin, dropping down like a Murphy bed as needed), sipping a tisane made from passion flower and pennyroyal, which was said to pacify the spirit without dulling the senses.

The first thing Granny told Selene was that if she wanted to take the Fair Lady again she should use fewer cherries, and cook them twice as long. Selene asked her how she knew; the weed woman tapped her temple. As soon as she'd seen the cherries, she explained, she'd recognized that what Selene called Fair Lady was a relative of the plant known as *con-com zombi*—zombi cucumber. The effects were the same as belladonna: soul flies, body dies. Or rather, body drops into a state of suspended animation indistinguishable from death.

"Wait a minute, Granny. You mean you don't have to be a witch to fly?"

Granny snorted derisively.

So much for witches and ithers. Selene put down her tea and inclined her head toward the weed woman as far as she could without leaning on the table suspended from the wall. "Help me, Granny Weed," Selene requested formally, before recounting what had befallen her in London, about Whistler's father having sent Aldo after both of them, about using the cure-root on the old man, about accidentally killing Mrs. Wah.

"Aldo? De devilish mon?"

"Same guy. That's why I need you to teach me what you can in the time we have, because in a day or two I have to go back to California, and in all probability, that devilish man is going to be either waiting for me, or coming after me."

Granny slapped the table, rattling the cups in their saucers, then leaned back, laughing. "Two day? Cheese and bread, girl, in dot time Granny cyan't teach you to fight Joe-Pie. How me ga send you off to battle de devil in Calif—" She cocked her head, listening. Selene did the same, and heard a sniffling coming from behind the curtain.

"You listenin' to women's talk again, m'son?"

A round brown head appeared from around the side of the

olive-drab blanket. "You got to help Miss Selene, Granny. You cyan't let de devil take her."

"Hush, boy. He ain' no real devil, just a poppy-show jumbie."

Selene took another sip of her penny-passion tea. "Well *that's* reassuring."

"It's de boy need assurin'," whispered the old woman as she rose from the table. "What you need is poison. Now dis Aldo, he mebbe don' want to eat what you give him to eat, nor drink what you give him to drink. So it must be on pin. First ting, me ga trade you de cure-root pins for zombi paste. Me ain' need to fly no more, and you ain' need to kill nobody else by mistake. Use one pin on any mon, no matter how big nor small, he sleep like de dead for a night and a day.

"Howsomever . . ." She returned from the drying rack over the windowsill with five pins. "If de devilish mon workin' for de old mon, he ga know about pins, ain' ga let you get close enough wit one to stick him."

She thought about it for a moment while Selene removed the three remaining curare pins from the "For Our Guests" sewing packet, and replaced them with the five new ones. "Unless he cyan't see it. You chew gum?"

"Sure. I bought a pack of Doublemint at the airport."

"You can spit?"

"Of course."

"Show Granny."

Selene took a sip of tea to moisten her mouth, then walked to the door of the cabin and hocked a decent, most unfeminine, loogie out into the backyard.

Granny nodded decisively. "Mashasha, den—if you don' mind a little pain and bleedin' from de mout."

"Mine or his?"

"Yours. But when you spit de juice in his eyes, even de devil go blind. Den, while he tearin' his own eyeball to shred tryin' to get it out, you strike wit de zombi-pin."

"And if I don't want him to wake up again in twenty-four hours—or ever?"

Granny shook her head. "One for sleep, two for dead, dey say. But dis Aldo, he be Drinker, yes?"

"I'm pretty sure."

"In dot case, make a pincushion out of de devilish son of a bitch, wit Granny Weed's compliments."

C H A P T E R

5

Around one in the morning, Pacific standard time, Len/Aldo brought the Toyota to a full stop at the intersection before turning onto Highway 1. "That was foolish of you," he informed Martha.

"What?"

"Waving at that car. From now on I want you to keep your head down."

"I thought it was somebody I knew," replied Martha. "Besides, who died and made you god?"

"I'm sorry, Martha. But I'm responsible for you now. And if anything happened to you—"

"Yeah, yeah, seat covers."

Aldo took his eyes off the road long enough to glance over at her. "I also—I know it's unprofessional, but I care about you. You're a gutsy kid—I want to get you through this."

Martha turned away, pressed her face against the window. She could see past her reflection to the black water of the lagoon, near the spot where she and her friends used to come to burn a bud and watch the sun go down. Those days were already starting to seem awfully far away. "You know what, Len?" she said into the window. "About an hour ago, if there was one person in the whole world who I was absolutely, positively, bet-your-lunch-money certain really truly cared about me, it was Selene. And now I find out that she's been lying to me all these years about knowing who my father was. So to tell you the truth, at this point people telling me they care about me doesn't exactly make my top ten list of crap I want to hear."

"Your call," said Aldo evenly. "If you want me to keep it on a professional basis, that's the way it'll be. So as bodyguard to client, miss, I'd like you to tilt your seat as far back as it goes, and keep your head below window level until we're through Stinson Beach."

Martha leaned forward against the tug of her seat belt harness; as she groped around for the seat lever she found herself feeling a little guilty. "I'm sorry, I don't mean to be so pissy."

"That's all right, miss."

"You can still call me Martha."

"That wouldn't be professional, miss."

"Oh give me a break! Can't we just be, like, friendly?"

Another sidelong glance from Aldo, accompanied by a charming smile. "I'd like that very much . . . Martha."

━

Aldo checked the dashboard clock as the highway wound down from the mountain—not quite one-thirty. The sun would be up around a quarter to seven. "Martha, I need a little input from you here." *Input*—he'd heard that word often on the local talk radio. "We need a place to stay. At least three hours away"—in the unlikely event that this fellow Carson had raised an alarm upon finding the old biker dead and his ward missing—"but not more than four or five at the most." In other words, well before sunset. "Somewhere with lots of motels, fairly steady tourist turnover . . . ?"

"Monterey," she answered promptly.

"Do you know anyone there?"

"To get hold of?"

"To *not* get hold of—or run into."

"I know a lot of bikers in Salinas, Hollister, like that."

"What about Monterey itself?"

"Not a soul."

"Monterey it is, then. How do we get there?"

"Turn right at Tam Junction, take 101 South. But I want to call Carson when we get there, explain what's going on, see how Daddy Don is doing?"

In a pig's eye, thought Aldo. "We'll see. I have to make a few calls first, see whether the line's being bugged. If it's clear you can talk."

"What if the line's not clear?"

"I'll have it swept," he lied nimbly. "Might take a few days, though."

━

Martha was wary when Aldo returned to the car from the office of a Best Western motel along Munras Avenue in Monterey bearing only a single key. She felt a little better when he assured her that the room had two queen-sized beds, but did not relax her guard entirely, and made *damn* sure the bathroom door was securely locked when she took her shower. She'd seen what had happened to Jamie Leigh Curtis's mother in the shower in that old movie.

But Len Patch remained a perfect gentleman in every respect. He changed into his pajamas while she was in the bathroom, and then when he was in the bathroom himself he even ran the water to cover the splashing noise while he was peeing: now that was class! He said he'd already tried calling her house, that the line was indeed tapped to trace incoming calls, and that his people were working on it, so she climbed into the bed nearest the TV, and fell asleep watching HBO.

When she awoke it was midafternoon. Len was burrowed deep into his bed with the covers pulled over his head; there was a note on the nightstand between the beds, warning her not to open either the door or the blinds, or call home until he had checked out the line again. His handwriting was outstanding—all neat and carefully curlicued—and he'd been thoughtful enough to add a nice post-script to the effect that he was a heavy sleeper, and she should go ahead and watch TV if she wanted.

Watching *Oprah* and snacking on the junk food they'd bought at a gas station minimart on the ride down last night—not a bad way to spend an afternoon, if only she'd been able to keep her mind off the circumstances that had brought her here. Fat chance of that, though: in addition to being in danger herself, there was the threat to her newfound father as well as her godmother (whom she couldn't help being afraid for, no matter how hard she worked at hating her). And of course Daddy Don . . .

That was the worst, the thought that Daddy Don might think she'd abandoned him. As the afternoon wore on, the urge to call him grew stronger. She started edging up the volume on the TV and banging things around to wake up Len, but it was no use: he didn't budge until sunset, a few minutes after five o'clock. Then when he did he dashed straight for the bathroom, so grumpy he wouldn't even return a friendly greeting.

When he came out, however, he was a charmer again. "I'll get right on it," he assured her when she told him she needed to call home. And sure enough, when she emerged from the bathroom after her shower he was shouting at somebody on the other end of the phone: "Put it this way: do you have an illustrated dictionary at hand? . . . Well, if you did, and you looked up *Somebody who gives a shit,* I assure you you would not find my picture. . . . No, no, sir, I don't want to hear any more excuses. I've got someone here who needs a clean line into— . . . Then call me when you do."

There was no one on the other end of the line, of course, but Aldo hung up before Martha was close enough to hear the buzzing. He'd had plenty of time by now to work on his contingencies. Presumably the old biker's body had been discovered last night, and by now they probably knew he hadn't slipped away of his own accord. The first question was, did they suspect Martha? And if so, had the authorities been notified?

Here's where it got complicated. The answers to those two questions would determine the nature of his first contact, but he wouldn't know what they were until after the contact had been made. Quite a conundrum. A catch-22, as the Americans were fond of saying. But until he worked it out, he would continue to stall.

Aldo pursed his lips and shook his head, looked up without meeting her eyes—he'd used Visine, but you could never predict how well it would work. "That was one of the best men in the business. Apparently the taps were placed by some highly sophisticated operatives. It's going to take him a bit longer than he thought, but I think I've lit a fire under him."

"But why? Does anybody know why all this is going on?"

Aldo rubbed his thumb and forefinger together in the universal gesture. "The money, I suspect. Up until they came after you, we couldn't be sure. But Jonas Whistler, your grandfather, is dying. If Jamey drops out of the picture, Jonas will have no heirs. And if you and Selene drop out of the picture, Jamey will have no heirs. What we're trying to learn now is just who will benefit from all the Whistlers dying without heirs. *Qui bono*, as they say in Latin. When we know that, we'll know who's behind it. When we know who's behind it, we'll be able to counterattack. In the meantime, we'll keep you out of sight, your father will keep his head down, and we'll do our best to contact Selene and get some protection for her. By the way, that last time she called you, did she happen to tell you where she was?"

"No. Only that she'd be back soon. But I'm still worried about Daddy Don. How long's all this going to take?"

"Somewhere between a few days and a few weeks."

"I can't wait that long. Daddy Don is dying. He needs me."

Aldo put on a gentle smile, sat down beside Martha on the edge of her bed, patted her hand. "I agree he needs you, but he needs you alive, not dead."

"Then I have to call him."

"And you will, I promise. But until my man can get that line clear, the moment your voice comes over that line, they'll have your location."

"Then we can split right after, and drive someplace else." She reached for the phone on the table between the beds.

He grabbed the receiver from her hand. "Please. Give my man a few hours."

"Just give me the phone, asshole!"

But she'd started to raise her voice; Aldo placed his free hand over her mouth. "I'm afraid I can't do that," he replied regretfully as he pinched her nostrils closed.

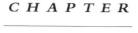

After staying up late talking with Granny Friday night, getting up before dawn on Saturday to hit the rain forest trail with Joe-Pie in search of the elusive stinging mashasha nettle and wild dumbcane, a Caribbean dieffenbachia that flourished only in the deep shade of the upper rain forest, then working with Granny again well into Saturday night doctoring a stick of gum, a long hot shower and then bed were all Selene was thinking about when Rutherford Macintosh delivered her back to the Kings Frederick and Christian Arms shortly before midnight. But as she slipped under the mosquito net it occurred to Selene that she hadn't checked on Martha since Thursday night. Thanks to the time difference, though, it still wasn't too late to call the West Coast. She pulled the phone under the net with her, and dialed Martha's number in Bolinas.

No answer. She gave it a half dozen rings, then hung up and tried Daddy Don's number. Martha's voice came on after four rings: *"Hi. We can't come to the phone right now, but if you'll—"*

A breathless man's voice interrupted the message. "Hello?"

"Hi, who's this?"

"Selene, is that you?"

"Carson?" Carson Young was Don Baechler's partner at the Point Reyes Chopper Shop; he and his wife, Carlene, a registered nurse, had been instrumental in arranging and orchestrating Don's home care.

"Yeah. Did you just call Martha's number?"

"That was me."

"Just missed you. . . . Okay, hold on . . . I gotta catch . . . my breath." Selene waited until he'd finished gasping. Carson was as close to being a chain-smoker as a roll-your-own man could get. "It ain't good news, Selene. It ain't good news at all."

"Daddy Don?"

"Gone."

Selene sighed. "I'm so sorry. But at least he's not suffering any—"

He cut her off. "That ain't all. We got what they call a situation here. Martha called me last night, all mysterious, told me I had to come right over, couldn't tell me why. When me and Carlene got here Don was dead in his bed—still warm, but dead—and Martha was nowhere around."

"Shit no!"

"There's more. Carlene noticed that Don's morphine infuser was wide open—full throttle. She says it couldn't of been an accident—somebody would of had to deliberately jimmy it."

"Somebody? You don't think Martha . . . ?"

"He couldn't of done it himself, not the shape he was in the last couple days. We figure maybe she couldn't stand to see him suffer no more, or maybe he begged her to help him end it, and then after it was over she panicked and ran away."

"Any idea where she might have gone?"

"We spent all day calling her friends, and her friends called their friends. . . . Nobody's heard from her."

"Has anyone gotten the police involved yet?"

"Naah. Carlene replaced the busted drip before we called his doctor, so there wasn't no trouble with the death certificate— they're gonna cremate Monday morning. If she hasn't shown up by then, we'll call in a missing persons."

"No!"

"Why not?"

Selene weighed how much to tell Carson. "You know about that fire up at my place two weeks ago? There's a pretty good chance that the man who set it was the same man who killed Don."

"What the *fuck* is going on here, Selene? What have you got that girl mixed up in?"

"Long story. I'll tell you all about it when I get there. In the meantime, whatever you do, don't call the cops, don't call in any missing persons. And if anybody, anybody at all who you don't know, calls asking any questions about Don or Martha or me or"—she started to say Whistler—"or anybody, you don't know a thing."

"Look, Selene, nobody has to tell *me* twice not to call the cops. It ain't exactly my natural inclination. But I promised Don when this whole tumor thing started that I'd help take care of Martha, and I ain't gonna let him down any worse'n I already did."

"I appreciate that, Carson. I made him the same promise, and I take it as seriously as you do. But you have to believe me when I tell you that right now I'm the best chance Martha has for getting out of this alive. Just sit tight, give me a few days—"

Carson interrupted her again. "Hold on, I just thought of something. If we have Don cremated, and Martha *didn't* do it, then whoever did will end up getting away with it."

Another expensive silence preceded her reply; even bounced off the satellite it had a weighty quality. "Not a chance he gets away with it," said Selene eventually. Then she remembered Jonas. *Or him.* Then, aloud: "W-word of honor."

She'd almost said something else. Caught herself just in time. Waited until Carson was off the line. Said it out loud—to Daddy Don, to Martha, Jamey, Lourdes, baby Cora:

"Witch's Word. You've got my Witch's Word on that—all of you."

ー

Ancient Checker to and from the rain forest Sunday morning. Blue Goose to St. Thomas Sunday afternoon. St. Thomas to Miami Monday morning. Make the connecting flight to San Francisco with minutes to spare. Gain three hours, arrive SFO late afternoon. Shuttle to the long-term parking garage. Find the Jaguar intact—minor miracle. Jaguar starts right up after lying fallow two weeks—major miracle.

Traffic was a bear from Candlestick to the Golden Gate. Selene crossed the bridge in the warm burnished glow of a Pacific sunset, but there was nothing left of the light save a greenish gold band on the far ocean horizon by the time she reached the Coast Highway and joined the conga line of northbound traffic; at each of the switchbacks she could see ahead to the long red line of taillights snaking along the side of Mt. Tam like the fairy-light procession at the end of *Fantasia*.

Selene extinguished her headlights just before turning into the driveway that led past Don's up to her own A-frame, then parked the Jag just past the turn-off so as to block the road up to her place. She left her suitcases in the trunk, and hiked up the rest of the way carrying only her purse and overnight bag. Her house appeared to be empty. She started up the flagstone walk, then circled around the side of the house to peek through the sliding glass door on the patio. Even in the dark she could see that the 'frame, cleaned up by the coven after the fire, had since been ransacked. Her heart in her throat, she walked around to the back door; it swung open at a touch, and as she felt around for the light switch she noticed the red light from her faithful old answering machine on the kitchen counter blinking insistently. Odd, how strongly the sight affected her: it was like being welcomed home by an old friend.

But the rest of the place was an unholy mess. She'd seen ransacked houses before; happened every so often on the outskirts of Bolinas—kids mostly—but the only place she'd ever seen that even came close to this level of thorough destruction had been tossed by cops looking for drugs. Every shelf had been swept clean, every sugar and flour and herb and spice container dumped out on the kitchen floor; books lay in piles in the living room, and the couch cushions had been slit open and were spilling their stuffing guts all over the place. Grimly she grabbed the magnetic flashlight off the refrigerator door and picked her way through the mess, heading straight for the paint-spattered wooden ladder that leaned against the front of the loft next to the charred remains of the old ladder.

A quick probe of the loft with the flashlight revealed another shocker. Her altar stood open and her tools were scattered around. She swept the beam this way and that and located her white-hilted athame and stag's horn chalice lying on the floor to the left of the altar, her thurible and cingulum on the floor to the right. The velvet garter took longer to spot; it had been tossed like a quoit over one of her black candlesticks. But no matter how hard she searched, no matter how desperately she prayed, her Book of Shadows was nowhere to be seen.

Numb with shock, unwilling to take in this new catastrophe, to deal with the possibility that Aldo had been through the book, and now knew the secret of Martha's paternity, Selene retreated down the unanchored ladder and made her way back to the kitchen, where the blinking light of the answering machine on the kitchen counter caught her attention again. She took a closer look. It was one of those clumsy old Code-a-Phones, the kind that gave you a readout of the number of messages since the last erasure (there were currently twelve), but you had to count the light blinks to see how many of the messages had arrived since the last time the machine had been cleared. She counted twice to make sure of the number —blinkblink pause blinkblink pause. Only two.

This was odd, because they should all have been new: she'd cleared the machine before daubing herself with the Fair Lady's ointment, but not since. Unless of course Martha had checked her messages for her. But she'd spoken to Martha half a dozen times and the girl had never mentioned it. Which pretty much left Aldo. She grabbed a pencil and pad from a drawer and pushed the "All" button: this would play both old and new messages in the order received.

She was chewing on the stub end of her pencil by the time the old motor finished rewinding. The first nine messages were from noncoven friends who were wondering where she'd disappeared to; she had just finished jotting down the last of these names when a familiar voice came on the machine, causing her to jam the pencil down so hard the point embedded itself in the pad before breaking off.

"Selene? Are you there? It's Jamey. If you're there, pick up. I haven't much time. It's Tuesday, the . . . what, the second? I'll try to call again."

That was all—but it was enough. Proof positive that Jamey had survived the fire at the Greathouse. Her heart soared, then sank again as she remembered that Aldo had probably heard the message as well. She hit the pause button while she tried to reason this through. Aldo had been trying to kill Whistler, but had failed so far—at least up to the point of the phone call. Then he'd learned that Martha was Jamey's daughter, killed Don, and abducted her. It was good news, in a twisted way. If Aldo had taken Martha hostage, she might still be alive.

Selene unpaused the machine to listen to the two messages Aldo hadn't heard. The first was from Carson—"Call me as soon as you get in: if I'm not home I'll be down the hill"—and pre-dated her contact with him on Saturday night, but the second made her grab for her pencil again and hastily gnaw the broken tip to a point.

"Selene? This is Nick Santos. I have some information about a mutual friend. I don't want to leave you my number—our friend doesn't trust the phones, and we can't either. For the next few nights I'll make it a point to be at the Prince Albert Club at four-oh-four-B Harrison Street between ten and midnight. It's a private club—I'll leave your name at the door."

The events of the past few weeks had evidently rung some profound changes in Selene's psyche; she found herself appreciating the efficiency with which her left and right brains immediately and simultaneously launched themselves upon their contrasting and complementary tasks. (Although which part of her mind was actually doing the appreciating was something of a conundrum—or a koan.)

Ten o'clock, reasoned left brain. *It's seven-thirty now. Take an hour and a half to get to the city, park, find the place . . . suitcases still in the car . . . Don't come back here. Sleep over in the city? Where?*

And while left brain was trying to come up with the name of the quasilegal bed-and-breakfast on Russian Hill owned by Balkis Rosenblatt, high priestess of a San Francisco coven, right brain was trying to make sense of it all. *Nick Santos. Of all people, Nick Santos.* Nick and Jamey had a relationship so complicated that it made Selene and Moll look like Ward and June Cleaver in comparison.

Impeding the efforts of both brain halves was the increasingly more obvious fact that jet lag and exhaustion had Selene's sidereal rhythms totally fubared—fucked up beyond all recognition. It was a term she had learned from Nick, a graduate of the Air Force Academy who'd served as an air force intelligence officer during the Vietnam War. Which, come to think of it, might well have been why Nick was the man Whistler had chosen to contact.

She pictured her body clock having gone *sproing*, springs and hands flying apart like a cartoon alarm clock. But whatever time it was in there, it was *late*, and she was exhausted. And careless: she jotted down the address of the club, then hurried out the back door without remembering to clear the Code-a-Phone. When she got to the Jaguar she took a suitcase out of the trunk, and there in the driveway she changed into jeans, a dark long-sleeved jersey with a silk-screened picture of Hildegarde of Bingen on the front, and a midweight Italian wool blazer she'd purchased during her second layover on St. Thomas. After putting the suitcase back into the trunk, Selene transferred her packet of pins and her pack of Doublemint to the inside pocket of the blazer, and by eight the Jaguar was back on the road.

Selene gassed up in Stinson and cruised back over the mountain on Highway 1. No traffic now; she gunned it for all she was worth, conscious as always of the fact that over the years the twisty cliffside drive had claimed several of her friends and acquaintances, including Connie, and might well claim her too some foggy evening.

But not tonight. Tonight for the first time in days she had real hope; tonight she was a drivin' fool. At least with her left brain; right brain was thinking about Nick Santos. After leaving the service, Nick, a devastatingly handsome gay man, had written a successful vampire trilogy before he even knew he was one (a blood drinker, that is: he claimed he'd always known he was gay, even during a short-lived marriage to a woman), and had moved to the Castro in the early seventies, just as the decadelong party there was gaining steam.

The three of them, Nick, Jamey and Selene, had remained the closest friends and lovers (or at least orgy partners) for another dozen years or so, a period that represented a golden age for the blood drinkers and witches of the Bay area. Selene's coven had formed an alliance with Whistler's Penang (from the Malaysian word for vampire): eight times a year, on lesser and greater Sabbat holidays, her coven and his Penang gathered in orgy.

The golden age had ended abruptly, however, on Yule night in 1987, when Nick overdosed on baby blood and "went werewolf," as the vampires called it. He'd very nearly murdered a witch from the Marin Coven, then tore a hole in Selene's throat with his teeth before drowning the Viscount, one of Whistler's dearest friends, in the icy waters of Lake Tahoe.

All of which might have been forgiven—some vampires just weren't meant to drink baby blood—if Nick, in the throes of remorse, hadn't founded V.A.—Vampires Anonymous—and misused the twelve-step principles in order to destroy the Penang. Nick and his V.A. mates had even gone so far as to kidnap Whistler himself and tie him to his bed for a night and a day to wean him from blood.

In the end, of course, Jamey and Selene had their revenge. Within three years Vampires Anonymous was only a bad memory, and every recovering blood addict who'd survived was now using again. In fact, by the time Whistler married Lourdes and moved to Santa Luz, even Nick had fallen off the wagon.

True, he was only drinking blood on weekends the last time Selene had seen him, but according to the rumor mill (aka Catherine Bailey), Nick had fallen on hard times of late: The Reverend Betty Shoemaker of the Church of the Higher Power in El Cerrito, another vampire, who'd conceived a baby with Nick through artificial insemination, had gone back into recovery, then eighty-sixed Nick from her and their child's lives when Nick refused to do the same.

The last Catherine had heard, Nick had given up his career as a systems analyst specializing in network security, moved back into the city, and begun hanging out with the "body art" crowd, a pierced, scarified, tattooed bunch who dwelled in San Francisco's SoMa—South of Market—partying and poking holes in themselves as the millennium came crashing to a close.

—

The Prince Albert Club was located above a leather bar across the street from the famous End Up bar. Apparently Catherine was right about Nick's current companions, for the doorman at the top of the stairs to whom she shouted Nick's name was pierced several times through both ears, both nostrils, and his tongue, and his nipples were bared to show their rings—and yet when he leaned over to unhook the velvet rope that barred the entrance, he had the nerve to give *Selene* a weird look. She winked and pointed to her crotch. "Both labes," she whispered; he nodded approvingly as she passed by him into a dark room—the only lights were the deep blue neon tubes framing the mirror behind the bar, and tiny hooded lamps at each of the Lucite café tables circling the dance floor.

Selene sat down at an empty table over by the far wall, trying not to wince at the sight of so much cruelly pierced flesh.

"Hi."

She looked up: Nick was sitting across from her. Dark brown hair cropped close; silver nose stud; from his left ear a Greek cross hung nearly to his shoulder; his earlobe had stretched like Silly Putty. And yet if she'd had to describe him to a friend, the words *divinely handsome* would still have to be in there somewhere.

"Hi Nick." She cocked her head. "Something's different—"

He started to laugh.

"No, not just— I've got it! You shaved off your mustache."

To her surprise his otter brown eyes misted up. "Who else would see past all this"—he gestured to his hardware—"to remember my Magnum P.I. mustache?" She could barely hear him. "You *are* an old friend, aren't you? There aren't many left, except the vampires."

Because only the vampires were immune to AIDS. She filled in the subtext, then took his hand across the table. "How's it going, Nick?"

"I've still got my money and my blood, and I'm making new friends as fast as the old ones are dying, so it could be worse."

Selene winced. "Don't say that. Things always get worse when you say that."

Nick leaned forward abruptly. "You know why we're here?" She started to say *Jamey*, but he stopped her with an upward flicker of his forefinger. "I saw him yesterday. He's either unbelievably paranoid, or else someone's trying to kill him."

"Oh, somebody's trying to kill him all right." Selene filled Nick in as best she could without mentioning Martha, interrupting herself once while the waiter took their drink orders, and once again when he returned, clanking, with Selene's Anchor Steam and Nick's Absolut.

Nick sighed more than once during the telling of her tale; he sighed again when she had finished. "In a way, that's almost better than what I was thinking, which was that he'd gone completely bonkers. It also explains the rest of his instructions. I have a number to call if you and I made contact; he'll call me back, and I'm to call you with instructions for meeting him."

But the deejay had just switched the dance music from Gothic death rock to ear-splitting Industrial. Nick had to beckon Selene forward and shout the rest directly into her ear. "After I speak to him, I'll get back in touch with you about the next step."

"I have to know, Nick," she called into his ear. "Is he still nearby?"

"I don't know. It's a local number, but that doesn't mean anything nowadays. Why, what's up?"

"There's a complication even Jamey knows nothing about."

"What?"

"I can't tell you until I've told him. Just let him know that we don't have any time to waste—there's a third life in danger."

"I'll call the number as soon as I can, and relay the message.

When he gets back to me I'll call you. Where are you going to be?"

Selene thought about it. "Maybe I'd better not tell you, just in case."

He nodded. "Your tradecraft's better than mine. How about if you call me first thing tomorrow morning?"

"Sounds like a plan."

He jotted his number on a napkin and slipped it into her hand under the table.

"What's the earliest I can call you?" she asked.

"Depends on whether I get lucky tonight. Say noon, just to be safe. Can I get you another drink?"

"No thanks, dearie." She rose. "I'm totally wiped—I'd better get this body to bed."

"Mother knows best," he said. "You take care of yourself, Selene."

"You do the same, Nick."

"Don't I always?" he said.

7

By the time Sunday evening arrived, Aldo was distinctly horny. Part of it was due, no doubt, to the period of time that had elapsed since his last sexual encounter, but the rest was the result of having Martha so completely under his control without trusting himself to have sex with her. It was important to know one's own weaknesses, Aldo thought. That first touch, for instance, when he had dropped her by shutting off blood flow to her brain for a few seconds, had been so delicious that he knew if he ever got his hands around her throat a second time he wouldn't be able to let go.

But he needed her alive, at least until he had snagged Whistler and the witch. After that she would be delightfully expendable— and he would be even hornier. But until then he would treat her not as an attractive young female, but as an object of potential value, he decided, and so kept her bound and gagged all Saturday night, allowing her only a little water and a visit to the toilet before he retrussed her and swallowed his customary handful of sleeping pills Sunday morning.

But no friendly contact. After waking up Sunday at sunset he let her have another sip of water and a pee, tied her up again, wrapped her in a blanket, stuffed her into the trunk of the Toyota, then drove her back through the night to San Francisco, where he found a motel on Lombard Street that would meet his new requirements—a parking space right outside the door, and the door facing a blank wall, in this case the back of a neighboring motel.

Even better, the Emperor Norton Motor Hotel had two ad-joining rooms available. Not that Martha would be getting a room of her own, but this would solve a potential problem: he could transfer the girl into the second room while the maid cleaned the first, and then back again without anybody getting suspicious, as sometimes happened if you stayed someplace more than two days without allowing the room to be made up.

And while Aldo had no idea how long he might need to stay, he figured that two days was the absolute minimum. So once he had Martha safely installed he loosened her bonds, and even had pizza and soda delivered to the other room. By the time they reached an understanding—that she was not to scream, strike out, or even raise her voice—the pizza was cold. But she was a smart girl; she only had to see the lit match, not feel it.

He let her good behavior earn her other privileges during the course of the night: as long as Aldo was in the room, Martha could have her bonds and gag loosened; he even let her handle the remote control for the TV. And while he wouldn't let her close the door to the bathroom when she had to pee, he promised not to peek.

He called housekeeping and had the rooms made up early Mon-day morning. Martha was most cooperative during the necessary room switching, and understanding when Aldo explained that he had to bind and gag her again while he slept in the other room. But he did allow her to lie on her back again, with her arms tied in front of her and the remote control in her hand. She seemed suitably grateful; another few days and the dynamic that binds victim to kidnapper would be fully in force: the kid would be eating out of his hand. And perhaps vice versa.

Aldo slept through the day, shared a Chinese dinner with the girl that was really quite good for take-out food, then tied her up on her back again, after allowing her to use the bathroom. "Un-fortunately," he explained, expertly adjusting her gag, "I can't let you keep the remote control."

She growled something unintelligible; he answered her confidently. "What do I think you might do with it? Why, you might turn up the volume until someone came to complain. You're a clever girl, you know—just not quite as clever as Len Patch. Tell you what I will do, though—I'll let you choose a channel before I leave. Blink for the channel you want . . . one, two . . . Channel two? Are you sure?" He clicked the channel select. *The Simpsons* was on.

"Ah, cartoons," said Aldo, adjusting the volume, then slipping the remote into his pocket on his way out. "How delightful." He meant it, too: in cartoons when you strangled somebody their eyeballs popped out on springs; then they recovered and you got to do it all over again.

—

Aldo had no way of knowing in advance that Selene was back. In fact, he hadn't expected much of this first night; he figured he'd set up a decent blind somewhere where he could watch the place, then set a few booby traps before he left—nothing she'd notice— just enough to tell him the next night whether she'd arrived during the day.

But for a man who'd arrived without much expectation, Aldo was frightfully upset when he discovered (after parking the Toyota down the hill and hiking all the way around through the woods again) that not only had she been there, but that he'd just missed her—the bulb over the back door was still warm. He stalked angrily into the kitchen, glanced around. It looked about the same as it had the last time he'd left it, except for . . .

Ah, but this was going to be almost too easy. The message pad next to the answering machine bore the faint imprint of a note that had been jotted on the previous sheet. All he could make out was a capital *N*—if he had to he might be able to bring up the rest with a graphite rubbing. But perhaps she hadn't erased the phone message yet. He tried to remember how this particular device worked. Last time it had been blinking; he recalled the red light in the darkness. Now the light was steady, and the counter was at 12 where previously it had read 10. He pushed rewind, then fast-forwarded through the first ten messages, gritting his teeth when Whistler's voice came over the machine sounding like a chipmunk—just what he needed, a cartoon reminder of his earlier failure. But then he reached the last two messages, and . . . how did they say it here? Ah yes: *Bingo!*

Once again Aldo had been blessed with the luck of the devil. And sheer luck it was—Aldo was well aware that he'd screwed up nearly every aspect of the job. First Whistler had somehow escaped the holocaust at the Greathouse, then Selene and the A-frame had both survived essentially intact; now a Chinese dinner had caused him to miss the striga by minutes. And yet here he was cruising back across the Golden Gate Bridge with La Divina's voice soaring from the Toyota's six speakers, and things were definitely looking up. Whistler *père* was in Aldo's debt (or under his thumb, as circumstances dictated), and might not have to learn that Whistler *fils* was still alive; Whistler *petite fille* was safely stashed away; Godmother Selene, to whom Aldo owed so much (and none of it good), would be waiting for him at the other end of this enchanting span; and best of all, so would the one man in the world who apparently knew how to contact Jamey Whistler.

Aldo grinned. It was enough to shake the Dalai Lama's belief in karma.

⬥

For all his air force intelligence training, the truth was that the former Captain Santos was now nearly fifty, perpetually stoned to the gills not only on blood but on whatever other drugs struck his fancy (and his was an easily stricken fancy), and hadn't actually worked in Intelligence since the sixties.

So it wasn't surprising that his tradecraft was a little rusty. For instance, while it was true that the Prince Albert was a private club, it was also true that to qualify for membership all one needed was the sponsorship of a current member, a hundred a year in dues, and a cover charge of ten bucks a night. Nor was the sponsorship a major obstacle: the doorman was a member. A needy member— Aldo slipped him fifty and was in like Flynn, with the sneaking suspicion that a twenty probably would have done the job just as well.

Having finished the last of the unfortunate Mt. Tam hitchhiker's blood in the car before entering the club, Aldo was high enough that neither the dimness nor the crowded dance floor was more than a momentary distraction. He spotted Selene almost immediately at the table by the far wall, conversing with a brown-haired man he took to be Nick. The brown hair he took to be Grecian Formula.

As far as he knew, Selene had never actually seen Aldo. He could have sworn she'd never opened her eyes Halloween evening. But then, he also could have sworn she was dead, so although he was now the darker-haired, goateeless (and much better looking, in his opinion) Len Patch, he didn't want to take a chance on her spotting him. Slowly he began working his way across the dance floor, taking such pains to keep his back turned that when he was finally close enough to eavesdrop he saw that Nick was now sitting alone. Selene had slipped away from the table. He looked around wildly, and caught a glimpse of graying hair descending the staircase by the entrance. "Goddamn it to hell!"

"Something wrong?" The brown-haired man was staring up at him with mild concern.

Aldo was torn. His gut instinct was to follow Selene, but his gut had been unreliable lately. The book said that when two subjects diverge, the operative goes with the one he knows to be closer to the source. He knew for sure Nick knew how to contact Whistler; the man might or might not have informed Selene. And it might or might not be a very unprofessional thirst for revenge that was urging Aldo to follow her.

He smiled down at Nick; the decision had all but been made for him. "Wrong? Nothing a little good company couldn't cure."

Nick laughed and gestured to the empty chair. "Have a seat."

Aldo sat down. "I thought you were with the lady."

"Just an old friend." He offered Aldo a cigarette.

"I also thought you could get strung up for smoking in this

town," said Aldo in the regionless, accentless diction of the television. He didn't want to pretend to be a Californian; he had the accent down, but not all the contexts—good enough for social, but not prolonged, contact. On the other hand a British accent might sound an alarm with the man, especially if he had Whistler on the brain.

"Private club," Nick replied. "Of course, if somebody complained . . ."

"Not *this* somebody." Aldo leaned over to light Nick's cigarette with his vintage Zippo. "By the way, I'm Len."

"Nick."

A waiter with a chromed-steel replica of a Fiji Island nose bone arrived while they were shaking hands, placed a fresh Absolut in front of Nick without being asked, and returned with Aldo's Stoli and a clean ashtray before they had finished their cigarettes. It didn't take Aldo long to figure out why the service was so snappy: Nick paid the fellow with a ten, then tipped him another five.

"So where you from?" asked Aldo. It was always best to be the first to ask that question, at least if you weren't planning to tell the truth in return.

"Detroit. You?"

"Know anything about the Miami area?" Aldo had spent enough time there to fake it if the answer was yes. (Ceaușescu and Castro had formed a short-lived alliance after Romania distanced itself from Russia and briefly became the darling of the Western democracies. The Cubans helped the Romanians inside the USSR; the Third Branch sent Aldo to Miami, which was too hot for most of the known Cuban operatives. On the international scene it was the equivalent of two paupers trading favors, but not so for the Cuban exiles Aldo dispatched during his several visits.)

"Not really."

"Lucky you."

"I hear the weather's nice."

"Sure. If you can tolerate sunlight." Aldo could sense the shift in the intensity of Nick's concentration. He wasn't sure whether he wanted Nick to turn out to be a blood drinker—it would make the pickup easier but the rest of the job more difficult—but it was something he would need to know in advance. Unfortunately there was no vampire equivalent of a Masonic handshake through which one blood drinker might identify himself to another—just this clumsy mutual feeling-out process.

"Not me," replied Nick. "Hurts my eyes."

"Me too, depending on what I've been drinking the night before—other than vodka, that is."

"*What* you've been drinking?" asked Nick. "Or who?"

Their eyes met across the table. "Who," replied Aldo. "Or is it whom?"

And the deal was done.

‹

Aldo was a tourist; Nick lived nearby. Aldo had little blood, Nick had a fridge full. Your place or mine, therefore, was not a question that needed to be asked. They walked the six blocks to Nick's apartment on Folsom Street. It was a cold night, but neither man wore a coat. As soon as they were inside the apartment they embraced; Aldo reached up and felt Nick's nipple rings through the thin fabric of his designer T-shirt. "Where else are you pierced?" he whispered throatily. It would have been better, he knew, to get started right away—tie him up first, before he was high on blood —but sometimes a dude just had to listen to his dick, especially here in California.

"You'll find out," replied Nick, turning away and making straight for the kitchen. Aldo took off his black pullover—he too was wearing a black T-shirt under it—and tossed the sweater over the back of the chrome-and-leather sling couch. The apartment itself may have been a dive, but the furnishings were expensive; the overall effect was an amalgam of Art Deco and *nostalgie de la boue*, slapped together with a little too much money and not quite enough panache.

Aldo followed Nick into the kitchen and watched him pouring

238 ■ JONATHAN NASAW

back in an instant; throwing a forearm choke hold around Nick's throat from behind, he rendered him unconscious in seconds, then stripped the coaxial cable from the TV and used it to bind his victim securely.

———

Nick opened his eyes. The blindfold had been removed. He was lying on his back looking up at Aldo; it took him only a few seconds of straining against the cable that bound him to understand that further struggle was pointless. He opened his mouth to scream, and Aldo, as if waiting for a cue, quickly jammed a handkerchief into it.

"Let's not waste time, shall we?" said Aldo, who was dressed again. "I'm here about Jamey Whistler."

Nick's eyes widened; he tried unsuccessfully to speak.

"Don't try to talk—just listen. I intercepted your message to Selene this evening, so I already know that you know how to contact the man. I tell you this just in case you were planning to try to bullshit me. Now what I need to know is how I can contact him myself. This you will tell me."

Aldo was vaguely aware as he spoke that his speech patterns were degenerating now that there was no further need for pretense. "The only question is, how much pain will you wish to endure before telling me? Personally, I'm quite sated sexually, so I have no particular interest in prolonging your agony. What do you say you make this easy on yourself?"

Nick took a minute to think about it, then nodded slowly and rolled his eyes down toward the wadded handkerchief stuffed into his mouth. Aldo reached in and pulled it out. Nick spat and coughed while Aldo waited patiently.

"Well?"

"I just wanted—" But Nick's voice was a hoarse croak. Aldo held a glass of water to his lips; Nick took a sip, then tried again. "I just wanted to let you know that you were absolutely the worst lay I ever had. You're hung like a gerbil and you kiss like a flounder."

"Are you quite through?" asked Aldo.

blood from a Clamato jar into two fluted champagne glasses. He took the glass Nick handed him and perched on one of the two high stools over by the counter. Silently they raised their glasses to each other before they drank; afterward they chatted while they waited for the stuff to come on. "To tell you the truth," said Aldo, "I don't know much about piercing. I've seen a few nipple and navel rings in my time, but as for the more extreme, er, extremities, I—"

Nick interrupted. "Before you say anything you're going to regret, I should inform you that I have a gold Prince Albert."

"I was about to say, I'd love to see some," said Aldo, reaching toward Nick's crotch. He had no idea what a Prince Albert was, but was willing to hazard a guess as to where one might be found.

———

There was nothing quite like sex between—or among— vampires. Gay, straight, lesbian—all the customary sexual self- identifications blurred on blood, or overlapped, or succeeded one another, until all that was left was pure lust, mental, physical, and emotional. At one point they even had a round of consensual stran- gulation sex, during which Aldo achieved his only orgasm of the evening.

As for the Prince Albert contraption that pierced Nick's glans, Aldo found it interesting but not compelling. Gradually he steered their lovemaking toward the bondage domain. First he let Nick bind him with velvet ropes from the bottom drawer of his bedside table, which had proved to be a veritable treasure chest of sexual para- phernalia. And after Nick had finished having his way with Aldo, he was more than willing to trade roles. The rest was embarrassingly easy. Aldo rolled Nick over onto his stomach and bound his wrists securely with the velvet rope—or as securely as velvet can bind a man on blood. Then came the blindfold, and as soon as that was in place it was but the work of a moment to yank the handy ex- tension cord out of the wall and whip it several times around Nick's wrists. Nick started to shout and buck, but Aldo was on the man's

"Not quite," said Nick; then he opened his mouth as wide as he could and began to scream.

The rest happened fast. Aldo jammed the handkerchief back into Nick's mouth; with a desperate gulp and a sudden convulsive intake of breath Nick managed to swallow the wadded-up cloth deep enough to completely block his breathing passage. Aldo quickly thrust his right hand as far as he could into Nick's mouth in an attempt to remove the handkerchief; he'd just gotten hold of it with the tips of his three middle fingers when Nick bit down as hard as he could. Now it was Aldo's turn to scream; he smashed down on the bridge of Nick's nose with his other fist, and kept smashing until Nick's jaws loosened.

Aldo yanked his hand free. His fingers had been bitten through to the bone both front and back just above the bottom knuckle; blood was spurting all over the bed. With an oath he grabbed the sheet from Nick and quickly tied a tourniquet around his wrist. Not an easy job, one-handed; he used his teeth to tighten the knot until the bleeding had stopped.

Nick's body, meanwhile, was flopping like a fish as he choked on the handkerchief. He was already unconscious from Aldo's pounding, but his penis had gone erect all the same, sending Prince Albert bobbing into the air one last time as the dying man achieved a final ejaculation before flopping over onto his side.

A heroic death, all things considered. Nick must have known it, too, because barely discernible beneath the bloody pulp into which Aldo had smashed Nick's face was the faint suggestion of a victorious smile.

8

Selene spent the night in a comfortable, if somewhat fussily deco-rated, room at Balkis's bed-and-breakfast on Russian Hill. Buoyed by the prospect of hooking up with Jamey, she slept soundly for a change, untroubled by dreams, and awoke at nine on Tuesday. The morning crawled by. At noon precisely she dialed Nick's number and reached his answering machine. She hid her annoyance with a joke. "Nick, this is Selene. It's twelve o'clock—do you know where *you* are? I'll call again in twenty minutes."

And twenty minutes after that, and twenty minutes after that, and then every hour until Nick's machine was no longer accepting messages. Shortly after four Selene packed her suitcases, loaded up the Jag, and drove back to the Prince Albert. The street door was locked; eventually she heard a "Hold on, hold on," from the top of the stairs, and the door was opened by a thoroughly pierced janitor-type young man who announced that he didn't know Nick from dick, but if she came back at seven when the club opened maybe the doorman or the bartender would be able to help her.

Selene spent most of the next two hours driving around the city, revisiting her old haunts. The basement apartment at Page and Central in the Haight; the Broadway house she'd finally sold at the height of the real estate boom in the eighties; Jamey's old Queen

Anne in Noe Valley; the Castro district where she used to hang out with Nick. She returned to the Prince Albert a few minutes shy of seven, but the doorman was in place, and remembered her. He also remembered whom Nick had left with, but his description didn't ring a bell with Selene. She asked him where Nick lived; he told her he couldn't give out that sort of information. "It's an emergency," she replied coldly. "If you'd like, I can make it a police emergency."

The address was then forthcoming, but as she approached the building on Folsom Street she began to suspect she'd heard the doorman wrong; surely Nick Santos would never have lived in such a dump. Yet there was his last name next to one of the three buzzers: apartment 301. She pressed the button. Waited. Pressed again. And again and again, then pressed the button for 201.

"Yes?" A man's voice over the intercom.

"It's an emergency—I'm looking for Nick."

"Ring his fucking bell then." The intercom went dead.

She rang 201 again. "I have been. No answer. Do you know where he is?"

"How the hell should I know?" was the reply. "Lady, life ain't a sitcom and I ain't the wacky neighbor. Welcome to the big city."

Silence over the intercom again. This time Selene leaned on the buzzer until 201 was sputtering at her again. When he quieted down she released the button. "You can either give me five minutes of your time or you can call the cops and swear out a complaint, which'll take a lot longer, and be a lot more trouble in the—"

But the peephole at the street door had darkened; a moment later the door swung open, and Selene found herself staring up at a burly bearded man in a frilly housecoat. One of those "only in San Francisco" moments. Selene was more than up to the challenge. "I'm so sorry to bother you," she said without batting an eye. "But I'm afraid something's happened to Nick."

He narrowed his eyes. "I didn't let you in," he said as he stepped aside just far enough for her to squeeze through. He then trotted up the stairs ahead of her, darted through the door to 201, and locked it behind him.

Wacky neighbor? thought Selene, hurrying past his door and up the second flight of stairs to the third floor. *Heaven forbid!* She knocked. "Nick?" And again. "Nick, it's Selene. Are you in there?" She tried the thumb-latch door handle, and was surprised when it yielded with a gratifying *ca-chunk*; the door swung open; Selene darted inside and locked it behind her.

The first thing that hit her was the smell of shit. It wouldn't be accurate to say that she knew what she was going to find before she found it, but on some level she must have, because her body more or less went on automatic pilot while her mind spun off into orbit. *He's just stuck on the pot. Montezuma's revenge—no wonder he couldn't answer the door.* Then, as she passed the kitchen area and saw the champagne glasses with the telltale red thread in the stems. *Hot date, hunh, Nicky?*

When she reached the bedroom door, whatever protective instinct was guiding her at the moment told her to keep her eyes down, not to look at the bed just yet. Bad enough that the hardwood floor was spattered with dried blood and the shit smell was so strong she was ready to retch even before she caught sight of Nick's body jackknifed onto its side with its back to her.

But she didn't; she swayed, she gulped, and yes, she called out to some power for strength as she forced herself to approach the bed. She couldn't take it in all at once; she started at the ankles bound with black cable, saw the thighs and buttocks smeared with caked feces, the hands bound behind the small of the back with the same black cord.

Her mind took one last irrelevant leap: *It's like a joke. He was doing b & d and the other guy left him tied up and he shit himself and he's embarrassed to say anything. . . .*

By then, however, she was close enough to see the edge of the pulpy mess the murderer had made of Nick's face, and denial was no longer an option. It was at that point that she realized she was not alone, that a man was now standing in the doorway behind her.

Panic flooded her as she spun around, but it was relief that sent her to her knees. Then Jamey Whistler was kneeling in front of her and his arms were around her. Words were not possible—or necessary. She began to sob into the familiar hollow of his shoulder; soon his shirt was wet with her tears, and her hair with his.

9

Aldo's trip to the emergency room had cost him nine hundred and
seventy-nine dollars—payable by credit card, fortunately—for
twenty-four sutures, eight in each of the three middle fingers of his
right hand, four above and four below, and an additional eighty
bucks at the all-night pharmacy for Len Patch's Percodan prescription. He'd discarded the prescription for antibiotics, despite the doctor's warnings about the septic possibilities of human bites, because
Aldo knew that as long as he had an ample supply of human blood,
taken orally, he'd heal swiftly, and infection free.

And blood he had; after stanching the wounds in Nick's apartment with pressure, then loosening the tourniquet, he had filled a
pillowcase with several of Nick's Clamato juice jars, none of which
contained Clamato juice, as well as a .38-caliber revolver he'd found
hidden in a cigar box in the bottom of Nick's bedside drawer.

Aldo was not in a mood to take any lip from his teenage charge
when he returned to their rooms on Lombard Street with less than
an hour to spare before dawn. Fortunately, she was asleep. Also
fortunate: their room was just down the hall from the ice machine.
It took him a dozen or so trips to fill the tub in the other
bathroom—clumsy going, one-handed—but by sunrise he had the
Clamato jars on ice. He then washed down three Percodans with a
water glass full of blood and retired to the other bedroom to watch

television. He'd rather have slept, but while he could never sleep on blood, neither could he heal as fast as he was going to need to without it.

Percodan and blood, however, proved to be a mellow combination; within an hour Aldo was pain free, and even in the mood for a chat. He wandered into the next room and found the girl awake. Her gray eyes were wide above the towel that held her gag in place, but she wasn't struggling. A good sign. He untied her, hand and foot, ungagged her, and let her take her toothbrush and toothpaste into the bathroom with her.

After everything Martha had endured—the unimaginable shock of being strangled back in Monterey, waking up trussed like a chicken, being stuffed into the trunk of the Toyota, spending that first day on the bed in the new motel, channel surfing frantically because she couldn't keep her attention focused on anything but the horror of it all for longer than a few seconds, and then, just when she thought it couldn't get any worse, being abandoned, half-suffocated, all night—after all this, being allowed to brush her teeth was like a day at the beach. "Can I take a shower too?" she called through the open door.

"I'd have to come in," he replied from the bed.

She checked out the shower curtain—flower patterned but transparent. "Never mind, then."

"I've already seen you in the buff, you know," he informed her. "You and your friends, in the hot tub the other night."

How long had he been watching her? she wondered, as she managed a shaky wisecrack. "See anything you haven't seen before?" It was a favorite line of Aunt Connie's.

"I'm really not in the mood for banter," he called back, not unpleasantly—these Percs really were quite good. "If you want a shower, I need to be there."

She rinsed her mouth out, then kept the water running while she looked around the bathroom for something she might use as a weapon. Maybe she could . . .

What? Soap him to death? She could feel the panic creeping up on her again. She stared into the mirror, into her own eyes. *Keep him happy, give him what he wants. Anything you can do to live is better than dying.* Then she remembered that she was a fully initiated witch now. *Besides, you have to stick around for the revenge.* She was grasping at straws, and knew it, but the option seemed to be a total and utter freak-out. "Okay, whatever."

Aldo wondered whether the sight of her might prove too tempting. He wasn't particularly horny, not after Nick at night (a good nineties American cable TV pun—Aldo gave himself a mental pat on the back), but he didn't want to leave her alone either. He thought of a compromise. "Let the shower curtain get steamed up, then call me when you're in."

Good decision, for once. The outline of her slim youthful body through the steamy curtain certainly proved pleasant enough, but not too arousing; it was like the soft-core porn on the so-called adult pay-per-view channels. "How old are you?" he called over the noise of the shower.

"Seventeen." She had donned the little plastic shower cap—dreads got better the less you washed them.

"Almost old enough to model. Ever consider it?"

She turned off the water. "Gimme a break. I'm not near pretty enough—or tall enough."

"For porno shots, I meant. You'll soon be the perfect age for that."

Despite her earlier admonitions to her mirrored self, Martha was starting to feel awfully weird about the turn things were taking. "Hand me a towel, would you?" she called shakily.

But he was a perfect gentleman again—he reached a bath towel around the curtain without peeking. Martha stepped out of the shower with the towel wrapped around her. Then she noticed that her clothes had disappeared. "What am I supposed to wear?" she asked him.

"That will do nicely," was his reply. He'd decided there was no sense denying himself a few innocent pleasures, not after the terrible traumas he'd been through recently.

—

Another compromise: for Aldo, knowing that the girl was naked under the bedclothes with her wrists and ankles bound was enough of a kick without being too much of a provocation. For Martha, the fact that he had let her keep the towel on until he had finished tying her up and covering her with the sheet gave her at least a breath of hope that he wasn't going to rape her after all.

He was even being a little kind, the way he had been the first night when he told her he cared about her. "Any pain?" he asked her when she was nicely tucked in.

"Only my arms and legs and back and neck and my shoulders from being tied up all—"

"Say no more." He patted her on the knee, went into the next room, and returned with a glass of ice water and a yellow tablet.

"What's that?" she asked.

"Percodan. Pain pill. Here." He brought it right up to her mouth; she kept her lips closed firmly while she thought about it. What if he was drugging her? Then it occurred to her: if you're going to get raped and murdered, you might as well get doped up first. She opened her mouth and swallowed; tenderly he held the glass to her lips and allowed her as much water as she wanted; even after the pill was down she gulped so greedily that the cold water gave her an ice-cream headache.

It took the Percodan about twenty minutes to start coming on. When Aldo returned from the other room to see how she was doing, she found herself feeling rather chatty. "What happened to your hand?"

"I was trying to save a fellow's life. Somehow he'd swallowed a handkerchief; I was trying to unblock his breathing passage and he bit me."

"But why—"

"Don't ask."

Martha was beginning to understand why the bikers liked pain pills so much. It wasn't just that they made the pain go away, it was that they replaced it with the mellowest feeling. *God's in his heaven and all's right with the world,* Carson Young used to say when he was kicked back and stoned. She thought of something: "Hey, could I have the remote back?"

"Soon, sweetheart. But first there are a few things we need to talk about."

"Like what?"

"Like vampires. I'm one, you know. And so is your father."

Whoosh! The good feeling rushed out like air escaping from a party balloon as Aldo pulled one of the motel chairs up close to her head and settled himself in for a bedside chat. *So much for God in his fucking heaven.*

CHAPTER

As if at a signal Selene and Jamey, still kneeling, broke their embrace, drew back, and looked into each other's eyes. A hundred irrelevancies sprang into Selene's mind. That Jamey's gray eyes were darker than she'd remembered—more like his father's. That he was no longer dyeing his hair; it was white now, cropped close with a suggestion of bangs, a Julius Caesar cut that cried out for a laurel wreath. That the furrows in his long meaty cheeks were deep enough to sprout wheat in. That he seemed to have aged more in the last year than he had in the last decade—or had it only been the past few weeks that had done this to him? Which brought her back to the moment, the terrible moment, Nick behind her on the bed, shit smell, blood spatters.

"How long have you been here?" she asked as they rose to their feet.

"Few minutes." Breathing heavily, wiping his face with the back of his hand. "Came in through the kitchen window. Whoever did this left that way. There's a trail of dried blood all the way down the fire escape."

"Do you know who it was?"

"I know fuck-all." But he read it in her eyes. "Wait—do you?"

"His name is Aldo, and he's working for your father."

Selene was already close to overdrawn at the astonishment

bank—Whistler's response wiped out her account entirely: he laughed. "What's that expression? No good deed goes unpunished?"

A ray of unwarranted hope for Selene—she knew it was foolish but found herself writing a little mind-screenplay nonetheless— Jamey one step ahead of them all, an elaborate plan, he'd faked all the deaths. Then she breathed in the smell of Nick and the moment ended. But just in case: "Lourdes and Cora?"

From a distance, though their faces were inches apart: " 'And I only am escaped alone to tell thee.' " There was still a trace of amusement in those narrow eyes. "I always thought that was from *Moby-Dick*. Turns out it's the Book of Job."

She wanted to shake him until the hint of a smile was gone from his lips. "Do you remember Martha Herrick?"

"The little girl who lives down the hill from you? Moll's daughter?"

"She's your daughter too."

A slow shake of the head, a mildly puzzled reply. "I often wondered about the timing. Though Moll never said a—"

"Aldo's got her, Jamey—I'm pretty sure he's got her."

Again his response was not what she'd have predicted, if she hadn't just gone out of the predicting Jamey business. "Ever been fingerprinted?"

She shook her head.

"Did anyone see you come in?"

She explained about the bearded man.

"Then let's get out of here before somebody calls the cops."

"Can we at least cover him up?" She gestured toward Nick's body on the bed without looking at it.

"I'm thinking about the legal implications," said the man who had been weeping into her hair a minute before. "As as of this moment neither of us has committed so much as a misdemeanor. But we will have, if we disturb the scene. I believe we're also required to inform the authorities, but we can always just dial nine-one-one on our way out and leave the phone off the hook."

"Jamey, that's *Nick* over there. We can't just—"

"The hell we can't." The glare in his eyes startled her—not

frightened her: Jamey could never frighten her—but she drew back, and he softened his tone. "I know that's Nick. Rather, that *was* Nick. Nick's dead now, and he's dead because of me. As is everyone else I care about except you. Right now my only concern is getting you away from here before you end up in a similar condition. And we certainly can't help—what was her name?"

"Martha."

"We can't help Martha from the police station."

It didn't take Selene long to think it over. "Door or fire escape?"

"Fire escape."

"Okay then. But Jamey?"

"What?" He had already started for the kitchen.

"It wasn't because of you that all those people died. It was because your father hired that man to kill them."

"Chain chain chain," he replied without turning around. "Chain of goddamn fools."

━

Considering the state of San Francisco's emergency response system—disrepair bordering on collapse—it was not surprising that after dialing 911 and leaving the phone off the hook, Selene and Jamey had time to slip out the window, sneak down the fire escape and up the alley, link elbows out on Folsom Street and stroll casually (or as casually as they could manage) for two or three blocks, then double back toward Harrison Street before they heard the first siren in the distance.

"Where have you been staying?" she asked him, tossing him the keys as they reached the Jaguar. She had already summarized her travels for him—she was getting awfully good at it—and told him all she knew about Aldo—not much, beyond the physical description she and Joe-Pie had stitched together. Then she realized that was obsolete; all they had to go on now was the Prince Albert doorman's roughest of sketches. Medium height, brown hair and 'stash. No apparent tattoos or piercings.

"With an encampment of homeless down by the Embarcadero."

"That accounts for the outfit." Jamey was clad in filthy denim jeans and jacket, like the goofy Reverend Jim from *Taxi*. "Are you broke, or just hiding out?"

"Both. Couldn't access any of my credit cards. They're all billed through the trust, and my father was the first man I suspected."

"So how have you been getting by?"

"By the skin of my teeth." He opened the passenger door for her. "But that's over now. No more hiding."

She leaned over and unlocked his door. "What do you mean?"

"I mean we need to be found," he explained as he climbed behind the wheel. "Contacted, rather. What other earthly use could this Aldo have for the girl? Or for you, for that matter? I'm sure they planned to use you both to get to me. When Jonas lost you, the other chap snatched Martha. And somehow he knew about Nick, too. Do you think he followed you to the club last night?"

"I don't—" But Selene stopped herself in mid-sentence. She did know. "Oh god, oh fuck, I forgot to erase the answering machine! The address of the club was on it, the time he'd be there— everything." Selene turned toward the passenger side window; she couldn't have faced Christ himself at such a moment. "It's my fault, Jamey. I might as well have killed Nick myself—I led that bastard right to him."

"If I may paraphrase one of my most reliable advisers?" One of Jamey's long-fingered hands patted her knee; she looked down and saw that his fingernails, which he'd always kept exquisitely manicured, were filthy, gnawed, and broken. "You didn't kill him, Selene. The man my father hired to kill me killed him. Can you access your answering machine from another phone?"

"No, but I'm pretty sure I forgot to erase—"

"That's not what I meant. If this Aldo knows your number, knows you're getting your messages there, that's probably how he'll be trying to contact you now."

"I could call Carson, ask him to check for—"

"No!" Again, after startling her with his vehemence he softened his voice. "It was bad enough losing Nick like that—let's not get any more of our friends involved. From here on in, it's just the two of us."

Funny, how she'd once longed to hear those words. "Are we heading for Bolinas?" she asked as the Jaguar pulled away from the curb.

He nodded, but did not speak again for several minutes. Then when he began, it was with a description of a recurring dream. . . .

Asleep in the hold of the smuggler's sloop, Whistler had dreamed of Lourdes on the island of Lamiathos the way Hemingway's old fisherman dreamed of the lions on the shores of Africa. Comforting dreams, disturbing dreams. On Lamiathos, Lourdes was alive, dancing on the patio of their villa, while behind her the Aegean glowed deep blue with the promise of false dawn.

He couldn't see Cora. Just as well: Lourdes, dressed only in a sarong, was improvising a sort of bare-breasted Filipina hula, while the Creature awarded her a standing ovation. But Cora was all right, he knew that. Knew with the sort of knowing that came in dreams that she was only sleeping somewhere nearby. Safe. Safe as the night is long.

He turned his attention to his wife. Her hips switched, and set the sarong swaying; her hands made graceful come-hither gestures. As he approached her she lifted her heavy breasts in her palms, hefting them, offering them to him, smiling invitingly but dancing away. He pursued her across the patio, down the stone steps, across the smooth raked sand; she let the sarong slip; in his dream he was high on blood, and heard the soft whisper of the silk as it fell to the sand at her feet. . . .

He had the dream again on Halloween night. The creak of the hatch awoke him from it; the hold was flooded with moonlight.

"Y'all secured down there, J. W.?" *Jay Dubya*—Buffalo Barry Klein, captain of the sloop, was from Georgia. "Looks like a squall's comin' up—might be some rockin' and rollin'."

"Where are we at the moment, Buffalo?"

Captain Klein stuck his head through the hatch. He had wide-set brown eyes and a shaggy head, wide at the brow, tapering to a narrow chin brush of a beard, hence the name by which Whistler had known him all these years. "Racin' the weather for Virgin Gorda. Figured we'd anchor till she blew over, but it don't look like we're gonna win the race."

"Okay, thanks for the warning."

The hatch closed, leaving him in darkness again. Whistler checked the bales of marijuana around him—they all seemed to be tied down securely enough—and leaned back against the curving wall of the hull. He sighed for his fading dream, but understood that it would have ended soon enough anyway, shortly after Lourdes dropped her skirt and danced into the darkening Aegean. For he'd had the dream twice before, and hadn't caught up to her either time.

Despite knowing better, despite knowing how much it would hurt, he allowed himself to think about his daughter, to remember Cora on Lamiathos, propelling herself across the patio with a sort of generalized baby wiggle that involved every muscle of her dumpling-shaped body. She was already showing signs of having inherited Lourdes's dramatic coloring; her hair was growing in black, and her eyes were turning a grave, thoughtful brown.

There, see, it didn't hurt too much to remember. He let himself think back to her first (and last—oh god, and last) birthday in September. The pink dress Selene had sent from California. The black hair long enough by then for a pink ribboned topknot. Cora had reached for the lone candle on the cake, trying to pluck the flame like a flower, flailing angrily when her mother leaned over the high chair and blew it out.

She didn't even know fire was hot. Whistler fought for control, told himself that surely Cora had been sleeping when the flames raged through the Greathouse. But Lourdes—Lourdes had almost certainly been awake at ten in the morning, waiting for him to return from the servants' quarters with his silver flask full of blood. He pictured her sitting on their enormous bed wearing that Victoria's

Secret thingie, powder blue lace and satin that complemented the brown sheen of her skin.

If it hadn't been for that damned thingie—what *was* it?—a chemise? a teddy? Something like that—he'd have to ask Lourdes. . . .

But he couldn't ask her, could he? Whistler felt the next thought creeping up, but was powerless to stop it, to turn his mind's eye away from a scene he hadn't witnessed, but would never forget: Lourdes in the flames, Lourdes in agony. He doubled forward as if he'd been kicked in the belly, and tried to stifle the sobs, but they were coming from too deep inside. Biting his lip to hold them back was like folding the top layer of skin over a deep welling wound. . . .

⟶

"That must have been when I saw you." Selene spoke for the first time since Jamey'd started talking.

He glanced over at her. "Must have been. I only cried that once. . . ."

⟶

After Jamey had cried himself out in the hold of the ship, he drew his knees up and wrapped his arms around them, rocking to and fro like an old Jew at prayer, unable to stop himself from thinking about Lourdes in that blue satin and lace outfit that was a good deal more lace than satin, and not much of either. The Creature, aroused anew when she stretched and yawned, couldn't take its eye off her.

And because it was as much the Creature's willful nature as it was size that had earned Whistler's member its nickname (when he was high, he had little more influence over it than Dr. Frankenstein had over *his* Creature), both Whistler and Lourdes understood full well that there would be no sleep that morning for either of them until it had been laid to rest.

But they had emptied Whistler's flask two hours ago. Lourdes could feel the crash coming on, and informed Whistler, in a tone of voice that Filipinas had used to subjugate Filipinos for centuries, that if he expected her to see to the Creature's needs, he'd better come up with some blood in the next fifteen minutes—"Fresh, not bottled"—or she'd have to down a few ludes and bid him a sweet good night. There were only two cures for the unbearable, unspeakable, soul-deadening depression that accompanied a blood hangover: one was more blood; the other was a good day's sleep, followed by more blood.

Ever obedient, especially when it came to drinking blood and having sex, Whistler ducked under the mosquito net canopy that surrounded the bed, and started out the door. "Not like that," called Lourdes, laughing, pointing. The Creature was poking out through the fly of his striped Dagwood pajamas, the costume for a little game they sometimes enjoyed together.

Whistler looked around the room, and on the floor at the foot of the bed (under Blondie's wig) he found the clothes he'd been wearing the previous night—black button-fly jeans and a vintage brown and black rayon Hawaiian shirt. He dressed, slipped on his watch out of habit, stepped out onto the balcony that ringed the second floor of the Greathouse on three sides, and padded barefoot down the wide curving stone staircase and out the front door of the Greathouse into a dark, cavernous courtyard. Even so late in the morning, not a shaft of sunlight could penetrate the dense rain forest canopy.

This impenetrable canopy, of course, was the major reason the vampires of Santa Luz had selected the centuries-old Danish sugar plantation for their principal dwelling. But for a Drinker even the muted light was far from comfortable. Whistler hurried across the courtyard and around the side of the house to the servants' quarters at the back of the compound.

All the other plantation outbuildings—the mill, the tower, the stables, the factory—had long since crumbled, or been subsumed by the rain forest, but the old slave cottages lined up abutting the high stone wall that enclosed the compound had over the years been remodeled, Luzan fashion, their corrugated roofs (tin or sheets of green fiberglass) raised up on poles, and the walls left open at the top around all four sides for ventilation.

"Josephina?" he called softly at the door of the last cabin. He could have simply peered over the top of the wall, but it would have been considered execrable manners. "Are you at home?"

"Boss?" Pronounced bass, like the fish. A willowy Luzan girl of eighteen, dressed in a long white cotton nightgown, answered the door, scratching her ribs sleepily.

"I'm sorry to bother you so late, m'dear, but Mrs. Whistler and I seem to have run out of blood."

If the girl was annoyed, she managed to conceal it. After all, it was part of her job description. And as an Eldest Drinker, Whistler, who paid well and ruled lightly, was a vast improvement over the late Nanny Eames, who had paid in lashes and ruled by fear. "To drink here, or wack wit?"

"To walk with," Whistler replied—that was Luzan for *to go*. He handed her his flask and watched with interest as she used a razor-edged utility knife to open a tiny vein in the heel of her palm. She evinced no pain; Josephina had been donating blood since infancy, and when she turned thirteen, in a ritual ceremony, Nanny Eames had severed a minor nerve in the girl's left wrist, permanently numbing the heel of her palm and the side of her hand.

When the flask was full, Whistler took it from her; she started to pinch off the wound, but he stopped her, brought the bleeding palm to his lips, and sucked a few drops out before stanching the flow himself. As he did so, Josephina reached down and touched the bulge at the front of his jeans. She knew the Creature well, had known it since she was sixteen. But when she started to unbutton the fly to free it, Whistler shook his head.

"Miss Lourdes'd have me bal's for breakfast, an' your titties for tea," he whispered, in a creditable Luzan accent. The Whistlers only screwed around with the servants during the full-moon orgies that were the centerpiece of the Luzan vampire culture; the rest of the month they attempted to be faithful to each other (in their fashion, which allowed for the occasional threesome—or foursome, or moresome).

But Josephina, who had been conditioned by Nanny Eames to

be aroused by the act of giving blood, deftly continued unbuttoning her employer; when the Creature sprang free she pulled her nightgown up to her neck and lay back on her cot.

"Oh what the hell," said Whistler, checking his watch as he knelt at the foot of the bed. "She gave me fifteen minutes. If I can't bring us both off in ten, child, then shame on me."

"Only ten?" moaned Josephina. The soft pressure of his lips made her squirm. So did the thought of how jealous the other servants would be when they learned she'd had Mr. Whistler all to herself two days before the moon was full.

Not long after that—certainly less than ten minutes—he heard a muffled explosion and jerked his head up from between her thighs. "Did you hear . . . ?" Then he caught a whiff of smoke and jumped to his feet, hopped out the door of the shack still tugging his jeans up, saw the back entrance to the Greathouse in flames, and started around the other way, toward the front of the old plantation house. But before he could turn the corner a hot percussive wind blew him off his feet; a microsecond later, still rolling, he heard the flat *whomp* of a deep basso explosion.

As he struggled to his feet, ears ringing, dazedly trying to figure out whether it had been the propane, the gasoline, or the oil tank that had gone up, the blast was followed by two more, and the point became moot. He was lying on his back looking up at the Greathouse. The back wall was gone—just gone, a ragged, smoking frame; the interior looked like the inside of a crematorium, red flames dancing in a white-hot glow.

Whistler rolled over onto his hands and knees, pushed himself up again. He staggered like a backsliding drunk around the side of the house, but when he reached the courtyard he could see the flames shooting out from a blackened dragon's mouth of a front doorway—the heavy mahogany door had been vaporized. His eyes traveled upward of their own accord and saw the bedroom curtains in flames; upward again to see the red-brown terra-cotta roof tiles beginning to blacken, resisting the flames themselves, but buckling inward as the beams beneath them gave way.

CHAPTER

11

"Damnedest thing, but as I stood there in the courtyard watching the Greathouse go up, my mind was as clear as if I'd been drinking baby blood," Whistler explained to Selene as the Jaguar turned onto Lombard Street, heading toward the Golden Gate Bridge. "With one part of my mind I understood everything: Lourdes, Cora, loss, emptiness. Grief—I realized, standing there, that I'd never truly experienced grief. It transforms everything, you know.

"Then the forest canopy caught, and began raining fire. I covered my head with my arms—still couldn't bring myself to turn away until the heat drove me back. I ran for the slave quarters, turned the corner just in time to see them go up, too. . . ."

But not from the flames. It was a powerful series of explosions that blew each of the huts apart in turn—*boom! boom! boom!* Josephina must have run to her doorway, because when the last hut, hers, went up, it blew her twenty feet in the air. Whistler saw her flying, heard the thump when she hit the ground, but by then he was ducking to avoid this new shower of debris, which included jagged shards of tin-roof shrapnel and flaming globs of melting fiberglass.

That's when Whistler understood that all this was not the result of some initial accident, that somehow the compound had been mined or wired or rigged, and was being blown apart building by building. Because he knew those cabins. No propane tanks there, no gas lines, no oil heaters. Only woodstoves. Cooking, heating, all done by woodstove.

Suddenly an odd picture popped into his mind—at least odd when you consider that the sky was at the moment raining sheer hellfire down upon his head. But he had remembered an unusually brisk evening last winter, just after Nanny Eames had died. He had looked out from one of the rear windows and seen a steady stream of servants shuttling armfuls of logs between the cabins and the woodpile stacked against the back wall of the compound. . . .

The woodpile! That stray image proved to be the key to Whistler's survival. For the first time he thought of the ancient Maroon tunnel that Nanny Eames and old Herbert Parrish, the two senior Drinkers, used to talk about. The entrance was said to be under the woodpile, but since the pile was never allowed to fall below the line chalked two feet above ground level along that rear compound wall, neither Whistler nor any other living Drinker had ever seen it.

He wanted to break into a run, but couldn't see for the smoke and dust and falling cinders. He stumbled barefoot through the debris, arms out in front of him, blind man's bluff. Twice he fell, the first time over a smoking chunk of two-by-four, the second time over Josephina's smoldering body. She lay facedown; her back was charred meat with shreds of white cotton nightgown stuck to the raw parts; he didn't bother to turn her over.

The forest canopy was fully engulfed by the time Whistler reached the woodpile. Six feet high and deep, ten feet wide, the top layer already smoking. Jamey snatched his newly filled flask out of his back pocket—it was badly dented from one of his falls, but the silver joins had held—and took a swig for strength, then began heaving wood from the top of the pile with desperate determination. Every so often he had to stop to brush live embers from his hair or back or shoulders; he could feel the heat beginning to build, feel the first stirrings of the firestorm.

He stopped for another swig of Josephina's blood, then redoubled his efforts; the firewood flew like kindling, until at last he'd reached the bottom row. He grabbed the nearest log, couldn't budge it; tried the next, same result. By the time he'd figured out that it was a false bottom, that this last layer of logs was nailed to a heavy trapdoor, the heat had grown so intense that his rayon shirt threatened to burst into flames. With a last desperate heave he hauled the trapdoor open and threw himself down into the cool darkness of the centuries-old Maroon tunnel.

━

"Maroon?" prompted Selene. "As in the color?"

"As in *cimarron*." Jamey rolled down his window to pay the toll, kept it down as they drove onto the bridge. "Spanish for fugitive slaves. Every island in the West Indies with a slave population and a rain forest large enough to hide in had them."

━

The heat drove Whistler on. Behind him the flames roared like traffic on a distant freeway; ahead of him in the unimaginable darkness he could hear the frenzied chittering of rats. It was hard to judge distance in the absolute blackness—not that he had any idea how far the tunnel led, or even if there was a way out at the other end. He counted his paces; after two hundred or so the path took a sharp left—Whistler's outstretched fingers brushed the hard-packed dirt of the tunnel wall just before he would have smacked into it—and began a downward slope that continued for another three hundred paces, leveled out again, continuing on another three hundred steps before taking another sharp bend.

But fifty paces after that the tunnel dead-ended.

━

"So what did you do?" asked Selene as the Jaguar breezed down the Waldo Grade.

Jamey shrugged. "Panicked, of course. Freaked large. But after I'd calmed myself with a swig from my flask, I started feeling my way around the cul-de-sac. The walls were solid dirt, but directly overhead my fingertips brushed what felt like wood. Hoping that it was another trapdoor, I squatted down, jumped straight up with my arms outstretched, hit the board with my palms. It felt as if it had budged just the slightest bit, so I took another whack at it. And another and another, slamming against the board overhead with all my strength, dirt sifting down on my head, until my palms were bleeding and my legs were turning to jelly. Once more, I told myself, and this time I gave it everything I had, and the board shifted, and a crack of sunlight came shooting through and damn near blinded me. I had to retreat all the way back around that last bend in the tunnel before my eyes stopped hurting. But it was well worth the pain to know there was a way out. Of course, I'd have to wait until sunset. . . ."

Whistler paused. What was there to say about the next seven or eight hours alone in the dark with only his grief and rage, his fear, and of course the goddamn rats, to keep him company?

"But how?" Selene prompted.

"Moved enough dirt to make a mound two feet high directly underneath the trapdoor. That gave me enough leverage to force the trapdoor open."

"And you went straight to Mr. Munger's?"

Jamey gave her a surprised glance as they approached the Tam Junction crossroads. "Who?"

"The Rastaman. By the way, he told me to tell you, if I ever caught up to you, to consider the bread and jerky as a gift, but you owe him five dollars for the spliff."

"Why, that old thief! It was barely a roach."

━

And the least of the debts Whistler incurred that night. There was only one other settlement within walking distance of where the Maroon tunnel ended, a village consisting of a half dozen geodesic domes built by a commune of Georgia hippies who had fled Calhoun County back in the sixties only steps ahead of a drug bust. After another pull on his flask he set out for it, limping down the dundo road on bare feet so burned and bruised and sore that he'd have needed a great deal more blood than he had available to him (the flask was by this time scarcely a quarter full) to still the pain.

Even before he'd turned up the long unpaved commune trail he heard the Luzan version of an intruder alarm—a pack of dogs in full cry—going off all over the village. When he reached the gate of the hand-split rail fence, a woman's voice informed him from somewhere in the dark that there were three guns trained on him.

"Shiner?" he called painfully. The sound of his own voice startled him; he hadn't heard it since that morning.

"Jay Dubya? That you, Jay Dubya?" A tiny white woman with a sixties-style whitish-blond Afro burst out of the shadows and came running to unlatch the gate, surrounded by yapping dogs. "We went up to look at the Greathouse just before dark. Fire truck's still up there—they said nobody got out. What happened?"

He stumbled forward; she caught his arm and steadied him with surprising strength for a woman whose bones seemed as light and hollow as a bird's. Long ago, back in the sixties, they had been lovers, Shiner and he. But then, back in the sixties everyone had been lovers.

"Are any of the others here?" he whispered urgently—it hurt less to whisper.

"Just the kids. Everybody else is down at the quay."

That would be Smuggler's Quay. "They're sailing tonight?"

"I didn't say that." She locked the gate behind them. "For God's sake, J. W., what happened up there?"

He could only shake his head. "Someone blew it up. Every building was wired."

"But who—"

"I don't know." He could feel his voice starting to falter as an image of Lourdes nursing Cora whizzed through his mind with subliminal speed. He quickly banished the unwelcome thought, a skill he'd had quite a few hours to perfect during that long afternoon. What he'd decided to do, every time a memory like that slipped through, was to replace it with purpose. Purpose, like grief, was one of those new companions that had come to live with him during those long hours in the tunnel. "But I'm going to find out,

Shiner. And when I do, they're going to pay. In the meantime I need your help to get off the island. Can you lend me a car to get down to the quay?"

"Can you drive?"

"I can do anything," he said through the pain. "Before I go, though, I need one more favor."

He didn't have to say what it was; that was another secret she'd kept for him for twenty-five years.

"On two conditions," she replied.

"Name them."

"One, Buffalo never knows. Two, you keep that thing in your pants, *in* your pants."

"Sex is the last thing on my . . ." Then something occurred to him. "You didn't know, did you?" he said softly.

"What?"

"I was married a year and a half ago. We had a daughter. They were both . . . up there."

Now Shiner's voice failed her; she threw her arms around him and hugged him with the side of her face pressing against his chest. Gently he pushed her away—rather, purpose pushed her away; grief made it gentle. "When do they sail?"

"With the tide—about an hour before sunrise."

—

"All I had with me was my flask and my watch," Jamey explained to Selene as they turned off Highway 1 to take the ridge route over Mt. Tam. "Shiner found a pair of deck shoes that fit me, threw some clothes and a toothbrush into a gym bag, dug up one of the kids' old *Sesame Street* thermos bottles, and gave me more blood than I should have allowed her to; when I left her she was pale as a ghost."

Selene patted his knee. "Times like these, you find out who your friends are."

"I know." He pressed down firmly on the back of her hand. "Believe me, I know. And Buffalo was a brick as well. He sent most of the crew back to guard the compound, in case somebody was just blowing up the forest for the hell of it, though neither of us really believed that, and we sailed short-handed, with only his brother Toby and Shiner's oldest son, Luke, for crew."

On the third night of the voyage (Selene had "visited" him on the second night) the *Layla* reached St. Croix and dropped off half its cargo; on the fourth night Whistler attempted to call Selene from St. Thomas.

"That was the second, right?" asked Selene, remembering his phone message. "I'd just flown out of St. Thomas that very afternoon. Talk about coincidence."

Whistler made no reply. He didn't want to talk about coincidence. He'd done more than his share of pondering about its role in human affairs during the past few weeks, and had decided, with the aid of his new allies, grief and purpose, that he could not, would not bring himself to accept any other explanation for the chain of events that had delivered him from Lourdes's and Cora's fiery fate.

Because if there was a God or a Fate or an angel that guided the affairs of mortals, that had arranged for Lourdes to wear that powder blue lace thingie from Victoria's Secret to bed that morning instead of more circumspect nightwear, thereby arousing the Creature and sending its servant/owner out of the Greathouse in search of blood just before the holocaust began, a Fate that had so carefully placed his face between Josephina's thighs while the Greathouse went up, then rushed him out of harm's way when the slave quarters exploded, that had led him to the tunnel, etc., etc., etc., then as far as James Whistler was concerned, It could pucker up and kiss his ass. And if there was more than one God or Fate or angel, They could stand in line.

Then something else occurred to him—he laughed mirthlessly.

"What now?" asked Selene.

"Remember I quoted from the Book of Job before?"

She nodded. "I remember I was surprised. You never were much of a biblical scholar."

"Well, the library aboard the *Layla was* rather limited in scope.

Four Tom Robbins novels and a Bible. Needless to say, I spent a good deal of time reading the Bible. Are you familiar with the Book of Job?''

"More or less. God takes everything away from him on a bet with the devil. Oh, and boils."

"Yes, everyone remembers the boils. But do you remember the end, when it comes time for God to even accounts with this man whose life he has destroyed?"

"I . . . no, I guess not."

"Neat trick. He replaces the children and doubles the livestock."

"Beg pardon?"

"At the beginning of the book Job has seven sons, three daughters, seven thousand sheep, three thousand camels, five hundred yoke of oxen, and five hundred she asses. God takes it all away, then at the end, after He's had his fun, He gives Job back fourteen thousand sheep, six thousand camels, a thousand yoke of oxen, a thousand she asses, seven more sons, and three more daughters. Replaces the children, doubles the livestock. Oh: *And every man also gave him a piece of money, and every one an earring of gold.* He lived another hundred and forty years, and died old and full of days— and earrings, I suppose.

"But here's what struck me funny just now. It occurred to me that when my father dies, which he will, soon, assuming I get him before he gets me, I'll receive the other half of the Whistler legacy—double my livestock, so to speak. Throw in this new daughter I never knew I had, and . . . well, you follow my drift."

" 'Tain't funny, Whistler."

"Tizzent," he replied.

She almost smiled. Would have, too, if she didn't still have the stench of Nick in her nostrils, and his image in the back of her mind.

PART 4

―

For Every Evil

For every evil under the sun
There is a remedy or there is none.
If there be one, seek till you find it;
If there be none, never mind it.

—MOTHER GOOSE

". . . But Selene was apparently a tad too clever for your grandfather," Aldo explained to Martha, toward the conclusion of their bedside chat on Tuesday morning. "Otherwise I wouldn't have had to involve you in all of this."

"Sounds like she was a *tad* too clever for you too," Martha retorted.

"Yes, well, we'll see about that," was Aldo's surprisingly mellow reply. It was not the girl's first dig at him, but he'd washed down another Perc with a little blood about halfway through the narrative, and could have tolerated any amount of irony.

As for Martha's sass, it wasn't that she was no longer afraid of him, just that the bizarre, scarcely credible tale he'd told her had more or less robbed her of any hope she'd had of getting out of this alive. Clearly he was going to kill her sooner or later. Sooner, maybe, if she had a vote; perhaps that was why she went on teasing him. "Yeah, we'll see. But as far as I can tell, so far the score is Selene two, wacko zip."

"And by wacko, you are referring to . . . ?"

"Guess wh— *Ow!* Cut that out!"

For he had seized the tip of her button nose and twisted it so sharply that the cartilage made a grinding sound. But there was no anger in his eyes, nor in his voice when he reprimanded her. "You forget yourself, child. Now you wouldn't want me to forget *my*self, would you?"

Martha's eyes were tearing from the pain, but she still had the strength of her despair. "How about if instead of forgetting ourselves, we just forget each other?" she joked nasally.

He laughed and released her nose. "How could I ever forget you, my dear Martha?"

He might have been smiling, but she wasn't watching his face; she was watching his unbandaged left hand. Somehow a scalpel had appeared in it. An ordinary surgical steel scalpel with a gently curved inch-long blade. It had no sheath—how he'd been concealing it she couldn't imagine, but there it was. And no matter how badly she wanted *not* to, she had to ask. "What's that for?"

"Do you remember how I told you we recognize each other, we strigoi?"

If you drink their blood and don't get off! thought Martha in terror. But her sudden decision to scream, no matter what the consequences, just on the off chance someone might hear, must have shown in her eyes, because Aldo's hand was over her mouth almost before she'd opened it.

"Foolish idea," he hissed; he was holding the scalpel in his clenched teeth like a pirate. "I can put you out in a second, but I couldn't guarantee you'd wake up again. Now are you going to behave yourself? It's hard enough doing this one-handed without you complicating matters."

He let go; she turned her face to the wall; he retrieved his roll of duct tape, tore off a six-inch strip using his teeth and his good hand, smoothed it over her mouth, then cut a slit in her gag with his scalpel so she could breathe through her mouth.

"As I was about to say," he went on, pulling her arms out from under the bedcovers and slitting the tape that bound her wrists, "now that you *know* about us, I'd better find out whether you're *one* of us." He was sitting on the side of the bed now; he took her arm in his lap, wrist up, nicked the web of skin between her thumb and forefinger, brought the hand up to his lips as the blood began to well, and began to suck. Had she begun to struggle at this point she'd have been a goner, all of Aldo's self-admonitions to the contrary. Instead she lay unmoving, eyes shut tight, face turned resolutely to the wall.

When he'd finished, he pinched off the wound. "The bad news is, you're not one of us," he said softly, feeling the hot blood begin to course through him. "The good news is, I have even more reason to keep you alive—several liters' worth, in fact."

But she refused to open her eyes.

"*Fine. Be* that way," joked Aldo—it was a turn of phrase he'd heard one of the girls use in the hot tub a week before. "I'll be in the other room—call if you need me." Another joke—when he left he did not remove the gag. But neither did he tie her hands again, and within minutes of retiring to the adjoining room he heard the TV click on. Some dreadful music—MTV, no doubt.

Aldo took his Discman out of his kit bag, settled the plugs into his ears, and dropped the CD of *Andrea Chénier* into place. The girl's live blood had excited him almost beyond endurance. Listening to Callas sing "Mamma morte" would calm him, or at least get his mind off the naked child in the next room, and back to business. His hand had begun throbbing again. He popped another Percodan into his mouth and washed it down with a belt of Stoli, then lay down on the bed and began rethinking his plans.

Clearly, he held the upper hand now. But he held it—excellent pun—one-handed, which might make it difficult to go after the striga again, much less the strigoi, should the two of them have joined forces. Fortunately, he didn't have to go after them. He could take his time, choose his ground, bring her—or them—to him.

Where, though, should that ground be? If Whistler was in the picture, he'd have to take him from a distance. No sense risking a hand-to-hand battle with another strigoi, *especially* one-handed. Which meant using Nick's .38, which meant he'd have to find someplace more isolated—certainly not a motel. And not the Bay Area, either—no sense hanging around until Nick's body was discovered. But he was familiar with only two other locations within driving distance, Monterey and Tahoe. He settled on Monterey, as it was more or less virgin territory, in that he had yet to commit a crime there, other than holding Martha against her will.

Aldo spent much of Tuesday afternoon on the phone chatting up realtors from a list provided him by a pleasant woman at the Monterey County Chamber of Commerce, scouting for properties, remote tear-downs or fixer-uppers (he'd quickly learned the lingo) where he could stage the next phase of the operation.

Eventually he reached a realtor by the name of William Honey, who was peddling what he carefully referred to as a *distressed property*, in a location known as *down the coast*, about halfway between Carmel and Big Sur.

Sounded perfect. When he had assured himself that the property was not only isolated but deserted and likely to remain so, Aldo schmoozed the realtor for a few more minutes, then made an appointment to see the place on Monday the 22nd, and obtained detailed instructions as to how to find it, along with Honey's assurance that he had no plans to show the place to anyone before then.

Immediately after hanging up, Aldo stuck his head through the doorway into the room where Martha lay channel surfing. "Just so you know, we'll be checking out right after sunset. In the meantime I'm going to try to catch a nap—if you behave yourself all day I'll let you ride in the front seat instead of the trunk."

"How ha-haw hunh?" Martha tried to enunciate through the tape covering her mouth. Apparently she had decided to abandon the silent treatment.

Aldo came over and loosened it. "Again?"

"I said how about lunch?"

"How about it?"

"Do I get some?"

"If you behave yourself."

"You keep saying that like I have a choice. What are you expecting me to do?"

"I don't know. But I'm sure you'd try to think of something —I just wanted to give you a bit of incentive not to."

Aldo kept his second promise to Martha—lunch, that is—Mexican food. They spent the rest of the afternoon quietly; Martha watched TV while Aldo rested and listened to Callas on the Discman and washed down Percodans with blood or Stoli, as needed. After the sun had gone down Aldo trussed Martha to the bed and went out shopping for camping supplies, including an ice chest for the bottles of blood now cooling in the tub. He'd realized he couldn't trust himself to drink from Martha again until it didn't matter whether she was alive or not.

As for Aldo's first promise to Martha, about letting her ride inside the car, he'd never had any intention of keeping it. He did let her get up to pee one last time after the car was loaded, then retrussed her. Her eyes were wild and angry over the shiny silver tape; he shrugged an apology, rolled her up in a green vinyl tarpaulin, hauled her over his shoulder out to the Toyota, and stuffed her back into the trunk. He left the tarp wrapped around her tightly so she couldn't pound for help, but peeled it back from her face so the fumes from the fresh vinyl wouldn't suffocate her. That had happened to him once in Timisoara, and wasn't Aldo's face red when Major Strada unwrapped the corpse he'd been planning to interrogate.

After Aldo had finished loading the car he returned to the room for one last chore. From the motel phone he dialed Selene's number, listened through her greeting, waited for the beep as bidden, and left his message:

"Hello Selene. My name is Len—or at least that's what Martha calls me. . . ."

2

The hospital bed was gone. Although it had been in Don's living room only a few months, Selene felt its absence profoundly. "Somehow I'd pictured the bed still there, but empty," she whispered to Jamey as they tiptoed through the dark toward Martha's door.

He held his finger to his lips, put his ear to the door for a moment, then opened it quietly. Selene could just make out the pale square of Martha's desk a few feet away; Jamey crossed over to it unerringly and picked up a heavy object, carried it back to Selene in the doorway. "This what you were looking for?"

She took her Book of Shadows from him. Somehow she knew without even feeling for it that Moll's letter was gone. She sat down heavily on Martha's bed. "I think we can assume that your secret is out," she informed Jamey.

"Wasn't *my* secret," he replied.

—

They left by the back door of Martha's room. The fog was thick enough that night to have obscured them even if they'd marched straight up the driveway, but Whistler insisted on leading them the long way around. At the edge of the woods above the redwood deck Jamey went as still as a hunting dog on point, watching, listening, smelling. "All clear," he whispered. "Except for—what's his name, your cat?"

"Dunstan."

"Dunstan's under the deck chewing on something."

Black cat in the dark, sixty feet away! It had been years since Selene had pondered seriously about what it must be like to be high on blood; now she found herself wondering again. Whistler took her hand and they hurried down the hill and around to the back door. In the dark kitchen they could see the red light on the answering machine blinking. One blink at a time. The counter read 13.

Selene pushed the play button, then took Jamey's hand and gripped it tightly all the way through the thirteenth message.

"Hello, Selene. My name is Len—or at least that's what Martha calls me. We've met once, though you didn't do me the honor of opening your eyes or acknowledging my presence. No matter— we'll meet again. It is now eight p.m. on Tuesday, November sixteenth. Martha and I are going to be moving now. I will call you tomorrow evening precisely at six-thirty p.m., and if we don't make contact, then every night thereafter at that time until we can make arrangements to trade her for her father. If you haven't located him yet I suggest you try harder, for your goddaughter's sake. Because if you can't find him within, let's see, shall we say two or three days, then I'm going to have to go looking for him myself. In which case I would consider Martha, not a hostage, but excess baggage. And I never carry excess baggage.

"One more point: about that murder of yours back in London? Good job, though rather quickly done for my taste. I bring this up only in case you're considering bringing the authorities into this. Of course, you can always have your barrister plead self-defense, but should it come to that, I'm afraid Martha's grandfather would be testifying otherwise—that you were and are delusional about vampires, that you went berserk and slaughtered poor Mrs. Wah, then stuck a needle in the old fellow when he tried to go to her aid.

"But don't worry, I'm sure you won't have any problem convincing a jury that it was self-defense—once you'd explained about the vampires and all.

"Ta-ta for now. Speak to you tomorrow at six-thirty. And remember, we're counting on you, Martha and I. Don't let us down."

━

Whistler removed the tape from the machine and slipped it into the outside pocket of Selene's blazer. "For your defense team, should it come to that," he explained. "Though I can't quite picture my father calling the police, much less testifying in a courtroom. I'm more worried about tomorrow night. It could be a trap."

"I don't think so," said Selene. "Sounds more like he wants to choose his own—"

But Jamey cut her off. "Let's forward your phone down to Don's just in case. You do have call forwarding, don't you?"

"Nope."

"Call Pac Bell in the morning and order it. Tell them it's an emergency."

"Okay, so we take the call at Don's," said Selene, slightly miffed: it had occurred to her that she was being demoted from Sherlock Holmes to Dr. Watson, and she wasn't sure that she liked her new role. "Then what?"

"Then we go where he tells us to go, rescue her, kill him, deal with my father." *Obviously*, implied his tone of voice.

"But wherever it's going to be, he's going to have things set up in his favor."

"I know. I'll just have to improvise."

"Wouldn't it be easier if we could find out where he was keeping her?"

Whistler sighed. "Yes, m'dear, it certainly would," he said patronizingly. "But somehow I don't think Aldo is going to be entirely cooperative."

"I don't need his cooperation," snapped Selene.

Jamey's wide-set gray eyes narrowed. "Oh?"

But she was still ticked off at the tone he'd taken, and would not reply. They locked up Selene's house and returned to the lower

A-frame, where they would sleep in shifts, Jamey informed her: that way he could stand guard over her all night, then sleep during the day when there would be less danger from Aldo, if he were indeed a blood drinker, which seemed increasingly likely.

And much as she disliked Whistler's attitude, Selene had to admit his plan made sense, so while Jamey went outside to move the Jaguar into the garage, she changed into one of the XXXL 49ers T-shirts Martha used for a nightgown, and crawled into Martha's narrow bed.

When he returned, Jamey perched on the edge of the bed and finished sketching out his adventures for her. Buffalo Barry Klein had advanced Whistler enough money to fly to Miami, using brother Toby's Virgin Islands driver's license—no passport necessary—to get through airport security, and it was from a cheap motel not far from the Orange Bowl that Jamey had first contacted Nick Santos and asked him to poke around cyberspace.

Nick, who had spent the past several years fighting hackers and crackers, was delighted at the chance to do some hacking and cracking himself. "News flash: you're missing and presumed dead in the Virgin Islands," he had reported back to Whistler within twenty-four hours. "In Contra Costa County they want to talk to you about an arson investigation—somebody torched your place in El Sobrante. It's a total loss. Meanwhile the Nevada State Police are investigating the fire in Tahoe—the manor's a write-off too."

"Also fire?"

"Also fire. At the moment, thanks to the sheer incompetence of all the official investigators, there are no warrants or requests to detain out for you, but if they ever get around to talking to each other, there will be. Now what can I do to help?"

"Send cash," Jamey had replied.

Of his adventures between Miami and San Francisco he had little to say to Selene, beyond the fact that the trip had taken over a week, and that upon arrival he had maintained his own surveillance on Nick to be sure no one was watching him before reestablishing contact. "We both knew what a dangerous game I might be drawing him into—or thought we did. He was due to check in with me this morning—when he hadn't contacted me by sunset, I went looking for him. I got there a few minutes before you did, came up the fire escape, heard the buzzer, hid out in the hall closet. I'm sorry you had to see the body. I wanted to stop you before you went into the bedroom, but I had to be sure you weren't being followed."

"I understand."

"Whoever this fucker Aldo is, he's good. Which reminds me —my flask is about empty. If I have to stay awake all night . . ."

He didn't have to spell it out for her. "I suppose it makes sense," she sighed, drawing back the covers and swinging her legs over the side of the bed. "What are you using?"

Jamey showed her the razor-edged utility knife he'd picked up in Miami. "I just put in a fresh blade this evening."

"I should hope so!" Selene crossed her right ankle over her left knee; he gave her a moment to go into her modified trance, then opened a small vein at the inside of her ankle. As usual, she did not flinch when he made the cut, though she did wriggle a bit with sensual satisfaction as he sucked at the small wound. "Not too much, now," she warned him. "I'm a little out of practice as a donor."

"Mmm-hmmm," he agreed; after another minute he withdrew his lips reluctantly from her ankle and helped her close the wound with pressure. She assisted by slowing her breathing, and thus her heart rate. When he stood up she couldn't help noticing the Creature swelling against the inside thigh of his Levi's. She gave it a pat for old time's sake, then a stroke.

Jamey pressed her hand against him. "Sure you want to do that?" he asked.

"Sure is not a word I use much anymore," she replied. Five minutes later Jamey, who should have been outside standing guard, was lying on his belly between Selene's outstretched feet, gradually nuzzling 49er red and gold up past her thighs, while Selene, who should have been sleeping, was raising her hips up off the bed to make his task easier.

"Missed you, missed you, missed you," Jamey whispered fervently when he'd reached the promised land, then bent to his work again, opening her with his tongue and lips as delicately as if the lips of her sex were the petals of a full-blown rose. She tightened her thighs around his ears, then pulled the 49er shirt up to her neck: soon he would reach up to roll her nipples between his fingertips like little nuggets of gold, the way he used to—she wanted her breasts to be bare for . . .

"Jamey, no! Wait! Stop!"

A muffled "What?" from between her thighs.

"We can't."

"Why not?"

"Come up here on the bed." She rolled onto her side and made room for him. "Have you ever heard of orgomancy?"

—

By the time she finished she was half expecting him to leap out of the bed, but he only laughed. "To tell you the truth, I've never put much stock in that sort of thing."

She stiffened in his arms. "Just what do you mean by *that sort of thing*?"

"I'm sorry—that came out badly. Coitus interruptus, y'know— I thought you were giving me the Wiccan equivalent of *not tonight dear, I have a headache*. The fact is, I don't even read my horoscope in the paper anymore. And as for the ravings of a crone in orgasm, I'd prefer to take my chances, no matter how well the verse scans. Or *are* you planning to betray me? Because we already are lying together, y'know."

Their noses were almost touching. "Yeah. But there's lying, and there's *lying*." Selene could feel the Creature nudging her thigh— he must have unbuttoned his jeans at some point.

"Let's *lie*," he suggested hopefully.

"Let's not."

"I'd much prefer to be the first man, *the man who must be betrayed*"—this last in a mock-portentous tone—"rather than *the man who must die*."

"I'm sure you would, especially if it gets you laid," she said, shoving him away from her, wriggling out from between Whistler and wall. But she knew full well that it was not *his* lack of faith that was upsetting her—talk about the pot calling the kettle black! And something he'd just said continued to nag at her as she climbed off the foot of the bed and stood with her back to him, rearranging her nightshirt. Something about the wording of the prophecy. All those musts. *Must lie . . . must betray . . . must die.* But why *must*? If a thing was going to happen, it was going to happen. You didn't say the sun *must* come up tomorrow. Unless . . .

Selene sat down heavily on the end of the cot. Behind her Jamey started to say something else. She shushed him.

Unless it hadn't been a prophecy at all, but rather a prescription. A plan of action: betray the first man you lie with in order to kill the second.

Far-fetched? Perhaps. But now there were three possibilities—the orgomancy might be nonsense, foreshadowing, or directive. But if it was nonsense, then she might as well make love with Jamey; it might be their last chance. If it was a true foreshadowing, then all this back-and-forth was only an attempt to manipulate the inevitable—if it was Jamey she was meant to lie with and betray, then it was Jamey; if not, not. And if the orgomancy was indeed some form of advice or instruction, if it was telling her she had to betray the first man she slept with in order for the second to die, if that was the only way out of this mess . . .

What was it Scrooge had asked the last ghost? "Are these the shadows of things that will be, or only things that may be." She couldn't remember what the Spirit had answered. Didn't matter, did it?

"You're right," she said, standing up again with her back to Jamey, reaching down cross-handed and pulling her nightshirt off over her head. "Let's do it."

Not long afterward—about as long as it took for Jamey to tug his jeans down the rest of the way, for Selene to find a jar of coconut oil moisturizer on Martha's dresser to slather over the Creature—she was lowering herself down upon it, down, down, down, until it filled her so that she could hardly breathe, hardly wanted to breathe. Jamey's eyes were closed. "Oh yes," he was murmuring. "Yes, yes, yes . . ."

Then he opened them, caught sight of her face above him, and ceased his upward thrusting. "Are you all right?" he asked her, reaching up to caress her cheek gently with a thumb.

"Wonderful."

"Does it hurt?"

"No."

He showed her the thumb that had just stroked her face; it was wet. "Then why are you crying?"

She could think of a few answers. *Because I missed this so much? Because I'm going to betray you? Because I have to do this again with Aldo?* She grabbed his damp thumb tightly in both hands, brought it to her mouth, and licked it clean of her salty tears.

"Tears of joy, dearie," she lied. "Tears of joy." At which point it occurred to her that perhaps the betrayal had already begun.

3

For the second time in two and a half weeks Selene hiked up the path to the herb garden on the southern slope of the hill behind her A-frame. This time, though, she wore her Mephisto sandals, and she had thrown on a long flower-print cotton Laura Ashley dress that absolutely cried out for a wide straw bonnet with a trailing ribbon. Some misguided relative had given the dress to Martha for her sweet sixteen. As far as Selene could tell it had never been worn.

The hedge of rosemary was in bloom, a dense green wall dotted with clumps of tiny Tuscan blue flowers glistening with morning dew. Selene drank it all in, the earthy colors, the dark bitter fragrance of the rosemary leaves, the rough feel of the blistered black paint of the iron gate latch against her fingers.

She'd already been up for hours, and made two phone calls, the first to Carson, whom she'd pacified with half-truths, to the effect that she'd heard from Martha indirectly, that by tonight she would know where the girl was staying, and would be on her way to pick her up. The second call had been to Pacific Bell. She explained her problem—emergency call expected, had to go out, sick friend, yadda yadda—anticipating a typical phone company blow-off, whereupon a kindly competent service rep quickly assured her there would be no problem adding the call forwarding feature to Selene's home number that very same afternoon, then *thanked* her for her business. The whole experience had done nothing to dispel Selene's mounting sense of unreality.

Nor did the sight of the deadly nightshade growing by itself in the center of the drought-ravaged herb garden. Selene's hand trembled as she began feeling the slightly wrinkled, purple-black cherries; she had plucked two before she realized that she had completely forgotten to ask permission of Hecate. Then she remembered that she'd also made her decision to lie with Jamey last night without consulting the Goddess—without even thinking of Her. Suddenly she understood that she was now instinctively, almost reflexively, practicing witchcraft without Wicca, tradecraft without the comfort of religion. The realization smacked her like a Zen master's stick; for a moment she felt as lost and lonely as one of Le Carré's post–cold war spies.

Then another smack—as Selene carefully dropped her five chosen cherries into the apron pocket of Martha's dress, she remembered that Hecate was Martha's chosen Wiccan name, and that yesterday, the sixteenth of November, had been Hecate Day on the Wiccan calendar.

"Oh give me a break," she said to no one in particular—but in the same tone of voice she'd once reserved for speaking to the Goddess.

—

Whistler dreamed his dream again that afternoon. But this time Lourdes did not dance away from him after dropping her sarong. Instead she took him by the hand and led him through the glass door into the bedroom. "You," she said. "Here, now." She lay back on the bed and reached up for him; it wasn't until he was on top of her that he remembered that she was dead.

But it wasn't a Stephen King moment by any means. The instant he realized that she had come to him in a dream both she and the dream evaporated, and he found himself lying alone in a bed that was much too short for him, nursing a bittersweet memory along with a stiff neck. He asked himself whether the joy of having her again, even for a moment, was worth the pain of losing her again.

Before he could decide on an answer it occurred to him that he might as well be asking the same question about having and losing both Lourdes and Cora the first time.

The question alone was enough to start the tears. Stupid question. Grief swells and purpose shrivels when you start asking yourself unanswerable questions like that. This much he knew, though: if Job forgave God before he died, then he didn't die old and full of days, he died old and full of shit. Beyond that, Whistler was sure of nothing, other than that it was time to take the advice that the exquisitely named Archie Bell and the Drells were giving out in 1968. Time to do the Tighten Up.

With his eyes still carefully closed, Whistler sniffed the air. It smelled like dusk, but Martha's room had venetian blinds, which were considered notoriously unreliable in vampire circles, and he didn't want any nasty sunbeams sneaking up on him. He tried a quick peek through slitted eyelids—no pain. He opened them the rest of the way, and saw that the light stealing in through the slits and around the edges of the blinds was violet-gray and fading.

Whistler sat up, turning his head gingerly this way and that, his neck snap-crackle-and-popping like a bowl of Rice Krispies. "Oh man, could I use a drink," he said aloud, throwing back the comforter and stepping out of bed; that's when he saw the note taped to the inside of the door. Purple marker on loose-leaf paper:

J.—Left you a waker-upper in the fridge. Enjoy! By the time you're awake my body will be in the loft. Please watch it for me until I get back. All my love, S.

Whistler hopped into his jeans on his way out the bedroom door. He fully intended to dash up the ladder to the loft first; he would have, too, if Martha's bedroom door hadn't opened out directly onto the kitchen only a few feet from the refrigerator. Besides, he told himself as he opened the door to the old Kenmore and removed a small silver creamer, whatever the hell was going on in the loft, he'd be better able to deal with it on blood.

He took a sip from the creamer. This was a moment he'd sworn to himself years ago he'd never take for granted, this first blood of the evening; even now, with no time to spare, he took an instant to appreciate the grateful shudder with which his body received its gift. Then he climbed the ladder to the loft and found Selene lying naked on her back under the skylight, her hands folded peacefully across her breast.

But as he approached he saw that the tendrils of her wild gray hair were damp and tangled and the thin bare mattress under her was drenched with sweat. If she was breathing, he couldn't detect it: no perceptible rise and fall to that pale chest, not even when he was kneeling at her side. But her skin was neither cold, nor blue, nor waxen like a corpse. Suddenly it all came together for him: Selene's tale of her first belladonna flight on Halloween; last night's "Wouldn't it be easier if we knew where Len was keeping Martha?"; her note; this body in suspended animation.

The blood hadn't hit him yet—cold blood took a little longer to come on. He checked his watch, the same Patek Philippe he'd stolen from his father so many years before. Quarter after five. An hour and a quarter until Len's phone call. He found himself wondering whether Selene had remembered to take care of the call forwarding. He had a moment of panic, but then, concurrently with the onset of the blood rush, a plan came to him. He found a blanket folded up against the wall and spread it over Selene, then returned to Martha's room and called Selene's number from Martha's white Princess-style phone; after three rings the phone in the front room, Don's line, began ringing, and did not stop until he'd hung up the bedroom phone.

Reassured, Jamey prowled around the A-frame checking out the bureaus and closets, and found clean socks, a pair of Ben Davis jeans that would be long enough for him, if a bit loose, a studded belt with a Harley buckle, and a Winged Rider Harley T-shirt. He chanced a quick shower, towel-dried and finger-combed his short white hair. When he checked himself out in the mirror behind Martha's door he saw that somehow he had managed to look nothing like a biker, despite all the paraphernalia.

Whistler made a few more trips up and down the ladder, hauling cushions from the couch in the front room, and a can of Colt 45 and a box of Snak Mix, then unhooking Don's phone and plugging it into a jack in the loft. He checked his watch as he settled down beside Selene's inert body: five forty-five. He took a deep breath and felt the blood rush spreading outward from the very marrow of his bones. The Creature stirred.

"Oh shut up," he told it. "Haven't you gotten us into enough trouble already?" He tried to remember that night with Moll seventeen or eighteen years ago. The Broadway house. Moll was there, Selene was off somewhere . . . Moll was carving runestones . . . cut her finger . . . *Oh Jamey* . . . ? Showing him the blood beading up on her fingertip . . . *No sense letting it go to waste* . . .

Whistler shook his head wonderingly, appreciatively. One minute you're sucking on a finger, next thing you know it's the nineties and you've got a teenage daughter. Had Martha inherited his blood-drinking genes, he wondered? Cora had not.

The Creature, which had been thrusting its head impatiently against the rough denim of the work jeans in memory of Moll's glorious bod, retreated at the thought of Cora. Whistler lay back against the cushions. Time to do the Tighten Up again.

Selene's hearing was the first thing to return, even before her consciousness of self. That was a particularly weird sensation: hearing a humming noise before she knew what hearing was. Or humming, or noise, for that matter, much less who was doing the hearing.

Jamey was beside her. It was his voice she had heard, humming an old Grateful Dead tune. When she spoke her own voice seemed equally distant: "Before I forget. Three falling-down shacks in a level clearing on a hillside. Knee-high grass around the shacks. A grove of cypress trees above the clearing, a ravine behind it. They're in the third shack, the one nearest the ravine. Martha was hogtied and gagged; Aldo was in a sleeping bag."

Selene sat up. She was shaky, and slightly feverish, but not nearly as confused or debilitated as she'd been after her last trip with the Fair Lady. Whistler steadied her from behind. She shivered; he tucked the blanket around her. "She was so frightened, Jamey. She's seen her own death and she was so frightened."

"Anything else—anything that might tell us where this hill is?"

Selene leaned back against him, trying to conjure up more memories. She shook her head. "Nothing's coming up. What time is it?"

"Just turned six." He felt her forehead. "You're still a little warm."

"I know. I'm going to go hunt up some aspirin to bring the fever down, then take a cold shower."

Jamey handed her Martha's Laura Ashley from beside the mattress, helped her pull it on, helped her to her feet. "You still look a tad shaky—here, let me spot you." He started down the ladder, waited for her halfway.

Selene made the descent easily enough with Jamey's arms around her from behind, not touching her but somehow steadying her nonetheless. *At least this time the ladder isn't on fire,* she thought.

CHAPTER

4

Aldo awoke at sunset on Wednesday night and enjoyed a swig of cold blood from the last jar in the cooler before unwinding the bandages from his right hand. The wounds were healing up nicely around the tiny black threads. There would be scars, he recognized, but other than that he'd been lucky—no nerves or tendons had been severed.

He rewound the gauze, then turned on his side to check out the girl. She was still asleep—or at least her eyes were closed—but she had wet herself overnight. Aldo's nose wrinkled up—the smell of cold piss always reminded him of the Orfelinat. He climbed out of his sleeping bag and went outside to relieve himself in the tall grass, then returned and scooped Martha up in his arms, leaning back from the odor of stale urine.

"Lucky thing I didn't feed you last night, you'd have shit yourself like poor Nick."

But her eyes, open now, were dull with stupor above the gag. Aldo hadn't participated in too many long-term kidnappings during his career (for some reason he was not the man his superiors would choose when the program called for keeping a subject alive for an extended period of time), but as far as he could tell the girl was currently in the surrender stage of victimhood. Which didn't mean you didn't have to watch them just as carefully, or confine them just as securely as in the more active stages, Aldo reminded himself as he slung the girl over his left shoulder, but there was also another problem to deal with—they had a tendency to die on you so very easily at this stage.

As he carried her out of the third shack, then up the two make-shift cinderblock-and-plank steps of the middle cabin, he tried to decide whether it mattered to him whether she died or not. Probably not, he concluded; still he would play it conservatively until he had drawn Whistler and the witch all the way into his trap. Better to have her alive and not need her than need her alive and not have her.

The floorboards in the middle shack were rotten-soft. With the girl in his arms, her pale eyes open and fixed on his face, Aldo followed the straight line of nail heads that marked one of the support beams, placing one foot carefully in front of the other in the dark until he'd reached the far wall. He set his burden down against the wall and began lifting out floorboards with his good hand, taking care to keep them level as he set them aside so that the dust and dirt didn't slide off. Fortunately she was a slender little thing. She fit into the long narrow space between the exposed beams with only a little cramming, and as he began to replace the boards he saw that there would even be a clearance of an inch or more between her chest and the underside of the rotten flooring. She would be able to breathe as long as she wanted to.

Of course, how long she'd want to keep breathing was problematical. Her eyes had gone round and soft in the dark; they were still looking up at him, but with surprisingly little reproach, as he painstakingly fit the last board into place over her face. It was a look he was more accustomed to seeing in the eyes of torture victims at the end of a long hard night, a look that meant that there wasn't much point going on with the torture—other than the sheer fun of it, of course.

Then he remembered that he'd decided to keep her alive. "I just have to make a phone call, pick up some supplies," he said loudly, while tightroping his way back along the trail of nail heads. "Be back in an hour or so and we'll get you out of there and cleaned up."

There, that should give her a reason to keep breathing for a while, without filling her with too much hope. Aldo didn't want her hopeful, just alive. He paused in the doorless doorway, remembering something William Honey had told him over the phone that morning.

"Two secrets to success in my profession, Len," the realtor had explained. "Location and timing."

Mine too, thought Aldo, looking over what to all appearances was one of three empty, humble, tear-down shacks on a half-million-dollar distressed property halfway between Carmel and Big Sur. *Mine too.*

➤

Martha watched the coffin lid closing over her and thought about all the things she'd never done. *Never had a baby* was the first thing that came to mind. She tried to imagine it, a life growing inside her. Must really be something. If she had a baby she'd strap it on like those Amazon Indian women do, carry it around with her all day and sleep next to it at night and nurse it whenever it was hungry . . .

She closed her eyes, tried to let that fantasy carry her off to sleep. But she'd slept so much lately, every time she dozed off she'd snap awake within minutes, and if she'd been asleep long enough to forget where she was—the motel, the trunk of the car, the other cabin last night—then the waking would be twice as painful.

As for how it would feel to wake up in your coffin? *Oh Goddess oh Goddess oh Goddess oh Goddess oh Goddess . . .*

➤

The first thing Aldo needed was more ice for the cooler. The Clamato juice jars were all empty, but with any luck he'd be refilling them again within a few hours. He drove north on Highway 1 to the shopping center he'd seen on the way down, and purchased several bags of ice at the supermarket, along with a ready-cooked barbecued chicken, a pint of potato salad, and a two-liter Pepsi. He also bought a clever plastic tub of pop-up Wash'n Dri's. He'd somewhat lost his taste for Martha, all dull and dirty, but perhaps after a good washing up . . . ? Be a shame to waste her entirely.

He made his phone calls from a booth near the supermarket entrance. After checking with the Monterey Marriot to be sure they had plenty of vacancies (it *was* a Tuesday night during off season), he dialed Selene's number and tried not to sound surprised when she answered, though he hadn't been at all sure she'd be there. "Why hello there! Is this Selene?"

"Aldo? Is Martha there? Let me speak to her."

"Nice to finally speak to you, too. No, she's not with me. But she's safe. And by the way, I'll be making the demands from here on out. Is Whistler there?"

"Yes."

"Excellent. Here's your next assignment. . . ."

—

As he approached the Carmel Highlands on his way back down the coast, Aldo set his cheap but reliable Casio to the stopwatch function. At the red-painted phone booth in front of the quaint little Mission-style gas station he clicked the start button with his thumb, and set the cruise control on the Toyota at fifty-five. He then selected a CD at random from the kit bag (couldn't go too wrong—they were all Callas), struggled with, but eventually managed to open, the case—talk about things that were difficult to do with one hand—slipped it into the slot without looking, and pushed the random button, a gesture of faith that was rewarded immediately by "Divinités du Styx" from *Alceste*.

Soaring horns, soaring voice—a fitting sound track for the wild coastal scenery. In places the highway seemed to have been hacked out of the side of sheer cliffs: to the left, above the road, majestic windblown pines and cypresses rose from bluffs and crags; to the right, far below, black surf battered itself into ghost-white foam against the rocks.

Aldo clicked the stopwatch again as he turned onto the dirt road immediately after the sign for the defunct Westmere rest home. Seventeen minutes at legal speed. He ran through the timing again: drive to the phone booth, make the call to the Marriott around eleven—Whistler and Selene would have had more than enough time to get to Monterey from Bolinas and check in—then drive back, arriving no later than 11:20, which would give him plenty of time to set up his ambush.

Timing: check. Location: check. Aldo held the bottle of Clamato juice between his knees while he unscrewed the cap, then drank a toast to William Honey.

—

Martha felt the floor shaking overhead; her eyes were sufficiently used to the dark by then that when Len lifted the boards away she could see his silhouette kneeling above her, and beyond that she could even make out a few bright stars through the holes in the roof of the shack.

She wasn't sure how she felt about being lifted out of her coffin. In a way it had been sort of a peaceful feeling, saying good-bye to her friends, forgiving her mom for leaving her and Selene for lying to her. And after the pain in her bound limbs had faded from sharp stabbing to a dull ache, from a dull ache to pins and needles, and from pins and needles to a dead absent sensation, it was not even a particularly uncomfortable experience, this waiting to die.

Then Len lifted her into the air and all the peace went rushing out of her. She closed her eyes against the sudden dizziness as he carried her out of the shack, felt her belly muscles clenching, tasted bile; she could feel it climbing her throat, filling her mouth, splashing against the inside of the duct tape gag. She tried desperately to swallow the vomit, but she couldn't force it back down again with her mouth taped shut: soon she was choking on the bitter stuff.

No, she thought, before the drowning sensation overtook her. *No, not like this.*

5

Low in the west Venus was a silver splash above the shallow ivory cup of the new moon. To the north and east, across the great crescent sweep of Monterey Bay, a luminous gray band softened the sky over the scalloped black ridge of the horizon; above the gray the stars were having themselves a high old time.

"Twinkle on, you bastards," muttered Jamey Whistler, pacing the balcony of the topmost corner suite at the Marriott. Selene was inside, sitting on the pink-and-cream-striped loveseat under an enormous print of a pastel-pink vulviform flower—Georgia Faux'Keefe—within arm's reach of the telephone. When it finally rang, just before eleven, she jumped as if someone had fired a starter's pistol, nearly spilling a glass of ice water down her good luck red-on-black "Surrender Dorothy" T-shirt.

"Yes?"

"Both there?"

Selene looked up as Jamey raced by on his way to pick up the extension in the bedroom. "Just a sec."

"Go on," said Jamey breathlessly into the phone.

"Strigoi and striga reunited at last. How lovely for you. Pencil and paper?"

"Just a sec." Selene picked up the Marriott notepad and ball-point from the coffee table. "Go ahead."

"The two of you are to leave your hotel at precisely eleven-thirty. I don't have to tell you what will happen to Martha should you attempt to leave early, or should anyone else accompany you, or even just happen to show up coincidentally. You are to proceed south on Highway 1. Approximately fourteen miles south of Carmel you'll pass a sign for the Westmere. Slow down. I want Selene behind the wheel. Take the first left after the Westmere sign. Kill your lights, drive a hundred meters or so up the hill until you come to a cattle gate. Whistler, I want you to step out and open the gate while she drives through, then close it behind her and wait just inside the gate with your hands behind your head. Selene, once through you are to stop the car just inside the gate, turn off the motor and headlights, step out of the vehicle, open the trunk and all the doors, leaving the dome light on, then step away from the car and stand by the gate next to your strigoi with *your* hands behind your head. Still with me?"

"Yes of course," said Whistler.

"Yissuvcawss." Aldo mocked his plummy Oxbridge accent. "It is now ten-forty-seven. I shall expect you between midnight at the earliest and twelve-fifteen at the latest. Got all that?"

"Got it," said Selene. "What happens next?"

"I hang up." And he did.

━

Selene looked up as Jamey returned from the bedroom awkwardly unfolding a map of Monterey County. "Sounds as if he's got all his bases covered, doesn't it," he drawled.

"Oh for crying out loud, Jamey," she snapped back. "Could we can the understatement for once?"

"Okay." He took the handset from her, and holding the mouthpiece in one hand and the earpiece in the other, snapped it in half like a dog biscuit. "We're fucked." He dropped the broken receiver in the general direction of the cradle on the parquet coffee table. "There. Is that what you wanted to hear?"

"Actually, I was hoping for something a bit more *engagé.*" But Jamey's outburst had, paradoxically enough, strengthened her own resolve. "To start with, what do we know now that we didn't know before?"

The earpiece of the phone, dangling by wires over the edge of the coffee table, began emitting an eerie death rattle of an off-the-hook signal. Jamey yanked the cord from the wall, then perched on the edge of the loveseat. "Building 'em better than they used to." Then, at an under-the-eyebrow look from Selene: "For one thing, he's Romanian—that bit about the striga and the strigoi?"

"I was wondering about that. *Strega* is Italian for witch."

"Yes. But *striga*, that's Romanian. So is *strigoi*. *Strigoi vii*, actually. Living vampire. Quite esoteric. Everyone knows about the *nosferatu*—that's the export version, Dracula and all that. The Romanian tourist board has made quite a little cottage industry out of it. They turned an old Customs station into Bran Castle, and built a rather garish hotel at the Tihuta pass. But *strigoi*—that's the real deal. The word itself is a derivation of *striga*. According to the legend, the *strigoi* were originally created by witches. When a striga and a vampire work together, their powers are said to be enhanced a thousandfold. Folk literature's full of tales of striga and strigoi finding each other, losing each other, searching for each other." Jamey finished up impatiently, then glanced down at his wristwatch and hopped off the arm of the sofa. "Let's go."

"But we're not supposed to leave yet."

"If we follow his instructions to the letter," said Jamey quietly, "then all three of us—you, me, Martha—we're all dead." He waited for Selene to disagree; when she did not he went on. "We've got to disobey him at some point—I think our best chance is to get there before he's expecting us. Thanks to you, we know the lay of the land—let's see if we can gain any advantage with surprise. Perhaps he won't even be there; perhaps he was calling from another location, and that's why he needs the extra time—to return."

"But he said he'd kill her if we left early." Selene was stalling while she tried to decide how this new development fit her own plans. "What if we're being watched?"

"Getting cold feet, Mademoiselle Engagée?"

Selene decided she'd have to make it work. She stood up,

slipped on her black blazer, and jerked her thumb toward the open sliding door. "Could you get us down that way?"

Whistler stepped out onto the balcony, glanced up at the celestial configuration known as Venus in the New Moon's Arms, then peered down over the edge of the railing. "I'd be a piss-poor strigoi if I couldn't, m'dear," he drawled.

⟶

Selene's internal rhythms had finally adjusted to Pacific standard time, but now that her body clock was working she was dismayed to discover that her thermostat had gone on the fritz—a little reminder from the Fair Lady, no doubt. She thought about asking Jamey to do something with the temperature controls, but decided not to bother him, inasmuch as he currently had the Jag screaming down Highway 1 at eighty-five miles per hour on the occasional straightaways, taking even the most murderous curves at a suicidal sixty.

When the Westmere sign came into view on the left, Whistler hit the brakes hard and cocked the wheel sharply; the Jag spun through a tire-squealing hundred-and-eighty-degree turn across the highway; centrifugal force threw Selene against the shoulder harness like a crash-test dummy.

Jamey yanked the emergency brake; the Jag shuddered to a stop facing north, at the mouth of the old road that led to the Westmere ruins. "It's got to be over that hill there."

Selene unsnapped her seat belt. "I'm going with you."

Jamey glanced at the dashboard clock and shook his head. "Doesn't make sense. It's already nearly eleven-thirty. On blood I can be over the hill and back in minutes—with Martha, if he's left her unguarded. If not, there'll still be time to work out a plan— and more information to work with—before Aldo's deadline."

"You need me, Jamey. He's a drinker too, remember? And younger than you, and in better shape, and probably more experienced at this sort of thing. When was the last time you even had a fistfight?"

He raised an eyebrow. "And what exactly are *you* planning to bring to the party?"

She reached into the inside pocket of her blazer and pulled out the sewing packet containing the zombi-paste pins. "These, for one thing."

"Potions and lotions aren't going to cut it, m'dear. Aldo's not going to let you within arm's length of him, after what you did to my father and his housekeeper."

"I have the mashasha."

"Same argument. Listen, we're wasting time. What I need here is your blood, not your advice." He reached into the pocket of his denim jacket and pulled out his utility knife.

Thanks for making this so easy, thought Selene as she took the knife. She started to loosen the nut that held the blade in place, then stopped, as if something had just occurred to her. "At least take one of the pins—*you* might be able to get close enough to use it." She put the knife down in her lap and carefully removed one of the pins from the packet. "It's called zombi paste. It will induce a state indistinguishable from death for twenty-four hours."

He appeared to be thinking it over. Finally, reluctantly: "Good idea. Thanks." He reached out his hand, holding the tips of his thumb and forefinger together loosely to receive the pin. "And thanks for listening to rea—"

Selene jammed the point straight into the center of his palm.

"—son." He looked down uncomprehendingly at his hand, which was frozen into the "okay" mudra—thumb and forefinger circled, three fingers sticking up into the air. He saw brown leather rising to meet him as he toppled facedown onto the seat, then a rather astonishing sight: his own lifeless body viewed from above as he floated up through the Jaguar's roof.

6

For Martha it had been almost a pleasant feeling, lying naked as a baby on the tarp spread across the floor of the other cabin, the one they'd first slept in. Almost pleasant to be bobbing in and out of consciousness to the smell of witch hazel and the soft swipe of moist towelettes as Len patted her down with Wash'n Dri's after she'd nearly drowned in her own vomit. She did try to stop him when he began to work his way down her lower belly toward her private parts, but her arms, though untied, hadn't enough strength. And besides, as Len explained to her so patiently, she was the one who'd been a naughty girl and gone and wet herself before—he was just cleaning her up.

Afterward he helped her sit up, and when she complained of the cold he helped her climb into his sleeping bag. Her arms were starting to work a little better now, but her hands were still numb. She did okay with a chicken leg, but Len had to help her with the potato salad. He let her have only a few sips of the Pepsi, explaining that he was going to have to tie her up again soon. "Not for long. I have to call your father and godmother, tell them where to come pick you up. But we don't want you pissing yourself again in the meantime, do we?"

"You're not going to put me back down"—she still thought of

it as her grave, there under the floor of that other cabin, but couldn't bring herself to say the word—"under again, are you?"

"I'm afraid I'm going to have to. But you'll be safe there."

From what? she thought.

—

"You get some rest now and I'll be back soon," Aldo whispered tenderly, as he replaced the last of the floorboards over Martha's tightly shut eyes. Nor was he being insincere. Stowing her away like this was giving him a warm feeling, like when he used to hide a piece of hard candy under his mattress to enjoy after lights out at the Orfelinat. He tightroped back across the floor, then hurried out to the Toyota he had parked in the clearing down by the cypress grove. One more visit to that quaint little phone booth at the quaint little gas station. Seventeen minutes up, the call to the Marriott . . .

. . . and seventeen minutes back. Aldo drove through the cattle gate at 11:14 and turned the Toyota around, then backed another twenty yards or so up the narrow rutted road. When he had the distance right he began edging the car forward and backing up again, making minute adjustments in positioning until the headlights were shining directly downhill onto the gate. Shutting off the engine but leaving the headlights on and the driver's door open with the window rolled down, he balanced Nick's revolver on the windowsill, then walked back down to the gate and stared up into the blinding glare of the high beams. Perfect—he could scarcely tell that the door was open, much less spot the gun resting on the windowsill.

Satisfied, Aldo returned to the car, pocketed the pistol, cut the lights, closed the door firmly but silently, and trotted up the curving dirt road, until it ended abruptly at a stand of towering cedars. Beyond the cedars, the path he'd worn going back and forth to the car through the tall sea of grass that surrounded the cabins was still visible, the bent and broken blades reflecting the starlight at an oblique angle, cutting a silvery ribbon through the dark grass. As he came around the corner of the first cabin Aldo swept the surrounding grass with his eyes and noted with satisfaction that there

were no other ribbons of bent grass leading down from the top of
the hill, or up from the ravine: if Whistler had attempted to approach the property during his absence, he'd have known it.

Just to be sure he checked out each of the three cabins in turn.
The first was only a stripped skeleton; a quick sweep with the narrow flashlight beam told him it was empty. The middle cabin also
appeared empty at a glance. If he hadn't put the girl under the
floorboards himself he'd never have known she was there.

The third cabin was undisturbed as well. Aldo took a sip from
his thermos. No sense conserving—soon he'd have all the blood he
needed, and when he was done with them there would still be
enough blood left in the striga and the girl to refill his thermos *and*
his jars. Besides, now was when he needed a picker-upper, and
perhaps a Perc too, as his hand was starting to throb again. He
washed down one pill on his way out, then a second on his way
over to the middle cabin. He had one more decision to make: bring
Martha down to the gate with him, or leave her under the floor?
The latter would be safer, less work, and easier on his injured fingers, but they might well demand to see her before getting out of
the car. And he needed them out of the car if he was to get a clean
shot at Whistler.

So: bring her. He had started to screw the cap back on the thermos, but changed his mind and left it uncorked on the floor beside
him, sipping from it occasionally as he set to work prying loose the
floorboards one last time. By the time he had the sleeping bag un-
covered Aldo was dreadfully ripped—feeling no pain, as they say in
America. Carefully he pried the lumpy bag out from between the
narrow beams, then unzipped it to reveal a stirring sight: the slender
body of a young girl, stark naked save for the silver tape that bound
her wrists and ankles and covered her mouth.

He took a few seconds to let the sight burn itself into his memory. For if ever there had been one image that summed up everything that made life worth living for Aldo Striescu, this was surely
it, this bound and naked child-woman staring up at him with gray
eyes gone all soft and quiescent. Only one thing missing to make
this a truly defining moment in Aldo's life—La Divina. He glanced

down at his watch. 11:44. Not enough time to fetch his Discman. *Oh well, perhaps later,* he thought, slinging the warm, naked body over his shoulder.

On his way down the hill Aldo amused himself by selecting individual arias for each of his victims. Possibly *Norma* for the girl. The "Casta Diva." Or perhaps something a bit more romantic. *Romeo et Juliette.* "Je veux vivre dans ce rêve." And definitely the mad scene from *Lucia* for the striga. But as for the strigoi—no Callas for Jamey Whistler. Just the "Serenada de Vierme"—the worm serenade.

━

Aldo set Martha down in the passenger seat of the Toyota bound, gagged, and naked, then reached in and sliced through the tape at her ankles. "Start trying to work some feeling back into your feet—I may need you to stand up and show yourself."

As he wiped his scalpel with his pocket handkerchief to remove the sticky tape residue from the blade, the idea began sounding better and better. As soon as the two of them were out of the car, he decided, he'd shove Martha out into the open. Even if she only managed a step or two, she would almost certainly distract their attention long enough to give him time to take proper aim. Especially if she was naked. The strigoi wouldn't be able to tear his eyes away, even if it *was* his daughter.

Kneeling behind the open door of the Toyota, Aldo removed the pistol from his pocket and balanced it on the windowsill again. He wondered whether he ought to chance a test shot, check the gun's rudimentary notched sight as well as the windage and angle of the downhill shot. Decided against it—the less gunfire the better. He would aim the first shot midpoint between Whistler's navel and sternum, the way he'd been trained, thus giving himself maximum leeway—a foot above and below for an average-sized man, and six inches to either side; a makable shot even without sighting in.

Aldo unscrewed the top of the thermos, popped the plug, took a swig. Soon he could see well enough in the dark, hear acutely enough, that there was no way even another strigoi could sneak up on him. Still the doubts beat like moths around his head as the minutes wore on. Anything might have gone wrong. They could have called the cops. An armada of helicopters might appear over the hilltop at any moment. *Or trackers and dogs. Or—*

Another pull on the thermos. Aldo tried to beat the fear back with sarcasm: *Or what? Villagers with flaming torches? Ha!*

On the other hand, an instinct for self-preservation might keep them from coming in the first place. Certainly would have kept *him* away from such an obvious trap. But in that case, what was the worst that could happen? He'd remove the girl somewhere, peel her out of the sleeping bag, slip on the earphones, and have at her to the tune of "Casta Diva." He fantasized about covering her face with the pillow he'd been saving for her godmother, suffocating her until he came, then reviving her and doing it all over again. And again and again—she was a young strong thing—might last through quite a few go-rounds.

And by tomorrow his hand would be healed enough that he could remove the stitches and bandages. Then he could go striga and strigoi hunting again, unencumbered. Not bad for a worst-case scenario.

But as he screwed the cap back on the thermos Aldo heard the whine of an engine ascending the dirt road in low gear; a moment later the dark shape of a classic Jaguar saloon crept into view, headlights dimmed. "Good for you," he muttered softly. No worst-case scenario this time.

But neither were they following the scenario he'd laid out. The Jaguar stopped according to instructions, and as best as he could tell through the glare of the Toyota's headlights off the Jaguar's windshield, it was indeed the striga behind the wheel. But she appeared to be alone. Aldo kept the pistol trained on her. He almost squeezed off a shot when she briefly disappeared from view—then the passenger door of the Jaguar opened and a body tumbled out onto the dirt.

A moment later the driver's door opened and the striga climbed out slowly, her hands in the air. "Aldo?" she called, stepping around to the front of the Jaguar, peering up into the blinding beam of the Toyota's headlights.

"That's far enough," he called back. "Now what's all this? And who's that?"

"It's Jamey," she called out boldly. "He wouldn't cooperate. Wanted to leave early, sneak up on you. I *had* to kill him."

"Hold it right there." She'd started to lower her hands. "Keep 'em up where I can see 'em." John Wayne would have been proud. "Dead, you say?"

"Come see for yourself."

"Not just yet, thanks." But the body by the side of the car still hadn't moved, and it was crumpled into a distinctly unnatural position. Aldo was confused. He began to wish he hadn't taken those last two Percodans. "What the hell is going on here?"

Selene shrugged. "I'm a striga. I need a strigoi. This one here" —she jerked her head contemptuously at the body crumpled in the dirt beside the car—"has been washed up for years."

"And why should I believe you?"

"I killed him for you, didn't I?"

About what he'd expected her to say. Not that it mattered; he was only stalling, trying to think this through. Of course he knew about the legendary connection about the striga and strigoi; he'd certainly used it to his advantage with Jonas. But beyond the basic etymology and the folktales, he'd never known a strigoi who actually worked with a striga. Until . . .

Until this one. Could there be some truth to the old legends? "Killed him?" he called. "We'll soon see about that. I want you to drag him up here, lay him out in front of my headlights, then lie down beside him on your stomach."

It took Selene several minutes to drag the limp hundred-and-seventy-pound man through the gate and up the hill by the collar of his jacket. Toward the end she could tug him only a few feet at a time before stopping to catch her breath. "How do you want him?" she said, panting, when she had hauled the body within yards of the Toyota's headlights.

"Pardon?"

She wiped the sweat out of her eyes with the sleeve of her blazer. "You said you want me on my stomach. How do you want him?"

"On his back."

She knelt by the body, flopped it over unceremoniously.

"Now you—but a few feet farther back."

When she was lying on her belly with her face in the clodded dirt of the road, he came around from behind the door of the Toyota, keeping the pistol trained on her. "First to move gets the first bullet," he announced loudly. Then, over his shoulder: "This means you too, Martha."

"I think I have to sneeze," said Selene.

"I'm sure such a powerful striga as yourself can manage to hold back a sneeze," Aldo replied. "And if you're not so powerful, who needs you anyway?" Awkward phrasing, sibilant s's—his California accent had evaporated entirely. He knelt at Whistler's side, placed two fingers at the side of the neck, feeling for a carotid pulse— there was none.

"Well?" Selene whispered.

Aldo rose to his knees, keeping the pistol trained on her. "He does appear to be dead, I'll give you that. But so did you, that first night."

"That was belladonna," she said.

Aldo was far from convinced. "And what did you use on him?"

"Here, I'll—"

"Don't move!" She had started to roll over. "Crawl back a few feet." She obeyed. "All right, go ahead."

The striga rolled over onto her back, then sat up, removed the sewing packet, pulled one of the pins out, showed it to him, then slipped it carefully back into the cardboard packet. "Curare," she lied. "Same thing I used on Mrs. Wah. She was dead enough for you, wasn't she?"

"But you also used it on the old man, and he woke up three hours later."

"I had graduated dosages. These are all the same, all fatal."

Aldo thought it over. "I think I'll blow his brains out anyway, just to be sure."

"Go ahead," replied the striga calmly, as Aldo placed the barrel of the pistol against Whistler's temple and cocked it. "But you'll be blowing off a hundred million bucks along with his head."

Aldo let the hammer back down slowly. "I'm listening."

⚊

"As my previous strigoi always used to say, if you can still count your money, you don't have enough yet. The last I heard, the Whistler trust was well into nine figures." Selene had, of course, guessed at the sum; Jamey never discussed his finances. She and Aldo were sitting in the middle of the dirt road under the wide and starry sky, leaning companionably against the front bumper of the Toyota. He had turned off the headlights before sitting down next to her with the pistol pointing toward her ribs.

"Half of it belongs to Jamey, the interest on the other half goes to Jonas. But when Jonas dies the capital reverts to Jamey, and when Jamey dies"—she looked down at the body lying at their feet—"officially, I mean, then the entire trust goes to his children, if any. As of a month ago, that would have been Cora. As of twenty minutes ago, it's Martha there." She jerked a thumb over her shoulder. Aldo waggled the pistol in her direction.

"Calm down," admonished Selene. "We're talking a minimum of fifty million in the pocket right now. Are you with me so far?"

He waved the barrel of the pistol impatiently. "If you're about to suggest we knock off the old man and double our money, then I'm ahead of you. But what does it matter whether I put a bullet through this one's head or not?" He nudged Whistler's body with the pointed toe of his ankle-high boot.

"We're going to have to produce the body at some point. If he was obviously murdered, there are going to be questions raised."

"He's already been murdered, and there'll be questions in any event—the fires and all that."

Selene shook her head. "You underestimate your new striga. Take a look at his right hand."

Aldo leaned forward, lifted Whistler's limp arm, turned it over to examine the palm. The pin was still embedded in it; the skin immediately around it had turned a dark purple with a ragged blue corona. "So?"

"So sad," she replied. "Wealthy man, everything to live for. Goes off the deep end. Murders his wife and child, sets fire to the Greathouse to cover the murders. We can work out the details later, but that's reason enough right there for a man to commit suicide." She looked down coyly at the sewing packet in her fingers. "Of course there'll be questions. But if they find him dead from a poison found only in the Caribbean, where he last lived, with the rest of these pins in his pocket, they'll be *why* questions, not *how*. And certainly not *who*."

"And what makes you think the girl is going to cooperate through all this?"

"Leave the girl to me. We strigas have our methods."

Aldo's thermos was at his side. He shifted the pistol to his injured hand, unscrewed the cap of the thermos with his good hand, peered inside. Only a little left. He polished it off. No need to conserve—after all, he had two live vessels to work with. When he looked over at Selene again his brown eyes were dark with broken capillaries, but thoughtful. "We strigoi have our methods too."

It was cold there on the open hillside; Selene buttoned her blazer, for all the good that did. "That's why we'll make such a good team. What's on your mind?"

Aldo drew a few inches closer. "What would happen if she died?" he whispered. "After she'd come into the legacy, I mean?"

"Do you mean could she will us the money? No. The way the trust is written, it's either children or charity."

"But if Martha herself had a child, and then suffered an untimely demise? Who would get the money then?"

"The child, of course."

"All of it?"

"If Jonas was dead."

"And the father of that child? Whoever he might turn out to be? Would he be able to access all that money?"

"I don't see why . . ." Then, as if she'd just caught on: "Why you clever devil, you." They were still whispering. "I do believe he would. Whoever he might turn out to be. The question is, would he share it with his striga?"

"He might," replied Aldo, as she flipped the packet in his direction. He plucked it out of the dirt, leaned forward, and slipped it into the flap pocket of Whistler's denim jacket. "In fact, I'm quite sure he would. What's the age of consent in California?"

"Eighteen."

"And the girl?"

"Seventeen." Then she smiled. "But she's got a birthday coming up in February."

Aldo nodded, recapped the thermos, rose slowly to his feet. "Martha, my dear," he called, slipping the pistol into the waistband of his black slacks as he walked around toward the driver's side of the Toyota. "How would you like to make an old Romanian very happy?"

7

Selene stood up slowly, a Beatles song going through her head. "Fool on the Hill." With the car lights doused, she could see all the way to the ocean on the far side of the highway. Whitecaps in the starlight. Behind her she heard the metallic click of the safety on Aldo's pistol.

"Who told you you could stand up?" he asked.

She knew without turning around that he had the gun pointing in the center of her back; she could feel a tingling between her shoulder blades. She sighed. "What's it going to take to get you to trust me?"

A derisive laugh. "How much did *he* trust you?"

"Not enough." She turned around carefully. Aldo was standing by the side of the Toyota; the pistol was now aimed at her heart. "How do you mean?"

"He wanted to come after you by himself. Told me my job was to supply him with blood and keep my mouth shut."

"Clever fellow."

"Not clever enough, obviously." She threw her hands open wide; his finger tightened on the trigger. "Damn it, Aldo, we've got the chance of a lifetime here, but we've got to work together to make it happen. And to work together we're going to have to trust each other."

"I suppose you're going to tell me now that *you* trust *me?*"
Another laugh.

"Of course I trust you—otherwise I wouldn't be here." She
glanced over her shoulder toward Jamey's body. "And he wouldn't
be there. So I'm asking you again, what's it going to take to get
you to trust me?"

He took a step toward her, raised the pistol until she was staring
down the barrel. "You're serious, aren't you?"

"As a heart attack," replied the fool on the hill. The stars froze
overhead; behind her, Selene knew, the waves were poised in mid-
rise, the breakers in midfall, the whitecaps hanging in the air like
swirls of white frosting on a wedding cake. A lifetime passed in
which nothing moved but the quivering black hole at the end of
the gunbarrel. She had just about decided that she'd made the very
last mistake of her life, *a real doozy,* when he lowered the pistol.

"In that case, I suppose I can think of something," he said—
but the pause had lasted so long she couldn't remember for a moment what it was he was going to think of. Then it came to her:
this madman standing in front of her, this arsonist, this kidnapper,
this murdering vampyromaniac, was going to think of some way
that she could prove herself worthy of his trust.

This should be good, she thought. *This should be a real doozy too.*

⟶

Doozy was not the word. There was no word. After Aldo loaded
Whistler into the trunk of the rental car, he backed it the rest of
the way up the winding dirt road with Martha slumped beside him
in the passenger seat, sagging into the shoulder harness. Selene followed in the Jaguar and parked it next to the Toyota under the
stand of cypress trees at the end of the road, then followed him on
foot through the high grass. He had Martha over one shoulder and
Jamey over the other; both bodies were limp.

Strange feeling, to be walking now over ground she'd seen from
the air earlier that same day. Selene followed Aldo through the grass
to the third cabin, and up two plank-and-cinder-block steps. Inside,
he propped both bodies up against the far wall, heads lolling. Be-

tween them a battery-powered Coleman lamp cast their elongated shadows out sideways and sent Aldo's dancing crazily ahead of him across the dusty wooden floor. "Ready?" he asked.

Selene forced herself to smile. "As I'll ever be."

He smiled back. "Stand over there by the foam pallet. Start by removing your clothes—slowly. Not that I'm an ecdysiaphile."

"Not a what?" said Selene, taking off her blazer, looking for something to lay it down on, settling for the ice chest, then kicking off her sandals.

"An ecdysiaphile, one who enjoys watching strippers. I just want to make sure you haven't any more pins secreted about your person." He shook his head sadly. "Disgraceful, how little you Americans know of your own mother tongue."

"And amazing how much of it you know. Did you learn it in school?" Selene started to turn her back to him as she pulled her "Surrender Dorothy" T-shirt over her head.

"Don't turn around," he said sharply. "And keep your hands in sight at all times." Then, conversationally, as if they were on a first date, as she unzipped her jeans and peeled them down over her hips: "School? After a fashion; I studied at the Institut Limba Strain in Bucharest. And you?"

"Barnard." She stepped out of her jeans and stood before him in her see-through lavender panties and bra. "Shall I keep going?"

"What do you think?"

Selene reached behind her and unhooked the bra, then slipped the shoulder straps down and let it fall; she slid her panties down and stepped out of them. Now she stood before him naked, feeling the goosebumps starting to rise across her shoulders and arms; her nipples had puckered up into hard cones. Her shoulders slumped forward as her body turned shy, tried to draw in on itself. Then she remembered the magazines she'd seen in Moll's office, forced her shoulders back, thrust her chest out. "Well?" she said, shifting her weight to one leg, cocking her fist on her hip.

He looked her up and down. "You'll do. But let's make sure you haven't any surprises for me. Hold your hands out to the side."

She obeyed, raised her arms as if she were being frisked—which she was. He started at her hair, sifting through it with the fingers of his good hand as if he were checking her for lice. That was bad enough, but when he forced her mouth open, peered into it, stuck his fingers in and began feeling around gingerly, she started to retch.

He jerked his hand out of her mouth and stepped back. "If you're going to vomit, do it out there."

"Just a gag reflex," she said, swallowing hard. "Had it since I was a kid. Dentists absolutely hate me. Course, I'm not so fond of them either."

"I understand completely," said Aldo, pulling her hair back so that he could examine her ears. "At the Orfelinat—the orphanage where I was raised—we had to visit the dentist once a year. *Care tort* . . . open your legs a bit wider, would you? There, that's the girl . . . *care tortureaza*, we called him. The Torturer. If he found a caries"—he knelt down—"he'd pull the tooth." Aldo was now going through her pubic hair with his fingertips. "Unh-unh, keep 'em up." She'd let her hands drop to her sides.

"My arms are getting tired."

"Just another few seconds now." He ducked his head to the side, spread the lips of her sex gently, and peered up into her like a man looking under the couch for his cuff links.

It was all quite matter-of-fact and clinical, and yet at the same time it was a vicious and deliberately humiliating invasion of her body for which Selene swore to herself she'd make him pay. First, though, she forced a joke: "Sorry I forgot my speculum."

"Mmm-hmmm."

"We don't really keep razor blades up there anymore."

"Mmm-hmmm."

"DAMN IT ALDO THAT'S ENOUGH!"

He stopped. "I agree. Turn around."

"No way José."

"I have to—" He started knee-walking around behind her.

"You're not going to find—" She began rotating, arms held straight out, turning to keep him in front of her as he scrambled around on his knees trying to get behind her.

"—check out all the—"

"—anything up there!"

"—orifices."

"I quit," said Selene, stopping in midpirouette, lowering her arms deliberately and covering her ass with both hands—a ridiculous posture, but no more ridiculous than the dance she and Aldo had just performed. "Forget it."

"Pardon?" Aldo looked up.

"I said forget it. It's not worth it, teaming up with you." With as much dignity as she could summon up, standing there naked, holding on to her ass with both hands. "My mistake—you're obviously not the strigoi I thought you were. So you can just go ahead and kill me, then drag your sorry self back home and collect however much chump change Jonas is paying you to kill Jamey—even though *I* had to do it for you. And when that money's gone, and you're sitting around crying in your beer, you can think about me, and how much you *could* have had. Then you can stick your thumb up your own ass, if there's room for it with your head up there."

Aldo was on his feet in an instant. "I love it," he said. "You're going to do just fine in the next part."

"I can't wait."

She didn't have to. With a swipe of his foot Aldo knocked her feet out from under her; she fell backward onto the thin egg-carton foam pad. Luckily her hands were already behind her to break her fall, but it jarred the wind out of her nonetheless. When she looked up again, Aldo was standing over her holding a pillow.

"Fight me," he said. "Fight me as hard as you can, and if you're still fighting when you pass out, I'll let you wake up. If not, you're not the striga *I* took *you* for."

Then without further warning he was on top of her, had dropped with his full weight, sending the air out of her lungs with a rush just as she had realized what was coming and started to take a deep breath to fill them.

No fair, she thought irrelevantly as the pillow approached her face. Her mind jumped back thirty years. She thought of how Stan Kovic had once tried to crush the air from her too. Then she began to fight.

Selene opened her eyes and took stock. Sore tailbone where she'd fallen on it. Egg on her forehead from skull-butting Aldo. Knocked him loosey-goosey—only for a few seconds, but it had been worth it for a gulp of air. Her hands sore from pounding on him, her heels from drumming them on the floorboards. Gingerly she rolled onto her side; Aldo was lying beside her on the floor next to the pad. Time to play the satisfied striga.

"How'd I do?" she asked.

"Not bad," he said, looking down with a goofy grin toward the wet stain at the front of his shiny black trousers. "I let you wake up, didn't I?"

"Aren't you going to ask me how it was for me?"

"Not my major area of concern, but all right: how was it for you?"

"Man, it was a *ruuush*."

He rubbed his forehead gingerly. "You did seem to—how do they say here?—to get into it."

"No shit."

"Next time I'll last longer," he said.

"Me too."

"Not if I've got two good hands. It was fun, though, wasn't it?"

"Oh, scads," she agreed languidly. Her real satisfaction lay in the knowledge that he hadn't even gotten his pecker out of his pants. She hoped their encounter would still count for the orgomantic prophecy.

Aldo propped his head up on his good hand, his elbow on the floor and his cheek resting in his palm. "You know, there are only three times in my life when I truly feel alive," he mused.

"Oh?"

"Yes. When I'm drinking blood, when I'm coming, and when I'm listening to Callas."

"Just Callas? Not other singers?" Selene's ignorance of grand opera was both wide and deep, but she wanted to keep a conversation going, and it seemed the least dangerous avenue of the three to follow.

"Just Callas."

"Really? Why just Callas?" Now Selene let herself shiver from the cold—not faking it, but not suppressing it either. "It's freezing in here—reach me my jacket, would you? Thanks." She draped it over her torso. "So why just Callas—is she that much better than all the others?"

"Don't know. Don't listen to any others."

"Then why?"

"It's personal; I've never told a living soul."

"Hey, if you can't tell your striga, who can you tell?" She reached into the pocket of her blazer, pulled out a green pack of Doublemint. "Gum?"

"Don't chew. Filthy habit—wait, let me see that."

"Oh for crying out loud, Aldo, are we going to spend the rest of our lives like this?" said Selene, reaching the pack toward him. "In the first place, I already offered it to you, and in the second place, it's going in *my* mouth."

He handed the gum back without looking at it. "Save your feistiness for our next go-round."

"Yes, great strigoi." She slid the center stick out of the pack, palmed it as she unwrapped the foil, popped it into her mouth. "Now tell me about Callas."

He propped his head on his palm again. "When I was brought to the Orfelinat as an infant, I had only three possessions—if an infant can be said to have possessions. At any rate, there were only three things that were delivered with me: the scrap of blanket that covered me, the basket I lay in, and a photograph in a small gilt frame. If it had been gold rather than gilt it would have been taken too. Times were hard in Bucharest back then. Of course, times are always hard in Bucharest.

"It was a photo of Callas, as it turned out, but I wasn't to learn that for quite a few years. And what my mother was doing with a photograph of La Divina at her bedside, I never learned—largely because I never knew anything about my mother, other than that she died giving birth to me. Instead I grew up in the Orfelinat believing that the woman in the photo was my mother. It was not until I was placed in the Institut Limba Strain that I learned the truth. I'd had the photo on my bedside table, and an older fellow down the hall admired it. 'That's my mother,' I told him. He laughed at me. 'So your mother is Maria Callas?' he said. 'Your mother is the greatest diva in the history of opera?' I wanted to crawl into a hole and die."

"Poor kid," muttered Selene, working her jaws.

"Yes, but it worked out rather well, actually. My new friend was an opera buff. Had a phonograph and quite a decent record collection, or stack of wax, as you Americans say."

"Not for forty years," remarked Selene.

"Thanks for the tip." Aldo was unfazed—better too much idiom than too little, that was his Institut training. "In any event, I was soon hooked on La Divina, as she was known. Saved my money, bought a reel-to-reel, taped every Callas in his collection, and began my own. It was the most peculiar thing: even though I knew in my mind that Maria was not my mother, on another level—my inner child, I believe you say in California—that's current, isn't it?"

"Close enough."

"On that level, then, my inner child still somehow thought of her that way. Whenever I heard her voice my heart opened up, like hearing my own mother sing me a lullabye. Still happens. In fact, I'm quite as hooked on Callas as I am on blood. Thank God for Walkmans and Discmans. I can be quite cranky without my Maria."

"You? Cranky?" said Selene, as her mouth began to burn. She had to fight the urge to swallow, lest the dumbcane paralyze her vocal cords.

Aldo chuckled. "Take my word for it."

Selene leaned over the edge of the foam pad, looked into Aldo's chocolate eyes. "Of course I take your word," she said, trying not to open her mouth, or let him see any of her spittle, which was by now pink with her own blood. "I trust you, remember. The question is, do you trust me yet?"

"As much as I trust anyone." His eyes opened a little wider as he stared back into hers—she'd been counting on that. "But I'm not in the business of—"

Ptoo. Ptoo. Quick as a viper, cool as if she'd been practicing the move for years, she spat a pink stream into first one of his eyes and then the other. He drew back, astonished; a second later his fingers, both bandaged and unbandaged, were clawing at his eyes as the poison began to take effect. Mashasha—stinging nettle—and Luzan dumbcane, with calcium oxylate crystals as deadly as ground glass, both held in a suspension that had been dissolved by her saliva. Once administered to the eyeball, Granny had assured Selene, there was no getting it out. "De more dey try to rub it out, de more dey rub it in," she'd said. "Tear dey own eyelids to bloody shreds."

I'd pay to watch that, Selene had thought at the time, but the truth was, she wasn't enjoying watching Aldo writhe in agony quite as much as she'd hoped she would. She spat out the gum, then glanced around the cabin for something to rinse her mouth with, found a half-full bottle of Stolichnaya standing by the ice chest, took a splash. The pain when the alcohol hit the irritated tissue inside her mouth was indescribable. She performed a spit take worthy of *I Love Lucy* and began hopping around the cabin nude, fanning her open mouth with her hand and making the sort of noises one makes after biting into a jalapeño. Meanwhile Aldo had begun emitting a high-pitched shriek; soon Martha, grunting frantically, joined the choir. Selene looked up; the girl nodded toward the ice chest. Selene hurried over and flipped back the Styrofoam lid, saw the big plastic bottle of Pepsi. She couldn't taste it, but groaned gratefully as the soda put out the worst of the fire inside her mouth. She drank, spat, drank, spat—the stuff might have been water for all she could tell.

"Thanks, dearie." She looked up at Martha, saw the girl's eyes go round with terror, turned to see Aldo struggling to his knees, eyes dripping gore: from road-show *Damn Yankees* to *Oedipus Rex*. Selene dashed over to Whistler, grabbed the sewing packet out of the front pocket of his jeans jacket. He started to topple sideways. She steadied him against the wall, turned back to Aldo, circled around behind him while removing a single pin from the packet, then darted in like a *banderillero* and planted the pin in the back of his neck just above the black collar of his shirt. He toppled forward onto his face.

Quickly Selene turned back to Martha and Whistler, propped up against the wall. She'd replaced Jamey's utility knife in the pocket of his jeans jacket earlier, and she used it now to slit the tape binding Martha's wrists. The girl's hands fell limply into her lap. "Shall I?" Selene reached toward the strip of tape that covered Martha's mouth and began peeling it off slowly as Martha tried to rub some feeling back in her hands.

"Is he dead now?" was Martha's first question.

"Only for twenty-four hours."

"What's in the pins?"

"Zombi paste. It's a way they have of preparing belladonna on Santa Luz."

"Let me see."

Selene handed her the packet; Martha had regained enough feeling in her fingers to pull the paper of pins out of the cardboard wrapper. "Help me up."

Selene slipped an arm around Martha's back and helped her to her feet. Martha swayed briefly, found her balance, tried a step, then another, and another, until she was standing directly over Aldo. Carefully she bent down; one by one she removed the three remaining pins from the paper and jabbed them into the nape of his neck. Only when three pins were firmly planted alongside the first did she turn to look at her godmother. "*Now* is he dead?"

With Granny Weed's compliments, thought Selene. Then she remembered the orgomancy. *Granny Bensozia's too.* She fought back a shudder, managed to nod in response to Martha's question; out of the corner of her eye she saw her shadow on the wall nodding grotesquely in tandem with her. Suddenly Selene wanted out of that cabin as desperately as she'd wanted out of the loft when her house was blazing around her. She knelt down, slipped her arms under Jamey's shoulders. "Grab his feet," she called to Martha. "Let's get him out to the car."

The skin around Martha's mouth was raw from the tape, mottled with a strawberry rash, and her lips were puffy; still she managed a weak smile as she looked over at her godmother. "Don't you think we ought to get some clothes on first?"

"Whew." Selene glanced down at herself, then across at Martha. "Do you know, I'd completely forgotten."

———

Once dressed, they struggled with Whistler's inert form for a few minutes, then gave up and dragged him out backward by the arms, letting his Topsiders drag on the ground. "It's true?" asked Martha as they hauled him down the plank-and-cinder-block steps with his heels bumping. "He really is my father?"

"To the best of my knowledge."

"You should have told me—or at least you shouldn't have lied to me."

"You're right. I'm sorry."

" 'S'okay. I already forgave you, back when I was, oh god . . ." *In there,* she started to say. They were dragging him past the middle cabin. It all started to catch up with her, the nightmare of the past few days. "I can't . . . I have to . . ."

Gently they lowered Whistler to the trodden grass; Selene put her arm around Martha and drew her close. "My poor baby, I can't imagine. . . ." She tightened her arm around Martha's shoulders.

"I'll say this for you, dearie: I do admire your instinct for revenge. You'll make a hell of a witch someday."

For a moment Martha was a child again in her godmother's arms. "Really?" she said shyly.

"The way you finished Aldo off? Absolutely positively. And what a Tale you'll have to tell." Selene wiped her own eyes with the back of her hand. "Ready to get started again?"

But Martha was peering past her, through the dark doorway of that middle cabin. "Have we got a minute? I have to do something."

When Selene entered the shack a moment later, she saw by the starlight pouring in through the holes in the roof that Martha was standing at the edge of a long narrow aperture in the floor. Selene took a step toward her; Martha wheeled, shouted a warning as Selene's right foot went through the dry-rotted floorboard.

"I was just about to tell you, you have to walk the beam," the girl explained. "See the line of nails?"

"I do now." Luckily the wood was so soft it had crumbled to sawdust. Selene yanked her foot free and retrieved her sandal.

When she joined Martha she could see where the floorboards had been removed and thrown to the side to reveal the dark, narrow cavity. Selene wondered what it must feel like, to be seventeen years old and staring down into your own grave.

"Len told me Daddy Don is dead. Is that true?"

Selene slipped her arm around Martha's waist. "I'm so sorry, honey. Len—Aldo—overdosed him with morphine."

"Must have been peaceful, hunh?"

"I can think of worse ways to go. So can you by now, I imagine."

"Did Aldo kill anybody else?"

Selene had to think about it for a moment. "Nobody you know." Not strictly true. Martha had met Nick a few times; she'd even seen her half sister Cora once, when the child was a few weeks old. But it didn't seem necessary to mention any of this at the moment. Perhaps the girl could talk about it with her father someday—might be healing for both of them.

Of course for now Martha's father was still lying out there in the tall grass, and Selene had nothing but the weed woman's assurances to tell her he wasn't as dead as all the others. "We'd better be going soon, dearie."

The girl looked up from the hole for the first time since Selene had joined her. "One thing I don't understand. What happened to"—she started to say *my father,* but the words wouldn't come yet—"Whistler? Did you zombi him too?"

"I did."

"How come?"

It occurred to Selene that she didn't quite know the answer to that question yet. Didn't know whether old Benny's orgomancy had been advice or prophecy. Then she realized that it didn't matter anymore: if advice, it had been heeded; if prophecy, it had been fulfilled.

"Long story, dearie," she replied, turning away from the empty grave. "I'll tell you all about it on the way home."

CHAPTER

9

Nick Santos's funeral took place at the Church of the Higher Power in El Cerrito on Saturday evening, November 20th. Twelve-Steppers (the recovered potheads still looked like potheads, the junkies like junkies, but the drunks had cleaned up nicely) mingled with computer nerds and tattooed body piercers. A fourth group of mourners, wearing sunglasses despite the late hour, had congregated on the lawn under the live oak tree before the service to sip a toast from flasks of various descriptions—more flasks than El Cerrito had seen in one place since Prohibition, though none of them was filled with bootleg whiskey.

The eulogy, delivered by the Reverend Betty Ruth Shoemaker, a major player in the recovery industry, dwelt rather heavily on the miracles that Higher Power could perform for those poor benighted souls among the mourners who were still among the afflicted addicted—or so it sounded to Selene, squirming uncomfortably in the rear pew. The Reverend spoke at length about how she and the departed had shared the same dreadful (but unidentified, to the relief of the sunglass-wearing contingent of mourners) addiction; how she had chosen to fight the dragon with a twelve-bladed sword, while poor Nick had attempted to tame it by using the (still unnamed) drug only on weekends.

"The Dream of the Occasional User," Betty Ruth declared

scathingly from the pulpit. "As well try to tame a literal dragon. And it turned on him, as it always does, and it killed him just as surely as . . ."

Selene never found out what it killed him as surely as. She had already slipped out the double doors at the rear of the white clapboard church. *Damn your sanctimonious hide, Betty Shoemaker,* she thought as she hurried down the walk. It wasn't blood that killed Nick—or vodka or weed or cock jewelry—it was Aldo, and although she understood where Betty was coming from (Betty and Nick had passed on their blood-drinking genes to their son, Leon, now fifteen months old: after kicking the blood habit herself, Betty had sworn to protect her child from his sanguinary inheritance), Selene still didn't want to hear Nick reduced to the sum of his addictions.

Who among us could pass such a test? she thought, writing her own eulogy on the way to the car she'd borrowed from Martha. *Nick lived fast, died relatively young, and it wasn't his fault he didn't leave a good-looking corpse.*

A somewhat sardonic frame of mind, but then, this wasn't the only funeral on Selene's calendar this weekend. Daddy Don's wasn't scheduled to begin until Sunday at noon, but the wake was already in full swing, and she wanted to get back to check on Martha. Not that the girl couldn't handle herself—and not that the bikers wouldn't be on their best behavior. But a tanked-up, cranked-up biker's best behavior could veer from maudlin to mayhem at the drop of a hat—or, in the absence of a hat, anything else that could be dropped.

Selene parked Martha's car by the side of the road, as the driveway was choked with motorcycles of every age and description save brand new or Japanese. A few Vincents and Indians, but mostly Harleys. Tiki torches lined the driveway, paper lanterns hung from the trees, one biker had passed out facedown in the rhododendrons, a middle-aged couple was dry humping against the side of the house, and the room where Don had died was wall-to-wall boogying mourners.

"Now *this* is what I call a *funeral*," shouted Selene over the sound of old Doobie Brothers blasting from speakers in the loft. "Anybody seen Martha?"

"I think she's up at your place," someone shouted back. Selene left via the back door and hiked up the driveway to her A-frame, where she found Martha seated at the kitchen counter eating Cherry Garcia ice cream out of the carton.

"When I was . . . you know," said the girl ("you know" meant with Aldo—it was the only way Martha referred to her captivity), "I kept fantasizing about all the stuff I'd eat when I got out. Now I couldn't care less."

"Then give it here." Selene climbed up on the stool opposite Martha, who slid the carton across the counter to her.

"It's a zoo down there, hunh?"

"Daddy Don would have liked it."

"Daddy Don would have *loved* it. How was the funeral?"

"Funereal. How come you split the party?"

"I got tired of everybody asking me what I'm going to do next. Next person that asks me that gets turned into a toad."

"We can arrange that," replied Selene.

"Yeah right. Like I believe there's a spell for that."

"Not per se. And not a spell. But there are quite a few substances that'll cause the body to break out in horrendous warts; put them in a verdigris base that turns the skin green, and you can see where the superstition came from about witches turning people into frogs." Selene polished off the last of the Cherry Garcia. Then, slyly: "So what do you tell them, these people who keep asking you what you're going to do next?"

The girl shot her a dart of a look. "I tell them I don't have to think about anything until after the funeral." Martha slid off the kitchen stool. "I'm going back down to the party."

"Want me to go with you?"

"Naah, I'll be fine." She tossed the empty ice cream carton into the trash by the back door, then turned to Selene. "*He's* up there, you know." Pointing up to the loft.

"I thought he might be. Did you two get a chance to talk?"

"You mean did we start bonding? I guess. Mostly he talked about you."

"Really?" She hadn't seen Jamey since shortly after he'd regained consciousness Thursday night. They'd had a beauty of an argument. He'd accused her of betraying him. She certainly couldn't deny it, but brought up his "What I need here is your blood, not your advice" speech by way of reply. He said he was only trying to keep her out of danger; she called him a liar; he'd stalked out as best he could on shaky legs. "Is he still furious?"

"Yeah, like!" replied Martha.

"I take it that means no."

"Selene, he's crazy about you. He kept talking about how much you meant to him, how much you guys have been through together. Hey, you know what?"

"What?"

"If you two ever do get married, that'll make you my godmother *and* my stepmother."

"Dream on!"

Selene locked the back door behind Martha, washed the ice cream spoon, straightened up the kitchen and living room, and was thinking about taking out the trash when it occurred to her that she was stalling. *Onward and upward.* Selene tugged on the fat tasseled rope hanging from the edge of the loft, and watched the new ladder lower itself smoothly into place. *Should have burned that old ladder years ago,* she thought. The new one *was* quite an improvement, if somewhat of a concession to age: three collapsible sections joined by springed hinges, the rungs wider and less steeply angled, the new handrails extending three feet above the floor of the newly shored-up loft.

Jamey was seated cross-legged on the foam mattress serving as a temporary replacement for the waterbed. He looked up. "Hello there. Hope it was okay that I let myself in."

"Mi casa . . ." she replied. "I thought you'd be in London by now."

"Had to get my passport replaced. My people greased a few

palms; I should have it by Wednesday, before they close for the holiday weekend."

"Amazing what money can do."

"Just a citizen in need."

"*Yeah, like!* as Martha would say."

"That Martha. Seems like a hell of a kid."

"To say the least."

"So how was Nick's service?"

"A drag. But everybody missed you. All your old drinking buddies were there. The good Reverend took the opportunity to lecture them about sobriety."

"I rather thought she might."

Selene had crossed to the dresser and was removing the tortoiseshell combs from her hair. "Where are you staying?" she asked, too casually.

"Bed-and-breakfast in Olema."

She picked up her brush and turned back to him. "I'm too tired for games, Jamey. Where do we stand?"

"Funny you should ask." He patted the side of the bed.

She sat down on the edge of the foam. "Hilarious."

"No, really. It's all I've been thinking about since I left. I don't want to lose you, Selene. I can't apologize for what I said, but I won't ask you to apologize for what you did, either."

"You'd better not," Selene replied, starting in on her hair again, brushing with short, angry strokes. "You have to admit, my way did work. We're all alive, and Aldo's not."

"Let's hope so. You should have cut his fucking head off, though, before you left. To be sure he was dead."

Oh, I'm sure, thought Selene. *He has to be dead—not only was he a pincushion, he was the second man in the orgomancy.* But she realized Jamey wouldn't have appreciated her reasoning. "By the way, you never did tell me what all you saw when you went flying."

"Only my body. From above. Couldn't bring myself to leave it."

Figures, thought Selene. *Found himself by the Fair Lady's light.*

He took the brush from her. "Here, let me help." His long-fingered hands were skilled and knowing—and manicured again. "I missed you, these last two days."

"Would you like to stay over?" She hadn't known she was going to invite him until just then, but it felt about right. Nobody should have to sleep alone after a funeral.

He pushed her hair aside and kissed her on the nape of the neck. "I was counting on it."

CHAPTER

10

After roaming the earth for what seemed like an eternity, Aldo Striescu's disembodied spirit had more or less reconciled itself to the idea that this was it, this was the afterlife. One thing sure, it wasn't hell: hell was down below where the people were. Every time he looked down from his restless flight they were up to something nasty: Hutus hacking up Tutsis with machetes, Serbs marching Muslims into mass graves—and all this during a time of relative peace on earth, as time and peace were measured down there.

Even apart from the large-scale slaughters, there didn't seem to be a square mile of inhabited earth where he couldn't find some form of cruelty being practiced. Murders, rapes, child abuse . . . He had just about decided that if this was the afterlife, he could live with it, when suddenly, against his will, he found himself hovering above his own battered, blinded body again; struggle as he might against the process, he could feel himself being sucked back into it; it was like being drawn down into a whirlpool, drowning into life. If he'd had a mouth he'd have screamed—then he did—he screamed and screamed and screamed, for though he now had a mouth, he had no eyes.

But if he had no eyes, how could they hurt so? He thought of the pistol. He could end the agony with the pistol. But as he began feeling around for the kit bag with the gun in it, his hand brushed against a small plastic pill bottle, and he remembered the Percodans. He tore off the rubbery plastic lid with his teeth and choked down a handful of pills.

"That ought to do it," he told himself, breathing hard, his voice hoarse from screaming. Of course, what would *really* do it was blood—he remembered how cavalierly he had polished off the last of his stash last night. Or was it last night? Just as it occurred to him that he hadn't the faintest idea what day it was, how much time had passed since the striga's betrayal, he heard the sound of an automobile climbing the hill in low gear. Friend or foe? But Aldo had no friends here. He scrabbled around frantically for the kit bag, found it just as he heard a car door slam, then a man's voice calling "Hellooo? Mr. Patch? Hellooo?"

Friend or foe? Neither—it had to be William Honey, keeping his appointment with Len Patch. And the day? Had to be Monday, 22 November, 1993. *"Drac noroc,"* whispered Aldo as he slipped the pistol under the waistband of his trousers. "The cavalry has arrived."

⬤

The realtor William Honey had climbed out of bed that morning with a song on his lips: "Timing and lo-*ca*-tion / Timing and lo-ca-*tion*," to the tune of "Some Enchanted Evening." Something about the date had been nagging at him ever since he'd made his appointment with the mysterious Len Patch last week. It wasn't until he saw the *Herald* that morning that it struck him: this was the thirtieth anniversary of the Kennedy assassination—the first Kennedy assassination.

But was it a good or a bad omen, that was the question. He played with the notion on the way to the office; he worked out of a small cottage on his place in the Carmel Highlands, so it was a short commute. Depended which way you looked at it, he decided, sitting down at his computer and accessing the Infolink program to print out a parcel map of the distressed property down the coast. Bad for Kennedy but good for Johnson. Bad for, what was his name,

Vaughn Meader, that comedian who'd done such a funny impression of JFK, but good for Oliver Stone.

And perhaps it would be good for William Honey as well—a comparable tear-down a few miles down the coast had sold for nearly four hundred thousand in October. He slipped the parcel map into his briefcase along with an abstract on the property, loaded a few tools into the back of his Volvo station wagon, and headed down the coast shortly before ten o'clock. The appointment with Patch wasn't until noon, but Honey hadn't been out to the property for months. By now the place might need a little fixing up just to qualify as a tear-down.

When he arrived he noticed the cattle gate was open—good thing there weren't any cattle within a mile of the place—and when he drove on up the dirt road he saw the beige Toyota under the cypress trees. He parked next to it. His first thought was that Patch had also arrived early, but if so, he saw upon closer examination, it had been very early: the car was crusted with sap and bird droppings.

"Helloooo? Mr. Patch? Hellooo?" No answer. In his blue blazer, khaki slacks, and brown loafers, Honey made his way through the tall grass, briefcase under his arm. Near shack looked about the same—still skeletal, stripped last year by squatters who were too lazy to gather firewood from up the hill. The first thing he noticed about the second cabin was the hole just inside the door—somebody'd put their foot through it for sure. He didn't know what to make of the other hole, though, the neat rectangular one from which the floorboards had been carefully removed and set aside. Perhaps Mr. Patch had wanted a look at the foundation, in which case he'd have been disappointed—there wasn't any.

It was the condition of the third cabin, the best of the three, that started him swearing under his breath. Someone had been camping out in it. Flies were buzzing around a chicken carcass, a bottle of vodka lay on the floor beside an empty Pepsi bottle. When he saw the body lying on its back behind the open Styrofoam ice chest, his first stunned assumption was that whoever it was was already dead—but then one of the arms waved feebly at the circling flies.

"Good Christ!" Honey dropped his briefcase and hurried inside. At the sound of his voice the mangled creature on the floor had groaned weakly; the realtor squatted down by the man's side, trying to keep his pants out of the blood that had pooled around the hideous head; the eyes were crusted with gore. "Don't worry, fella, it's going to be all right—just hang on."

"Bluh!"

"What's that?"

"Blood. Need blood."

"I've got a cell phone in the car. I'll tell them when I call for the ambulance. I'll be right back, I promise."

"No . . . your . . . blood."

"What about my blood?" Honey bent over the body and put his ear to the lips to hear the reply.

"Need it."

"Well I don't know—"

Those were William Honey's last words—appropriate enough, for he never did know what hit him. Just a muffled explosion and a blow to the midsection that drove the air out of him. He felt no pain as he pitched forward across Aldo's body: mercifully, the .38-caliber bullet that had torn through him had severed his spinal cord on its way out.

November 22nd, 1993. Bad day for William Honey, good day for Aldo Striescu.

⏤

By the time he crawled out from under the body of the realtor some fifteen minutes later, Aldo was feeling almost chipper, for a newly blinded man. It wasn't only the blood, but also the memory of roaming the earth as a disembodied soul that had him feeling so bubbly. For one thing, he was no longer afraid of death; he wasn't yearning desperately for it anymore, the Percodans having finally kicked in, but now he thought of it as an ally he might or might not have to call upon, rather than an enemy to be avoided at all costs. For another, more than just Aldo's relationship with death had been affected by his spiritual journey. Like Ebeneezer Scrooge after his experience with the supernatural, Aldo's entire outlook on life had been transformed. Always before he had felt himself cut off from the rest of humanity. The way other people, even the most virulent agents of the Securitate, were always going on about good and evil, Aldo had taken it for granted that some sort of moral absolute existed, and that he was outside it. Nor had it ever occurred to him to deny its existence, any more than it would have occurred to the tone-deaf Major Strada to deny the existence of music.

But now, after—quick math—four days and nights of watching humanity in action, Aldo finally understood that *Do unto others* had always been the whole of the golden rule, and that the only reason he had felt himself outside the pale of humanity was that he'd been in the vanguard all along. The feeling of well-being didn't last long, however. No sooner had he realized that there was no moral absolute than it hit him that it was too late for him to take advantage of his new understanding: he was only a poor blind man lying on the floor of a tumbledown shack on a deserted, albeit half-million-dollar, hillside, with a corpse for company.

Aldo buried his face in his hands. He would have wept—for the first time since childhood Aldo Striescu would have wept—but he couldn't. As if the irony inherent in the situation weren't already cruel enough, he soon discovered that whatever the striga had spat into his eyes had evidently destroyed his lacrimal apparatus as well: he had no tears to shed.

He turned his sightless face to his cooling companion. "So, William Honey? Are you up there laughing at me? I don't blame you —you've certainly had *your* revenge. But now I'm going to have mine, eyes or no eyes, and when I'm done I'll join you up there, and together we'll fly around and look down at *all* the bodies, our own included. Then we'll have ourselves a *real* laugh."

⟶

Chores that should have taken minutes took hours. Locating the thermos, transferring as much of William Honey's blood into it as he could before the stuff went bad. Crawling around the bloody floor of the cabin, slipping and sliding and swearing, searching for his kit bag again, finding it not by touch but by smell—comfortable leather smell. Packing—he would take only the kit bag with him, along with his black-lensed glasses and collapsible white cane. Funny, how all those hours of pretending to be blind turned out to have been practice for the real thing.

Not so funny, but equally necessary: finding the box of pop-up Wash'n Dri's, gritting his teeth as he soaked and dabbed the clotted blood and gore from around his ruined eyes. Searing pain, like pouring turpentine over an open wound, but it had to be done—didn't want some well-meaning Samaritan driving him straight to the hospital; bound to be questions asked.

Also necessary, but seemingly impossible: sanitizing the scene. And what a scene, thought Aldo: inside, he had the body of a local man who would presumably be missed sooner rather than later. Outside, he had the man's own car. No sense trying to hide the body if he couldn't hide the car. Even worse, the Toyota was out there too, and could easily be traced to Leonard Patch of Croyden, whose belongings and fingerprints were strewn about the floor of the bloody cabin. And any fire large enough and hot enough to cleanse the scene would only bring the authorities that much sooner. This would be the greatest professional challenge of Aldo's career.

Clearly the automobiles out there were at the root of the problem. He mulled it over as he fumbled around in his suitcase for a change of clothes, and a possible solution came to him as he pulled on a fresh-smelling shirt. He remembered the card clipped to the inside of the sun visor of the Toyota, a card he'd seen every time he'd flipped the visor down to check out his bloodshot eyes in the courtesy mirror. IN ORDER TO MEET OR EXCEED CALIFORNIA EMISSION CONTROL STANDARDS, it declared, THIS VEHICLE IS EQUIPPED WITH A CATALYTIC CONVERTER, and went on to warn of the danger involved in parking an automobile equipped with such a device directly over dry leaves or brush.

Or high grass? High, dry grass? Aldo felt through Honey's pockets for his car keys, then tapped his way out of the cabin and started down the hill. He soon found that by keeping the buildings close on his right, staying in their shade, occasionally brushing the walls with his right hand—which had healed up nicely while he was off flying, thank you very much—he was able to make his way from cabin to cabin with relative ease. At the far corner of the third cabin, however, there was nothing for it but to launch himself headlong into the fearful sea of darkness with only the cawing of the crows in the cypress trees, the degree of slope to the hillside, and, once he'd left the shade of the cabins, the angle of the sun against his right cheek to orient him. Several times he fell; the last fall sent him sprawling against the side of the Toyota—he had reached the cypress grove.

Next challenge: moving the vehicles. He tapped his way around them in ever-widening circles, trying to ascertain how the Corolla and the other car—a station wagon, by the shape of it—were aligned in relation to each other and the trees, how much room he'd have to back out, what sort of angle he'd need to cut the wheels before driving forward into the grass. He decided to try driving the Toyota first—it had an automatic shift—but turned on the Volvo's radio in order to be able to find his way back to it.

Aldo started up the Toyota and backed it a car length or so, cocking the wheel tentatively to the right, listening for the shriek of metal on metal which would tell him if he'd cut the angle too close to the station wagon. When the front bumper had cleared the other car he straightened the wheel, then drove forward until he could hear the tall grass whispering against the front bumper, then brushing the undercarriage.

He left the Toyota in park with the motor running, followed the sound of the station wagon's radio back down to the cypress grove, and repeated the process of backing and cutting and shifting, with a great deal of clutch grinding and gear slipping and bucking and stalling, until finally the front grille of the wagon fetched up against the rear bumper of the Toyota with a satisfying thud. He set the hand brake, grabbed his kit bag, and climbed out without shutting off the engine. Then it occurred to him that perhaps the wagon had some sort of manual choke. He reached in through the open door and fumbled around the dashboard, found a knob that pulled outward, and adjusted the idle speed until the engine was whining like a dentist's drill.

There, he told himself, backing away from the car, then turning around slowly like a dog about to lie down in high grass, until the sun was warming his right cheek again. *That ought to get that catastrophic converter heated up nicely.* He set off down the hill, kit bag in one hand, white cane in the other, chuckling at his fine English pun.

Laughing in the dark? Sure, but when everything was dark, where else was there to laugh?

11

Selene should have been enjoying herself more. What was not to enjoy? Almost every night she and Jamey dined in another fine restaurant, took in another show, had fabulous sex in (and out of) her new top-of-the-line Simmons Beautyrest. Mornings were spent with Martha, talking over old times while Martha copied out her own Book of Shadows by hand. They reminisced about Daddy Don, whose funeral Sunday afternoon had gone off without a hitch, though the roar of a hundred hogs had sent residents of Stinson Beach scurrying into doorways seeking shelter from an earthquake. The riders carried small paper bindles of ashes; as the procession wound up Highway 1 past Dead Woman's Curve, each sent his or her few grams of Daddy Don wafting over the side of the cliff to join Connie.

Selene's afternoons were full as well. Luncheon with one or another of the most noble ladies, then a few rounds of serious shopping—couch, chairs, lamps, rugs, wall hangings, knickknacks —she had decided to redecorate the A-frame top to bottom.

If she got home before sunset Jamey would still be asleep under the blackout tent in the loft. Selene would bring him a waker-upper from one of the bags in the fridge (he had renewed his connection with Blood Bank Bev, the former doyenne of Vampires Anonymous), and together, fog allowing, they would watch through the

Plexiglas bubble of the skylight as the sky darkened and the stars came out. Then off to dinner at a fine restaurant, and so on. Not a hard life.

So why the vague sense of dissatisfaction that colored her days and nights? Probably equal parts post-traumatic stress disorder resulting from the events of the last few weeks, and what might be called pretraumatic stress disorder, stemming from the inescapable knowledge that by the end of the week she and Jamey would be off to London to confront his father.

But there was something else troubling her as well, the same question that had been nagging at her since long before Halloween: even if everything went smoothly in London, she still had no idea what she was going to do afterward. Jamey seemed to be assuming the two of them would take up where they had left off before he had married Lourdes. He hadn't proposed to her again yet, but it seemed pretty clear to her that it was only a matter of time. He'd already dropped a few hints to the effect that, given her current disaffection with Wicca, there really wasn't anything holding her back from resigning her position as high priestess now, was there?

Mrs. Jamey Whistler—she could see herself slipping into that sort of life easily enough. But every time she thought about it, she remembered Moll's scornful words in the limo on the way to the airport. Needlepoint, marriage, volunteer work with the Cancer Society.

At least Martha had finally decided on *her* next move: over the phone she had let her mother talk her into spending Christmas in Tuscany. Moll's friend Gianni had a villa there that would be idyllic for a mother-and-child reunion. Selene had only one piece of advice for them: if they ran into a countess named Theresa di Voltera, they were to give her a wide berth.

Theresa di Voltera—odd the details that stayed with one. During her futile effort to talk Jamey out of going to London in the first place, Selene had given him a slightly sanitized version of the story of his father's fall and his mother's death—it had certainly given *her* a better understanding of the mad old fellow's motives. Of course, she wasn't the one whose spouse and child had been

murdered, but after spending a little time with Aldo—shudder—
Selene thought she had attained some insight into the dynamics of
the relationship between Jonas and Aldo, and was tending toward
the view that the more culpable partner had already been dealt
with.

Jamey wasn't buying it, however: "Somehow the knowledge
that my father was responsible for my mother's death in addition to
all the others does not exactly incline me toward clemency."

Which was yet another reason why Selene felt she needed to
be there when Jamey confronted Jonas; it seemed to her that there
had been quite enough killing already in this affair.

So after a mellow Thanksgiving dinner at Catherine and Sherman Bailey's house in Mill Valley, attended by most of the coven,
as well as several members of Whistler's old Penang, Martha drove
Jamey and Selene to the airport in the Jaguar, which she promised
to treat in their absence as if it were her own. This was a promise
that Jamey found less than reassuring. Somehow he had become the
father of a teenager—he was about as ready for it as Martha was to
find herself the daughter of a vampire.

—

Despite her own far from modest means, Selene had never flown
first class before. Didn't take her long to get into the spirit, though.
Swaddled in fluffy blankets, her feet in comfortable slippers, she
found herself leaning back against fat pillows, sipping a very decent
chilled Chablis and glaring at the peasants from coach who dared
to poke their heads through the curtains to inquire about using the
upper-class toilets.

As for the VIP treatment when they arrived at Heathrow late
Friday morning—the deference of the Customs officials, the waiting
car and driver—Selene decided she could get used to that as well.
She told Jamey as much when they were safely ensconced in a
luxurious Park Lane hotel suite with the blinds closed and the heavy
drapes drawn.

"I imagine you could," he remarked after the bellboy had been
dismissed. "Where's my white box?"

Selene had started for the bedroom—she turned back to Whistler. "You're not really blind, you know."

"Quite right—I'd almost forgotten." Jamey took off his opaque wraparound shades and began unwinding the strip of black cloth tied around his head as a second line of defense for his eyes. Aldo Striescu wasn't the only photophobic blood drinker to have hit upon the idea of masquerading as a blind man when circumstances forced him to travel during daylight hours.

Jamey found the hard-shell white bio-hazard ice chest with the big red cross on top near the minibar where the bellboy had deposited it, and loaded all but one of the thick plastic bags of whole blood labeled with his own name and blood type into the small refrigerator. It was a concept pioneered by Jamey in the mid-eighties, when most nations' blood supplies were considered compromised by the HIV virus: even now, with new strains of AIDS being discovered every year, the role of a wealthy hypochondriac traveling with his own predrawn blood in case an emergency transfusion became necessary was not so far-fetched or eccentric a pose that it provoked more than mild curiosity among border guards and Customs officials.

While Jamey enjoyed his first drink on British soil, Selene finished unpacking and ran herself a bubble bath in a Romanesque tub. When Jamey came wandering in, glass in hand, she slipped beneath the suds until only her head was visible—didn't want the Creature getting any ideas.

"I'm having our lunch sent up." He perched on the edge of the tub.

"What did you order?"

"Damned if I know. They asked me if I'd like what I'd ordered during my last stay—seemed ungracious to tell them I didn't remember what that was when they'd gone to all the trouble of keeping track."

The main course at luncheon turned out to be something called gravlax, thin slices of marinated salmon served over rice. "The height of English cuisine," Selene conceded when the last morsel was history. "Of course, that's sort of like being the tallest mountain in Ohio."

After lunch Selene went into the bedroom and napped for a few hours. When she came out Jamey was watching a soccer match on the telly. Selene had rarely seen him so animated outside of the bedroom. "I didn't know you were such a rabid soccer fan."

"Oh yes. Quite a respectable striker in my day. Might have gone in for it professionally if only they didn't insist on playing during the daytime."

She sat down next to him on the sofa. "Jamey?"

"Mmm?"

She took his hand. "It's not too late to change your mind."

Without taking his eyes from the screen. "It certainly is, m'dear. There are no fifty-year-old soccer—"

"You know perfectly well what I'm talking about."

"And you know perfectly well I'm deliberately ignoring you." There was a bowl of mixed nuts on the coffee table. Jamey tossed a cashew in the air and caught it in his mouth. When he turned to look at her his eyes were glittering red. "It's going to be dark soon. I've had the concierge book us a table at L'Odeon on Regent Street. By all reports they've a saddle of rabbit to die for, and a black pudding to bring you back from the dead. After we dine I'm going to pay a visit to Number Eleven and have a chat with my father. You can either accompany me, or return to the hotel and wait. Now if you'll excuse me, I believe the home team is about to— Oh, good stop, good stop."

That last was to the goalie of the team in blue. When there was a break in the action Jamey turned back to Selene. "I don't mean to sound inflexible—if there's another restaurant you'd prefer, just say the word. I'm told the Connaught still has a lovely mixed grill."

It is possible to look at, say, a rack of lamb and not think about the lamb; it is, however, quite impossible to see a saddle of rabbit and not think about the rabbit. What little appetite Selene had worked up quickly fled at the sight of Jamey's entrée. She scarcely touched her scallops, just shoved the food around on the plate so as not to offend the chef, and waved away the dessert trolley. She and Jamey hardly spoke during the meal, nor was there much conversation in the back seat of the cab on the way to No. 11. Selene kept to her side, Jamey to his. One joke: she asked him who'd made his leather bomber jacket. "Dolce et Gabbana est pro patria mori," he replied. Nothing more until the cab had turned onto the Belgrave Road—then Jamey asked her something in a whisper.

"What?" Selene turned to him. She'd been looking out the cab window, but not paying much attention; mostly she was trying not to think about what might be waiting for them at No. 11, because when she did, even though she knew it was unlikely, she couldn't help picturing Mrs. Wah's corpse lying there rotting on the floor of the atelier.

"Have you brought any of your poisoned pins with you?" he repeated.

"I'm not going to help you kill your father, Jamey."

"I'm not asking you to. I was more worried about the possibility of your using one on me again."

"Well don't be. I don't have any pins left anyway."

"Why didn't you just say so in the first place?" replied Jamey in a mildly annoyed tone. Then: "Next corner will be fine, driver."

They were still three long blocks from Cranwick Square. Was Jamey so sure there'd be bloodshed, then, that he didn't want his whereabouts traced? Selene gave it one more try as the driver pulled over to the curb. "Nothing you can do in there will bring Lourdes and Cora back."

"Oh really? And I was so counting on their sliding down from heaven on a moonbeam." His plummiest tone. But when he turned to face her the pain in his eyes stopped her in mid–*up yours*.

"I'm sorry, Jamey. You didn't need me to tell you that."

He reached out and brushed her hair back from her forehead where it had come loose from her tortoise-shell comb. The gesture reminded her of their first meeting twenty-five years before, in Morgana's parlor; she pressed the hand tightly against her cheek.

"Aren't we a pair to draw to?" said Jamey, tears welling in his bloodshot eyes. In the darkness in the back of the cab, the irises were only a little grayer than the whites.

"Always were."

"I have to see this through, you know. One way or another I have to see this finished."

"I know." Then, to her own surprise: "Me too."

CHAPTER

12

Aldo Striescu hadn't truly understood the impact the sight of his eyes would have upon others until the third or fourth ride. The driver was a kid, from the sound of his voice.

"Look, man, I just gotta ask—are you really, you know . . . blind, or is this just how you get rides? Don't make no difference to me—I mean, I ain't gonna kick you out or anything—but . . . Oh. Oh Jesus."

For Aldo had lifted his dark glasses by way of reply. With a squeal of brakes the car veered to the right, shuddered to a stop; the driver's door flew open. They must have been on a narrow shoulder of the highway—Aldo could hear traffic rushing by just a few feet to the left as the boy vomited onto the pavement.

After that he left the glasses on. Soon the rides began to blur together in his mind, undifferentiated by the modality of the visible. Voices, smells, snatches of conversations. Standing by the side of the coastal highway, sometimes in the heat of the sun, more often shivering, his windbreaker zipped up to his throat, in the all but palpable fog. Blood would have helped, but he had to ration his remaining store a sip at a time. A woman bought him supper and put him up in her motel room the first night, but lamentably her motives were charitable, and nothing came of it. He considered killing her for her blood, but escaping afterward would have been somewhat of a problem.

The second day was even worse. An old man in an old sedan who kept blathering on about the view (for Aldo, of course, the scenery never changed) finally dropped him off somewhere between El Something and San Something Else, and he stepped off the side of the road to urinate into the bushes. But afterward he must have gotten disoriented, taken a wrong turn somehow, and couldn't find his way back to the highway. He tried following the sound of traffic and walked into a chain-link fence, then followed the fence and found himself in a cul-de-sac. Fighting against panic now, he tried to backtrack and stepped onto what proved to be the highway off-ramp, directly in the path of an oncoming truck. A horn blared. *What are ya, bl— Oh*, was the shouted comment.

From then on he kept to the shoulder of the road. Sometimes a car radio would give him the hour, but it didn't mean much; time measured itself out in increments of riding and waiting, hot and cold, crashing and high, hungry and less hungry. Mostly he ate candy bars from gas stations when someone would help him with the vending machine. But as the days melted into nights it seemed as if the rides were getting shorter and the waits in between longer, and it occurred to him that perhaps his personal hygiene was suffering. He decided to chance using his credit card, telling himself that if the cops were indeed looking for one Leonard Patch, they'd surely nab him at the airport anyway; he asked the next ride to drop him off at a motel that fronted the road—one with a restaurant, if possible.

There proved to be a whole strip of these lining the highway at a town called Cambria. The desk clerk walked him to the coffee shop; unable to read the menu, he ordered a burger and fries in his best Californian. Finger food; cutlery was too unwieldy. The waitress walked him back to his room. After that he was on his own. He banged his old football knee against the corner of a table, nearly scalded himself in the shower, and later, as he lay in what he presumed was the dark, he found himself wondering, not how the blind managed to get along, but why? Then he remembered that most people, the sightless included, were still as afraid of death as he used to be—before he knew about the afterlife, that is.

But it was dangerous to think too much about flying, too tempting, with the pain starting to build again where his eyes used to be, and the pistol only a few feet away in the kit bag by the foot of the bed. Aldo allowed himself a small sip of Dutch courage from the thermos, chose a CD at random (how else, now?), and listened to Callas until the batteries of the Discman had gone dead and his bowels had come alive.

And no wonder, on a diet of burgers and candy bars, he thought as he climbed out of bed. He'd left his cane by the side of the bed, but it went flying when he tripped over his kit bag. No time to feel around for it, either; his innards were cramping now. He started on hands and knees in what he thought was the direction of the bathroom and crawled headfirst into a table leg, lost his bearings entirely, and ended up scrambling around the floor, desperately afraid of soiling himself (toilet training at the Orfelinat had been a brutal affair) until he'd found the wall, then following the wall by touch around two corners until he reached the open bathroom doorway.

Made it, though. It was his first bowel movement since he'd been blinded, and when, after a great deal of stink and commotion, it was done and he had located the roll of paper in the recess next to the toilet, he found himself confronting one of the world's greatest mysteries: how do the blind know when they're done wiping themselves?

It struck him as hilariously funny: sitting there on the throne with a wad of bum-paper in his hand, he began to laugh. How long he went on he couldn't have said, but every time the hilarity started to subside he'd reach back to wipe himself and off he'd go again— harsh, barking laughter bouncing off the tile walls. Eventually someone in the adjacent room started banging on the wall and threatening to call the desk, so Aldo swiped and sniffed until he was reasonably certain he was clean, and shuffled back to bed giggling quietly.

But as he lay there listening to the radio and thinking ahead to the next morning, thinking about going *out there* again, his good humor deserted him, along with most of his courage, and he went so far as to take the pistol out of the kit bag. Just wanted to feel its reassuring weight in his hand, he told himself. Then he wanted to see how it felt against his temple. Then in his mouth, cocked, safety off; then farther in, angled up—*blow a chimney hole straight up through the roof of the mouth that way, take out the entire cerebral cortex. That was how Major Strada had done it, according to a later émigré. Characteristically thorough, but uncharacteristically messy. Have to leave a fiver for the maid. How to tell one bill from another? Didn't matter—leave her all his money. Be flying over Bosnia or Burundi by then anyway. Or Bucharest or Bolinas . . .*

Bolinas—now there was the fucking rub. Slowly Aldo slid the barrel out of his mouth. It was the one thing that would make eternity unbearable—to be flying around knowing that somewhere down there the victorious striga was still enjoying life, eyes and all. Then a sudden realization: the strigoi was almost certainly alive as well. She hadn't killed him—not permanently, anyway. He'd probably been flying around up there watching the whole thing—and now the two of them were together, laughing about poor Aldo coming in his pants, tearing his own eyes out in agony.

Not yet, thought Aldo, regretfully slipping the pistol back into his kit bag. *Not yet.*

—

Aldo spent the next few hours working things out in his head. He would need help, he knew. First thing he would do when he got back home (no, second thing—his first stop would be his apartment, where he had left himself a welcome-home present in his refrigerator) would be to cab over to Cranwick Square, tell the old man he needed more money, scare him, tell Jonas the striga was coming for him. Then, if Selene hadn't simply gone back home, he could hire a good skip tracer to find her. Once he'd located her, he'd hire one of his old field buddies to help him go after her. Anton Roman—Tony Rome, they called him, after an old Sinatra movie—was always looking for work. Third stool from the end at the Cock and Fender.

Aldo even managed to catch a little sleep that night, with the aid of his last two sleeping pills and a relaxing fantasy of having Selene under him again, fighting just as hard as she'd fought him last time, but this time knowing there'd be no waking up for her. . . .

➤

The next morning Aldo's hitching luck changed. The waitress at the motel coffee shop helped hook him up with a retired couple driving down to San Simeon to see the Hearst Castle, and they in turn passed him on to another retired couple who'd just finished the tour and were driving down to L.A.

So Aldo finished the overland portion of his Incredible Journey in the backseat of a new-smelling Eldorado, listening to two old farts droning on and on about the wonders of the Castle. His thermos went dry south of Oxnard. By the time they'd reached the Los Angeles airport, though they'd gone far out of their way for him, he would gladly have slaughtered both of them just to shut them up, and the hell with their blood.

Not that he wasn't desperate for a drink when they finally dropped him off. It was with the courage of that desperation that he had the curbside skycap bring him to the front of the nearest ticket queue, where he slapped his passport and his credit card down on the counter and announced loudly, in his best Croydenese, that his name was Leonard Patch and that he had to get back to England as quickly as possible.

All the while, though, he had the cold feel of the pistol against his belly fueling his bravado; he had slipped it into the waistband of his slacks, covered only by his windbreaker. But there was no need for the melodramatic sort of you'll-never-take-me-alive maneuver Aldo had in mind as a last resort—no J. Edgars materialized from out of the walls. The ticket agent asked him for another piece of identification, something with a picture, and accepted the blind man's fine Manny the Mocker driver's permit without comment.

Once he'd been ticketed, things started moving almost too fast. An electric cart was summoned to carry Aldo to his gate—he didn't know whether this was standard procedure for the blind, or only for blind first-class passengers. They were within yards of the metal detector when Aldo remembered the gun and called for a detour to the men's room. The toilets there, unfortunately, had no tanks; he had to try a bit of sleight of hand with paper towels to drop it into the trash receptacle without being seen. A difficult assignment: how could you be sure you wouldn't be seen when you didn't know who was looking?

No subsequent problem at the metal detector, once the security guards had determined that the white cane was not a weapon of some sort. Aldo's cart driver picked him up at the other side and drove him straight to the first-class lounge, where he quickly downed a succession of first-class vodka martinis.

As for boarding the plane, Aldo could scarcely remember it; they must have poured him on. He could vaguely recall having a seat-mate at one point, a woman who would simply not . . . stop . . . talking . . . about her grandchildren until finally, driven to desperation, Aldo turned his face to her and lifted his dark glasses just long enough to shut her up in mid-sentence. . . .

——

"Mr. Patch? Mr. Patch, sir?"

A gentle hand tugged at Aldo's sleeve. He awoke, confused—he'd been dreaming in Romanian, but the voice was English. *"Iertare?"*

"Beg pardon?" replied the man.

"Yes."

"What?"

"Yes. *Iertare* means beg pardon. In Romanian. Where are we?"

"Over the Atlantic, sir. We've run into a bumpy patch. Here, let me help you with your seat belt." A body leaned across him; scent of talc. "So you speak Romanian, then?"

"I'm fluent in every European language with the exception of Finnish." Aldo leaned forward; knowing hands tightened his seat belt across his lap.

"Are you, now?"

"I can make myself understood in Finnish, mind you, but I've been told I sound rather like a Russian with a cleft palate."

"You don't say? By the by, Mr. Patch, do you have anyone meeting you at the gate when we arrive?"

"I don't think so. What day is it?"

"Friday."

"And the date?"

"The twenty-sixth. Shall I arrange for someone to—"

"Of November?"

"Yes, sir, November. Shall I . . ."

But Aldo was no longer listening. *Four days,* he was thinking. Seemed more like an eternity. Then he remembered the previous eternity, when he had eyes, when he'd flown. That had lasted four days as well.

"Perhaps I'd better arrange for someone, then." The voice seemed to be coming from farther away; the smell of talc definitely was.

"Yes, please do." Aldo was so tired again. *If only I could close my eyes,* he thought. But his eyelids were in shreds, along with most of his eyeballs. "What's your name, friend?"

"Peter, sir."

"Peter, could I ask you to bring me two of those clever little bottles of vodka and a large empty glass?"

"I'm afraid I can serve each passenger only one drink at a time, sir."

Aldo thought for a moment. "Where's the lady who was sitting next to me?"

"Still in the loo with a cold washcloth on her head."

"Good," said Aldo. "Bring me her drink, too."

—

It was the helpful steward himself who walked Aldo through the nothing-to-declare door at Heathrow, where the Customs agent pawing through Aldo's kit bag unscrewed the top of the empty thermos—and immediately wished he hadn't.

"Whew, what a stink. Good heavens, man, what was in there?"

"Clamato juice," replied Aldo. "Gone rather off by now, I should imagine."

"And what on earth is or was Clamato juice when it's at home?"

"Clam juice and tomahto. I'm afraid I've grown rather hooked on the stuff."

"Clam juice and tomahto—what won't those Yanks think of next?"

—

Peter next volunteered to help Aldo at the autoteller; he'd given the skycap at LAX the rest of his American money. Afterward they shared a cab into London. Dropped Peter at his door first. "I'd invite you up," said the pleasant-smelling fellow, "but my roommate wouldn't be at all pleased. Perhaps I could give you my number, we could get together for a drink sometime?"

Aldo, who by then was so miserable he could no longer distinguish between the effects of his hangover and those of blood withdrawal (though he'd have offered to keep either for life if only something would take away the pain where his eyes used to be), was nevertheless strangely touched by the obvious come-on. After all the apparently disinterested kindnesses of the past few days, he was glad to know that at least one Samaritan had ulterior motives. Restored his faith in human nature. He pretended to memorize the number, then gave a phony one in return. *Nothing personal, Pete, but Len Patch is about to disappear from the face of the earth. Can't have anyone following him to Aldo Striescu's door.*

—

The taxi driver, energized by a generous tip, saw Aldo to the front door of his apartment house. Once inside the vestibule Aldo tried to picture the layout. Stairs to the right. His was the door to the right of the first landing. Almost there. Door key . . . deadbolt key . . .

Home at last? Not quite. He shoved the door open, locked it behind him. Dusty, comfortable, coming-home smell of an empty apartment. Tapping carefully, feeling for anything he might have left lying on the floor, leaving in such a damned hurry nearly three weeks before. End of carpet. Cane tip clicking across linoleum. Refrigerator dead ahead. Feel for the handle. Blast of cold air in his face. Vegetable bin, bottom left. Under a green pepper gone squishy with age, under the rotted spinach . . .

Almost home now. Two sealed plastic bags. Teasing himself now . . . located a pewter goblet in the cabinet. Carried goblet and one bag into the sitting room, set them down on the table beside his armchair. Tapped his way over to the CD player. He'd operated that in the dark often enough—no trouble turning it on. Heard the whir of the CD carousel. Tapped his way back to the armchair. Unsealed the bag of blood as the instrumental music began. Placed the tip of one finger inside the rim of the goblet—the right forefinger, the one Nick had come closest to biting clear through. Poured until the liquid reached the fingertip, took his first sip as the first glorious notes of the Voice came ringing out of the doghouse-sized speakers. La Divina as the treacherous Delila: "Mon coeur s'ouvre à ta voix."

Aldo Striescu was home at last.

13

Lights were blazing in every window of No. 11 Cranwick Square; disco music blared from the second-floor drawing room. As Jamey and Selene turned up the short walk they heard snatches of raucous conversation, a man shouting in a foreign language, the high-pitched shriek of a woman's drunken laughter.

"Sounds like Pop's made himself a few friends since my last visit," remarked Jamey. As he started up the shallow tiled steps the front door flew open and a small dark man staggered out under the portico, bounced off one of the Tuscan columns, and would have fallen headlong to the street if Jamey hadn't caught him by the shoulders of his zippered khaki workingman's jacket.

"Steady there, old sport."

"*Va multumesc.*"

"Pardon?"

The man looked up at Jamey blearily. He resembled the younger, scrawnier Peter Lorre, but with one dark eyebrow running the width of his face, and the hairline of a chimpanzee. "Multumesc. Means thanks. Thanks you very much."

"In what language?"

"Romanian, what you think?"

"You're Romanian?" In a friendly, surprised, what-a-coincidence sort of way. "You must know Aldo, then."

"Striescu? The *strigoi*?" He started to pull away, but Whistler had a firm hold on his arm, just above the elbow.

"Yes."

"Didn't heard of him."

"But you just told me his last name."

The drunk tapped the side of his nose slyly. "I only wanted to be sure we was both talking about the same man I didn't heard of." He looked down at Whistler's hand on his arm. "Now look, mister. Either you got to let me go now, or you got to come home with me, tell my *femeie* why I'm coming home so late for supper."

◦—

Stepping over the threshold of No. 11 Cranwick Square was no longer like stepping back into the nineteenth century. The parquet floor and the Oriental rugs were tracked with mud, and the green and gold flocked Morris wallpaper scored with short but emphatic black scratches as if someone had been striking matches against it; the mahogany coat rack lay on its side, one arm broken off; the elegant walnut hall table was buried under fast-food garbage and dirty highball glasses, some with the ice still melting in watery whiskey, others with cigarette stubs floating in days-old scum; overhead cobwebs were strung like hammocks in the corners of the corniced ceiling, and what appeared to be a negligee and a pair of crotchless panties hung from the Beethoven gasolier.

Selene took off her Lady Burberry trench coat and folded it over her arm, then followed Jamey up the stairs, skirting a vomit stain over which someone had dumped a box of baking soda; the empty carton lay beside the sodden white pile of powder. From the first landing they peeked into the drawing room, where a stout middle-aged man in a cheap wide-collared shirt open at the throat to show his gold neck chain was dancing what might have been the frug with a heavily made-up younger woman wearing a black spaghetti-strap cocktail dress that had been fashionable back when Jackie O. was still a Kennedy.

Whistler took a sharp right and marched into the drawing room; Selene, puzzled, followed after. There were another dozen or so partygoers in various stages of inebriation scattered around the room, but Jamey made straight for the woman in the black dress. "Where'd you get this?" he demanded coldly, ignoring the man.

"Upstahrs in big wardrobe." She looked down, then met Jamey's eyes. "Nice, da?" Then, checking Selene out frankly: "There's nice St. Laurent up there, color of *safir*, look like it might fit you, darling. Why don't you—"

"Take it off!"

Jamey hadn't raised his voice, but there was no mistaking his tone. Bewildered, the woman turned to her dance partner. "Manny! You going to let him—"

But Manny, after a glance at Jamey's eyes, had backed away, holding his hands up in the air, a playful surrender. "Sorry, amorez, none of *my* affair."

The woman turned back to Whistler, fingered the lapel of his butter-smooth Italian leather bomber jacket. "Here? Or more private? We can—"

She had obviously decided to make the best of it, but Jamey cut her short again. "Take it off or I'll rip it off your fucking back."

No one spoke. The Bee Gees were screeching about staying alive, staying alive, as the young woman shrugged the narrow straps off her shoulders. Jamey looked around for the source of the music, saw a boom box perched on the antique writing desk, strode over to it, and yanked out the plug so hard the outlet sparked. "Party's over," he announced. "Anybody still here in ten minutes leaves through the window—headfirst."

He looked around the room, clearly hoping someone would challenge him, but no one did. The party girl had stripped down to her strapless bra and panties; he glanced at her disinterestedly, then stalked out of the room. "That was my mother's dress," he said over his shoulder on his way up the stairs.

"I gathered as much," Selene replied, hurrying after him. He had always taken an interest in fashion: of all the men she'd ever known—straight men, anyway—only Jamey would have been likely to recognize a thirty-year-old dress, mother or no mother. What had really surprised her was his behavior in the drawing room:

she couldn't remember Jamey being rude to a woman, hooker or duchess, in all the time she'd known him.

One thing hadn't changed since Selene's last visit—the old bedstead still creaked. They could hear it from the stairs, a steady counterpoint to the grunting and the groaning and the giggling and the moaning emanating from the bedroom. *If somebody in there is wearing something of Whistler's mother's, there's going to be hell to pay,* thought Selene.

No need to worry. At first glance none of the women whose reflections Selene could make out in the mirror of the massive ebony armoire appeared to be wearing much of anything, and certainly nothing likely to have belonged to Alice Whistler, unless Jamey's late mother had shopped at Victoria's Secret. She followed Jamey into the room. The first thing that hit her was the good old orgy smell, a mélange of lubricity and lubricants, stale perfume, sheets damp with sweat and semen. She caught a quick glimpse of the Joanie-on-the-pony pile squirming on the bed—three women, no, four: there was a little one under the old man—before Jamey began hauling bodies off the pile and heaving them onto the floor, quite heedless of where, or how hard, they landed.

"No!" Selene dropped her trench coat and threw herself at Jamey from behind, tried to pin his arms. "It's not their fault, they're just—"

He shrugged her off violently; she fell to the floor beside the bed, and a moment later had the wind knocked out of her as one of the women—the little one, fortunately—landed on top of her. Her eyes met a pair of startled hazel eyes in a face not much older than Martha's; then the girl scrambled up and fled the room.

Selene peered over the edge of the mattress, saw Jamey staring down at Jonas, who was returning his gaze evenly though he was unclothed save for a condom.

The father spoke first. "And Ham, the father of Canaan, saw the nakedness of his father," Jonas Whistler declared sepulchrally, pointing a trembling forefinger toward his son's face like some Old Testament prophet, albeit a naked one whose rubber-sheathed penis lay semi-engorged and twitching athwart his skinny white thighs.

"And Noah awoke from his wine, and knew what his younger son had done unto him. And he said, 'Cursed be Canaan, a servant of servants shall he be unto his brethren.' "

Instead of replying, Jamey looked down at Selene, peeking over the foot of the bed. His fists were clenched but his voice was steady. "I think my father and I need to have a little chat, Selene," he said. "Could you give us a few minutes?"

Lifting his head, Jonas appeared to notice Selene for the first time; he glanced from her to his son and back again. "Well I'll be buggered," he said conversationally. "Didn't that arsehole Striescu manage to kill *anybody*?"

It was Jamey who answered. "Only about a dozen or so innocent people, including my wife and my little girl."

Again the sententious, sepulchral voice: "Remember, I pray thee, who ever perished, being innocent?"

"Job four seven." Jamey turned back to Selene. "Now if you don't mind. . . ."

Still she hesitated.

"Don't worry, I'm not going to kill him," he assured her. "That's exactly what he wants me to do." Then, to his father: "Isn't it?"

An aristocratic shrug of the bony old shoulders. "Wherefore is light given to him that is in misery, and life unto the bitter in soul, which long for death but it cometh not?"

"Job three twen—"

"Oh for shit's sake, will both of you please shut the hell up?" In the astonished silence that followed, Selene climbed wearily to her feet. She'd suddenly had quite enough of both Whistlers—but at least she'd finally figured out why she'd accompanied Jamey to London, to this house, to this bedroom, what she'd come here to say to the old man.

"I've got something to tell you, Jonas Whistler," she began. But the Creature's father had begun to bobble erect again, distracting her. Selene grabbed the edge of the sheet hanging over the side of the bed and tossed it over him. "Aldo Striescu is dead. I killed him myself, and I can assure you he died in unspeakable agony. But you, old man, if you ever try to harm me or mine again you won't get off nearly so easily. I will hunt you down wherever you are, I will follow you to the grave and beyond. If you don't think I can do it, by the way, I suggest that you check out First Samuel, since you're so goddamn fond of your Bible, and reacquaint yourself with the Witch of Endor. And I will personally see that you spend eternity in such torment that it will make whatever pitifully inadequate Christian hell you've been so terrified of all these years seem like Club Med in comparison. On that, I give you my Witch's Word."

She glanced up, saw herself in the wardrobe mirror. With her gray-black hair gone all wild again, and the long black dress that Moll had insisted on buying for her during one of their shopping sprees the other week still in disarray from her fall, she could easily have passed for the woman of Endor—the Bible never actually calls her a witch—though the dress was from Bergdorf's and the matching pumps from Saks. Then she caught a glimpse of Jamey, who was glaring at her over the rumpled expanse of his father's bed with his arms folded lightly across his chest, and understood suddenly that he'd been intending to deliver a similar sermon to his father all along. But now whatever dramatic parting speech he'd had planned would come out more like *Yeah, that goes for me too.*

Poor Jamey—she had stolen his thunder yet again.

—

Selene let herself out quietly, closing the door to the bedroom behind her. Neither Jamey nor his father had spoken yet. She was vaguely curious about what they'd have to say to each other, now that she'd let the air out of Jamey's planned jeremiad, but not curious enough to stick around to hear it. Her business here was done—of that much, and that much only, she was sure.

It was quiet out in the hall—clearly the revelers on the second floor had taken Jamey's threats to heart—but when Selene started down the stairs she saw the littlest prostitute, the one who'd fallen on her earlier, sitting on the landing with a throw rug wrapped forlornly around her.

"My clothes is in there," the girl wailed, in what Selene was coming to recognize as a Romanian accent. She drew back her feet as Selene passed her. "How I can go home without my clothes?"

Selene turned back, handed her the expensive Lady Burberry she'd bought at Heathrow three weeks before. "Here," she said. "Now if I were you I'd get the fuck out of Dodge while I still had all my blood. Either that, or give it about fifteen minutes, then march on in there with your pretty little titties high. You'll be weak and sore when you come out tomorrow morning, but if you play your cards right, by Goddess you'll be rich."

"If you telling me the truth . . ." The girl handed the coat back. "Here. Weak I know, sore I sure God know. But that third thing —I could stand a little rich for a change."

"Good luck, dearie," Selene replied. Then, on an impulse, she stooped down and planted a dry firm kiss on the young lips before trotting down the stairs and out into the London night.

14

No. Not home. Aldo Striescu, lying in his darkness, in his own bathtub, goblet of blood at hand and *Norma* on the stereo, began to understand with mounting dread that he could never go home again, at least not to that place where blood used to take him. True, it had done wonders in easing his physical hurts: the hangover head-ache and sour stomach were gone, along with the pain where his eyes had been, and the lesser aches of the body's fenders—bruised shins and forearms, knees and elbows.

But that was all. No matter how much he drank, that was all. It wasn't just the visuals that he missed, either, the bright colors and subtle shadings, the depth of field, the *presence* of every object that came into sight, the sense of living inside a starry night, not just looking up at one. All that had been stolen from him. He had already accepted that, filed it under lost loves—and given his sexual predilections, Aldo had lost a lot of loves in his time.

What he could not accept was the deeper loss. Always before, with blood had come a feeling of almost magical well-being, a warmth spreading from the inside out until it engulfed the world, imbuing even the most pedestrian of environs—a concrete block of flats in Bucharest, a small apartment in Chelsea—with a rosy sense of all-rightness. But no matter how deeply Aldo drank—and by Friday evening the first of his two bags was an empty plastic husk on the bathroom floor—he couldn't get it back: he was only a blind man in a bathtub.

He thought back to the cabin, when he still had eyes. What was it he had told the striga? Three things to make him feel alive: blood, coming, Maria. But in his bleak darkness not only did Aldo not feel horny, not only could he not summon up so much as a hard thought even by recalling his most intense orgasms—as long ago as that Algerian girl in Marseilles who'd fought him to the death, screaming in silent orgasm at the end, as recent as Georgie in flames—but as he could no longer bring to mind or body the why of desire, the what and how left him hopelessly limp.

Having checked off the first two items, Aldo turned his full attention to the music, and found that no matter how hard he tried, he could no longer summon up the face of La Divina. He'd always been able to do that before, blood or no blood. But now in his eternal darkness the voice was only a voice—in a way, it was the worst blow of the three.

Blood, coming, Maria: clearly the luck of the devil had run out.

Good thing that Aldo had always had a memory for numbers, because his address book was certainly no use to him now. He called Danny Dimitriu first. Danny's *femeie* answered the phone in English, but called Danny to it in Romanian, to the effect that one of his lowlife friends wanted to speak to him.

"Well, speak of the devil and he shall appear," said Danny in Romanian when he recognized Aldo's voice. The phrase was much the same as in English. "I just got back from the party at old Whistler's. That's why the wife's so pissed—"

"Wait a minute." Also in Romanian. "What party?"

"You *have* been out of town, haven't you? Why, it's been going on for weeks. Incidentally, thanks for that clean-up job—we'll be eating beefsteak through the New Year. Anyway, to get back to what I was telling you: I was just on my way out when I bumped into this fellow coming up the steps. Asked me out of the blue if I was a Romanian. And proud of it, I told him. Asked me if I knew Striescu. Never heard of him, I said. The strigoi, he says. And the way he grabs me, and the look of his eyes, I'd say he was strigoi as well. Let me tell you, I got out of there fast as my legs could—"

Aldo interrupted eagerly. "What did he look like, this strigoi?"

"Tall, lean, white hair cut short. Money: I could pay my rent for three months on what his coat must have cost. And the woman's Rolex—"

"The woman? There was a woman with him?"

"Little thing. Late forties, early fifties. Gray hair done up in a, I don't know, a twist, a braid. You know me, all I saw clearly was that lovely watch. I'd have had it off her in a minute if she'd been alone, and her none the wiser."

"You didn't tell them anything, did you? About me, I mean."

"Aldo!" Reproachfully. "How could you even ask such a—"

"And they were on their way inside?"

"As surely as I was on my way out."

Aldo hung up. He could hear his heart beating in the darkness. *Perhaps,* he thought, *the luck of the devil hadn't quite run out after all.*

—

"Here we are, sir, eleven Cranwick Square. Thank you, sir."

"Keep the change."

"In that case, thank you *very* much. Sure you don't need some help up the steps?"

"Just tell me how many there are."

"Four, sir. Door's to the—"

"I know where the bloody door is."

Aldo waited until he heard the sound of the taxi engine receding down the street, then tapped his way up the front steps, kit bag in his free hand, trying to make as little noise as possible with the cane tip, which was a challenge, as the steps were tiled. The front door was unlocked. Aldo closed it softly behind him, trying to visualize the interior of the house. He vaguely remembered a long hallway with some furniture, at the end of which a carpeted staircase led up to the left and a doorway at the right led through to the dining room.

But the hallway, he soon learned, was now a minefield of litter and unmoored carpets. After stumbling on the overturned coat rack, Aldo took the thermos from the kit bag and drank deeply before replacing it: as the blood came on his senses sharpened until he could feel what was at the end of his cane through his fingers. At the end of the hall Aldo stopped and listened. Silence in the dining room, no one on the stairs, no noise from the second-story drawing room. Whatever party Danny'd been talking about was apparently over. Aldo's heart sank—had he missed them?

But as he made his way up the stairs, passing the smell of vomit on the first turning of the staircase, he heard voices above him. Slower now, taking infinite care, holding his kit bag so it wouldn't bump the banister, testing each step with half his weight to be sure it wouldn't creak, he approached the third floor. The voices were coming from the bedroom. He couldn't tell whether the door was open or not so he kept his head below floor level.

He made out the old man's sly voice first: "Not planning to lecture me about women, are you now?"

Although Aldo had only heard his voice on Selene's answering machine, and once over the phone, there was no doubt in his mind that it was a somewhat incredulous Jamey Whistler who spoke next: "Do us both a favor—just tell me you're insane. If I could believe that, I could almost begin to make some sense out of all this."

"Nonsense," replied Jonas. "Haven't needed my medication since I started drinking the damned blood. . . ."

Aldo held his breath. Both strigois, the old man who'd gotten him into this, the son who'd escaped him twice. An unaddressed prayer arose in his head. If only the striga were up there. . . . Please let the striga be up there.

"Would that I were, though," Jonas's voice continued from the bedroom. "If I were insane, you see, there'd have been no need for all this. Done myself in long ago. Sick mind, blameless heart. Madman can meet his maker with a clear conscience. Now if you're going to kill me, get on with it. If not, leave me alone with our little naked friend here and get on with your life, and I give you my word I'll leave you alone to get on with yours. But *don't* tell me you don't want to fuck her every bit as much as I do."

Little naked friend? thought Aldo. *Could it be . . . ?*

Jamey spoke next: "I've got to get out of here before I do something I'll regret and you'll be glad for." Then, a gentler tone: "Honey? You want to come with me, or stay here with that?"

The reply must have been nonverbal, but Aldo didn't need to hear her voice: that *honey* had clinched it for him. *Damn,* he thought. *I should have tried prayer years ago.* He started back down the carpeted stairs. The door to the bedroom opened above him as he reached the second-floor landing; he heard a single set of footsteps descending the stairs, and ducked around the corner. So the striga had elected to stay with the older strigoi! Good—make things all that much simpler.

Aldo grabbed the thermos out of the kit bag, cocked it like a cricket bat, waited. He would only get one swing, he knew, but decided it was worth the risk. Couldn't let Jamey escape him time after time: from the sound of that last conversation, he might never have the three of them together in the same place again. And without the comfort of blood—the high, the bliss, not just the absence of pain—Aldo didn't want to prolong his stay on earth, at least down here and eyeless, a moment longer than absolutely necessary.

Six, five, four . . . He timed the rhythm of the descending steps *. . . three, two, one . . .* Aldo swung the heavy thermos.

—

Leaving Whistler lying on the second-story landing, Aldo hurried down the stairs, turning left when he reached the bottom, feeling his way through the doorway and into the dining room, then circling the mahogany table, shoving dining room chairs out of his way until he'd reached the wall on the far side. Followed that wall until he reached another doorway; cane-tapped through that, found himself in the kitchen, and began feeling around until he came upon an enormous range. Felt for the knobs along the front, turned one, heard a hissing noise, then a pop as a burner ignited. Gas, not electric. Oh, good luck! Wouldn't be long now.

There were three knobs on the left, one in the center, three on the right. He turned on the other five outside knobs, then leaned over the stove and began blowing out the flames until all six burners were extinguished, but hissing madly, merrily. He backed away from the stove as the hissing turned to a ringing in his ears and he realized he was blacking out from the gas.

Couldn't let that happen, he thought, fumbling in his kit bag for the tube of jellied gasoline he'd brought with him. Had to see this one through to the end. He unscrewed the top of the tube, tapped his way back to the doorway, then stooped over and began walking backward, squeezing the gel out with a steady pressure onto the floor until he'd backed into the dining room table. He dropped to the floor and crawled backward under the heavy-legged table, one hand dragging his kit bag, the other continuing to squeeze the tube steadily until it was empty.

Aldo stood up again on the other side of the table. He'd left his cane on the floor on the far side of the dining room, but reminded himself it was no great loss. Another minute or so to let the gas build up in the kitchen, then light the trail of napalm, and in another few seconds, *boom*—he'd never need the damn white cane again anyhow.

Aldo found his Zippo in his pocket, flicked it open, sniffed the comforting smell of the lighter fluid, then began counting off the seconds the way they'd counted back in the Orfelinat Gheorghiu-Dej when he was a kid playing hide-and-seek. *Un-u o mie, do-i o mie, tre-i o mie . . .*

When he reached *seizech-i o mie,* Aldo knelt and flicked the wheel of his lighter with his thumb, lit the end of the long bead of jellied gasoline, and stood up, listening to it begin to sizzle its way across the floor. He started to open the kit bag to take out his Discman. He'd already cued up the cut he wanted: third act of *Medea.* Took him an hour to find it back at his apartment—his CD collection was scattered all over the living room floor by the time he'd located it—but it would be worth it. All he had to do was slip the earphones on and punch the play button, and La Divina's would be the last human voice he would hear.

But the kitchen went up before he even finished opening the kit bag. "Ma—" he screamed in the breathless instant of eternity that bridged the sound of the explosion—a dull *whomp!*—and the hot blast that blew him off his feet, sending him flying backward through the air with his hair and eyebrows on fire, clutching the bag in both hands.

He must have lost consciousness briefly when he hit the wall. He awoke on fire and staggered to his feet, his clothes fully engulfed. Miraculously, he still maintained a death grip on the kit bag, even after bouncing off the wall a few more times, trying to find the doorway. Then he was through it, reeling down the hall, flesh melting from his bones. He heard a voice shouting; a moment later he was knocked to the floor, felt himself being wrapped in something heavy, then dragged down the hall. He tried to open the kit bag, but his arms were trapped at his sides. "Maria," he cried in agony, in rage and frustration, charred fingers clutching and unclutching impotently. "Momma. Momma. Maria."

━

The problem was, Selene hadn't been able to get the image of the girl on the stairs out of her mind. The littlest prostitute. Could she have been much over seventeen? Martha's age?

"What *could* I have been thinking of?"

The cabbie who'd picked Selene up on the Belgrave Road glanced over his shoulder. "Ma'am?"

"What? Oh—never mind me. Just talking to myself." It was one thing to make a mistake, a wrong move. To err is human, and all that. But in this case, Selene knew, with sudden conviction, she'd not only *not* done the right thing, which would have been to follow her first instinct, give the kid her coat, and get her the hell out of that house, but she'd gone in the exact opposite direction, all but pimped the child. And for what? A smart remark? A desire to wash her hands of both Whistlers?

She thought of Birgie, a German girl who'd joined the coven briefly in the seventies. Most inept witch Selene had ever known. Screw up the simplest of spells. Then would come the midnight phone call. "Selene? This is Birgie. Please could you help me? I *up-geh-fucked* again.*"* It was still a catch phrase for the coven long after Birgie had returned to Munich.

Selene? You up-geh-fucked it good this time. She glanced at her watch—fifteen minutes had gone by since she'd left the girl on the stairs. "Driver, I've changed my mind. I don't want to go back to the hotel."

"Lady's privilege, innit? Where to instead?"

"Cranwick Square, please. Number eleven Cranwick Square."

—

The front door was still unlocked. Selene picked her way down the littered hallway, started up the stairs, saw the white-haired body in the leather jacket lying facedown on the second-floor landing, and thought of Nick. *Not again. Please not again.* But when she reached him she saw he was breathing. No shit, no blood. "Jamey?" No answer either.

She turned him over and found a knot just under his hairline, a lump oval as an egg, dark as an eggplant in the dim staircase light. "Jamey, what happened?" She raised one of his eyelids with her thumb; the eye was rolled back in his head, only white showing (of course the white was bloodshot red). She sat down, cradled his head in her lap. Her first thought, naturally enough, was that Jonas had done this to his son. She raised her head, listening, heard the now-familiar squeak of the bedsprings again. Had they quarreled over the girl? Had Selene *up-geh-fucked* even worse than she'd thought? "Jamey, it's Selene. Can you wake up for me, dearie?" Trying to keep the panic out of her voice. "I need you to wake up for me, Jamey." She patted his cheek, pinched him. "Please, Jamey, try to wake up. Try to come back to me, Jamey. Come on, let's go—"

Home, she'd been about to say, when the explosion rattled the house. Sounded as if it had come from the downstairs back, leaving a deep echoing silence in its wake. Even the creaking of the bed-springs overhead had stopped. Selene grabbed Jamey under the shoulders, tried to lift him but couldn't. She was about to drag him headfirst down the stairs when the bedroom door opened above her.

"What was that?" called the old man. "Jamey? Are you still—"

Then a second explosion, and a third, and the smell of smoke and the distant crackle of flames. The old man's slippers came in sight above her on the stairs, then the hem of his quilted dressing-gown. "What in the name of— What are you doing here? What's happened to Jamey?"

Selene looked up. "I don't know. Here, help me get him up."

"I've got him." Jonas knelt, slipped his arms under his son, scooped him up as easily as if Jamey were still an infant.

Selene stood, started up the stairs. "Get him outside—I'll get the girl."

But the girl was already on her way out of the bedroom, car-rying her blouse, tugging on her miniskirt. "What—"

Selene grabbed her by the arm. "Fire. Get out quick—move it, move it, move it!" Tugging from below, ushering the girl past her on the landing, then urging her on from above, Selene followed the young Romanian down the stairs. Smoke was billowing out of the dining room. Selene shoved the girl to the right, hustled her down the long hallway and out the open front door, but as she turned to close it behind her she saw a human torch come staggering through the smoke at the far end of the hall, beating at the flames that engulfed it with one hand, holding a smoking black bag at arm's length with the other hand.

"Drop and roll!" Selene raced toward the reeling figure. "Drop and roll!" She stooped by the fallen coat rack, seized the tasseled fringe of an Oriental rug and yanked it with all her strength, top-pling the antique hall table over onto its side. Holding the stiff rug in front of her like a shield, she threw herself at the burning man, knocking him over easily, falling on top of him, wrapping him in the rug, then dragging him back from the inferno.

Now someone was beside her—the girl. Together they hauled

the heavy carpet down the hall and over the doorsill, stopping only once to stomp out the fringe of the rug as the tassels began to singe and spark.

Then they were down the four tiled steps and out into the cool air; they laid the smoldering carpet down on the sidewalk and Selene began beating at it with her bare hands, vaguely aware of sirens in the distance, the buzz and murmur as people streamed out of the neighboring row houses in nightclothes.

Only after the last tendrils of smoke from the rug had dissipated did Selene notice that the girl was gone. She raised her head to look around, and saw Jamey lying on the sidewalk, his head cradled in his father's lap. She was about to call to him when she heard Aldo's voice in her head.

It had to have been in her head—hard to tell for sure in all the confusion, but when she began to unwrap the carpet from around him—the plastic frame of the dark glasses had melted to his face, saving her the sight of those ruined eyes—she saw that what was left of his mouth could not have formed the words she had heard so clearly: *Maria, Momma. Momma, Maria.* Not without lips.

When she finished unwinding the carpet she saw the charred fingers clutching the kit bag. The moaning began again. She had to look away as the jaw began to open and close, but there was no turning away from the voice in her head—*Maria, Momma. Momma, Maria*—as the burned thing struggled feebly to pry open the satchel with fingers like blackened sticks.

The leather was warm to the touch when Selene reached down to help him; bits of his burned flesh tore away like shreds of steak clinging to a grill as she spread the handles. Nothing inside but a Sony Discman and a thermos.

Maria, Momma. Momma, Maria.

All at once she understood; carefully she lifted the portable CD player out of the kit bag. She hesitated for a moment with the earphones in her hand, then decided that nothing she could do at this point was likely to worsen his pain, and forced herself to slip the earphones over what was left of the ears.

⬮

"Numi! Venite a me, inferni Dei!"

Gods! Come to me, infernal Gods! It was a miracle of sorts—La Divina's voice cutting through the fiercest agony like a soft golden light shining through crimson flames. Best of all, he saw her face again. It was all he'd wanted at the end. He thought she had been stolen from him, but now he had her back. "Va multumesc," whispered Aldo to his unseen benefactor.

⬮

Selene could hear a tiny voice squeaking out from under the little plastic earphones. *That Sony makes a hell of a product,* she thought numbly. Then the jaw opened and closed again; again Selene heard the voice in her head: *Va multumesc.*

The phrase was familiar: it took her a moment to remember the little man on the steps earlier that evening. *Multumesc. Means thanks. Thanks you very much.*

"You're welcome." Then strong gloved hands were tugging her away from the body. She found herself in the arms of a fireman in a black rubber coat, turned back to see another fireman kneeling by the body, feeling at the throat for a pulse.

Don't bother, she started to say; she could tell by the silence in her head that he was gone. To hell, she hoped—and yet she was not at all sorry to have helped him at the end.

EPILOGUE

Mill Valley, California
December 21, 1993

Midway through the backward Lord's Prayer, Selene knew it would be all right—she could get through it this one last time. She looked around her at each of the naked witches in turn as she recited—Ariadne, the Barbaras, old Faye, and so on around the circle until she reached plump, rosy Catherine on her left—trying to fix each of their images in her memory. The coven numbered only twelve for this Yule Sabbat—Martha was off in Tuscany with her mother.

". . . Neveh nitra chiw, rethaf rau." She waited until the others had opened their eyes, then crossed her hands over her breast and began the charge: "Now listen to the words of the Great Mother. . . ."

The rest of the general Sabbat forms, the charges, invocations, balancing of the elements, setting of the watchtowers, took longer than usual to complete. Selene would not hurry through them, not *this* night. The forms specific to the Yule Sabbat, the ritual birth of the sun/son, seemed to take forever as well, but finally they reached the last *So mote it be,* and Selene took Ariadne's and Catherine's hands to begin the Yule Spiral, a clockwise circle around a giant wreath of smooth stones and dark green juniper branches known as the Yuletide Ring.

A stately turning at first—step, pause, step, pause, joined hands held high—then faster and faster, lengthening their steps until they were running in a tight circle holding each other's hands, stumbling, laughing, fleshy parts bouncing and slapping until, inevitably, one of them lost her footing and went down, dragging the others along with her like a fall of dominoes until the entire coven lay giggling and panting on the thick white wall-to-wall carpet.

When she had her breath back, Selene took her place inside the Yuletide Ring, sitting with her legs crossed in front of her tailor-fashion and her hands at her sides, palms up; before her lay her opened Book of Shadows, a lighted black candle in a tall silver candlestick, and a small silver bell. Slowly the others joined her inside the giant wreath, some sweating, chests still heaving, all with their color raised and their eyes bright; they settled themselves in a tight circle, sides of their knees touching lightly, their hands joined.

"Before we call for our cakes and wine," Selene began, "there's a bit of coven business to be gotten through. As you know, it has always been the tradition of this coven that the high priestess, the first among equals, cannot be a wedded woman. I would seek your permission to change this tradition."

The words were scarcely out of her mouth when the coven— everyone except Catherine—burst into excited chatter: "At last." "Of course." "Congratulations." "Absolutely." "So happy for you." "A Wiccan wedding!" "Who's the lucky . . . ?" "When's the happy . . . ?"

Selene ignored the outburst. "I take it there are no objections? So mote it be!" She closed the book, blew out the black candle, rang the silver bell sharply. The witches kissed each other, then broke the circle and retrieved their forest green robes from the dining room before inviting their guests to join them for cakes and wine. Orgy to follow.

➤

Selene watched from the couch as Sherman Bailey, his graying walrus mustache flecked with crumbs from the traditional Yuletide crescent cakes, lapped ruby drops of a cheeky but immodestly priced Napa Zinfandel from his wife's freckled bosom. She couldn't help comparing the rather circumspect scene unfolding at her feet with other orgies she'd attended over the past thirty years: sweet Sapphic saturnalias under the Gypsy fortune-teller's tent in the back room of the Covenstead Bookshop; Morgana's elaborately choreographed debauches in the Circle Room; cluster fucks and daisy chains under a painted frieze of satyrs and nymphs in the orgy pit at Whistler Manor.

And now? *Mine anomie grows older,* as Nick used to say. Poor Nick, how he'd loved the coven orgies. *No better time to seduce a hetero than when he's surrounded by naked women,* he would crow, climbing into bed with Jamey and Selene for a postorgy spoon and dish as dawn approached. She remembered the first time she'd seen him, at a black-tie Halloween at Whistler's place in Noe Valley. A shy dip of his gorgeous head as Leon introduced them. Jesus, but he was a handsome man.

A hand caressed Selene's bare ankle; a voice interrupted her reverie. "Hey Sel, want to join us?" Catherine, lying on her back spread-eagled in the star position, was smiling up at her.

Selene smiled back through her tears. "Thanks all the same, dearie. I think I'll just watch tonight." Then she looked up and saw Jamey Whistler standing in the archway, a suitcase in one hand, the white hard-shell bio-pack ice chest with the red cross on top in the other. "Or not, as the case may be."

———

"I didn't think you were going to make it." Selene pulled the hood of her robe up over her head. It was a clear cold night out on the Baileys' patio, one of those rare California nights that almost makes you believe there's going to be a real winter.

Jamey turned up the collar of his new camel-colored cashmere topcoat. "You said you'd give me your answer at the Yule Sabbat. Where else would I be?"

"How's your father doing?"

"Moved him into a rest home for the fearfully rich near Tunbridge Wells. I visited him a few nights ago—they're keeping him heavily sedated."

"Any chance of his getting out?"

"Not so long as he keeps insisting he's a vampire, and demanding blood to drink. He's already been declared *non compos.* I'm having myself appointed his guardian, with complete power of attorney over his portion of the trust."

"So you did double your livestock after all."

Jamey was confused for a second, then the reference registered. "I suppose I did. Not much of a sense of closure, though. Like I told you, I don't think I'll ever get over the shock of seeing him like that, that night. It was like going forward in time and meeting some nightmare version of myself. Christ in a basket, Selene, I don't want to end up like him."

He reached out to cup her face in his hand. She pulled her chin back and turned away, leaning against the railing. "I don't blame you, Jamey. But like *I* told *you,* that's your problem. I don't see what it has to do with me."

"It has everything to do with you. How did it go, that little ditty? Something about finding your path by the Fair Lady's light? You said it yourself, Selene, I'm your path. And you're mine. Together we can—"

"No, Jamey." She cut him off without raising her voice. "Saving you wasn't my path, it was my task. And in performing it, I've seen my path, and it does not include matrimony—to you or anyone else. Remember the rest of that little ditty? 'The deeper the dark, the truer the sight.' Jamey, my path was right there in front of me all the time. I was already on it; I couldn't have been anywhere *but* on it."

This time he interrupted her. "Are you about to click your heels three times and tell me there's no place like home?"

She almost smiled. He seemed to be taking it pretty well— perhaps there was still a chance to salvage the rest of her plans for the evening. "You want to hear or not?"

"Of course I do."

She turned away from the railing, looked up into his bloodshot gray eyes. "I'm going to be a crone."

The wide-set eyes narrowed in amusement. "Let me just see if

I've got all this straight. You had me fly in from London in order to turn down my proposal of marriage because you want to become a crone?"

"More or less."

"And what precisely does this entail, this . . . *encronement?*"

"I'm not sure. There aren't exactly any manuals on the subject. But the first thing I'm going to do is resign as high priestess and appoint Catherine as my successor—"

"But she's married."

"Already taken care of. Then after that I'm flying down to Santa Luz for a combination postgrad course in Caribbean ethnobotany and vacation. Next: the Big Apple. I can't start studying orgomancy with Benny and Moll until after I've missed three periods in a row, but there are plenty of other things to study in the meantime. And who knows, maybe I'll even do a spread for *Foxy Forties* while I still qualify; might be kind of fun."

"I'll look forward to the issue." Again the flash of contained amusement. "But couldn't you have told me all this over the phone, saved me a six-thousand-mile journey?"

"Nope." She slipped her arms around him, snuggled her cheek against the impossibly soft cashmere of his topcoat.

"Why not?" he asked her; she felt his chest rumbling against her ear.

"Because you *do* mean so much to me. Because our lives *are* so tangled up together."

He stiffened—and not in a good way. "Don't you *dare* give me that old 'Can't we still be friends?' kiss-off. Don't you dare reduce all that we've been through, all that we've meant to each other, down to that."

Selene sighed—but it was a sigh of relief. "That's it, Jamey. I *knew* you'd get it."

"Get what?"

"Why I wanted to say good-bye to you here, tonight. I don't want to cut off the part of my life that you represent—that *we* represent—and just leave it dangling like it didn't mean anything."

"Then what *do* you want to do?" But the gentle way he said it, the knowing way of his hands in her hair, led her to suspect that he already knew.

"I want to end it the way we began it. I want to bring it around in a circle. I want to tie it up in a beautiful ribbon."

"In other words . . . ?"

"In other words, I want to take you inside, and lay you down on that couch in there, and screw your brains out in front of all the most noble ladies at the Witch's Sabbat."

For a minute there she thought she'd miscalculated: he let her go. "And it would be the last time?"

"Witch's Word," she replied, surprising herself.

"In that case . . ." He looked away sheepishly. "I don't suppose you have Moll's number in Tuscany? I've often thought about getting back in touch with her."

She felt a quick flush of outrage, then caught the amused glint in his eyes. A little payback chain-yanking.

"Just kidding," he said.

"No you're not," she replied. "But I think Moll's pretty much spoken for." The bent nose gesture. "You might be able to get her to introduce you to the other Selene, though."

"There's another Selene?"

"Sure is. One of her most popular models."

"I'll keep it in mind," said Jamey. He offered her his arm. "Shall we go inside?"

She took it; he turned to her as they started across the patio. "A word of caution," he said. "That bit about screwing my brains out? It's been tried."

She patted his arm. "I'll take my chances."

· A NOTE ON THE TYPE ·

The typeface used in this book is a version of Bembo, issued by
Monotype in 1929 and based on the first "old style" roman typeface,
which was designed for publication, by the great Venetian printer
Aldus Manutius (1450–1515), of Pietro Bembo's *De Ætna* (1495).
Among the first to use octavo format, making his books cheaper
and more portable, Aldus might have grown rich printing as he did
a thousand volumes per month—an extraordinary number for the
time—had his books not been mercilessly pirated. The counterfeits
did, however, spread the new typefaces throughout Europe, and
they were widely imitated. The so-called Aldine romans were actually designed by the man who cut the type for Aldus, Francesco
Griffo (d. 1519). Griffo fought with Manutius over credit for the
designs and was later hanged after killing his brother-in-law with an
iron bar.